Rhine River

TEUTONS

ALPS

CISALPINE GAUL

*Ligurian
Sea*

*Adriatic
Sea*

*Tyrrhenian
Sea*

THE DRUID KING

❧ THE ❧
DRUID KING

NORMAN SPINRAD

ALFRED A. KNOPF   NEW YORK

2003

THIS IS A BORZOI BOOK
PUBLISHED BY ALFRED A. KNOPF

Copyright © 2003 by Norman Spinrad

Library of Congress Cataloging-in-Publication Data
Spinrad, Norman.
The Druid king / Norman Spinrad. — 1st ed.
p.   cm.
ISBN 0-375-41110-0
1. Vercingetorix, Chief of the Arverni, d. 45? B.C.—Fiction.
2. Gaul—History—Gallic Wars, 58–51 B.C.—Fiction.
3. Druids and Druidism—Fiction.
4. Kings and rulers—Fiction. I. Title.
PS3569.P55 D7 2003
813'.54—dc21   2002027539

Manufactured in the United States of America
First Edition

For Jacques Dorfmann
and
Richard Shorr

THE DRUID KING

I

THE COUNTRY of the tribes of Gaul extends from the sere and rugged cordillera of the Pyrenees in the west to the grandeur of the snow-capped Alps in the east, from the dank fogbound coast of the northern sea to sunny southern reaches where the balmy tang of the Mediterranean can be smelled drifting up through the mountain passes.

But in truth, the lands of the Edui and the Arverni, the Carnutes and the Belovaques, the Turons and the Santons, and all the rest, their farmsteads, their cities, their pastures, are but islands in an ocean of trees. For it is the mighty green forest, cresting over hills and rolling down valleys, that fills the greater part of their world; it is the oak that reigns supreme, not man.

Deep within this endless oak forest is a round clearing, its grass sprinkled with wild flowers, mushrooms, mossy rocks. Waiting silently just within the ferny undergrowth fringing its margin is a circle of leaders of a score and more of the tribes of Gaul, wearing pantaloons in their tribal colors, woolen shirts, leather jerkins, their scabbards empty of swords. Each of these vergobrets stands beside a pole bearing aloft the sigil animal of his tribe—boar, hawk, bull, bear, stag, wolf, and the like—roughly carved in wood or cast in subtly modeled bronze or silver.

In the center of the clearing, illumined by the bright noonday sun, stands Guttuatr, Arch Druid of all Gaul, a tall, slightly stooped man in early old age. His hair and neatly trimmed beard are silvery gray. He wears a white robe with no tribal colors. The cowl of the robe is drawn over his head, but does not hide his face, with its hawk-beak nose and its deeply set green eyes that seem to look through this world and into another. He bears, but does not lean upon, a gnarled oaken staff as tall as he is. Atop the staff is fixed a fallen star, a roughly spherical piece of dark-gray pockmarked iron twice the diameter of an apple.

He looks up at the sun, then down at his own shadow, severely foreshortened as the sun passes through its zenith. Then he raises his staff one-handed, the fallen star now a quarter of a man's height above his head.

From the four quadrants of the wind, their white robes trimmed in the many colors of the tribes of Gaul, druids emerge silently past the vergobrets and into the clearing.

They form an inner circle around the Arch Druid, then stand immobile. Guttuatr grounds his staff once more upon the earth. No one moves. No one speaks.

And then the ghostly-pale midday moon begins to move across the face of the golden sun.

The vergobrets gasp as a shadow begins to cross the clearing and the forest beyond, as the sky slowly turns a deeper blue.

The Arch Druid Guttuatr speaks.

"As in the heavens, so upon the earth. The gods of night seek to conquer the day. Those who serve the dark war against those who serve the light. As upon the earth, so in the heavens."

The moon, like a mouth open wide, swallows an ever-growing portion of the golden sun, as if bent on devouring it entire.

The tribal leaders moan and shuffle their feet in distress. The druids stand silent, knowing eyes fixed upon Guttuatr, as if waiting for some signal.

Nothing is to be heard but the shuffling feet and softer and softer moans of the vergobrets, then the confused cries of day birds returning to roost and night birds awakening and the faint far-off baying of dogs and wolves, as the blood-red light of false sunset falls upon the forest.

Then the night itself descends. The sky turns black and the stars appear, but the sun is still visible, its face a void of darkness, but rimmed in a gauzy light like hair and beard aflame or the fiery crown of a celestial god.

"The night destroys the day!" Guttuatr shouts, and brings forth cries of terror from the men beside their tribal standards. "The dark devours the light!"

And the druids begin a stately circling round him.

Guttuatr begins a slow chanting.

"But the Great Wheel turns and we turn with it. . . ."

The circling druids answer.

"That which is eternal, that which passes . . ."

"As in the heavens, so upon the earth . . ."

"As upon the earth, so in the heavens . . ."

"Let the Great Wheel turn with us!" Guttuatr shouts, raising his staff high above his head as if to command the heavens. "Night into day! Darkness to light! Let the Great Wheel—"

Suddenly vergobrets and druids alike cry out, a great collective shout not of terror but of wonder. The druids abruptly cease their circling, and turn to stare at something above and behind Guttuatr. All at once the solemn spell is broken, and an unruly crowd is pointing at the sky, shouting and babbling.

Guttuatr himself whirls around, looks up to see—

A point of light emerging from nothingness, growing brighter, and brighter, and brighter.

A new star being born.

Guttuatr's jaw drops slack, and his eyes widen in awe, as those of a man beholding the visage of a god.

"Once in a thousand years . . . ," the Arch Druid whispers.

The vergobrets do not move, but the druids crowd close to him, and one of them dares to speak.

"What means this, Arch Druid?"

With enormous reluctance, Guttuatr slowly turns from this mighty portent.

"This is the sign of a Great Turning," he tells his fellow druids uneasily. "This Great Age will die to give way to the next."

"But what will—"

"No man of the age that is passing can see clearly into the age that is to come," Guttuatr says quickly and more firmly. "We have conjured more than those of the world of strife should know. We must finish the rite before the heavens finish it for us!"

And he raises his staff aloft once more.

"Behold!" he shouts. "The heavens themselves declare their favor! Light from darkness! Day from light! The Great Wheel turns!"

The druids hastily and somewhat clumsily resume their circling and chanting. The vergobrets draw back.

"We turn round, and round, and round. . . ."

"Let the Great Wheel turn with us!" Guttuatr commands.

And, as if to obey, the moon begins to disgorge the light it has eaten, and the sky begins to brighten in a gloriously luxurious purple-and-gold false sunrise. The forest awakens, and blue skies and bright sun once more look down upon a world of verdant green. The rite has succeeded.

Or so it might seem.

Half a dozen roasting boar and as many sheep dripped their fat on crackling log fires, perfuming the air with deliciously pungent smoke. Boys pulled planks of steaming loaves from the ovens and set them out to cool. Peasants brought in wicker baskets overflowing with ripe red apples, white turnips, and dark-green nettles, savory and freshly picked. Bards toyed with their harps, and here and there servants sang with them.

It was the happiest day of Vercingetorix's young life, trotting to keep up with the mighty strides of his father, Keltill, as they crossed the outer courtyard of the family homestead in the bright afternoon sunshine. It was the day of the great feast to be given by Keltill to celebrate the inauguration of his year as vergobret of the Arverni.

Though robust and brawny, Keltill was but of average height for a Gaul, yet, in the eyes of his fourteen-year-old son, he was a giant.

His lands and his riches and his rule might have been passed down to him by the will of the gods, as the druids proclaimed, but what Vercingetorix saw in the eyes of his father's people was something no god could bestow. Nor were the smiles that greeted him bought solely with the gold coins he tossed with gay abandon into the air, as if they were so many sprigs of mistletoe.

Keltill was loved by his people.

Keltill grinned and made a great show of smacking his lips as they approached the brew master's cart. Seeing this famous enthusiast of his wares, the balding, fat-bellied fellow drew two foaming horns of beer from two different barrels.

"This one I would say has rather more flavor, Keltill," he said, offering the horn in his left hand, then raising the one in his right. "But this one has a bit stronger spirit."

Keltill quaffed the first, then the other.

"Well, which one do you favor?" asked the brew master.

"When did I ever taste a brew I didn't favor?" said Keltill. He laughed, then grinned at Vercingetorix. "What do you say, Vercingetorix, would you care to favor us with an opinion?"

Like any boy of Gaul, Vercingetorix was familiar with watered-down beer, given when hot weather made milk curdle or cows went dry. But this would be his first taste of the full-strength manly brew. He took a hesitant sip of the "more flavorful" beer. It was thick and sweet. Under the watchful eye of his father, he took a more manly gulp. Now a bitter aftertaste emerged, which he found less than pleasant.

"Well?" asked Keltill.

"Uh . . . good. Nice and, uh, foamy."

Keltill handed him the second horn. This time, Vercingetorix took a full adult mouthful straightaway, and made a show of rolling it around in his mouth thoughtfully before he swallowed. Less bitter, less sweet too, and not as thick.

"Even better!" he declared sincerely.

"Like father, like son!" Keltill said, fetching him a mighty clap on the shoulder. "My sentiments exactly! You heard our beer-taster, we'll have twenty barrels—of each of them!"

"Of each?" said the brew master, eyeing Keltill skeptically. "About the money . . ."

"Name your price! I'll pay you double whatever it is when we've both died and gone on to the next world in the good old Gallic fashion!"

"Very generous, Keltill, but if I, my family, and my brewers don't eat in this world, we'll find ourselves there for a good long while before you, so, if you don't mind . . ."

"Well, if you're going to be that way about it . . ." Keltill said impishly, reaching into the leather pouch from which he had been so freely dispensing largesse, and extracting but a single coin.

The brew master was not amused.

Keltill laughed at his sour expression.

"Come along, then," he said. "There's plenty more where that came from!"

He held the coin, which Vercingetorix knew bore Keltill's own portrait, closer for the brew master's inspection. "Handsome, are they not?"

They passed through a gate in the wooden palisade that enclosed the inner courtyard. Within was the great round house, with its well-hewn plank walls caulked with wattle, its tall conical roof freshened with newly cut thatch for the occasion, and still redolent of earth and hay. The roof, as always, was crowned with a carved wooden bear, sigil animal of the Arverni, but now a bear cast in bronze stood on a pole before the doorway—the standard of their new vergobret.

At the front of the house, trestle tables had already been set up and servants were setting out benches, dressing the tables with platters, and piling up logs for a bonfire.

Keltill crossed the courtyard to a wooden shed. Vercingetorix had been inside and so knew what to expect, but the brew master didn't. Two artisans were beating lumps of soft gold into sheets with heavy, broad-faced iron-headed mallets, and two more were stamping out coins from the sheets with round-faced dies and tossing them into big leather sacks already brimming with the fruit of their labors.

Keltill led the gaping brew master to one of the sacks. "Take what you consider just," he said. "No more and no less."

The brew master gave Keltill a look of amazement, which transformed to greed. He dipped both hands in the sack and came up with as much as he could carry.

He froze. He looked at Keltill.

Then he slowly dribbled half his load of coins back into the sack and departed.

"You just trusted him to take what he would!" Vercingetorix exclaimed.

"I trusted his honor. This is our way, Vercingetorix. Honor is to be trusted. Fortune is to be shared. Else what are we?"

He scooped up a great handful of coins and stuffed them in the leather pouch tied to his belt.

"Of course, it does not diminish a man's reputation for generosity that his likeness appears on his largesse, so that those who receive it never forget whence it came," he said. Then he laughed. "Not *every* notion of the Romans is foolish."

Keltill picked up another handful of coins and held it up before Vercingetorix's eyes. "On the other hand, the way they whore after this stuff to the point where they will even let it buy their honor is pitiful!"

"Pitiful, Father?"

"Indeed! They forget what gold is for. Do you know, Vercingetorix?"

Vercingetorix could only shake his head.

"Consider," said Keltill. "You cannot eat it, you cannot drink it, you cannot ride it, you cannot even forge a sword from this pretty but otherwise useless metal."

"But you can buy food and drink and horses and swords and more with it!"

"Exactly!" cried Keltill. "Life is not to be spent in the making and hoarding of money! Meat is to be eaten! Beer is to be drunk! Horses are to be ridden! A year as leader of your tribe is to be celebrated freely!"

With a wild laugh he tossed the whole handful of coins into the air. "Money is to be spent on the pleasures of living!"

By the time the sun had set, the festival had begun, and it could fairly be said that much money had indeed been spent on the pleasures of living.

A horde of guests had arrived. Most were Arverne nobles, their families, and warriors, and the ordinary folk of Keltill's holdings who had been favored with admission to the outer courtyard for the feast. Some few were invited nobles from other tribes of Gaul; some fewer still were druids, who had the right to invite themselves to any feast, anytime, anywhere, in the lands of the Gauls.

The drinking of beer was already well under way. Everyone had a foaming mug of copper or pottery, open barrels had been set out everywhere, and the fumes alone were enough to make the very old and the very young lightheaded.

Not that they were relying on their noses to get the beer to work its happy magic. Nor, having savored his first true taste, did Vercingetorix fail to quaff his fair share and then some. The torches seemed to him haloed, the final handful of coins tossed by Keltill cascaded through the syrupy air like flurries of golden snow, and the music and voices melded into the wordless song of a burbling stream.

Keltill's entry was greeted by a collective cheer. And though this was not lacking in wholehearted affection for the man himself, stomachs spoke as loudly as hearts when Keltill strode up to the bonfire.

A warrior handed Keltill a torch. Keltill made a grinning show of hesitation. "Surely, my friends, you have not yet drunk enough beer to truly whet your appetites?" he said. "Best we wait a bit longer before going on to the meat."

This was greeted by a mighty collective groan.

Keltill shook his head disapprovingly. "When Brenn was king and we were all heroes, Gauls would not even remember they *had* bellies until enough beer had passed down their throats to wash Ariovistus and all his Teuton tribes back across the Rhine on a river of piss!" he declared to a roar of laughter.

He shrugged. "But now I can hear your guts rumbling even over my own mighty words of wisdom, and so . . ."

Keltill tossed the torch through a gap in the loosely built pile of seasoned logs into the kindling at its core, which burst into flame with a whoosh of air and puff of smoke. Logs then caught fire, and the piney aroma mingled with the odors of roasting meat to drive all present into a state of joyous famishment.

Vercingetorix wobbled behind his father to the host's table, his knees performing a clumsy dance, his head reeling, his belly growling, his vision glittering from the torchlight and the bonfire.

The table was an oaken top set on trestles in front of the house, with a bench on one side only, so that those seated behind it faced the festivities. Upon it were laid loaves of bread, knives, and planks laden with roasted fowls, as well as bowls of turnips, carrots, boiled nettles, apples, ribs, and joints of mutton and boar, and, for this special feast, whole roast suckling boar, obtained at great expense and with no little difficulty.

Vercingetorix had not yet achieved such an exalted state that he could fail to recognize his own mother, Gaela, among those seated behind the table, and was even able to discern his uncle Gobanit and Gobanit's wife, Ette, seated to her right. To Gaela's left were the empty spaces reserved for his father and himself, and beyond that was a stern-looking woman in middle age who seemed vaguely familiar, and to *her* left—

Once Vercingetorix's gaze fell upon the girl who sat there, it had no interest in lingering elsewhere.

She looked to be about his age, with long golden tresses held off her fair, rosy face with a garland of flowers, and slim, graceful neck arising from the bodice of a yellow dress gathered tightly enough to reveal budding breasts. Her eyes were of that elusive hue that seems green one moment and hazel the next, her nose was straight, her chin was strong, and both were elevated to send a haughty challenge that set Vercingetorix's teeth on edge and his blood aflame.

Something in his eyes must have betrayed his state, for she met his gaze with a look that was enough to wilt crops in the fields. It was certainly enough to banish any notion of summoning up the courage to speak to her.

The feasting began with a will. The legs of fowl were ripped off with bare hands, ribs of pork and boar torn into individual morsels, everything else carved up with knives, and all was conveyed straight to devouring mouths as efficiently and quickly as possible, washed down by endless mugs and horns of beer kept full by servants.

Vercingetorix gobbled up his fair share of food and swilled at least that much beer, but throughout the meal stole long glances at the blonde girl, who displayed an admirable appetite, a sign that her appetite for other pleasures might prove equally hearty.

But he wished she would sip less daintily at her beer, for, the drunker she got, his fantasies proposed, the more likely they would pass from the realm of dreams into this one. The only thing he could think to do was set her a proper example.

"Is there enough meat?" Keltill bellowed. "Is there enough beer?"

The drunken roars and collective table-thumping of approval roused Vercingetorix from his dozing torpor.

"It is the tradition for the new vergobret, upon beginning his year as leader, to praise the wisdom of the Arverne nobles in electing such a hero as himself," Keltill declaimed, "but as you all know, my single flaw is that I'm far too modest to do my own proper boasting—"

Howls of good-natured laughter and amused hoots and jeers erupted from his audience.

"—so I'll let a better man do it for me—my noble son, the silver-tongued Vercingetorix!"

Vercingetorix, who had never made a speech before, whose head was reeling, and whose tongue, far from being silver, felt like a piece of dead wood in his mouth, sat there stunned and quite terrified.

But Keltill yanked him to his feet, and there he stood, the glow of the torches gauzed by his drunkenness, the bonfire nearly blinding him, staring into a field of faces, eyes sheened red by the firelight, as all sound died away into a dreadful expectant silence.

He found himself glancing sidelong at the blonde girl, who met his gaze for an instant with eyes as blank and impenetrable as polished jewels and an expression of amused contempt.

And then it was that the magic happened.

He looked away, his gaze following the sparks from the bonfire skyward. The roaring firelight washed away the glow of all but the brightest star, which in turn seemed to be gazing down at *him,* bestowing, so unlike the girl, its favor. And when he looked back earthward into all those eyes which a moment before had terrorized him, the silence had been transformed into an invitation to speak.

"As . . . as Keltill is my father, so now is he yours, Arverni, for the vergobret is the father of his people. And to have such a man as Keltill as your father makes you the most fortunate tribe in all Gaul. But I am more fortunate still. I am the most fortunate boy in Gaul. For you will have him as a father for but one short year. I will have him always."

He paused, lifted a horn of beer in a toasting gesture, a horn of beer that seemed to have been magically placed in his hand by the same gods who had given him this moment.

"To Keltill! To the vergobret of the Arverni! To honor that is to be trusted, and fortune that is to be shared, and a life that is to be spent on the pleasure of living!"

The roars and cheers were gloriously deafening. They seemed to grow even louder as Vercingetorix gulped down his entire horn of beer in five continuous swallows.

This, however, finally proved too much for him, and the last things he heard, before collapsing unconscious into the arms of Keltill, were good-natured laughter and the amused voices of his mother and father:

"Like father, like son!"

"My sentiments exactly!"

II

A LL ROME IS WAITING to watch you fall," said Decimus Junius Brutus as they made their way toward the baths, past eyes that looked away and backs that always seemed conveniently turned to them.

"Jackals are good at smelling blood, Brutus, but they lack the courage to attack even a wounded lion," Gaius Julius Caesar told him contemptuously. "And this fox still has a few tricks left, to mix a predatory metaphor."

Brutus gave him a quizzical look.

Caesar laughed. "I mean you would do well not to wager on my defeat, my young friend."

So young, so naïve, so innocent, Caesar thought. Was I ever thus? Perhaps suckling at my mother's teat? More likely, I was simply unaware of the political intrigue already swirling all around me, as a fish fails to notice that it is swimming in water.

Caesar's clan, the Julii, were old patricians, but by the time he was born rather threadbare ones, and the only road to riches in Rome for a scion thereof was politics. Unfortunately, the reverse was also true: any office in Rome worth having was won by election, and winning the favor of voters cost money—to finance feasts, games, bribes, favorable attention in the Forum. Thus, unless a politician was born to riches, he was constrained to replenish his depleted coffers from whatever office he had achieved in order to finance his election to the next rung up the political and economic ladder. Since this was the only means by which a man such as Caesar could pursue a career of public service, as far as he was concerned it was the height of cynicism to call it corruption.

Not that cynicism was ever in danger of going out of fashion in Rome, Caesar thought as they entered the thermae.

The baths were divided into three large main chambers: the cool frigidarium for those who sought the illusion that they were rugged Spartans; the tepidarium, where the temperature was kept at the civilized level of a fine spring day; and the caldarium, too hot for Caesar's taste but, fogged with steam from the central hot pool, an appropriate venue for a political assignation with Marcus Licinius Crassus.

Crassus was not the sort of figure displayed to best advantage without his toga. Blubbery and out of shape, he lay on his belly on a poolside couch with only a towel over his behind as a gesture to aesthetics, sipping wine from a golden goblet.

"Hail, Crassus!"

"Hail, Caesar . . ."

"You know my young friend Decimus Junius Brutus?"

"Hail, Brutus. I believe we may have met somewhere," Crassus said, looking the poor boy up and down as if it might have been in a brothel where Brutus had served as a catamite.

He raised a bushy eyebrow at Caesar and gave him a look that seemed to assume that Brutus was presently serving him in the same capacity. "I thought this was to be a private conversation, Caesar."

"It would not be wise for it to *seem* so, now, would it, Crassus?" Caesar said smoothly, masking his displeasure. "And Brutus enjoys my full confidence."

"Does he, now?" said Crassus in a lubricious tone of voice.

Caesar knew that his propensity for mentoring promising youths was often taken for boy love in the Greek manner. But he had found nothing a boy could do to please him that a woman could not do better, and by his lights sex with a protégé like Brutus would be all too akin to doing it with one's own son. Indeed, he suspected that the Greeks who extolled the intellectual communion of such love above all others did so out of pining for male progeny.

"Brutus is like the son I unfortunately do not have," he said pointedly, without letting his true feelings show, an art at which he was adept, and particularly around Crassus.

"And what is the subject of this conversation, which you have so urgently requested?" Crassus asked fatuously.

"We have reason to discuss these ridiculous charges of embezzling public funds," Caesar replied.

"Do we?"

"Really, Crassus," said Caesar, "any Roman over the age of ten knows that anyone elected to anything requires money to oil the machineries of the Republic."

Crassus took a slow sip of wine and regarded Caesar ingenuously. "I see," he said, "you've simply appropriated public money to do the public business. None of it, of course, managed to find its way into your private coffers."

"Whatever may find its way into my private coffers exits soon enough in the service of election to my next public office," Caesar replied. "And since I am acknowledged to be among Rome's most able political leaders, it may justly be said to serve the interest of the Republic."

"You always were a diligent student of the Sophists, Caesar."

"Better a skilled practitioner of Sophist rhetoric than a devotee of the philosophy of the Cynics, Crassus."

"Even as we have a god for every taste, the Greeks had a philosophy for every purpose," said Crassus.

"Spoken like a Pragmatist!" said Caesar. "And, one Pragmatist to another, Crassus, you do not really want the Senate delving too deeply into my finances—now, do you? Do you really imagine our mutually advantageous dealings would remain hidden?"

Crassus put down his goblet, rose into an upright position, and regarded Caesar with a colder eye.

"Is that a threat, Caesar?"

"Not at all, my friend, I merely seek to protect you," said Caesar. "After all, we both know that what may have stuck to *my* fingers since you and I and Pompey were elected consuls has also stuck to yours."

"What do you want?" Crassus said sharply.

"The proconsulship of Cisalpine Gaul," said Caesar.

"Governing a sleepy province in northern Italy where nothing much has happened since we threw out the barbarians seems quite a comedown after a consulship in Rome," said Crassus, eyeing Caesar narrowly.

"The only reason the Senate hasn't charged me yet is that a consul is immune from prosecution during his term of office—"

"And yours is shortly to run out—"

"But the proconsul of a Roman province is *also* immune from prosecution by the Senate."

"I had forgotten you were a lawyer," Crassus said dryly. "But why a backwater like Cisalpine Gaul?"

"Because it's available," Caesar said. "Because it's a backwater. Meaning that enough of my enemies would vote with my friends to grant it to me just to get me out of Rome."

"Very clever." Crassus smiled at Caesar smarmily. "But . . . how can I put this delicately. . . ? It seems I can't." He shrugged "What's in it for me?"

"Aside from avoiding an unpleasant investigation into our previously profitable dealings?" replied Caesar. "More of the same profitable dealings, of course. Much more."

"Cisalpine Gaul is hardly a cornucopia of riches," Crassus said skeptically.

"But the rest of Gaul is," Caesar told him, baiting the hook.

"Gallia Narbonensis? Wine, olives, fruit, good ports. A little better, but not by much, and besides, you said—"

"No, no, not our old Mediterranean province! The whole thing, Crassus! *Transalpine* Gaul! What lies to the *north* of Gallia Narbonensis! The great heartland of *true* Gaul! A vast territory rich in gold, silver, iron, jewels, rare dyes, cattle, grain, and prime slave material!"

"Inconveniently inhabited by tribes of warlike Gauls and savage Teutons."

"The Teuton tribes may be savages," said Caesar, not bothering to add that they were going to provide the perfect casus belli, "but the Gauls are rich, and sophisticated enough to be eager for the benefits of commerce with us. Why, they've got a trade delegation in Rome even now."

"Rich naïfs ripe for the picking," said Crassus, rolling the baited hook around in his mouth thoughtfully.

"First come our merchants," Caesar told him, "then our engineers to build roads for the commerce, and artisans to build the rich Gauls proper Roman villas and dress them in style, and slave dealers, and of course they will need skilled Roman bankers to manage their new economy."

"I see," said Crassus, taking the hook. "A proconsul of Gallia Narbonensis who understood this could reward his friends with handsome concessions."

"Indeed!" said Caesar. "Those whom I favor will become richer than Crassus—I mean Croesus."

"But wait!" said Crassus. "It's the proconsulship of *Cisalpine Gaul* that's vacant, not Gallia Narbonensis."

"True," said Caesar, "but if the proconsulship of Gallia Narbonensis should become vacant later, it would be easy enough to persuade the Senate to combine the posts, would it not?"

"I suppose so."

Caesar cast a sidelong glance at Brutus, considering how far he cared to go in corrupting youth in the service of political education.

"And it will become vacant," he said. "Soon after my appointment, the present proconsul of Gallia Narbonensis will develop a fatal illness."

"How do you know this, Caesar?" asked Crassus.

"You forget I was not only once a pontifex, but elected pontifex maximus," said Caesar. "I read the omens in the entrails of last night's roast chicken."

"Food poisoning?"

"It's a hot climate. Hang a pheasant a day too long, or eat a bad oyster in the wrong season . . ."

Caesar glanced once more at the shocked Brutus. But the boy's face quickly became an unreadable mask. And that showed promise. Everyone had to rid himself of his virginity sooner or later.

His appointment as proconsul of Cisalpine Gaul had left Caesar with little need of strong drink to buoy his spirit, and he, Brutus, and Junius Marius Gisstus reclined on couches around the banquet table, awaiting the arrival of the Eduen envoy, sipping at well-watered wine.

"Well, my friends, farewell to the pit of vipers that is Rome," he fairly burbled. "We're off to win fame and fortune in glorious Gaul!"

"I can believe the *fortune* part," Gisstus said sardonically.

His lips seemed carved in a permanent ironic grimace; there was something about his eyes that said he had seen twice as much as any other man of his middle years and had not been particularly impressed by any of it. Caesar's spymaster's face was one only his mother would trust. And even she not very far.

Nevertheless, he was utterly loyal to Caesar out of pragmatic self-interest, for Caesar had raised him from centurion to his present position, and there was no way a man of his modest and shady background could rise any higher.

"But *fame*, Caesar?" said Brutus. "By holding down Cisalpine Gaul, a province in Italy that's been pacified for a hundred years?"

"You're forgetting Gallia Narbonensis."

Brutus frowned. "I wish I could," he muttered glumly.

"What's troubling you, my young friend?"

Brutus shrugged. "Perhaps my conscience."

"Have it removed at once," suggested Gisstus. "I know a good surgeon."

"Perhaps it can be eased without the knife," suggested Caesar.

"Don't you intend to . . . remove the proconsul of Gallia Narbonensis in order that you might replace him?" Brutus said queasily. "Which is to say, murder him."

"The proper term is 'assassination,'" corrected Gisstus.

"There's a difference?"

"Indeed there is," said Caesar. "A murder is personal act. An assassination is the killing of a man for reasons of state. An act of political necessity."

Brutus seemed less than convinced. Perhaps a bit of Socratic dialogue . . .

"You are eager to attain the rank of general and win glory by defeating the enemy?"

"Of course, Caesar."

"And how is the enemy to be defeated?"

Brutus' silence was eloquent.

"Yes, my young friend, by killing as many of them as possible."

"But that's *war*!"

"Thousands of killings for reasons of state. Thousands of assassinations performed out of political necessity."

"It's not the same thing!" Brutus insisted. Then, a good deal less certainly, "Is it?"

"Perhaps you'd care to elucidate the moral difference?"

There was a long moment of awkward silence.

"I still don't see how holding down even two thoroughly conquered provinces will do much to enhance your reputation," said Brutus in an equally awkward attempt to break it.

"Explain it to him, Gisstus," Caesar said.

"There are bound to be Teuton attacks on the trade caravans we send into the lands of the Edui and the other tribes of Gaul, and of course Rome can hardly let such outrageous banditry go unpunished. Order will have to be established up there in Transalpine Gaul, and since the Gauls have not proved up to it . . . ."

"We will have to teach the Teutons a lesson," said Brutus, beginning to get it.

"Many lessons, I'm afraid," said Caesar. "They may be relied upon to be slow learners. Unfortunately, in the end we will have to dispatch many more troops than we originally anticipated to secure the trade routes and save Rome's friends from these bloodthirsty monsters."

At last the light of comprehension dawned on Brutus' visage. "And, once established in the lands of the Gauls, we will be in no hurry to leave. . . ."

"You'll make a general yet," said Caesar.

"But I still don't see how something like that is going to make you a famous hero in Rome."

Caesar laughed. "Never fear, Brutus, it will sound like Great Alexander's march through Persia into India in the dispatches sent back to be read in the Forum and the Senate!"

"How can you be so certain?"

"Because I intend to write them myself. And perhaps collect them in a book to preserve the glory of my conquest for the ages."

Gisstus made a show of choking on his laughter. Brutus obviously didn't know whether to regard this as boast or jest, and, truth be told, neither did Caesar.

He habitually led his legions from the forefront, wore a cloak dyed crimson with rare and costly Tyrian purpura, and forbade the hue to his generals and lieutenants otherwise entitled to wear the purple, thus turning the color into his personal ensign, and thereby proclaiming his position on the battlefield to friend and foe alike.

For like it or not, leadership in war was part of statecraft.

And gods help you, Gaius Julius Caesar, like it, you do.

"What do you think of *Gaius Julius Caesar, Conqueror of Gaul* as a title?" he asked.

"Too cumbersome," said Gisstus. "Why don't you just call it *The Conquest of Gaul*?"

"You may be right," Caesar said dryly. "People do favor a certain modesty in their heroes."

As Gisstus laughed, Calpurnia entered to inform Caesar that the Eduen envoy, Diviacx, was arriving.

"Remind the slaves not to water his wine," Caesar told her as he rose to greet his guest at the gate like a proper host.

"Of course," said Calpurnia. "After all, water rusts out iron. Imagine what it would do to a Gaul's insides. Whereas wine may preserve them by pickling."

"The more the better," Caesar said, giving his third wife a wink as he departed.

Calpurnia might not have quite the beauty of Cornelia or the sexual hunger of Pompeia, but she was the only one of the three with the intellect and instincts to become his confidante.

Caesar had never before met the leader of the Eduen delegation, but he knew that the Edui were perhaps the most powerful and civilized of the Gallic tribes, and he had been informed that Diviacx was a member of their grandiloquently self-styled "Senate." The man he greeted at his portal was tall and robust, with near-shoulder-length iron-gray hair, big matching mustache, and a saturnine visage—your typical Gaul, from all he had been told. But his cowled white robe trimmed in blue was something of a shock, and Caesar had to exercise his thespian skills to avoid showing it. The leader of the Eduen trade delegation was a druid!

Little was known about these Gallic priests, if that was indeed what they were. There seemed to be many more of them than were needed to leech off an equivalent population of Romans. It was said that they were also magistrates. And perhaps tax collectors. It was also said that none of them paid taxes, an advantage, alas, that Caesar had not enjoyed during his brief stint as pontifex.

Priest? Senator? Merchant? Some bizarre combination? This might complicate things. Best be wary.

It seemed prudent to greet him with a simple "Hail, Diviacx." "Hail, Caesar," Diviacx replied, and they left to join Calpurnia, Gisstus, and Brutus at the banquet table.

Though styling the repast a "banquet" would have been hyperbole—there were only five diners clustered on couches toward one end of the table, and not so much as a single musician to distract from the conversation. Caesar had, however, laid on an impressive display of Roman cuisine. Impressing the Eduen with the civilized luxuries of Rome was certainly called for, never mind the expense.

The first courses were brought out with the wine as soon as Diviacx was seated—honeyed dormice, figs poached in wine and cinnamon, assorted smoked songbirds, grilled langoustine served in warm saffroned olive oil, red peppers stuffed with whole sardines, a paste of spiced mashed eggplant served with four kinds of bread for dipping, plates of both vinegar- and oil-cured olives, nuts, fruits, small pies of pheasant and lamb forcemeats, pickled octopus, fried squid.

Diviacx went at it like a good diplomat, trying everything, visibly turning up his nose at nothing—an impressive feat, as Caesar knew from his travels, since one people's delicacies might very well be another's abominations. While it was obvious to the careful observer that he regarded the squid, langoustine, and octopus as species of loathsome sea monsters by the way he picked listlessly at them, and though he turned a bit green around the edges when constrained by politesse to sample the dormice and songbirds, Caesar had the feeling that Diviacx had steeled himself to at least nibble gingerly at a turd should one be placed before him. The rest of the appetizers he wolfed down as if they were the only course, displaying an impressive barbarian appetite, and equally barbaric table manners.

During all this, Gisstus, not much for small talk, and Brutus, somewhat overawed by the company, said little, as Caesar and Calpurnia kept the conversation light—the nature of the cuisine, the relative merits and flaws of Gallic and Roman climates and of beer versus the wine that the slaves poured so freely, and which Diviacx seemed to favor, judging by the diligence with which he sampled it.

Caesar did not venture into deeper waters until the slaves began clearing the detritus from the table in preparation for the main course.

"If I understand correctly, Diviacx, your robe indicates that you are a druid. . . ."

"This is so," said Diviacx, reclining torpidly, but nevertheless sipping at his wine goblet.

"And yet here you are, a priest, at the head of a trade mission."

Diviacx carefully placed his goblet on the table, as if now sensing it would not do to befuddle his brain further. "Not all druids are priests," he said.

"My husband was a priest for a time, you know," said Calpurnia.

"But, like myself, more a man of this world than the other?" said Diviacx.

"Like yourself?" blurted Brutus. "I had heard you were all magicians."

"In our tongue, 'druid' means not 'priest' but 'man of knowledge.' And as there are different kinds of knowledge, so are there different kinds of druids. Magistrates. Teachers. Many bear the knowledge of this realm, a few bear the knowledge of the other."

"The other realm?" said Brutus.

"The Land of Legend."

Diviacx turned from Brutus to lock eyes with Caesar, and though his eyes were rheumed and bloodshot with wine, they had the power to hold Caesar's own.

"*You* know whereof I speak, do you not, Caesar?"

"Do I?" said Caesar, staring back unwaveringly, for he had learned this trick too, not as a pontifex, but from his studies of oratory on Rhodes under the master of the art, Molon.

"I have heard it said you consider yourself a man of destiny. . . ."

"Guilty as charged," said Caesar.

"And the spirit of Great Alexander reborn."

"That, my friend, is metaphor," said Caesar, dismissing the notion with a laugh, albeit one that sounded hollow to his own ears. This druid had seen more deeply into his soul than he found comfortable. For, although he had had difficulty taking the gods and their otherworldly realm seriously even when elected to perform their rites, he did feel a lineal connection between his own spirit and that of the long-dead Alexander.

Not that he believed he was Alexander reborn; on the contrary, he believed that Alexander had been his primitive forerunner, as Alexander's own father, King Philip, had been a more modest version of the great man himself. Caesar believed that his destiny was to succeed where the Macedonian had failed.

Alexander had conquered the largest empire the world had yet seen, and it was said he had wept for lack of more to conquer. This Caesar doubted, since all he would have had to do was turn his attention westward—toward Gaul, for example. If he had wept at all, it was probably because, being a great general but no genius as a political craftsman, he had no notion of how to turn his conquests into a nation that would long survive him. He started as a king and died as an emperor, leaving the posterity of what he had built to be inherited and squabbled over by the usual royal mediocrities.

Caesar would start with a republic and build upon that not an empire but something yet nameless, ruled not by his heirs but by a political system of his creation. This would be his monument, greater than the Pyramids or the Colossus of Rhodes or the Library of Alexandria. Greater because it would be built not of the stone and cement of the material world but of the immaterial stuff of the world inside his own cranium. Caesar shuddered. How deeply did this druid see? For that realm of future destiny was indeed his Land of Legend.

"Are you all right?" asked Calpurnia, leaning closer to whisper in his ear in some agitation. "Not the falling sickness?"

"Perhaps he has had a vision?" suggested Diviacx, a shade too knowingly for Caesar's equilibrium.

"Perhaps," said Caesar, shaking his head, both to return his focus to the here and now and to reassure Calpurnia with the same gesture. "In a metaphorical manner of speaking."

Fortunately, a moment later four slaves carried in a huge bronze platter bearing the main course, and it was Diviacx's turn to be discombobulated. Caesar had ordered up one of those layered mixed roasts designed to impress dignitaries at state banquets or, as in this case, to impress a foreigner with the wealth and lavish style of his host, and hence his economic power. At large banquets, the outer layer was usually a whole ox or stag, though Caesar had heard stories of elephants, but for such a small dinner a boar sufficed, glazed with honey, holding an apple in its mouth, and wearing a crown of laurel. Inside this was a whole lamb roasted over rosemary branches, mouthing an orange. Inside the lamb was a peacock with a plum in its beak, inside the peacock a pheasant with a grape, inside the pheasant a pigeon with a wild raspberry, inside the pigeon a tiny thrush with a single currant impaled on its beak.

Caesar watched in amusement as Diviacx's eyes fairly bugged out while the slaves sliced this nested confection of beasts and birds open with swords and ceremony, stepwise revealing what was hidden within, extracting it, and laying it out upon the table.

"Fortunately, Diviacx," said Caesar, when this had been completed, "you had the foresight to pick delicately at the appetizers."

Diviacx made a heroic effort at least to sample everything, washing it all down with more wine, and by the time he had consumed what politesse required, his face was sheened with sweat, his eyes were glazing over, and it was time to negotiate.

"As you know," Caesar told him, "I've been elected proconsul of Cisalpine Gaul, and am therefore in a position to greatly enhance trade relations between your people and Rome."

Diviacx managed to perk up at this, though it obviously took quite some effort. "It is no secret that that is indeed the purpose of my mission."

"Well, consider it a success, my friend!" Caesar exclaimed. "You will return home a rich man!"

"I am here to enrich my people, not myself," Diviacx replied huffily.

"Of course, of course. Still, there's no reason why a man should not do well by doing good. It is what makes Rome great and makes its friends prosper."

Diviacx levered himself into an upright position, a magical feat in itself, considering how much food and wine he had consumed. "What are you proposing, Caesar?" he asked.

"My intent is to shift the route of exports of dyes, chariots, horses, metalwork, and so forth from the lands of the Edui south through my territories to my Mediterranean ports and thence to Rome by sea rather than overland—"

"A rather circuitous route—"

"But a more secure one, passing as it does only through the lands of the Gauls and my own and then via sea-lanes pacified by Roman galleys. And since it will be more secure, it seems to me only just to levy taxes on their passage—say, the tenth part of their value for passage through the territories of the Gauls, and the tenth part for passage through mine. I have heard that the writ of the druids crosses tribal boundaries. . . ."

"This is true," said Diviacx.

"I have also heard that there are circumstances under which druids collect such levies. . . ."

Diviacx's eyes lit up with a greed that seemed very much of this world and not some other. "This too is true," he said.

"May I thus presume that I can leave it to you to find administrators to take care of the collection on the Gallic end . . . ?"

"That should prove no problem."

"Likewise, the same taxes will be collected on the Roman wine, furniture, foodstuffs, arts, marble, instruments, and tools of architecture, medicines, and everything else moving in the other direction by the same route. . . ."

"As is only just," agreed Diviacx.

"Moreover," said Caesar, "the flow of trade will increase from the present trickle to a mighty torrent, for I will send Roman engineers to build roads to speed this commerce. Why, we will—"

"You're forgetting a few things, Caesar," Gisstus interrupted, as had been previously arranged. And Caesar gave him a prearranged scowl of annoyance.

"What, Gisstus?" he demanded harshly.

"In the first place, there are other tribes between the lands of the Edui and Gallia Narbonensis, who may not appreciate—"

"Why not allow them the benefit of the same arrangement?" Diviacx interrupted hastily.

"He's right, Gisstus," Caesar said. "You just heard our friend say that the law of the druids crosses tribal boundaries."

"Well, what about Ariovistus and the Teutons?" said Gisstus. "We can hardly send engineers to build roads through territory overrun by savage marauders."

"There *is* that . . ." mused Caesar.

"The threat is highly exaggerated," Diviacx said. Unconvincingly. "Our warriors will protect them."

"They haven't been doing that well protecting your own people lately, now, have they?" Gisstus said dryly.

Diviacx had no answer to that, and Caesar let the ensuing unhappy silence go on a while before he deemed it appropriate to display his spontaneous inspiration.

"I have an idea!" he exclaimed.

"You do?" said Gisstus.

"I'll dispatch a Roman legion or two to rid your lands of the Teutons once and for all, Diviacx! I'll lead it myself! I personally guarantee that Roman troops will make short work of such marauding horse barbarians! And since it won't take long, the cost to you will be modest."

"The cost. . . ?"

"The Senate of Rome can hardly be expected to finance an expedition to rescue a foreign land from rapine and plunder. *Someone* has to pay for it."

"I don't know about this, Caesar . . ." Diviacx said unhappily.

"Believe me, Diviacx, getting the money out of the Senate is a political impossibility," Caesar said, quite truthfully. Having gotten him safely out of Rome, the last thing his enemies were about to do was finance his raising of an army at whose head he could return in triumph.

Once more, Caesar let a silence go on for a long moment, then brought the drama to its happy climax.

"Of course!" he cried, whacking his forehead with the heel of his hand as if angered at his own stupidity. "We'll do it at a *profit*! To both of us!"

"We will?"

Now Caesar locked eyes with the druid, and if he lacked the power to peer into Diviacx's soul, he lacked not the power to grant him a vision.

"Why think of the Teutons as a liability, when they are in fact a valuable and abundant commodity?" he purred. "Physically robust, not excessively intelligent—ideal slaves for quarries, galleys, farm labor, if not households. And the best of them will fetch great prices as gladiators. You will pay the expense of collection, and we will split the profits right down the middle."

"Sell the Teutons into slavery?"

Caesar favored Diviacx with a vulpine smile. "Have they been so gentle in the process of pillaging your lands and raping your women that selling into slavery the ones we do not slay would not sit well on the conscience of your people?"

"Hardly," said Diviacx, and broke into a grin himself.

And Caesar knew that the deal was sealed.

III

THE SIXSCORE HORSEMEN in the Roman cavalry formation retreated down the valley in good order, standard held high, as if this were a triumphant parade. Yet less than a mile behind them and gaining was a horde of Teutons numbering at least a thousand.

The valley broadened out into a grassy plain behind the Teutons, but here it narrowed into a defile between lightly wooded hills, and whereas the Romans galloped along six abreast down the center, the Teutons surged forward in a wide front across the valley floor, jostling and racing one another to gain the front rank.

The Romans wore identical black-brush-crested helmets, leather breastplates, and brownish-red cloaks, and were equipped with identical swords, shields, and lances. The Teutons were armed with weapons of every sort, and each of them boasted his own taste in attire—helmets of brass, bronze, iron; leather kilts, plaid Gallic pantaloons; furred capes, and capes of cloth; sandals, leggings, boots; wool shirts, leather jerkins, bare chests. They wore their hair long, some braided, some blowing like golden pennants in the wind of passage, some greased up in jagged crests.

Most of their horses carried one warrior, but some carried two, the second mounted behind the horseman and armed with a lance, a battle-ax, or a long sword. There were even a few chariots.

The din they sent up was terrific and meant to be so; the clattering thunder of hooves, the rumble of chariot wheels, and, most fearful of all, the massed berserker rage of battle cries, bellowed at the top of a thousand and more sets of lungs. But no Roman deigned to glance back, as if even to acknowledge the onrushing presence of that which was gaining on them would be an offense to their dignity.

As the valley narrowed, the hills confining it descended and it became a small meadow at the margin of a dense lowland forest. The Roman cavalry fled toward it, apparently seeking to disperse within the trees, where a large formation of mounted warriors would find it difficult to run down scattered single horsemen.

Or so, no doubt, thought the Teutons.

Instead, as the meadow curved to the left, they found themselves confronting a formation of Roman infantry. This might be only three cohorts of a full legion's ten, no more than a thousand men, but their front rank confronted the Teutons behind an impenetrable wall of shields barbed with short thrusting swords. About thirty yards behind them, another such rank of swordsmen was visible, and in between were legionnaires armed with javelins. The flanks were guarded by smaller squads of sword-bearing infantry backed up by modest detachments of cavalry.

The front rank of Roman infantry quickly opened a gap to allow the cavalry to pass through their line to safety, and just as quickly re-closed it.

By now the Teutons were familiar with Roman infantry, and prudence would have dictated retreat. But their pride would not allow them to flee a force no larger than their own, and one not even mounted like proper warriors.

The Romans greeted them with a barrage of javelins as soon as they came within even extreme range. The first volley did little damage, but the second and the third, delivered at closer range, caused considerable carnage and great confusion, as men fell screaming from horses or lost control of their mounts, as wounded horses reared and dying horses thrashed and whinnied on the ground, as other horses tripped over them and fell, spilling their riders.

The front rank of Roman infantry marched toward them, followed by the javelin squads, then by the second rank of shielded swordsmen.

The Teutons charged.

This neutralized the Roman javelin squads, as the Teuton cavalry closed with the Roman infantry. But their swords and axes and lances were largely ineffective at penetrating the Roman shield wall to get at the swordsmen behind.

The Teutons hacked away at the Roman shields with broad sweeps of mighty swords and battle-axes, but the Romans hunkered behind them, wielding short, double-edged, and sharply pointed gladii, thrusting straight at soft targets—the bellies of horses, the legs and groins of their riders. Soon scores of horses had their guts pierced and scores of Teutons lay dead beneath their fallen bodies. Men writhed on the ground screaming, bleeding, as they died in slow agony.

Then a group of Teuton horsemen at the right of the Roman line found the wit to retreat far enough to regroup and try a flanking maneuver.

They managed to round the right end of the Roman front line, and fight their way through the flank guard to attack the javelin-throwers and the front line's vulnerable rear.

But the javelin throwers had retreated behind the second rank of Roman infantry. And the Roman front rank *had* no unprotected rear.

To the befuddlement and dismay of the Teutons, what had appeared as a simple rank of Roman infantry was now revealed as only the front sides of a rank of small square formations of legionnaires, protecting themselves with shield walls in all four directions. Within these little mobile fortresses, the Roman swordsmen hid like turtles in their shells. Worse, attacking them was like falling upon *porcupines* inside the shells of turtles, for these turtles bristled with sharp metal quills and knew how to use them.

The Romans allowed the Teutons between their lines to clash against the turtles long enough to set up an encouraging din, then they allowed another group of Teuton horsemen to come around their line on the left. Only then did their rear rank, more turtles, march forward and catch them like grapes in a wine press.

By now, the berserker rage of the Teutons had been cooled by the disastrous turn of events, and the majority of those remaining were ready to turn and flee back up the valley.

Turn they did, but flee they couldn't.

Blocking their escape route was another wall of Roman infantry, advancing implacably toward them.

"Pathetic," said Gaius Julius Caesar, as he and Brutus rode through the battlefield toward Marcus Tulius.

The grass of the meadow had been churned up and pools of blood were everywhere, drying to the color of the exposed earth beneath. The clearing stank with the aftermath of battle, with the reek of burst bowels and intestines, the death-dunging of hundreds of horses. Moans and shrieks rent the air as legionnaires dispatched the dying. Other legionnaires stripped corpses of their weapons. Chattels of the slave dealers went about inspecting the wounded, dispatching those too far gone to recover to a marketable condition, yoking the lucky ones together into strings of men and leading them away.

"A horrific sight," agreed Brutus, turning a greenish shade of pale.

Caesar shrugged. "A battlefield . . ." he said diffidently, kindly restraining the urge to laugh at the boy's expense. "I was referring to the pathetic battle tactics of the Teutons."

"Unfortunate for them, but fortunate for us," said Brutus.

"In battle, yes, my young friend; afterward, no. If they were a little less inclined to volunteer to be butchered and a little more inclined to surrender rather than fight hopelessly to the death, we'd be taking a lot more slaves. They just have no idea of civilized warfare."

Of course, this had been just a minor skirmish against one of the remnants left behind after the main forces commanded by Ariovistus— a barbarian who at least had *some* flair for tactics—had been beaten back across the Rhine.

The Teutons, like the Gauls, were larger men in general than Romans, and great horsemen, and Caesar knew (but would never admit) that an equal force of Teuton or Gallic cavalry would prove superior to his own. But whereas infantry was the main force of a Roman legion, neither the Teutons nor the Gauls had true infantry. The nobles and their warriors thought it beneath their dignity to fight afoot, and so their foot troops consisted of dragooned and untrained peasants or even slaves; Roman infantry consisted of professionals who had volunteered for the full twenty-year term and well-trained citizen conscripts.

That well-disciplined and well-commanded infantry could be more effective than the bravest and best of cavalry was a concept as foreign to Teuton military doctrine as tactical retreat, which they regarded as an act of cowardice and an offense to honor.

"Well done, Tulius," Caesar told the general upon arriving outside his tent, where Tulius sat on a stool beside a great pile of Teuton weaponry being tallied by a scribe with a stylus and tablet.

"Hail, Caesar," said Tulius, starting to rise.

Caesar stopped him with a gesture of his hand and did not bother to dismount. "Mostly worthless, I'd say," he said, casting a dismissive glance at the pile of captured weapons.

Tulius, a short, dark-complexioned, wiry man of few unnecessary words, simply nodded. Marcus Tulius was that rarity, a twenty-year legionnaire who had taken five years to make centurion and seven more to rise to command of a legion. He was an exemplar of the Roman professional soldier, and therefore a special favorite.

It also made him the sort of general you could assign necessary but inglorious or even odious tasks and know that he would get them done. Which was more than you could say for Titus Labienus, Caesar's second-in-command, a greater leader of men and tactical thinker by far, but one who fought for the joy of glorious battle alone, like a Teuton or a Gaul.

"Sort out Roman swords and armor and the Gallic swords, and leave the rest to rot," Caesar ordered. "It wouldn't fetch enough to justify the bother of hauling it away."

Tulius nodded again.

"Slaves?" inquired Caesar.

Tulius' shrug may have been all too eloquent, but Caesar pressed him for more detail anyway. "How many?"

"Fewer than two hundred able-bodied ordinaries," Tulius told him. "They *do* find it difficult to surrender in a condition suitable for mines or quarries." His expression brightened somewhat. "But the same will to fight to the death does make these Teutons great gladiator material when you can capture them intact. I'd say we have twenty or twenty-five, three or four of them potential favorites in Rome itself."

Caesar nodded without any great enthusiasm, saluted, then rode slowly toward his own field headquarters to be alone with his own thoughts.

Teuton gladiators did command handsome prices, but he had counted on taking many more slaves during this phase of the war. Thus far the war was running at a loss, for the slave trade was not covering the difference between what the more and more reluctant Edui were paying him to support his expanding army, and his own mounting costs.

Worse, by now Caesar had learned enough to know that able-bodied warriors in the prime of life would never be plentiful slave material here. Both Gauls and Teutons preferred fighting to the death even to a chance to fight their way to a retirement of riches, fame, and Roman citizenship in the arena. Odd, since, if one was going to fight to the death anyway, one had nothing to lose by giving a career as a gladiator a try.

Indeed, the Gauls and the Teutons, though both would slit your throat for saying so, were really cousins in the same family of peoples. Both had arrived as marauding bands of nomads from the endless eastern plains. The Teutons kept mostly to the north and west of the Alps. The Gauls had pillaged their way through Italy all the way to Rome under their so-called King Brenn. But once they were driven back here by Rome, Brenn's "kingdom" had degenerated back into a collection of tribes, each ruled by a vergobret, leaving "Gaul" a nation that really only existed on Roman maps.

Yet, whereas the Teutons had remained much as they had always been, the Gallic tribes had become more civilized. They farmed, were husbandmen, mined, and smelted ores. They were excellent smiths and produced jewelry as good as most in Rome. They guarded the secrets of dyes whose hues no one else could yet produce, and they built rude but usable roads and cities of a modest kind; some had even learned to write their language in the borrowed Greek alphabet.

Give them a coherent system of government, and you could fairly deem them civilized. Indeed, they were already beginning to copy the style of the Roman Republic. Vergobrets, although they weren't yet called "consuls," were elected by tribal councils for short fixed terms; a few such councils had begun to call themselves "Senates."

What made the Gauls different from the Teutons?

This was a conundrum that Caesar knew he would do well to fathom before he turned his attention to them. Which would have to be fairly soon. He was running out of Teutons. Already there were mutterings to be heard among the Edui's most powerful rivals, the Arverni, that the legions of Rome had completed their task and it was time for them to leave.

Logic told him that the difference between the Gauls and the Teutons must have something to do with the druids, since the Teutons had nothing like them. Nor did any other people Caesar had encountered in his travels or readings. Not only did they perform the rites and sacrifices, they administered the law throughout Gaul. But nowhere was the law written down, nor did anyone seem to know quite what it was but the druids themselves.

The druids were recognized by all Gauls as the ultimate authority, yet they did not seem a priestly theocracy, for they did not rule. But they somehow made sure that no one else did either.

It was a paradox worthy of Zeno.

It was early afternoon when Gisstus arrived at Caesar's camp from the Eduen capital, Bibracte. Caesar was sitting on a stool in the pleasant sunlight, composing his latest dispatch with stylus and wax tablet before committing it to the permanence of paper, since he had found that turning an account of a minor skirmish into a tale of glory usually required several revisions.

"Hail, Caesar," Gisstus said, then peered over his shoulder. "Still writing *The Conquest of Gaul*, eh? Let's hope it won't be long before you can write the final chapter. And then on to—what?—the first chapter of *Julius Caesar, King of Rome?*"

"No, Gisstus, the gods forbid that such a volume ever be written!"

"But the whole purpose of this war is to seize power and—"

"To *rule* as dictator as the law allows, Gisstus, not to *reign* as king. The king who founds a dynasty is a hero and a statesman, his son is a mediocrity, his son a half-wit or a monster, and *his* son probably both!"

"All this for six months as dictator?" Gisstus said sardonically. *"As the law allows?"*

"Laws can be changed when inconvenient to the health of a state," Caesar told him.

"Spoken like a lawyer."

"By a lawyer, as I am, who is also a general with a sufficient force behind him to be decisively persuasive in debate. As I will be."

Gisstus laughed. "Spoken like Gaius Julius Caesar," he said. "But changed to what?"

In truth, Caesar hadn't decided yet. "Perhaps dictator for life?" he said tentatively.

"That might turn out to be a shorter term than it might seem, since it would leave only one means of retiring you from office," Gisstus pointed out dryly.

"Appointed for some long fixed term, then? Ten years? Twenty?"

"A modest enough ambition . . ." Gisstus said dryly.

"Indeed. When Alexander the Great was ten years younger than I am now, he had conquered the entire civilized world."

"When Alexander the Great was your age, Caesar, he was dead."

"All the more reason to hurry."

Gisstus' sardonic mien warped toward an expression of worry. You had to know him well, as well as Caesar did, to read it.

"What is troubling you, Gisstus?" he asked.

"We may have a small problem with the Arverni. Or perhaps not so small . . ."

"I thought this Gobanit they've just elected vergobret is a greedy and pliable fellow. . . ."

"Oh, he is, and he's not all that clever either," Gisstus told him. "But he's not the problem . . . the possible problem. It's his brother."

"His brother?"

"Keltill, the outgoing vergobret . . . and the omen . . ."

"You mean the new star?" Caesar asked in no little perplexity. According to the locals, a new star had appeared in the heavens shortly before his arrival, a sign of a change of destiny or some such thing. Caesar's attempts to claim it as a sign of the good fortune of his own coming might not have been exactly a great success, but he couldn't see how this omen could become a problem.

"Not the *new* star," Gisstus told him, "a *falling* star."

"They take falling stars for omens too? But at certain times the night skies are full of them."

Gisstus shrugged. "This isn't one of them, and apparently there was an unusually large one," he said. "Large enough for some of the ignorant to call it a comet."

"I still don't—"

"According to our druid friend Diviacx, the Gauls believe that comets are the omen of the passage of kings, some say the death of a king—"

"But there isn't any king of—"

"—and someone seems to be encouraging their bards to say the *coming* of a king."

"Oh," said Caesar. "But why would Diviacx be spreading such stuff around?" As a former pontifex privy to the tricks of the trade, he knew only too well that omens could easily enough be interpreted to mean whatever might serve the purpose of the interpreter.

"He isn't."

"It's this Keltill?"

Gisstus nodded. "So it would seem. It can hardly be a coincidence that he's convened a meeting of all the tribal leaders—"

"I thought only the druids had the authority to do such a thing."

"That's why Diviacx is so worried. Keltill can't command attendance at such a meeting, but he's famous as a lavish host, and when he invites you to a feast, it's an invitation that few Gauls are abstemious enough to refuse."

"But surely the druids could forbid it."

"They could," said Gisstus, "but although he wouldn't quite admit it, Diviacx seems to be afraid that, what with Keltill's popularity among the minor tribes, and their fear of us, and the money he has to toss around, it would be a dangerous move for them politically, especially if *he* did the forbidding. . . ."

"And he wishes us to weigh in against it somehow . . . ?"

"Diviacx has unclearly made it clear that he believes it would be to our mutual benefit if Keltill were to . . . retire from public life."

"Thus speaks the druid Diviacx," said Caesar. "But perhaps the Eduen Diviacx fears that the Arverne Keltill might be able to make a favorable alliance with me. After all, a king of Gaul who swore an oath of fealty to Rome would allow me to—"

"Keltill is no friend of Rome, that much is certain!" Gisstus replied. "Sooner would a lamb swear an oath of fealty to the wolves."

Caesar pondered the situation without being able to attain any clear vision through the murk; indeed, perhaps the murk itself, so characteristic of the tribal politics here, was all that there was.

"You said this Keltill is famed as a host, Gisstus?" he finally said. "Perhaps you might like to enjoy his hospitality?"

Gisstus eyed him narrowly. "Keltill's hospitality toward any Roman arriving uninvited would probably consist of roasting me on a spit and serving me up as the main course."

Caesar looked Gisstus slowly up and down. He shook his head disparagingly. "You have no color sense, Gisstus," he said. "A man of your complexion would be a much more pleasing figure garbed in blue. *Eduen* blue."

The last flaming sliver of the sun sinks below the horizon, and the sky, deep purple above the treetops surrounding the clearing, is already black at the zenith and toward the east. It is a lightly clouded and moonless night, and the brightest stars are already visible, among them one younger than a child who has not yet learned to crawl.

Within the dark depths of the forest, glowing orange lights, like enormous fireflies, converge on the clearing from the wind's four quarters, emerging into it as flaming torches in the hands of a dozen druids.

All wear robes of white unmarked by tribal colors. They form a small circle in the middle of the clearing, facing outward. Torchless, bearing only his staff of office, the Arch Druid emerges from the western margin of the clearing, strides toward the circle of druids.

As he enters the circle, they turn inward, so that when Guttuatr halts and plants his staff upon the earth he is the center of a circle of fire, a circle of inward-turned eyes, expectant, waiting.

"I have called this convocation of Druids of the Inner Way to consider . . ."

"The portents in the heavens—"

"The new star—"

"The Romans—"

"Keltill—"

The Arch Druid does not seem truly displeased by the interruption, by the cacophonous confusion of diverse voices, but he does not let it go on long before he demands silence by raising his staff and bringing it down again.

"To consider the chaos in the heavens that brings chaos to the earth!" the Arch Druid intones. Then, in quite another voice: "Or, as you have just demonstrated, the reverse."

He smiles, as if he has made the driest of jests, but does not laugh. No one else does either.

"The heavens have given us one true sign," he says, "the birth of a new star. . . ."

"Sigil of the Wheel's Great Turning," says the druid Zelkar.

Guttuatr nods. "But now there are those claiming to have seen a comet and sowing chaos and confusion."

"Easy enough for those without knowledge to mistake a large falling star for a small comet," scoffs Zelkar, nodding toward the fallen star atop the Arch Druid's staff.

"The sign of the death of a king, time out of mind," says the druid Polgar.

"Or a king's *passing*," says the druid Gwyndo. "Easy enough, in the absence of a king, for someone to claim it means the *coming* of a king first. The same sort of someone who would thus benefit from calling a falling star a comet."

"If so," says Zelkar, "like his falling star, one who will flash across the sky for a brief moment and then be gone."

"Let us hope—"

"—that it's a sign of the return of Caesar to Rome!"

"There are those who say the omen points to Keltill—"

"Nor does he discourage such talk—"

"Nor does he claim it—"

"Not openly!"

"Enough!" shouts Guttuatr, slamming the butt of his staff down hard. Then his voice becomes intimate. "No Gaul has worn the crown of Brenn since before the time of our grandfathers' grandfathers. There have been myriad falling stars since, and some few comets, but as long as the land was at peace, no one thought to mistake the one for the other, whether by ignorance or by design. But now, when there is no peace, the people stare up into the sky and see what they might wish to see."

"Or what those who might wish to be king might wish them to see," says Gwyndo.

"So might Keltill or anyone else be accused by his enemies," points out Polgar.

"This is true!"

"Silence!" commands Guttuatr. Then he shrugs. "We are men of knowledge, and yet we have seen how these portents, both real and false, bring even ourselves deep into the chaos of the world of strife. . . ."

"May I speak now, Arch Druid?" Polgar asks in a chastened tone of voice.

Guttuatr nods.

"We know that we stand on the cusp of a Great Turning from one Age into the next," says Polgar. "Might it be . . . might it be . . ." He hesitates, as if what he is struggling to spit out is a morsel so enormous that it sticks in his throat. "Might it be that in the Great Age to come the heavens will speak in a different tongue?"

"In which false comets become true signs?" sneers Zelkar.

"A tongue that no man born in this Great Age can understand . . ." Guttuatr says softly. "Might it be that they speak it already?"

There is no sound but the hissing crackle of the torches, the faint rustle of tree crowns in a light breeze, the far-distant hoot of an owl.

"It may be so," Guttuatr finally says. "And as men of knowledge, we turn with the Great Wheel lest we be crushed beneath it."

"But *how*, Arch Druid?" asks Zelkar.

Guttuatr sighs deeply, and there is no answer in his words, nothing like assurance written on his visage. "I do not know," he says.

These simple words, spoken so many times by so many men, now call forth gasps of dismay from these men of knowledge.

"I *cannot* know."

He turns to look upward, skyward, into the star-speckled black depths of elsewhere, of elsewhen, of a time yet unborn.

"For no man of an Age that is passing can ever see clearly into an Age that is being born. And so we must seek out he who can. He who destiny will choose to lead the people of Gaul into it."

IV

"WHO ELSE would be generous enough to put on a feast to celebrate the *end* of his year as vergobret?" Vercingetorix burbled gaily as father and son rode toward Gergovia.

"This is less than a celebration, and more," Keltill told him. "If the gods will it, *much* more."

The words revealed the existence of secrets without more than hinting at what they might be.

A year as vergobret had wrought changes in his father. He had spent less and less time in the pleasures of the hunt, with his horses, out-of-doors like a natural man, and indeed less time with Vercingetorix, and more and more time within the house huddled with nobles, military craftsmen, collectors of taxes and tributes.

At first Vercingetorix put this down to the natural order of things, for, after all, Keltill was not just *his* father but the father of his people. After his term was over, things would return to what they had been.

But in the last three or four cycles of the moon, the changes in Keltill had become stronger, had changed in kind. Keltill, whom everyone loved, had found enemies.

Namely the Romans, whom nobody loved, but who, according to Keltill, were seen as benefactors and sources of riches by all too many Gauls who should know better, rather than as the treacherous and cunning invaders they were.

This had turned Keltill, the most hale and open of men, secretive. Moreover, he had taken to spending hours listening to the tribal lays, ofttimes alone with the bard.

Vercingetorix found this atmosphere of mystery exciting, but it was frustrating for a boy so close to manhood to be kept outside the swirling mists of that secret purpose.

The road from Keltill's homestead to Gergovia was far older than any living man, wide enough for two carts to pass, beaten smooth by lifetimes of passage, and free of mud in this fair weather. It embraced the land as it wound around grassy hillocks and skirted the margins of the great forest. It lay rooted in the earth and made of it, a living thing.

The closer the road got to Gergovia, the more traffic there was on it, almost all headed toward the city: carts bearing kegs of beer, heaps of fruits and vegetables, grains and loaves, butchered deer and wild boar, dun chickens and more brightly feathered wildfowl; drovers herding sheep and pigs; bards, harlots, musicians; purveyors of jewelry, cloth, even Roman wines; Arverne nobles and warriors, and those of other tribes; the occasional druid.

As was his custom, Keltill tossed coins here and there from the leather sack tied to the saddle of his horse, taking care not to insult nobles or druids or warriors or any folk of tribes other than the Arverni by flinging money in their direction, but favoring all with his great winning smile.

But Vercingetorix sensed that there was something deliberate about it, more like a rite than an expression of pleasure.

"Everyone seems to be in a mood to celebrate," Vercingetorix ventured.

"And why should they not?" Keltill exclaimed. "They are to be guests at the greatest feast in the history of Gaul!"

"Why, then, do you say that this is less than a celebration and more?"

"The *more* is what I'm paying for it, and the less is what *they* are not!" Keltill told him, with a great laugh that went straight to Vercingetorix's heart.

"And this *much* more that it will be, if the gods will it?" Vercingetorix presumed to ask.

Keltill reined his horse into a slow walk, leaned closer to Vercingetorix. "Can you keep a secret?" he said in a voice so soft as almost to be a whisper.

"Certainly not," Vercingetorix told him archly. "Whatever you tell me, I will shout at the top of my lungs in the marketplace of Gergovia when the sun is at its zenith and I may be sure all the world is there to hear."

"Like father, like son!" Keltill cried, clapping Vercingetorix on the shoulder, roaring with laughter. When his mirth had subsided, he leaned close again. "I can tell you that the true purpose of this fête is to gather together the leaders of the tribes of Gaul, something that would be impossible otherwise, and not to a *celebration*. What is there to celebrate? The raids of the Teutons? The plague of Romans invited up from the south by the Edui to save us from them? The loss of our freedom? Of our honor itself?"

"Our honor?"

"Where is the honor in summoning the mercenary army of this Caesar to do our fighting for us? Where will our freedom be when he finishes with the Teutons?"

"But we are few and the Teutons are many."

"No, Vercingetorix, alone each tribe is few, but we *Gauls* are many! Fighting together, we could throw the Teutons back across the Rhine, and the legions of Rome into the sea!"

"But that hasn't happened since the time of Brenn, since we last had a . . . king."

"Did I say that?" Keltill said sharply. Then, with a wink, "Don't you say it either!"

He brought his horse up into a trot. "At least not before the fact!" he called back over his shoulder as Vercingetorix urged his mount to catch up.

"And now I will offer you the strangest advice ever to escape my mouth," he said when they were riding abreast again. "Stay sober tonight!"

Vercingetorix stared at his father in amazement.

"Take care to stay sober enough to remember this night, Vercingetorix, so that you will be properly able to boast to *your* son that you were there at a moment the bards will sing of forever!"

Gergovia was built on a hilltop, the better to defend, and if the hill had in the dim past been wooded, now it was grassy and stood above a wide meadow, with a stream shaded by flanking copses meandering through it. The broadness of the meadow and the treelessness of the hill were the works of men, for forest had been felled not only to provide logs for the palisade and buildings of the city, but to render potential attackers plainly visible from afar.

The city was enclosed by a wall four men high built of stones set in a framework of sturdy timbers and strengthened at intervals by low towers constructed in the same manner. The gates, now invitingly open, were flanked by taller parapeted towers, from which invaders attempting to batter their way in with a ram would be subject to a rain of arrows, lances, stones, boiling pitch, and scalding water.

Today Gergovia was surrounded by the most marvelous sight that Vercingetorix had ever seen, a second city almost as large, extending halfway down the hillside—the encampments of the nobles of the visiting tribes and their entourages, surely the greatest gathering of the peoples of Gaul in the lifetime of even the oldest of living men.

The leather tents of vergobrets were pitched beneath tribal standards—bear, hawk, boar, wolf, horse, and more—carved in wood or cast in bronze or, in the case of the Eduen boar, even silver, and held high on wooden poles. The tents of their nobles and warriors pitched around them flew pennants in their tribal colors.

The spaces between tribal encampments were clogged with the hustle and bustle of servants, grooms, bards, musicians, artisans, and tradesmen. All around them were stalls selling beer, bread, meats fresh and cooked, even jugs and amphorae of Roman wine.

Vercingetorix's heart nearly burst with pride as he rode up the hill and into this joyous pandemonium at the side of the man who had called it all into being.

Keltill's sack of coins was soon empty, and he could only wave and toss smiles to his admirers as they rode past the tribal encampments, displaying his knowledge by reading off the identities of each from the standards and pennants as they passed.

"The stag, the Cadurques . . . Brown, the Sequani . . . The owl, Bituriges . . . Green and yellow . . . uh, that's a bull, so it must be the Turons . . . Ah, here we are, the Carnutes!"

Keltill rode past the largest of the Carnute tents, displaying the horse standard of their vergobret, and reined in before a somewhat smaller one flying a red-and-black pennant.

"Why here first?" asked Vercingetorix.

"As a favor to you, Vercingetorix, for this is the tent of Epona, widow of Arthak, vergobret of the Carnutes, slain by the Teutons in battle, and an old friend—"

"I don't understand—"

"Oh, you will," Keltill told him with a wink and a laugh as he dismounted, bidding Vercingetorix to do likewise.

"Greetings, Epona, we are here!" Keltill shouted when they reached the entrance.

A stern-looking woman with more gray in her hair than brown

emerged, wearing a somber black tuniclike dress nevertheless secured at her right shoulder by a large and ornate filigreed silver broach in the form of a horse.

"Greetings, Keltill," she said much less loudly, and they embraced fraternally as Vercingetorix dismounted.

"You remember my son, Vercingetorix. . . ."

"Who could forget the silver-tongued Vercingetorix?" Epona said in a dry tone.

"We've met . . . ?" Vercingetorix stammered.

His father and Epona exchanged amused glances, which only made his discomfort worse.

"Your attention, as I remember, was elsewhere at the time," said Epona.

Keltill laughed. "If you don't remember Epona," he said, "I'll wager you remember her daughter, Marah."

Indeed he did.

For the girl who then emerged from the tent had been the first object of his boyish lust. The girl who had so disdained him at his father's inaugural feast. The girl he had not found the courage to speak to, but whose presence had somehow conspired with much beer to turn a tongue of wood to one of silver.

Her face had tanned to a golden hue, and her long blond hair was now worn free and wild. She wore a plain white shift, snug enough to reveal breasts that had blossomed into womanhood. Her lips were if anything fuller, and there was a new . . . something in her eyes. All in all, the sight of her was now even more intoxicating to Vercingetorix sober than it had been when he was drunk.

Keltill gave the gaping Vercingetorix an elbow in the ribs. "Why, if I were a few years younger . . . and, on the other hand, even so—"

"Don't even think about it, Keltill," said Epona.

Keltill exhaled a great false sigh. "Well, there's always my son here to carry on. . . ." And then, more seriously, "They make a fine couple, do they not? And your family is without a man to head the household. . . ."

"Now, there might be an alliance," mused Epona. She continued, more sharply: "But we have something more pressing to discuss right now, don't we, Keltill?"

"Indeed," said Keltill. "So why don't we discuss it inside and leave them alone to see if they'll do what comes naturally?"

Vercingetorix blushed, for nothing could have been closer to his mind.

"Not *too* naturally, Marah," Epona said, and the maiden in question blushed likewise. Then Keltill and Epona went into the tent, leaving the two of them to stand there staring at each other in red-faced mortification.

"Shall we go walk down by the stream?" Vercingetorix summoned up the courage to suggest.

"Well, I suppose so," said Marah. "At the moment I seem to find myself with nothing better to do."

The stroll through the encampments together had been awkward, but not as awkward as Vercingetorix found himself when at last he had Marah alone under the trees fringing the stream.

There, he could at least break the long silence pointing out the identities of the tribes whose encampments they passed, and boasting of the extent of Keltill's holdings, and of his good fortune in being the son of such a great man.

But here, alone with her in the cool brown shadows, with no sounds but the burbling of the stream through its rockier reaches, the chirping of the birds, and the breeze in the trees, the silver-tongued Vercingetorix found himself entirely at a loss for words. Only one thing filled his mind, and he only hoped the pantaloons he wore were loosely cut enough to conceal the extent to which it filled *them*.

On the other hand . . .

"Do you know what your name means—Marah?"

"The she-horse, a mare."

"I would be happy to mount you, mare."

The look that Marah gave him was enough to freeze the stream in its bed.

"There's a little more to what's supposed to happen between a boy and a girl than matching up the right bloodlines in a stable!"

"I . . . I meant that someday you will be my queen," Vercingetorix blurted.

"Your *queen*?"

"Uh . . . I mean that, were you mine . . . it would make me *feel* like a king," Vercingetorix said. It was the best he could do to recover, without revealing that which he must not, and, however lame it sounded to him, it seemed to have the desired effect.

"Well, at least that kind of talk's a little more silver-tongued," Marah said, regarding him with a bit more favor than she would a passing cur on the road.

"Silver-tongued. . . ?" he said teasingly, and, nothing ventured, nothing gained, took both her hands, pulled her to him, kissed her boldly upon the lips, pressing the point of his tongue between them.

Marah seemed to resist for a moment, but when he persisted, her mouth opened like a flower, and a bolt of lightning went from his mouth to his groin as he felt her tongue reach out for his for the briefest of moments, before it shyly retreated and she pulled away.

"That's not exactly what I had in mind!" Marah complained, not entirely convincingly, or so he was pleased to believe. "But not so bad for someone who's probably never kissed a girl before."

"Who says I've never kissed a girl before?" Vercingetorix cried, then attempted to mask his dismay at her voicing of this truth with bravado. "Who says I've never made love to a girl before? Say the word, and I'll prove it!"

"The word," said Marah loftily, "is 'crude.' It is to be hoped that the haggling over my dowry will take long enough to give you time to grow up a little."

Vercingetorix's ears burned. "It . . . it was only an offer . . ." he stammered.

"Very generous, Your Majesty," Marah said dryly. Was that the thinnest of smiles on those lips he longed to kiss again, or was he only seeing what he wished to see? Without knowing, Vercingetorix dared only stand and stare.

For a long moment Marah stared back, revealing nothing. Vercingetorix found himself leaning closer and—

Marah laughed, pecked him on the cheek, took him by the hand.

"Come on, Your Majesty," she said. "Time to return to the city. I wouldn't dream of keeping you from your royal duties."

The Great Meeting Hall of the Arverni was the largest building in Gergovia, a tall oblong structure of rough blocks of sand-colored stone mortared together and embellished with gray wood facings and an entryway so weathered that it was difficult to tell the grain of the wood from the ghosts of the swirling floral carvings.

It faced the main plaza of the city, ordinarily given over to the stalls and kiosks of the market. Today these had been removed, and a good thing too, for, by the time Vercingetorix and Marah arrived, it was quite jammed with jostling and contending people. Some were servants carrying provisions to the Great Hall and sure to gain entry. Others were nobles of the Arverni and other tribes, there by invitation, likewise not to be denied. But there was also a crowd of the curious, the already besotted, and the forlornly hopeful clamoring to get in, no few of whom were harlots, musicians, bards, jugglers, and even a fellow with a trained bear cub, ardently insisting that the festivities within could hardly be complete without their assistance.

The crush and tumult were not improved by the two Arverne warriors who stood guard at the entrance of the Great Hall, perusing each would-be entrant with a dubious stare, turning back the many and admitting the few, and, strangely enough, even giving the same slow and deliberate examination to fellow warriors of their own tribe.

Vercingetorix, determined to seize the opportunity to impress Marah, yanked her into the crowd.

"What are you doing?" she cried, bouncing off a man bearing a beer barrel on his shoulder, and into a cursing whore.

"Getting us inside," Vercingetorix told her. "Make way for the son of Keltill!" he shouted, to less-than-magical effect.

Swallowing a small sour portion of his pride, he resorted to the use of his smaller size to slip serpentlike closer to the entrance through the crowd in a less honorable but more effective manner, tugging the protesting Marah behind him. They emerged into a small pocket of calm around a man with a hawk-beaked nose, whose lined face and deep-set green eyes seemed far older than his black hair and beard, and whose moth-eaten purple-and-yellow robe seemed older still. He was juggling three delicate-looking tinted glass balls: red, white, and blue.

The space accorded to the juggler by the crowd was not at all large and not all that calm. A Sequane warrior brushed by him, he lost concentration for the briefest moment, and the glass balls went flying toward Vercingetorix. Without thought, Vercingetorix snatched them out of the air—one, two, three!

"Well played, Vercingetorix!" shouted the juggler.

"You know me?" exclaimed Vercingetorix in no little surprise.

"What bard in Gaul does not know of Vercingetorix, noble son of the great Keltill!" the juggler roared at the top of his lungs.

The crowd, which had been pressing in, began to open a respectful space. Vercingetorix eyed the bard suspiciously, certain that the man was after some advantage, but on the other hand, the bard had already gifted *him* with the respect of the crowd, and, better still, with the new look of admiration on Marah's face.

"So you're a bard too. . . ?" he said.

"Among other things," said the juggler.

"Then where is your harp?"

"Skill in games of chance is, alas, not among my many talents," said the juggler-bard with a shrug. "At least not lately. In fact, my finances might be greatly improved if I could gain entrance to yonder feast by the grace of some noble guest such as yourself. . . ."

Aha! thought Vercingetorix, eyeing him narrowly. Still, why not? Let this clever fellow open the way, and earn his reward.

"Why not?" he said. "Announce my presence to clear the way, for I am far too modest to do it myself"—at this Marah groaned—"and I will grant you entry. What did you say you were called?"

"I didn't. . . ."

Just then a fluff-winged seed drifted by through the air.

"Call me . . . Sporos," said the bard, "for I am a spore of the wild mushroom of the forest, a seed of legend, floating on the wind."

Vercingetorix laughed. "Well, come along, then, Sporos," he said. "I'm sure we can find you a harp within."

"Make way for Vercingetorix!" shouted Sporos. "Make way for the son of Keltill!"

Vercingetorix took Marah's arm and proudly escorted her through the crowd behind Sporos, in the void created—half from respect, half in amusement—by his threadbare and trumpet-voiced crier.

When this entourage reached the Arverne warriors guarding the entrance, however, it was another matter. He recognized neither of his father's men, and, stranger still, they didn't seem to recognize him.

"Where do you think you're going, boy?" said the one on the left.

Vercingetorix's outrage took precedence over his puzzlement.

"What do *you* think *you're* doing?" he demanded. "How dare you speak thusly to the son of your commander?"

"The son of Gobanit. . . ?" said the other warrior.

"The son of Keltill, fool!" Vercingetorix snapped. "And this is Marah, soon to be my betrothed, and this bard enjoys my favor!" Hearing this, the first warrior trod nervously on the foot of the second. The two warriors exchanged chagrined looks and seemed properly chastened. "A thousand pardons, O . . . *son of Keltill*," said the one on the left, "this man is new here. I promise you it will not happen again." There was something about the way he said it that Vercingetorix did not like at all.

Still, he nodded graciously and motioned for Marah and Sporos to precede him within. "Fear not my wrath," he told the guards reassuringly. "It shall not fall upon you."

For Keltill had taught him that openhearted forgiveness of minor faults built loyalty among one's troops in the end.

The Great Hall was already half full when Vercingetorix entered with Marah and Sporos. Vergobrets and other important guests were already taking their places at a long sturdy oaken table that dominated the center of the hall, with those in Arverne orange on the benches nearest the entrance, facing the many-colored cloaks and pantaloons of the visitors from the other tribes.

Immediately behind each tribal contingent at the central banquet table were the modest number of guards allotted them as a courtesy, and behind them were ranks of smaller tables and benches set up for the lesser guests now slowly trooping in: nobles of rank and their attendant subordinates and wives, a few druids; the Arverni on their side of the hall, the rest on the other.

Serving girls were already bustling everywhere, refilling tankards, mugs, and horns from barrels of beer as soon as they were emptied, which was as rapidly as possible.

It seemed to Vercingetorix that he had entered not a building but a twilit glen in the deep woods of legend, for the stone walls had been plastered smooth in the long ago and painted in bright colors with complex patterns of intertwining vines, trees, flowers, creatures both familiar and strange, rendered dusky now by years of smoke and soot from the great stone fireplaces at either end of the hall. The crepuscular atmosphere was enhanced by the rays of the waning sun streaming in through the tall, narrow window slits and the long, wide shadows between them.

Along the walls, the shadows were banished by torches set high in brass sconces. Captured shields, spears, swords, axes, lances, pennants, standards all but covered the walls, and more of the same hung on ropes and thongs from the rafters, along with a good collection of the skulls of former enemies. Arverne tribal treasures were piled up beneath them: chests of gold and silver coins, gemstones, jewelry; statues of unknown gods in white marble or painted in lifelike colors; bolts of cloth, plain and embroidered, some shot through with threads of gold; great casks of salt from the sea.

A spitted boar and a sheep were roasting in the big fireplaces, their dripping grease crackling and hissing off the burning logs; just about ready, to judge from the crispy brown skin and the delicious aroma of meat and oak smoke.

Keltill stood by the roasting boar, hacking off a slice with a battle-ax. He bit off a piece and chewed it thoughtfully as Vercingetorix led Marah and Sporos toward him.

"All this will be ours one day!" Vercingetorix told her as Keltill swallowed his morsel, nodding his approval to the roasting crew, and, still clutching the ax in one hand and the slice of boar in the other, swept forward to meet them.

"Well, Marah," he said, "has my son yet proved to you that he's a sturdy branch off the gnarly old tree?"

"Uh, I'd better take my place with my mother," Marah said, and departed somewhat hastily in the direction of Epona, already seated at the table among the Carnutes.

Keltill did not seem to take much notice of her embarrassment or even her departure, fixing instead a questioning gaze at the shabbily dressed Sporos, and then at his son.

"This is *your* guest, Vercingetorix?" he asked dubiously.

"The bard Sporos," Vercingetorix said nervously, suddenly all too aware of how unsavory his guest must appear to his father in the midst of such company.

"But where is your harp, bard?" asked Keltill, returning his gaze to Sporos.

Instead of looking away or even blinking, the bard met the gaze of the vergobret of the Arverni with an unwavering stare of his own.

"Lost on the winds of ill fortune now blowing through our lands," he said. The words seemed to hold no magic to Vercingetorix's ears, yet Keltill's eyes showed him to be uncannily transfixed.

"Then how to sing us the old tales?" Keltill said.

"Truth be told, I hope to learn a new tale tonight."

Keltill's gaze became if anything more intense, but now there was suspicion in his voice. "From whom?"

"Why, from whoever might dare to enter the other world. . . ."

Vercingetorix beheld something strange passing between them.

"The other world . . . ?"

A new and deeper resonance came into the voice of Sporos. "The eternal world hidden in plain sight," he said. "The world of deeds that shape an age, of valiant heroes . . . and noble kings. The Land of Legend. Perhaps tonight someone may enter. Who knows? Perhaps even you, Keltill."

Vercingetorix started at that last. Did this bard know? Had he unwittingly brought a spy into the Great Hall?

"Do you know something you're not supposed to?" said Keltill, mirroring Vercingetorix's thoughts.

Sporos continued to stare into Keltill's eyes, but his mouth now creased in a smile, though one with no mirth in it.

"We . . . bards have been accused of having forbidden knowledge from time to time. From time out of mind, Keltill."

Now Keltill gave him the same smile back. "Well, then, we who hope to have our stories sung in legend should not be inhospitable to such masters of the, uh, noble arts. So be seated . . . Sporos. Any guest of my son is a guest of mine."

So saying, Keltill handed the ax to a servant and, munching on the slice of boar, took his place to the left of his wife at the center of the Arverne side of the table. When Vercingetorix made to seat himself at his father's left, Keltill directed him to seat himself one place farther over, to the left of his uncle Gobanit, instead.

Gobanit—flabby where his brother was hard, dour where his brother was expansive, tight-fisted where Keltill was magnanimous— was no favorite uncle of Vercingetorix's, and, moreover, to be separated from his own father at the table could be deemed a demotion in honor. Vercingetorix was not at all pleased.

Until he realized that Keltill had placed him directly across the table from Epona and Marah, who sat next to the Eduen vergobret Dumnorix, and his druid brother Diviacx.

The sun had long since set, and the only light in the Great Hall, dusky orange, flickering and shadowy, was that provided by the fires in the hearths and the torches on the walls. Still the eating and drinking went on, though the zest for it was waning. Dogs were favored with choicer scraps, beer was flowing more slowly. The diners at the long table slumped torpidly, eyes glazed and bloodshot.

Of those on the Arverne side of the table, only Keltill, who had been drinking far less than his custom, and Vercingetorix, whom he had enjoined to stay sober, seemed alert, the son's eyes fixed upon Marah, the father's darting here and there.

Directly across the table from him, Dumnorix, the blond, burly, mustachioed Eduen vergobret, relaxed at his ease. But his druid brother Diviacx kept exchanging sidelong glances over his shoulder with a blue-cloaked Eduen warrior directly behind him: a short, wiry man, black-haired and darker-skinned than most Gauls, with a saturnine mien.

Keltill raised his voice above the general murmurings in the tone of a host about to toast his guests, though there was no horn or tankard in his hand.

"Good food, good beer, a generous heart, the love of our families, and the admiration of our friends!" he declaimed. "What more do warriors of Gaul need for our lives to be perfect?"

He suddenly pounded his fist hard upon the table.

"Except of course to crush our enemies in honorable battle!" he roared.

"Well spoken!" shouted a beefy iron-haired warrior at the far end of the Arverne table, and guzzled down a mighty swallow of beer to punctuate his enthusiasm. "And, fortunately, we lack not enemies for the pleasure of crushing!"

"Well spoken yourself, Critognat," Keltill declared. "We let the Teutons ravage our lands, and now we let the Romans do our fighting for us! Where is the honor in that?"

"Nowhere!" Critognat shouted woozily. "Let's slay them all!"

There was a hush in the Great Hall. All conversation ceased. The bard Sporos, seated behind Vercingetorix, gave over his desultory plucking at a borrowed harp. Even the dogs ceased their scavengers' squabbling. All eyes were upon Keltill.

It was Epona, as if by arrangement, who finally broke the silence. "The Teutons slew my husband, but at least he was favored with an honorable death in battle."

Diviacx shot her a quick suspicious look, but his attention immediately turned back to Keltill.

"No one here loves the Teutons," he said, "but I don't see—"

"It's time to deal with them ourselves, once and for all!" Keltill shouted, not merely at the druid, but in a voice that fairly shook dust from the rafters. "And if we have to change our ways to do it, then so be it!"

"Change our ways, brother?" said Gobanit, looking at Keltill, but glancing meaningfully across the table at Diviacx.

"Indeed, Gobanit, we must change our ways enough to preserve them!"

"Those who cannot find a way to turn with the turning of the times will be crushed beneath it!" blurted the bard Sporos.

The nobles on both sides of the table shot him poisonous looks for this presumptuous incursion, but Keltill half turned to smile at him strangely.

"Well spoken . . . bard!" he said.

Then, louder, to all present: "Like it or not, we can no longer survive this lack of real leadership!"

Diviacx and Gobanit exchanged longer looks. Behind the two of them, their warriors came nervously alert.

"Surely you would not seize another year as vergobret of the Arverni beyond your rightful term and deny me my own?" said Gobanit.

Keltill laughed. "Surely not, my brother. We must rise above these petty tribal rivalries if we are to preserve the way of life we cherish!"

Gobanit glanced behind him at his guards. Diviacx shook his head slightly and spoke soothingly. "Where is the problem? Caesar's legions will soon completely rid us of the Teutons."

"What next, Diviacx?" Keltill roared. "Do we invite the wolves into our farmyards to protect our chickens from the foxes?"

The rude laughter was not shared by Diviacx or Gobanit.

"Better the forces of Rome, who bring order and wealth, than the Teutons, who bring nothing but death and ruin!" declared Diviacx.

"Better we are rid of both of them before your friend Caesar turns true Gauls into fawning false Romans and our lands into nothing but another enslaved Roman province!"

"Or before you use the situation to do what, Keltill?" said Diviacx. "Usurp power against all sacred tradition?"

"Sacred tradition! What sacred tradition do you imagine we will have left as a province of Rome? The only way to preserve who we are is to unite all the tribes and drive Teutons and Romans alike from our lands, as the great warriors of Gaul we were when Brenn was king and made Rome tremble!"

"And will again!" roared Critognat. "After we slay the Teutons, let's march on Rome again and do it right this time! No mercy! No ransom! Burn it to the ground!"

Fists and tankards pounded the table. Arverne warriors behind Keltill pounded the pommels of their swords on their shields. Roars and cries

of approval went on for long moments before subsiding enough for
Epona to make herself heard. "Well spoken, Keltill! But only words!"

Keltill spoke crooningly into the pregnant silence.

"It's deeds you want . . . ? I'll show you deeds!"

And he reached down into a leather sack that had lain previously
unnoticed beneath his feet and under the table.

Keltill withdraws from the sack a dusty old golden crown, a band thin at
the rear, rising into filigreed peaks in front, as if to adorn the brow of its
wearer with a miniature range of mighty mountains.

He raises it high above his head at arm's length, and as he does, the
bard in the purple-and-yellow robe rises to his feet, his eyes wide at
what he beholds.

"The Crown of Brenn!" croons Keltill. "Worn in the long ago by
what we need now—a king!"

He reaches for a mug, anoints the dirty crown with beer, and begins
to clean it with the hem of his cloak. "Time to clean the cobwebs off
this dusty old crown and make it shine! Time to do what these dark
days demand."

Keltill holds up the crown, gleaming now in the firelight.

"Time the tribes of Gaul fought Teutons and Romans alike under a
single leader."

No one dares speak save the bard. "You, Keltill? You would wear
the Crown of Brenn? The crown that no one has worn within living
memory?"

Once again, his presumption is met with glares of outraged anger.
But not from Keltill, who turns to lock eyes with him.

"Someone must, or we are lost . . . bard."

"The price might be higher than you can imagine. . . ."

"Whatever the price may be, someone must pay it," Keltill says,
offering the crown to the room in a slow, sweeping gesture. "Would
anyone care to pay it in my stead?"

The silence is total. No one moves.

"I thought not," says Keltill, and he raises the crown above his head.

"You would crown yourself king of Gaul by your own hand?" asks
the bard.

"I would prefer the crown be placed on my head by the Arch Druid,
according to sacred tradition," Keltill tells him, and then leers at him

like a wolf who has cornered his prey. "But tradition is crumbling, the hour is now, and he is nowhere to be seen—now, is he . . . bard?"

"Do not do this, brother," shouts Gobanit, glancing behind him, then at Diviacx. But Keltill pays him no heed.

"Epona of the Carnutes has called for deeds. Deeds that shape an age, eh . . . Sporos? You hoped to learn a tale tonight of one who dares to enter the Land of Legend . . . ?"

Diviacx glances questioningly at the short, black-haired, dark-skinned Eduen warrior behind him, who nods, as if issuing or confirming a command.

"Sing, then, of *this,* bard!" says Keltill.

And lowers the crown onto his brow.

"Your brother usurps the will of the gods, Gobanit!" Diviacx shouted at Gobanit. "Seize him!"

Gobanit hesitated for a moment, then turned to issue the order to the warriors behind him. "Do as the druid commands!"

The Arverne warriors behind Gobanit rose somewhat uneasily to their feet and drew their swords. Keltill's guards immediately leapt up, some with their swords drawn, some not, both sides unwilling to strike the first blow against fellow Arverni.

Keltill, the crown still on his head, leapt up onto the table, drawing his own sword. "Would you obey the command of an Eduen that sets Arverne against Arverne in our own Great Hall?" he shouted.

"I obey the command of a *druid*!" cried Gobanit.

The Eduen warriors on the other side of the table were now on their feet with drawn swords too.

The Eduen vergobret Dumnorix whirled around to confront his men. "No!" he ordered. "The Arverni must do this themselves!"

For a short moment no one moved or spoke.

Then—

"Take him!" Gobanit shouted. "Do it! Obey the druid!"

Half a dozen of his men rushed at the table.

Critognat lumbered drunkenly to his feet, drew his sword. "Don't just stand there!" he shouted at Keltill's warriors.

"Father! Behind you!" Vercingetorix shouted.

Keltill whirled just as three of Gobanit's men were climbing up on the table. He sliced the first one's head nearly off and kicked him backward, sliced the second across the face on the return stroke, then stabbed the third under the sternum.

Vercingetorix sat there frozen as Arverne warrior fought Arverne warrior behind him. On the other side of the table, warriors of every tribe were on their feet, swords in hand. Marah regarded him with terror as Carnute warriors formed a protective shield around her, her mother, and their vergobret, Graton.

Dumnorix screamed something at his Eduen warriors, who then took positions along their side of the table, backs to Keltill, a palisade of swords preventing any of the Carnute warriors or those of the other tribes from coming to his rescue.

Four more of Gobanit's men advanced on the table where Keltill stood, these not attempting to mount it but, rather, slashing at his feet as best they could from where they stood, as Keltill jabbed down at them with equal futility.

Thus distracted, however, Keltill did not see two more climb up onto the table on the far side, then scramble to their feet, amidst tankards, beer kegs, platters, slabs of meat, half-gnawed bones, much of which clattered off the table loudly as they stumbled through the detritus toward him.

Keltill turned at the sounds, in time to parry the first blow with his sword and kick the first man backward into to the second, but Vercingetorix saw that Gobanit had summoned up the courage to draw his sword and come up unseen behind Keltill. As Gobanit stepped up on a bench to stab Keltill on his blind side, Vercingetorix jumped to his feet and grabbed Gobanit's sword arm with both hands, yanking it backward and downward with all his weight behind it.

Gobanit screamed as he teetered backward and sideways. Keltill whirled at this, saw Vercingetorix struggling with his brother, and kicked Gobanit square in the jaw, knocking him to the floor and out of Vercingetorix's grip, and as he did, the Crown of Brenn went flying off his head—

The golden crown tumbles through the smoky firelight.

And a boy's hand plucks it out of the air before it can fall.

And holds the Crown of Brenn high above his head.

As a ray of torchlight behind gives momentary birth to a blazing new star. And when he brings the crown down to clutch it to him, the star disappears—not falling, but seeming to rise.

"Not the father but the son?" whispers Sporos. "Not the passing of a king but . . . but . . ."

Grasping the Crown of Brenn in his left hand, Vercingetorix picked up a fallen sword with his right and, as a dozen or more of Gobanit's men began climbing up on the table, sought with great difficulty and little success to wield it one-handed in aid of his father.

"No!" shouted Keltill. "You can't save me! Save *yourself*! Go! *Go!*"

"But—"

An Arverne warrior smashed the sword from Vercingetorix's hand with a two-handed stroke and decided matters for him. He rolled under the table and out the other side.

V

I HEARD SOMETHING down there, I tell you!"

The fearful pounding of his own heart seemed as loud to Vercingetorix as the approaching footfalls as he crouched in a narrow alley.

Clutching the Crown of Brenn with his left hand, he reached down for something, anything, with his right. His hand closed on a stone. He picked it up, leaned out into the cross-street, threw it with all his strength, and ducked back into the alley.

The stone smacked against a distant wall and clattered down the street; a dog began barking.

"I told you!" a voice shouted, and a few moments later, three Arverne warriors ran right by the mouth of the alley where Vercingetorix knelt. As soon as they had passed, he rose and ran away, deeper into the maze of dark streets where he had been eluding his pursuers for what seemed like a nocturnal lifetime.

He could not leave Gergovia, for the gates had been closed and were guarded by Gobanit's warriors.

And even if he should somehow succeed in mounting the ramparts unseen and dropping down over the wall unhurt, he could not seek sanctuary in the tribal encampments outside, for he was now the son of a prisoner outlawed among all the tribes of Gaul.

And so warriors of all the tribes were searching for Vercingetorix. Or, rather, for the talisman that he had captured and which Keltill had entrusted into his care.

It's the crown they're after, not me, Vercingetorix told himself once more, though I can count on no mercy if they have to take it from me by force. But . . .

There *was* one way he could end this nightmare pursuit. He could slink around back to the plaza, where he had some hours ago seen Diviacx gloating over his father confined in a wicker cage. He could hand the druid the Crown of Brenn before witnesses, and, having remedied his only breach of the law, he would live, he would be free.

But such an ignoble and dishonorable betrayal of Keltill would make his craven flight from the scene of his father's capture seem like an act of heroism that would be celebrated by the bards for a thousand years.

Down a street, through another alley, another street, going to nowhere, simply fleeing from the sounds of pursuit, Vercingetorix felt that he had been down all these streets and alleys before. Perhaps he had, for in the dark the shapes of the buildings all looked alike; Gergovia was not so large that all of it could not be run through in a hour or so, and he had been running for much longer than that.

And when dawn came and with it the light, the advantage would pass from the singular pursued to the many pursuers. . . .

Lost in these thoughts, Vercingetorix suddenly found that he had blundered down an alley that led into a cul-de-sac.

Or, rather, he saw, a corner where the street into which the alley led ran along the city wall and dead-ended to his right, up against a tower of the palisade.

And then he heard the sounds of feet coming toward him down the street from the left. He turned around to flee back up the alley—

—and he saw that it was blocked by a robed figure visible only as an ominous black silhouette against the dim starlight behind it.

"*Not* so well played, Vercingetorix," a familiar voice said.

"Sporos!"

But when the figure stepped forward under the greater panoply of stars illumining the intersection, Vercingetorix saw that the robe he wore was the purest unadorned white. And his hair and beard had become iron-gray.

"You're no bard! You're—"

"About to make us invisible!"

So saying, he reached down, grabbed the hem of his white robe, pulled it up over his head to reveal a scrawny and pale form clad only in a breechclout, and made motions that Vercingetorix could not follow in the near-darkness; when he had donned it again a moment later, he was wearing filthy rags, his face was cruelly twisted by some horrid disease or accident, and spittle leaked from the corners of his trembling lips.

"What magic is this?" Vercingetorix cried.

"Invisibility?" cackled Sporos in the voice of a feeble and demented ancient. "A minor art. Which you are about to learn."

And he grabbed the astonished Vercingetorix by the tunic, ripping and tearing at it. He reached down and picked up a handful of shit-smelling gray-and-brown filth, smeared it all over Vercingetorix's clothing, then mashed another handful of the putrid stuff on his face.

He threw Vercingetorix backward and down against the palisade wall, and as he squatted down beside him, laid a hand on the tendons linking his left shoulder to his neck, did something that felt like the searing bite of a hawk's talons, then grabbed Vercingetorix by the jaw with both hands, causing an even greater pain, all in less than a minute, while the approaching footfalls got louder and louder.

Spying a loathsome old bone in a heap of offal, he picked it up and shoved it into Vercingetorix's hand.

"Gnaw on this as if you like it, idiot child—and, oh yes, drool!"

Three warriors in Eduen blue cloaks running along the palisade wall stopped, noses wrinkling in disgust, before two foul beggars sitting on the ground and leaning back up against it—a filthy old man who immediately raised a palm for alms and a drooling, deformed, half-wit child gnawing a bone rejected by the local curs and for good reason.

"You see a boy—?"

"A thief with a stolen crown?" gabbled the old man.

"Yes! Thief? Where?"

The beggar thrust his stinking paw in the warrior's face. "The little bastard took my last coin too!" he shrieked in addled outrage. Then, more shrewdly, "Perhaps you'd care to replace it?"

One of the Edui raised his sword angrily, but the one doing the talking fished a small gold piece out of a pouch and held it above the beggar's palm.

"Over the wall and into the woods!"

The warrior dropped the coin into the old man's hand, and the three of them reversed direction and ran back toward the city gates as the beggar tested the coin by biting it between his front teeth and yanking it down with his fingers.

It was base metal inside, and it broke.

"The Arch Druid himself, are you?" scoffed Vercingetorix, as he sat against the city wall beside the beggar who had once called himself the bard Sporos and now called himself the Arch Druid Guttuatr. "Why should I believe such a ridiculous boast?"

"I made us invisible, did I not?" said Guttuatr, or Sporos, or whatever his true name was, assuming that he had one. "And invisible we remain. Is that not magic?"

Vercingetorix gave him a scornful look. "Magic such as might be performed by anyone with a pile of rags and a handful of shit," he said.

"Magic as might be performed by anyone who knew how," said the beggar, his deformed face so warping his smile that Vercingetorix could not tell whether there was any mirth in it or not. "Magic lies not in a pile of rags, or a handful of dung, or a mandrake root, or any talisman, but in knowing how to use them. Magic is not a thing. Magic is knowledge."

These words seemed far deeper to Vercingetorix than the man who spoke them appeared to be. And if he did not believe that this was the Arch Druid Guttuatr, he found himself wishing to believe it was true, for if it was, he was talking to the one man in all Gaul who could save Keltill.

"Prove you are the Arch Druid," he demanded with a challenging sneer. "Show me now *true* magic."

"There is always a price," said the man who called himself Guttuatr.

Vercingetorix picked up half of the false gold coin that the beggar had discarded and tossed it to him. "Guttuatr" threw it aside. "You do not choose the price you must pay," he said. "It chooses you."

He laid a bony hand on Vercingetorix's shoulder once more. "Rise," he said, applying a complex but only slightly painful pressure. "Or try to."

Vercingetorix willed it, but his body did not obey; it was as if he had been turned to stone.

"Do not move," said Guttuatr, and suddenly changed the grip of his fingers and stood up.

Against his will, Vercingetorix found himself bolting to his feet.

Guttuatr—and Vercingetorix was beginning to believe, beginning to have hope, that it was he—released him, and he regarded the "Arch Druid" with new respect, not untinged with fear.

"That *is* magic," he admitted. "Magic that I would learn."

"You have already learned the first lesson," Guttuatr told him, waving his hand. "The magic is neither in my hand nor in your body."

"But in knowing how to use them . . ." whispered Vercingetorix.

Guttuatr nodded. "There is in you the making of a druid," he said. "If you are willing to pay the price."

"You *are* really a druid?" Vercingetorix said. He was beginning to be convinced, not by magical feats, but by something else he did not quite understand. And perhaps that too was a kind of magic. "You are really the Arch Druid Guttuatr?"

"What would be my purpose in lying?"

"What is your purpose in saving me?"

The beggar's mask suddenly fell away. The previously almost comically overlarge nose was transformed into the noble prow of an eagle by the intensity of the predator's eyes that now seemed to bore through his own and deep into his soul.

"That you may not yet know," said the Arch Druid Guttuatr in a deep, resonant voice, and Vercingetorix no longer doubted it was he. "The price for that knowledge may prove more than you will be willing to pay."

"Is that not for me to decide?" Vercingetorix said angrily through what he recognized as fear, though he could not say of what.

"Not in ignorance," Guttuatr told him. "That is knowledge only a druid may contain. And therefore I offer you the chance to learn to become one."

"How long will it take?"

"Years. An age."

"We don't even have a day to save my father!" Vercingetorix cried. "They'll burn him when the sun reaches its zenith."

"Your father cannot be saved, Vercingetorix."

"If you're the Arch Druid, you can save him with a word!"

"Your father should not be saved," said Guttuatr.

"How can you say such a thing to me!" Vercingetorix demanded.

"Your father *must* not be saved," said Guttuatr in a cold, even voice devoid of all pity.

"*Why?*" shouted Vercingetorix.

The Arch Druid now hesitated, and when he spoke again, it seemed to Vercingetorix that, despite the certainty in his voice, he was dissembling.

"Because it is written in the heavens that he will not be saved," he said.

"Not by you!" Vercingetorix shouted at him in a fury. "So I'll have to do it myself!" And he took a half-step away, into running flight, before—

—the bony hand of the Arch Druid had him by the shoulder again and froze him in place where he stood.

"Now I will speak and you will listen, Vercingetorix, son of Keltill," Guttuatr said, and Vercingetorix found that he could no more speak or avert his gaze from those eagle eyes than he could move his limbs.

"Keltill ignorantly sought to make magic with the ring of metal that you conceal beneath your tunic. Give it to me, Vercingetorix, son of Keltill."

Without looking away from those coldly burning eyes, without his own volition, Vercingetorix handed the Crown of Brenn to the Arch Druid.

Guttuatr placed the crown on his own head.

"Am I now a king?" he asked. He placed the crown on the head of Vercingetorix. "You are not a king either."

He removed the Crown of Brenn and tucked it under his own robe.

"Magic is not a thing. A crown does not make a man a king."

Guttuatr removed his hand from Vercingetorix's shoulder, and Vercingetorix found he could move his legs, his arms, could flee if he so chose. And yet he did not.

"Keltill sought to become king by making a forbidden magic. But he believed the magic was in a crown. He tried to make magic without knowledge, and so that magic was false, and failed. But even though it failed, he must pay the price."

"He . . . he must die . . . ?" Vercingetorix found the strength to whisper.

Guttuatr's gaze seemed to soften slightly.

"Your father knew that would be the price of failure, Vercingetorix," he said. "But now he will make the greatest magic that a man can make."

"The greatest magic that a man can make . . . ?"

"The magic of his death. Which belongs to him alone. The greater the magic, the greater the price that must be paid."

As the sun crawled up a sky grayed with a glowering overcast, the plaza of Gergovia began to fill with equally sullen people. Guttuatr had insisted that, disguised as a beggar or not, it would not be safe for

Vercingetorix to pass among them until it was well crowded and all eyes were drawn to the wicker cage at the center of the plaza; by the time they arrived at the edge of the plaza, it was densely thronged.

From here all Vercingetorix could see was the top of a wicker cage, and he despaired of making his way close enough to get even a parting glimpse.

"This is your fault, *Arch Druid!*" he said scathingly, rounding on Guttuatr in a fury. "What magic will you use to get us through *this*?"

Guttuatr placed his hand on his shoulder, but lightly this time. "Even a crowd awaiting a burning will allow a poor sick blind man to pass. Lead on, boy!"

He rolled his eyes back into his skull so that only the whites showed, an unwholesome sight that Vercingetorix himself did not care to view, and that did work its magic: the crowd gave uneasy way to a muttering, spittle-spraying, and possibly diseased blind beggar staggering through it, guided by a ragged urchin smeared with malodorous offal.

It was mostly Arverni who had gathered to witness the death of Keltill, his former guests from the tribal encampments outside the city walls wisely choosing to stay well away from them during this somberly unwelcome rite. Vercingetorix overheard little conversation of consequence as he wormed his way across the plaza, for nobles and lesser folk alike seemed to be taking care to guard their thoughts and their loyalties.

Vercingetorix understood why the Arverni thought it best to keep their opinions to themselves, for allegiance to Gobanit and the gods must be divided from allegiance to Keltill and the heart, even within the same soul, and who could tell which side his neighbor might be on. Keltill was greatly loved, but Gobanit was at best unenthusiastically respected. And though Keltill had committed a great offense against the gods and had been condemned by a druid for it, that druid was an Eduen.

And when Vercingetorix finally led his blind beggar to the front ranks, he saw that the Arverni had good reason to suspect Diviacx of something less than druidic detachment from the affairs of his tribe.

A rectangular pyre of oak logs like a tiny wooden hut had been erected in the center of the plaza, its interior filled with kindling, and atop this had been placed the wicker cage confining Keltill. Arverne warriors surrounded the pyre, and Gobanit stood to the left, as was his proper station as the new vergobret of the Arverni. So too was it correct for the presiding druid, Diviacx, Eduen or not, to stand beside him. But what was Dumnorix, the Eduen vergobret, doing standing next to his brother? And why were they screened from the Arverne crowd by a score of Eduen warriors?

But all this was banished from Vercingetorix's mind by his first full sight of his father since the battle in the Great Hall.

Keltill's tunic was freshly stained with not-yet-dried blood seeping redly from hidden wounds in his chest and side. There was a long cut on his left forearm. One eye was badly blackened.

Vercingetorix's heart was breaking, and yet it was also bursting with pride, for Keltill stood there within his wicker cage upon his pyre neither cringing in fear like a man about to die a horrible death nor sighing in regret like a penitent who had offended the gods; his arms were folded across his chest, his feet spread wide, his shoulders erect, and his gaze was fierce and fearless and as unwavering as that of a lion.

Like a king.

Diviacx took one short step forward. The crowd murmured, a sound like the lowing of a cranky bull. Diviacx's Eduen bodyguards tensed.

Diviacx looked uncertain and nervous as he began to speak. "Keltill of the Arverni has offended gods and men—"

"Speak for the gods, druid," a voice from back in the crowd shouted, "but not for the Arverni, *Eduen*!"

Grunts, roars, shouts of sullen approval.

"Keltill of the Arverni has offended the gods by seeking to crown himself king of Gaul with his own hand!" Diviacx shouted angrily. "And for this sacrilege he must die!"

"Keltill!" shouted the voice of Critognat from within the cover of the crowd. Others picked it up. "Keltill! Keltill! Keltill!"

The Eduen bodyguards brandished their swords. The Arverne warriors surrounding the pyre brought their hands to the hilts of theirs, and that reluctantly, but went no further.

"This is not a dispute between Edui and Arverni," Diviacx insisted, "this is not a dispute among men! It is not Edui or Arverni who demand the death of Keltill! It is the gods whose will he has defied, and the gods who demand his death, and the gods for whom I speak!"

A groan replaced the chanting, like that of cattle knowing there is after all no escape from the slaughter.

A short, dark-haired Eduen warrior whispered something in Gobanit's ear. Gobanit frowned, shook his head no. The Eduen whispered

to him again, and he stepped forward. The same man shot a commanding glance at Diviacx, and the druid stepped back.

"It is my own . . . my own brother who must die to . . . to appease
the wrath of the gods . . ." Gobanit declaimed hesitantly. "And Keltill
has also violated the sacred traditions of the Arverni . . . and so . . . and
so . . ."

Gobanit succeeded in reducing the crowd to silence, but it was a
merciless silence, a void which the assembled Arverni opened up and
an invitation for him to fall into it. The Eduen warrior who had been
directing Gobanit and Diviacx nodded a sign at one of the Arverne
warriors. The man lit a torch and handed it to Gobanit.

It seemed to Vercingetorix that every man beholding his father in the
wicker cage, gazing upon the torch in Gobanit's hand, felt what he felt.
Surely he had but to leap forward and demand it of them and they
would rush to Keltill's rescue.

A claw of pain bit hard into his left shoulder, and a voice whispered
in his ear. "No," it said. "The magic of his death is his alone. You can do
nothing save what you must—endure!"

And Vercingetorix found that he could neither take a single step forward nor look away.

Gobanit regarded the torch in his hand fearfully.

"And so . . . and so, my brother, whom I love . . ."

Diviacx stepped forward, his brow creased in exasperation.

"And so in fire must die *any man* who would crown himself king of
the free tribes of Gaul!" he shouted.

Gobanit offered him the torch. Diviacx shrank back.

Keltill had regarded this disastrous attempt at solemn ceremony in
lofty disdain, standing in his wicker cage upon his funeral pyre with his
gaze upon his people and eternity, as if he had already left the world of
men and composed himself into an image fit for the Land of Legend.

But now he laughed.

And spoke into the stunned silence.

"Edui! Arverni! Slaves of Rome! Even on this you lack the courage
to agree? You're not fit to call yourselves Gauls! You're more afraid to
kill me than I am to die at your hands! So hand me the torch, you cowards, and I'll light the fire myself!"

The crowd laughed, then cheered, and at this Gobanit finally tossed
the torch onto the pyre, a convulsive gesture owing more to chagrin
than to newfound resolve.

Vercingetorix watches in stone-still silence as the kindling within the pyre catches with a crackling burst of orange flame, and then the inner logs, not knowing whether the magic in the hand of the Arch Druid restrains him or not, for now nothing in this world or any other could make him move or look away.

For as Keltill stands erect and unmoving in his wicker cage, as the bonfire begins to roar and blaze beneath him, as the flames begin to lick at his feet, the pain in Vercingetorix's heart is burned away by the fiercer flame of the passion to gaze upon the fire consuming the best man he would ever know and love. He watches with the same unwavering courage, so that perhaps he might prove worthy of having some small portion of his father's spirit pass into him, and one day people might say, "Like father, like son," and speak the truth.

And perhaps the gods look upon him with their cruel favor, for as the flames rise higher and higher, and his face contorts with pain, Keltill's eyes scan the crowd, and while the smoke rises to obscure his blistering body and his tunic catches fire, they find what they seek.

Vercingetorix finds himself looking directly into the eyes of Keltill and doubts not that Keltill sees him. As his hair ignites in a crown of flame, his visage becomes a mask not of pain but of the iron resolve to triumph over that pain, and Keltill's eyes burn far brighter than the fire consuming him as they gaze from the next world into his own.

And if there is any doubt in Vercingetorix's heart, it is gone when Keltill speaks from within the flames, loud and clear, for all the world to hear, reciting his own funeral ode from his funeral pyre.

"In fire do I become the tale the bards will sing.
In fire I enter the Land of Legend as a king!"

The flames mount higher, and there is nothing in Vercingetorix's vision but the fire and the eyes peering out of it into the depth of his soul.

"As the fire sets my spirit free
So in fire will you remember me."

And something passes from those eyes into those of Vercingetorix, the eyes of a filth-smeared boy dressed in rags with love and pride filling his burning heart.

It lasts but a heartbeat.

And when it is gone nothing remains but the flames.

And Vercingetorix knows that the boy he was has died with the father he had loved.

He swears a silent oath by the flames that consumed them both that the father would live on in the man the son must become.

VI

WHAT ARE THE THREE necessary virtues of the man of knowledge?"

The voices droned on.

Vercingetorix heard, but did not listen.

He squatted on the well-beaten earth within the semicircle of students around Gwyndo, seated before the evening bonfire. Behind the fat and balding druid was a small square temple of roughly dressed granite. Beyond that were the wattle-and-thatch huts where he had lived with his fellow students for twenty cycles of the moon, and beyond the huts the darkening oak aisles of the forest. And outside this hateful and ignoble refuge was the world from which he was banished, the world where he longed to be.

But Vercingetorix's attention was captured by the flames alone.

"The courage to follow the will of the gods in this world . . ."

The words were willow-bark bitter in his ears. What craven gods willed that he endure these lessons, which taught him nothing of the warrior's way? What cruel gods willed that he endure the contempt of the sons of vergobrets and nobles of many tribes as an outcast who had gained refuge here only by the will of the Arch Druid himself? Where was the courage in that?

"The will to make his own destiny in the Land of Legend . . ."

Oh, I have the *will*! he thought bitterly. I have the will to finish the great task Keltill died to begin. I have the *will* to be my father's son. But where is my courage to act?

"Vercingetorix? *Vercingetorix?*"

Gwyndo was shouting at him. Some of the students were laughing.

"If you have returned to this world from the other, Vercingetorix," Gwyndo said, "perhaps the wisdom you have gained there will now enable you to answer the question."

More laughter.

"The third of the necessary virtues of a man of knowledge?" Vercingetorix muttered. "The wisdom to tell the one from the other," he grunted sourly, knowing the proper response, but finding it worse than meaningless to his own heart.

"To tell which from what?" sneered Viridwx. "This world from the one you seek to enter in the fire?"

Viridwx, three years older than Vercingetorix, was the son of an Eduen noble who had once been a famed warrior, served a term as vergobret, and was now waxing richer and richer through commerce with the Romans. He did not have to say "like your father" for Vercingetorix to hear it in his voice.

"We must all enter the other world sooner or later, Viridwx," he said, his hands balling into fists. "Some of us with honor, some without."

"You insult my honor, Vercingetorix?"

"I only meant that some of us will enter later and others sooner than they might wish or expect," Vercingetorix said in a false tone of sweetness.

"Is that a threat, Arverne?"

"Do you *feel* threatened, Eduen?" Vercingetorix asked with the same mocking sweetness, glaring at him menacingly. Viridwx might be heavier and taller by half a hand, but Vercingetorix had given as good as he had gotten in their previous bouts, and was eager to take him on again.

"Enough!" shouted Gwyndo.

"Perhaps the son of Keltill has just wandered too deep into his dreams to notice that we are now learning the virtues of the man of knowledge, not the arts of combat," said another Eduen, to a round of laughter at Vercingetorix's expense.

This was Litivak, Vercingetorix's size and build, but dark-haired and, like Viridwx, both his elder and the son of an Eduen noble. But where Viridwx was dim, Litivak was bright, and where Viridwx was forthrightly hostile to him and all things Arverne, Litivak's barbs were far more finely pointed, often as not delivered with a mirthful grin.

"Must the man of knowledge listen quietly and grind his teeth to stubs while the honor of his father is insulted?"

"I heard no insult to your father's honor," Litivak replied mildly.

"Perhaps I was mistaken," said Vercingetorix, turning his gaze back on Viridwx. "Viridwx need merely say that Keltill was a man of honor and a hero and I shall be happy to apologize for my error and hail him as my brother."

Litivak groaned.

And then there was a long moment of tense silence as Viridwx sat there befuddled by the trap Vercingetorix had set for him.

Guttuatr might command that Vercingetorix not venture into the world outside the forest, but he learned of events there from those who came and went.

Among the Arverni, there were those who found it expedient to support Gobanit, and according to these men, Keltill had been justly condemned by the druids for defying the will of the gods. But to those who were eager to do battle with not only the Teutons and the legions of Caesar but the Edui as well, Keltill was a hero.

Most of the other tribes accepted that Keltill had offended the gods, but, thanks to the depredations of Caesar, more and more had come to agree that uniting long enough to drive off the Romans was becoming a necessity. Only the Edui, waxing richer, stronger, and by their lights "more civilized," thanks to their cooperation with the Romans, were united in their approval of things as they were now.

And since the druids mingled students from all of the tribes in their schools, the world inside this forest mirrored the world outside. Except here the memory of Keltill had a living heir and champion. It might be a petty game, but Vercingetorix had no other worth playing. Viridwx might not be very clever, but he was clever enough to realize that whatever he did now would be wrong.

If he acknowledged Keltill as a man of honor and a hero, he might be hailed by those who believed it, but he would be scorned by his fellow Edui as a traitor speaking out of cowardice. But if he did not, the Arverne students would be given a fine excuse to come to blows with the Edui, and Vercingetorix's esteem would be raised in their eyes no matter who won the fight.

But Gwyndo saw Vercingetorix's intent and spoke before Viridwx was forced to. "Observe what your words are about to kindle in the name of your father's honor, Vercingetorix, and then tell us you have nothing more to learn of the wisdom of the man of knowledge."

"Must the man of knowledge be without honor?" Vercingetorix countered angrily.

"Would the father whose honor you seek to defend be proud of a son who sowed strife among the tribes of Gaul to do so?"

To that Vercingetorix had no reply, for he could not deny that Gwyndo had spoken truth, and a truth which shamed him.

"Well spoken, Gwyndo," he was forced to mutter sullenly.

"Spoken like a man of knowledge who is also a man of honor."

"And yet . . ."

And yet you *men of knowledge* killed my father! Vercingetorix thought, but he found himself hesitant to so challenge a druid.

"And yet?" Gwyndo asked him encouragingly.

But Vercingetorix still lacked the courage to speak the angry words in his heart. "You invoke the honor of Keltill to shame me, and justly so, and yet . . . and yet . . ."

"And yet he was condemned to burn by the law of the druids," Gwyndo said for him.

Vercingetorix could only nod meekly.

"Keltill was not condemned for lack of honor," Gwyndo said, "for Keltill acted as he did with a pure heart, believing his cause was just. Keltill lived and died a man of honor, let no one mistake that."

Then he dampened the warm glow he had built in Vercingetorix's breast.

"But Keltill was not a man of knowledge, and so he defied the will of the gods and the way of our people out of pure-hearted and honorable *ignorance*," the druid said, "and for *that* was he condemned."

Gwyndo looked directly at Vercingetorix. "You have just demonstrated that it is possible for a man of knowledge to be a man of honor, Vercingetorix," he said. "But your father demonstrated that it is necessary for a man of honor to be a man of knowledge or heed those who are if he would be a man of destiny. Else he will enter the Land of Legend as your father did—an honorable *failure*."

"Like father, like son," sneered Viridwx.

But in that moment Vercingetorix lacked the will to reply.

Strangely enough, it was Litivak who rebuked his fellow Eduen with a poisonous glance.

Litivak came up beside Vercingetorix as the troop of students ambled through the forest to the gaming field.

"Why do you forever goad poor simple Viridwx?" he demanded.

"It is Viridwx who is forever goading *me* by dishonoring the memory of my father," Vercingetorix replied testily, the calm deep-green boughs and cool shadows of the oak groves doing little to slake his ire.

Litivak gave him a lidded look of gentle scorn. "True enough as far is it goes," he said, "but why do you use the fool to set tribe against tribe?"

"I do no such thing!"

"Oh yes, you do!"

"I do not!"

"You bring every lesson and conversation you can around to the subject of Keltill in such a manner that those who do not praise him become your foes," Litivak told him. "Most men seek to accumulate friends and allies. You seem avid to accumulate enemies."

"I am not!"

"But that is what you are doing all the same, Vercingetorix. Who here among us, other than the Arverni, can you count an ally? And even among them—"

"Do I really do that?" Vercingetorix found himself asking this Eduen with unaccustomed sincerity.

"Would you have me believe that you do not know that the honor of Keltill is a subject sure to arouse bitter contention? To many of your tribe, he was a hero; to others and to mine, a usurper—"

"You call my father a usurper, Litivak?" Vercingetorix demanded angrily.

Litivak laughed. "You see, you're doing it again!"

Vercingetorix could not help laughing at himself, something he did not do often. "But you still haven't answered my question," he said, softening it with another laugh.

Litivak shrugged. "An Arverne crowning himself king of Gaul can hardly fill my Eduen heart with joy," he said. "But—"

"No doubt your Eduen heart would prefer an Eduen king!" Vercingetorix snapped.

"By the balls of the gods, you're doing it yet again!" Litivak said, and now there was real anger in his voice. "You accuse me of saying something I haven't said, and you won't even hear me speak!"

"Speak then, Eduen!"

"*I was going to say* that your father was right about the need for us all to unite to rid ourselves of the Romans before we all find ourselves prancing around in togas, drinking soured grape juice, and worshipping Jove and Venus!"

"You were . . . ?" said Vercingetorix in a small voice, feeling very much chastened, and no little bit a fool.

Litivak nodded. "Thus speaks not the Eduen heart but . . ."

He shrugged.

"The Gaul?" Vercingetorix suggested.

Litivak shrugged again.

"That was what my father was about, I think," Vercingetorix told him earnestly. "And why I do what I do, Litivak. Not to set tribe against tribe, but to unite those who feel thus, whatever their tribe."

"You're not exactly doing any better at it than your father did—now, are you, Vercingetorix?"

"What do you mean by *that*?" demanded Vercingetorix, his ire once more aroused.

"You wield words like a sword," Litivak told him. "Even against yourself."

"Against *myself*?"

"When you wield words against one whom you might win over, whom do you really wound?"

"Meaning *you*, Litivak of the Edui?" said Vercingetorix. It was a novel thought.

Litivak laughed. "Take it as you will," he said. "But some advice, Vercingetorix of the Arverni. The best way to win over men to your way is not with words, but with noble deeds that display its virtues."

These words both troubled and teased at Vercingetorix's spirit, but there conversation ended, for they had reached the gaming field, a grassy meadow created by the damming of a stream by beavers in the long ago, then expanded by men clearing the forest at its margins. Young trees, clumps of blackberry brambles, half-buried boulders had, however, been left where they were—obstacles to make the game of war more interesting.

A large, crudely carved wooden statue of a horse had been set out at one end of the gaming field, and a similar statue of a wild boar at the other, both now so weathered and splintered by rain and wind, and moss-grown with time, that they appeared to be growing out of the earth even as the years slowly absorbed them back into it.

The rules of the game were simple. The students would be divided into two equal "armies," the "horses" and the "boars." They would line up facing each other in the middle of the field in "battle formations" of each army's choosing. A pig's bladder stuffed with straw would be tossed between them, and the game would begin as the armies fought to capture the ball and retain it long enough to move it down the meadow to touch it to their sigil animal. The first army to score twelve "touches" won the war. Biting and blows to the head or testicles were not allowed.

In order for the warriors of each army to recognize each other during the fray, the "horses" retained their shirts while the "boars" played bare-chested. Sides were chosen by the drawing of straws held by Salgax, the youngish, muscular druid who taught the arts of the body and the lore of forest survival—short for the horses, long for the boars. When the lots had been chosen, Vercingetorix became a boar, Litivak became a horse, and so did Viridwx.

Salgax threw the stuffed pig's bladder between them, both sides rushed forward—grabbing for the ball, and pushing, pummeling, and punching at each other—and the game of war began.

A boar seized the ball and ran a short distance toward his statue before a horse slammed into him from behind. But as he fell, he tossed the ball to another boar, who planted an elbow in the ribs of a horse trying to intercept it as he caught it, ran forward a few steps, kept his balance as a horse kicked him in the buttocks, knocked his way past two more horses, only to be tripped by another horse.

He went down hard, the ball rolled free, and half a dozen young men scrambled on the ground for it, punching and kicking, before a horse grabbed it up, ran toward the other end of the field—

—and right into a boar, who suddenly stepped out from behind a tree, crouching low, bracing himself, and letting the impact flip the ball-carrying horse over onto his back.

In the cool forest shade just beyond the edge of the meadow, the Arch Druid Guttuatr stands watching the game of war with Gwyndo.

"They remain boys on the gaming field," says Gwyndo, half ruefully, half affectionately.

On the green field in the bright sunlight, the pig's bladder has been knocked free again, and a dozen boys rush together after it, tripping each other, kicking, elbowing, crawling beneath each other on the grass, as they fight for the ball.

"All too often in the world of strife as well," says Guttuatr. "We may teach them the ways of the man of knowledge here, but even when we succeed, the man of knowledge always contains a man of action. Alas, the reverse is seldom true."

"You speak of Keltill's son?"

"He is filled with anger and a lust for vengeance. And yet . . ."

The Arch Druid's shrug is belied by the intensity with which he regards the game of strife.

"And yet his wit is quick, if slower than his tongue . . . and he *is* still a boy. . . ."

The ball bounded free in the middle of the field, boars and horses dashing after it, the former outnumbering the latter. But a horse got to the pig's bladder first, scooped it up, ran a few steps forward, looked over his shoulder.

Behind him, fellow horses had knocked down some of the pursuing boars, but there remained three more coming up fast. The horse with the ball looked far down the meadow and saw Viridwx run out into the open from behind a stand of blackberry bushes not far from the wooden horse where he had been lurking, waving his arms frantically, and clapping his hands for the ball.

The horse with the ball reared back and tossed it high and hard with all of his might.

Vercingetorix had run almost the full length of the field, chasing down a previous horse ball-carrier and knocking the pig's bladder free, then had been knocked down himself by four other horses, who gave him a good angry pummeling for preventing the touch. Out of breath and sore, he had ducked behind a tree to recover for a few moments, and saw it happen.

Viridwx ran out from a stand of bushes, waving his arms for the ball. A long, high throw brought it almost to him. The ball hit the ground in front of him; it bounced, once, twice; and Viridwx had it.

He whirled around, dashed for the horse statue. Vercingetorix saw that he himself was the only defender visible between him and a sure touch, so, out of breath or not, as Viridwx angled toward him he prepared to leap out of cover and bring him down. But before he could—

—a boar, the Arverne Fragar, slid from behind a nearby boulder as Viridwx ran past him and, instead of tripping him fairly, fetched him a blind-sided kick in the balls.

Viridwx went down screaming, but managed to hold on to the ball as he rolled on the ground, writhing in pain.

Without thought, Vercingetorix ran across the field as—

—Fragar punched Viridwx squarely on the brow and pried the ball from his hands.

Vercingetorix arrived just as Fragar turned to carry the ball to the other end of the field, grabbed him by the arm, spun him around, punched him in the sternum, kicked him to the ground, and took the ball himself.

Time seemed to stop as Litivak ran toward the bizarre tableau. He saw Viridwx, clutching at his aching groin, staring up at Vercingetorix in puzzlement and the Arverne boy glaring at him in a fury. Vercingetorix stood there uncertainly, with the strangest look on his face as he clutched the pig's bladder, as if he too, no less than Fragar, had entirely forgotten the rules of the game.

But then Keltill's son, like his father, seemed to have little regard for rules handed down by either gods or men. Litivak's own father often enough declared that this was typical of the Arverni, which was why the gods frowned upon them and favored the Edui, an opinion generally shared by most Eduen warriors of a mature age.

Why the gods of Gaul should choose to smile on a tribe who had achieved wealth and strength through craven alliance with the Roman worshippers of Jove and Venus was a question that some of Litivak's generation might ponder unsuccessfully among themselves, but not one they would dare broach to their fathers.

Perhaps this was what fascinated Litivak about this callow Arverne. Vercingetorix was free in a way that Litivak both feared and envied, for his rage at those who had rendered him fatherless and disinherited freed him to give the heat of his blood full voice, to challenge all the rules of fathers and tribes and even druids.

Vercingetorix looks down at the furious Fragar and the dumbfounded Viridwx, a frozen moment that seems both a serious conundrum and quite ridiculous.

Fragar the Arverne is "on his side."

Viridwx the Eduen is "on the other side," and is his personal enemy too.

Yet he has thoughtlessly fought his "ally" to avenge an act of injustice against his "enemy."

Ally?

Enemy?

This is not a war. This is only a game.

And he is holding not a sword but a pig's bladder stuffed with straw.

And he remembers Litivak's words of not very long ago: Better to win over those who oppose your way with noble deeds that display its virtues.

"You cheated, Fragar," he says, and he pulls Viridwx to his feet. And hands him the ball.

"Which side are you on?" Viridwx mutters in utter befuddlement.

And Vercingetorix finds the words to fit the deed.

"The side of honor, Viridwx. Is that not the side of us all?"

"The boy of action contains the seed of a man of knowledge, Gwyndo," says the Arch Druid, Guttuatr, smiling at what he has seen.

"You truly believe we can mold this angry boy into a druid?" Gwyndo asks skeptically.

"Angry or not—and who is to say he has no cause?—I do believe we have just seen him take the first true step to becoming a man—"

"—of knowledge?"

"Let us hope so, Gwyndo," Guttuatr says more darkly. "We must certainly do our best to make it so. For if not . . ."

A tiny shudder passes through the Arch Druid's body.

The druid Gwyndo knows the worldly reason for Guttuatr's presence here yet not the deeper why of it, just as he knows the story of the tribes of Gaul as passed down by generations of tellers thereof like himself, and the laws of the druids, but not that which connects them, that which flows through, the slow, unseen river shaping all things.

The Arch Druid has come to "observe" his teaching of the story of Brenn, and there he stands behind the circle of nervously squirming students discomforted by his presence, implacable and immobile in the shade of the temple entrance like some marble Roman statue of himself.

Gwyndo knows that Guttuatr seeks to bend a vengeful boy, whom the heavens may have singled out, away from the path of action and onto the path of knowledge. Gwyndo knows that Guttuatr fears the coming of a king. Gwyndo knows that the law of the druids declares that Gaul must not *have* a king. But he knows not the why of it.

For this is knowledge that lies deep within the Inner Way. And he is one of the many, not one of the few. He is a keeper of the annals and the law and a teacher thereof. He is not a druid of the Inner Way. When he was offered that knowledge he refused, for the price was greater than he was willing to pay.

He is a druid. He is a man of knowledge.

But not the knowledge of the oak.

Of all the students seated before Gwyndo and sweating from more than the noonday sun, only Vercingetorix was anything like at ease. The Arch Druid might be a daunting apparition to the rest of them, but he could not cast eyes upon Guttuatr without seeing also the bard Sporos in his threadbare robe.

Gwyndo was expounding the story of Brenn, and, this being a tale he well knew, Vercingetorix was listening with half an ear when, without warning, Guttuatr strode forward through the gasping semicircle of students, stood beside the squatting Gwyndo, thumped his staff hard on the ground, and looked straight at Vercingetorix.

"Tell us the true lesson of the story of Brenn, Vercingetorix," he demanded.

And this was no Sporos, no blind beggar, no fellow ordure-smeared fugitive playing games of invisibility, this was the Arch Druid in all his solemn grandeur. Vercingetorix felt the pressure of every eye upon him in the rapt silence that followed. He knew that this was a test. Or a trap. Or both. He knew what he was expected to say, for he had used this tale to extol Keltill and what he had died for many times, and he knew all too well that the druids who had condemned his father used the very same tale to condemn also his just cause.

"Brenn was the last king the Gauls have had," he said slowly. "After him, we have had no other. . . ."

"And can you tell us why?" asked the Arch Druid.

"Because since then we have had no need of a king," Vercingetorix said sullenly, not adding "until now," but knowing that all would hear those words' unspoken ghosts.

"And why have we had no need of a king?" he asked.

Vercingetorix's silver tongue failed him utterly.

"What is the purpose of a king?" said Guttuatr.

"To lead his people."

"To lead them into what?"

Vercingetorix stared into Guttuatr's eyes for a long silent moment. Those eyes revealed nothing. And yet . . . those eyes seemed to be looking out at him from a world of flame, and something seemed to speak through him.

"Into war!" he said. "King Brenn led the tribes of Gaul against Rome in order to unite them!"

"Did he?" said Guttuatr. "Or did he unite the tribes of Gaul in order to lead them into war on Rome?"

"There's a difference?" Vercingetorix blurted.

Several of the students choked on titters. Gwyndo laughed openly. Even Guttuatr smiled fleetingly. Vercingetorix's ears burned, and his teeth ground against each other in chagrin.

"What did Brenn do after he had led his army of Gauls to Rome and gained his great victory?" Guttuatr demanded.

"He turned around and led them home," Vercingetorix admitted reluctantly.

"Why?" asked Guttuatr.

"Why?"

"Why did Brenn not crown himself king of Rome instead?"

"As Caesar would crown himself king of Gaul and Rome and of the whole world and the heavens beyond if we allowed him!" Vercingetorix interrupted hotly.

"Exactly," said the Arch Druid.

To this, Vercingetorix had no answer, for it seemed to him that Brenn, though a great war leader, had in the end been a fool. He had defeated and humiliated the Romans but refused to conquer them. And for that mistake in the long ago, Gaul was paying dearly now.

Guttuatr strode to an oak at the margin of the clearing.

"Here is an oak growing out of the soil of Gaul," he said, laying a palm on its rough bark. "Would it prosper in the hot lands across the southern ocean? Yet in those lands are other trees that thrive in the broiling heat. Would they flourish here?"

"What do *trees* have to do with the story of Brenn?" Vercingetorix demanded.

"The Romans believe that any land they conquer belongs to them. But men too are rooted in the soil of their own land. Sooner or later— even if it takes a thousand years—the tree of Gaul will die in the soil of Italy, and the tree of Rome will die in the soil of Gaul. Brenn knew that we could not forever rule Rome. Nor can Rome forever rule Gaul."

"One does not have to be a man of knowledge to know that men are not trees!" Vercingetorix said contemptuously. "Trees have no choice but to stand there defenselessly and bow to the woodsman's ax! Is that what you would have us do? Meekly keep our swords in their scabbards, bow to the will of Caesar, and become just one more enslaved province of Rome?"

At this there were scattered cheers, and Vercingetorix believed there would have been more had it not been the Arch Druid that he had challenged.

Guttuatr scowled, and Vercingetorix, as a warrior should, pressed his advantage home. "Are we *trees* or are we *Gauls*?" he demanded. "I say we must unite to make war on the Romans to drive them from our lands!"

Now the cheers were louder, and the Arch Druid's discomfort verged on open ire. "Behind a king?" Guttuatr said grimly.

"Is not a comet the sign of the coming of a king?" demanded Vercingetorix. "And was not one seen in the heavens?"

"Is it?" said Guttuatr. "Was there? No man of knowledge saw any such thing. A comet endures long in the firmament; a falling star, no matter how brightly it burns, is gone in a few heartbeats. And so— might not what was seen be the sign of the *death* of him who, in his prideful vanity, would place a crown upon his brow in defiance of the law? For did not this very thing come to pass?"

Vercingetorix's hands balled into fists, and for one mad moment, he almost stepped forward to menace the Arch Druid of all Gaul.

"All hail Vercingetorix, king of Gaul!" some Eduen bastard shouted mockingly, and the ensuing roar of laughter was enough to prevent the unthinkable.

Instead, Vercingetorix found himself fleeing the unbearable, fleeing the harsh, hot sunlight of the clearing to hide his tears and cool his blood in the calm, quiet, shadowy depths of the woods.

Caesar gazed down at a broad valley that narrowed gradually as it rose into the mild, grassy foothills leading up into the great rocky gray-brown ridges of the Maritime Alps. The green of the grass was only beginning to wither toward brown, but there was white to be seen on the higher crests, and a cool breeze blew down from the mountains, ruffling the banners, whirling the dust kicked up by the carts and wagons and horses, a harbinger of autumn.

This was a sign that it was indeed time to begin to move south to Aix for the winter, before snow began to clog the passes.

Caesar had marshaled all his legions here, save the garrison forces being left behind under Titus Labienus, and as he sat on his favorite horse surveying them from a low hilltop, it was almost as if he beheld vast fields of crops that he had sown, ripe now, and ready for the harvest: the brazen helmets slung across the chests of the infantry formations like gleaming yellow sunflowers, the upraised spears and standards like rows of giant asparagus, the brush-crested helmets of the cavalry bobbing like rushes in the wind. And, indeed, in the midst of these fields of his fancy were the real rich crops he had harvested—long strings of yoked slaves, wagons and carts loaded with dyes, metalwork, pelts, silver, gold—the spoils of this season's booty and tribute.

But Caesar was not content.

"Well, it will be good to be getting back to civilization," said Gisstus, reined up beside him. "Or at least what passes for civilization in Gallia Narbonensis."

"Will it?" said Caesar glumly.

"What ails you, Caesar? The tribute has been rolling in, the only resistance left is minor and fragmented, and the Senate has voted you another term as proconsul of Cisalpine Gaul and Gallia Narbonensis."

"And when that one's over, they'll be all too happy to vote me another, and then another! I have only to ask and they'll make me proconsul of Gaul for life! Julius Caesar, permanent proconsul of this barbaric country, permanently and safely far from Rome!"

Gisstus shrugged. "So it's going more slowly than planned," he said. "But you do have six legions, and enough money to—"

"To keep them here forever as an army of occupation!" Caesar snapped irritably. "And these miserable tribes will keep them occupied with their endless petty rebellions just as long! No, Gisstus, I need to finally conquer Transalpine Gaul, so that the three parts of Gaul can be formally incorporated into a single Roman province. Only that will force the Senate to allow me the full triumph in Rome I need to bring this army unopposed to the border of Italy."

Gisstus nodded in comprehension. "To persuade the Senate to elect you dictator . . . ?"

Caesar nodded back, but he found himself measuring Gisstus out of the corner of his eye. How much can I tell even him? he wondered. Gisstus knows me better than anyone save Calpurnia. But even she doesn't know everything. Best not to tell him all.

Best not to tell *anyone* that I am not about to blindly obey the law that no proconsul may take his legions beyond the borders of his own province, let alone across the frontier into Italy itself.

A man who would *make* history cannot not be bound by the history that has been made before him and frozen in place by senatorial law. The law is no more than the ancient residue of the politics of the past. The law is not meant to constrain destiny.

If the fools in the Senate call my bluff, they will find that Gaius Julius Caesar does not bluff, that he has the courage to follow his own star. If the presence of this army on the frontier between Gaul and Italy is not enough to convince them . . .

Well, I'll cross that bridge if I come to it.

And I'll allow no lawyerly Horatiuses to bar my path.

"You know, Caesar," said Gisstus, "if what you need is a formal conquest, when we return in the spring why not just sack the major towns, execute all the vergobrets, and declare victory?"

"Not funny, Gisstus!" Caesar snapped.

But he felt that the seed of something had been planted in the soil of his fertile mind.

"Perhaps," he said, in a slightly better humor, "not so funny at all . . ."

"Could we have read the signs wrong, Zelkar?" asks Guttuatr, to the amazement of the druid Salgax.

Zelkar shakes his heavy, jowly head. "The sign of the new star proclaims a Great Turning as clearly as a mighty flash of lightning proclaims a coming clap of thunder."

"But does it really point to the boy?" Kifris mutters dubiously.

"Vercingetorix defies all laws *because* they are laws," says Polgar. "The law commanded the death of his father, and so the law itself is his enemy, or so he sees it."

The five druids sit on wooden stools around a stone brazier within the school's small stone temple. Although waning golden afternoon light streams in through the oblong entranceway in a solid sharp-edged beam, it does not penetrate the shadows, and the little fire in the brazier augmenting it has not been well built, so its acrid smoke thickens the air, adds to the atmosphere of gloom, mustiness, confinement. Salgax does not like this place. He does not like to be enclosed by walls and roofs at all.

Kifris keeps the knowledge of the rites. Polgar keeps the knowledge of the law. Zelkar keeps the knowledge of the heavens. Salgax does not know why the Arch Druid has included him in this council. His knowledge is of the forest, of the trees and men and animals who dwell within it, who are the parts of its living body, as fingers are living parts of a man's hand. He has little knowledge of and less interest in heavenly portents, laws, rites, and none in what those known as Druids of the Inner Way call "knowledge of the oak." Rather would he be rewarded by the gods for his service to them in this life by being *born* an oak in the next.

"The boy would sooner become a brigand than a druid," Kifris says scornfully.

"The boy is a boy," Salgax finds himself saying, speaking out for the first time, much to his own bemusement. "And, like all natural boys, he would be a warrior. Would you expect a wolf cub to seek to become a sheep?"

"I fail to see—"

"Let Salgax speak!" the Arch Druid commands sharply, and turns an approving smile upon him; now Salgax understands the wisdom of Guttuatr in summoning him here. The others bear knowledge of rites and stars and laws, but have long since forgotten the knowledge of what it is to be the spirit of a boy on the cusp of manhood within a healthy young man's body. But this is part of the knowledge that he is meant to remember and pass to the generations to come.

"As a colt must become a horse before he can be ridden by either druid or warrior, so must a boy first become a man before he can *choose* to become a druid or a warrior," Salgax explains. "The body becomes a man before the spirit does, so, before being faced with such choices, the boy inside must satisfy his natural desire to learn the way of the warrior and thus become that passion's master rather than its slave."

"You are saying that we should give Vercingetorix what he wants?" Polgar says skeptically.

"Or what he now thinks he wants . . ." muses the Arch Druid.

"You must first give the boy what he thinks he wants," Salgax says, "if you would have the man want what you wish to give."

The Arch Druid nods. "Wisdom," he says simply.

"But who here is to teach him?" protests Zelkar. "No druid knows the warrior's way."

"But do we not shelter one who does?" says Salgax.

"More wisdom, Salgax," says the Arch Druid. And, to Salgax's astonishment, he laughs! "Greater wisdom than you think!"

An autumn's morning mist obscured the treetops as Vercingetorix was led by Guttuatr through the woods, away from the druid school to a deeper part of the forest, where he had never been before. Awakening day birds chirped, now and again unseen animals crashed through the underbrush. Other than that, and the soft sounds of their own passage, the silence lay heavier than the light fog.

Guttuatr had rudely awakened Vercingetorix at dawn with a thump of his staff and, before he could rub the grit of sleep from his eyes, had handed him a sword.

"Like all . . . boys, you seek to learn the warrior's way; then so be it," Guttuatr had said, and led him away, and would speak no more.

"Where *are* you taking me, Guttuatr?" Vercingetorix asked yet again.

At last the Arch Druid deigned to answer, with a look that chilled Vercingetorix more than the dank morning fog.

"To confront the most dangerous animal known to man!" he said.

Vercingetorix drew the sword from its scabbard and gripped it tightly, eyes suddenly alertly peering through the mist, ears registering every distance-muffled sound.

"A boar? A bear? A lion?" he said, unsuccessfully trying not to show his fear.

But Guttuatr remained silent, and Vercingetorix spent the next half hour or so darting at shadows, startled by rabbits, whirling his sword at every distant thump. By the time they had reached a small clearing before a cave mouth in a rock face, the fog had lifted, and a wan sun was attempting to shine.

Guttuatr approached the cave entrance. "We are here!" he shouted. "Come forth!" And then he stepped to one side, well clear of the cave mouth, so that Vercingetorix would confront whatever lurked within on his own.

Vercingetorix spread his legs, braced himself, raised his sword two-handed and upright before him.

A woman with long raven-black hair, wearing a white robe, emerged from the cave.

"Behold the most dangerous animal known to man!" Guttuatr exclaimed. And laughed.

"Her?"

The robe hid all but the woman's face. She was a head shorter than Vercingetorix and seemed several years older. Her hair was lustrous, her brown eyes were hard and unwavering beneath a noble brow, her nose was a bit overlarge, her lips were thin and creased in an expression that might be mirth or might be determination. It was a compelling visage, but too strong for a man to deem beautiful.

"This is Rhia, Vercingetorix," said Guttuatr. "She will teach you the way of the sword. And other things besides."

"You jest!"

"Fear not," said Rhia in a cool, even, soft voice. "I will inflict no pain you cannot learn to bear."

And she pulled the robe over her head and tossed it aside.

Beneath it she wore nothing but a white breechclout and a leather belt from which hung a sword.

Vercingetorix had never seen a woman naked, but he had caught enough glimpses of this and that to form a picture of what one should look like in his mind.

Rhia's body was nothing like it.

She was not heavily muscled, but every muscle stood out as though sculpted by a master. Her breasts were not large but were held upright by the muscles of her chest. The nipples were small and hard and brown. The strangely masculine beauty of her body was marred—no, not marred, but somehow enhanced—by old sword scars across her hard stomach and the thigh of one of the mighty legs, which seemed to guard a treasure trove that only a hero might enter.

Rhia drew her sword one-handed, a motion so rapid and fluid that Vercingetorix could hardly follow it, then put the other hand on the hilt and pointed it straight at him. Judging from the way she handled it, it must be lighter than his own: if not, she must be the stronger.

"Come at me with your sword," she said.

"I can't do that. . . ."

"Don't be afraid to hurt me."

"Why should I want to?"

Rhia licked her lips, arched her pelvis forward. "Draw but a single drop of my body's blood," she said, "and you shall have the blood of my virginity."

Vercingetorix hesitantly lifted his sword and edged forward.

Rhia stood still, gazing into his eyes with a force that at once went straight to his groin and yet constrained him to look away.

"Don't be shy," she said seductively. "I'm waiting. I've been waiting for a long time."

Vercingetorix aimed a tentative crosswise slash at Rhia's sword, still unable to aim at her flesh. Rhia dropped her sword beneath it, whirled around in a low crouch, ducked under his sword, and, in a rapid motion he could not quite follow, came up behind him and whacked him humiliatingly on the rump with the flat of her blade.

Angered, Vercingetorix found himself turning to slash blindly at his tormentor, but Rhia ducked under the blow, came up behind him again, and teasingly ran the point of her sword lightly between his shoulder blades. Vercingetorix whirled around furiously, but this time stepped back and, anticipating her move, slashed low at her ankles. But Rhia hadn't tried to spin behind him this time; rather, she stood her ground, leapt over his sword toward him, and brought the edge of hers up against his throat.

"Watch the eyes, not the sword," she said.

She leapt away from him, pointed her sword at him in challenge again. Vercingetorix ignored her sword, thrust straight forward, and, watching her eyes and seeing Rhia glance left and anticipating her parry, bent his move to the right in mid-course.

Rhia's sword was under his unexpectedly. She brought the flat of her blade up hard against the edge of his, flipping it out of his grasp into the air, then caught it on the way down and handed it back to him. "Trust nothing your opponent says or does," she said.

Once again, Rhia stepped back and pointed her sword at Vercingetorix. Chagrined, enraged, the blood pounding in his ears, he ground his teeth, forced himself to slow down and plan his next move, decided to look right, slash left, and then—

—Rhia's sword turned into a whirlwind of metal, forcing him backward in terror, faster than he could keep his balance, and he fell over backward. Rhia stood over him astraddle, and he found himself staring straight up between the muscular pillars of her legs into her breechclout and at her breasts beyond, with the tip of her downthrust sword lightly resting on his groin, a position that he found both humiliating and enormously exciting.

"Stop thinking," she said. "It slows the mind."

"I have never known a woman like you," Vercingetorix whispered.

"Have you ever known a woman at all?" Rhia said, teasingly running the point of her sword round his pelvis, circling inward.

Vercingetorix burned in silent shame, for in truth he had not. "No shame," said Rhia, reading this. "I have never known a man."

"Then this shall be your lucky day!" cried Vercingetorix, as he suddenly rolled out from under her, tipping her off balance, and, scrambling to his feet, thrust his sword at—

—where she had been.

Somehow Rhia had not fallen, and had come up behind him yet again. With a quick sideways leap, she was once more before him, sword upraised this time.

"Not so bad," she said, "for a *boy.*"

Beside himself with lust, fury, shame, Vercingetorix did as she had advised, or perhaps he could not help doing so, for a red tide overcame his thinking and he found himself slashing, thrusting, clanging metal against metal, without regard to harm, either to her or to himself.

Somehow, and he could not remember how, it ended with his back up against a tree, his sword crossed with hers, hilt to hilt, and blocking it, both of them leaning against their weapons, Rhia's nipples pressed hard against his chest, and her face close enough to his that he could feel her warm breath when she spoke.

"Hot blood can cloud the warrior's mind."

"Then let me cool my heat in you!"

"Hot blood can also give power to him who knows how to use it and is willing to pay the price."

"Can you truthfully say you do not want me now as I want you?"

Rhia brought her pelvis against his, and Vercingetorix ached cruelly with lust.

"No," said Rhia, moving against him, "I burn with desire. All of the time."

"Well, then—"

Rhia shook her head. "That fire is my strength," she said. "To burn with lust and yet keep the virgin's vow is a mighty source of power."

"I . . . I don't understand. . . ."

"I will teach you," said Rhia.

And she stepped back to release him.

"You promised that if I drew a drop of your blood I could have you! You lied!"

Rhia shook her head. "I spoke truth," she said. "For, if you take a drop of my blood, you shall take all of it."

"I would never do that!"

"My virginity is my magic. He who takes it takes also my life. And so I must defend it with my sword, must I not?"

And she raised her sword in challenge again.

"Every magic has its price . . ." whispered Vercingetorix. "The greater the magic, the greater the price to be paid. . . ."

Rhia nodded. "But the greater the price you are willing to pay, the greater the magic you will be able to make. And now I will show you how to break your hot blood to harness, turn foe into partner, and make his struggle your dance."

And she did, or at least she began to; until the autumn sun had reached its zenith, he and Rhia danced with their swords.

First she would show him a move very slowly, then invite him to find a counter in like manner. Then she would invite him to try his own attacks and offer her own counter. With the same exaggerated slowness, the moves were strung together.

Vercingetorix found himself indeed moving from figure to figure without plan, without thought, as Rhia had bidden; letting her moves call forth his own, his moves lead into hers, until the thrust and parry, the leaps and dodges, became a slow, fluid dance, the touches of sword on sword caresses.

And finally, without Vercingetorix's realizing when or how it had begun, the rhythm of the dance became faster and faster without losing its fluid grace, until they were performing it at full fighting speed.

It was exhilarating, it was arousing, it heated the blood, it warmed the heart, and when at length it became quite exhausting, they stood there leaning toward each other, covered in sweat and panting for breath like spent lovers.

Vercingetorix leaned almost imperceptibly closer.

Rhia stepped back, shook her head, gave him a sad, knowing look, and disappeared back into her cave.

"You seemed to have . . . enjoyed your lesson," Guttuatr said as he led Vercingetorix back through the forest toward the druid school. "More dangerous than any lion, now, isn't she?"

"*You* seemed to have enjoyed watching," Vercingetorix replied sourly. "Just who is she?" he demanded.

"Our sorceress of the sword," said the Arch Druid.

"That is not an answer!"

"The right questions are the tools you need to pry the answers you seek out of their shells."

Tired, sweaty, his body taut with frustrated desire, Vercingetorix was in no mood for lessons or riddles.

"There are no other women like her in Gaul," he said.

"That is not a question," said Guttuatr. "Still, it is true."

"So—from whence did she come?"

"From somewhere across the northern waters," Guttuatr said. "She landed on the beach in a boat with the corpse of a woman dressed as a warrior and bearing a sword. She was perhaps ten years old. She could not speak. When fisherfolk approached, she took up the sword, terrified them with a fierce attack, and fled."

Guttuatr shrugged. "Of her next years, there are only tales and legends of a girl child with a sword wandering in the forest like a wild beast, driving off those who sought to succor her, slaying those who sought to violate her or take her as a slave."

"A small girl!" exclaimed Vercingetorix. "What sorcery is this?"

"The sorcery into which you have just been initiated," Guttuatr said dryly.

"But where did she learn this magic? From whom?"

"She remembers nothing of her life before she arrived on this shore, and of her years in the forest, only . . . visions."

"Visions?"

"She now remembers only sights, sounds, smells from that time, for she knew no human tongue to bind their meaning to memory with words."

"Bind their meaning with words?"

"The animals of this forest see, hear, smell, but without words they cannot think as we do, and so cannot remember the meaning of what they have seen, heard, and smelled. Words are the first and greatest magic. They made men and women from beasts."

"Then she was like an animal?"

Guttuatr nodded. "When at last she was taken as she slept by fearful farmers and given to the druids, we had to teach her to speak. To become human again."

"What could have done such a thing to her, Guttuatr?"

Guttuatr shrugged once more. "Perhaps the girl's spirit saw more than it could contain, and so died while her flesh yet lived. Or . . . or the gods emptied her out so that they might fill her with . . ."

The Arch Druid stopped in mid-sentence.

"With what?" Vercingetorix demanded.

"There are matters that cannot be spoken of to those without the knowledge of the oak," said the Arch Druid.

Vercingetorix stopped dead in his tracks. Had it been anyone other than the Arch Druid, he would have grabbed him by the shoulder and spun him around.

Guttuatr continued to walk at the same pace, forcing Vercingetorix to trot to catch up.

"With visions!" Vercingetorix cried.

Guttuatr stopped suddenly, rounded on him. "How did you know that?" he said sharply.

"What else could make a strong woman in her prime torture herself with a vow of virginity?" Vercingetorix told him.

Guttuatr laughed. "You mean what else could make her spurn the ardor of a fine young stallion like yourself?" he said.

Vercingetorix felt his face flush red. "Tell me what they were!" he said.

"There are matters that cannot be *understood* by those without knowledge of the oak."

Gaius Julius Caesar had gone to Rome at the beginning of winter, but though he enjoyed his reunion with Calpurnia and the luxury and sophistication of true civilization, enemies, rivals, and creditors had swarmed all over him like flies, the Senate had asked too many pointed questions, and he finally arranged to be "summoned" back to his provincial capital at Aix to deal with the nonexistent threat of pirate raiders.

There he had lolled about his villa, dealing with the tasks of proconsulship, recruiting yet another legion, and taking a hand in arranging the curriculum of the "hostage school."

As Gallic custom allowed and Roman practice mandated, he had taken children of potential adversaries as hostages to good behavior, and it had occurred to him that styling the captivity of these young Gauls as an "educational opportunity" could serve two useful purposes. Assuring their parents that they would be attending a Roman grammaticus made their captivity go down a lot smoother. And in the long run, giving the young hostages a real Roman education would be an excellent means of creating a Romanized elite which would make Gaul a lot easier to administer.

So Caesar took care to see to it that their introduction to Roman civilization was seductive rather than coercive, establishing pleasant quarters, laying on true Roman cuisine, decent wine, and good teachers, and doing his fair share of the seducing himself by providing a sophisticated Roman erotic education to the comelier and more promising students.

Still, all this was merely passing the time until spring came and he could return northward to finish the conquest of Gaul once and for all. But now that the time to prepare to move his legions back over the mountains had finally come, he found that his impatience had become anxiety.

"The problem is, the Gauls' weakness turns out to be their strength," he complained to Gisstus as they sat alone in the courtyard of his villa on a balmy night after he had dismissed his servants.

Gisstus, not being a commander of troops, was the only man to whom he could voice his misgivings without risking the poisoning of morale. Gisstus was the closest thing he had here to a mirror of his own mind.

"Is that one of your riddles, Caesar?" Gisstus asked dryly, sipping at the local wine, which, though rough and of lesser quality than that of Italy, had the virtue of not being tainted by a sea voyage sealed in amphorae.

"A true conundrum, Gisstus," Caesar said, pausing to sip at the stuff himself. It relieved his thirst, but it also reminded him of where he was, and where he did not belong, here in the provinces far from the finer vintages of Rome.

"If the Gauls united, they could raise an army that would outnumber us, and their cavalry is fearsome," he said. "I say this to no one else, but I fear that if they did we would be hard-pressed to hold our ground."

"You worry too much, Caesar. There are more tribes than anyone can count, and they shift alliances more often than they bathe."

"That is the weakness that prevents them from defeating us," Caesar told him, "but also the strength that prevents us from truly conquering Gaul."

Gisstus gave him a quizzical look, cocking his head to one side.

"How can you conquer something that doesn't really exist?" Caesar said, hearing the tone of exasperation in his own voice. "How can you conquer a country without a ruler? How can you conquer Gaul when the Gauls don't even have anyone with the power to surrender it? It's like trying to pick up water in a sieve!"

Caesar felt his blood pounding, his ire rising. Take care, he told himself. Exercise control. Breathe deeply. The stars above do not yet sparkle with gauzy auras, the moon does not waver, my vision remains clear. The falling sickness does not yet approach, but do not tempt it with rage.

He took a long, slow sip of wine, and when he spoke again it was more calmly. "Easy enough to make any alliance with some greedy noble in each of the tribes, like Gobanit or Diviacx, but as soon as you do, four other factions use it to plot against him. And the cozier we get with the Edui, the more restive the Arverni become. . . ."

"The ideal situation for an army of occupation. Divide and conquer."

"No, Gisstus," Caesar snapped angrily, "divide and *don't* conquer!"

Gisstus shrugged. "Well, we could always try my plan. . . ."

"What plan?"

"Sack the cities, slay the vergobrets, enslave the nobles, and declare Gaul conquered," Gisstus said dryly.

"You're serious?"

Gisstus shrugged. "If we acted quickly and ruthlessly, we could get it done before they could organize to stop us," he said. "If they ever could."

"And then what? It would be a Pyrrhic victory, Gisstus. Every hand in Gaul would be turned against us forever, and we'd need an army half again as large as what we have now just to collect tribute at sword point. Gaul would never be pacified enough to become a Roman province, and the Senate would reward me for creating such a quagmire by allowing me to preside over it until I was old and gray or decided to fall on my own sword, whichever came first."

"You have a better idea, Caesar?"

Caesar shrugged and drank deeply of his wine.

"Maybe we were too hard on the Teutons," said Gisstus. "It would certainly have been convenient to have someone else rid us of all of the troublemaking bastards."

"Why not?" Caesar exclaimed. It was as if a fog had lifted. Suddenly Caesar's mind was clear, and his spirit filled with an energy that owed nothing to the mediocre wine. "It's perfect!" he cried.

"*What* is?"

"What do all these vergobrets and would-be vergobrets have in common, Gisstus?"

"A thirst for gory glory and a greed for gold?"

"Exactly," said Caesar. "So we give it to them!" And he found himself laughing in delight at the beauty of it all.

"You must be feeling your old self," said Gisstus, "since I can no longer see where you're going."

"Britain," said Caesar, and he laughed again.

"Britain?" said Gisstus. "As I remember, your foray there was less than an edifying experience. 'Inhabited by savages beside whom the Gauls appear as the populace of Athens in the Golden Age of Pericles,' I believe was how you put it."

"But Britain is also rich in metals and a good source of prime slaves."

"Conquer Britain? Not worth the cost of conquest in men, or money even, I believe was your final judgment."

Caesar found himself laughing yet again. "We don't really try to *conquer* Britain, we just invade, win a quick series of easy victories, and depart with the loot."

"I don't understand . . ." said Gisstus.

"Perfect!" cried Caesar "If *you* don't, neither will the Gauls!"

He got up, began pacing as he spoke, brimming with self-confidence. It was like welcoming himself back as an old friend.

"We bring along an army of Gallic auxiliaries led by the chieftains and major nobles of all the tribes and let them do most of the fighting," he said.

"I didn't know you were a magician too," Gisstus said dubiously.

"They'll be falling all over themselves to take part when we offer them half the booty we take," Caesar told him. "Even those who deem themselves enemies of Rome will be forced to come along or be scorned as cowards for the rest of their lives!"

"Nice," said Gisstus, "but don't let your natural generosity carry you away, Caesar. A quarter of the take will surely do."

Caesar laughed. "Fear not, Gisstus, we can afford to be generous with the fortunate few."

"The fortunate few?"

"Our good friends the survivors. For only our good friends *will* survive," Caesar said. "Mars is a fickle and unpredictable god, after all. Such an invasion could prove to be a lot more costly in lives than planned. It wouldn't surprise me if most of the leaders who are *not* friends of Rome met glorious deaths in battle."

Caesar could not keep from laughing once more. "And can you guess what the most amusing part is?" he asked slyly.

He saw the full light of comprehension dawn in his spymaster's eyes. Gisstus smiled; he even gave out a short barking laugh.

"The Gauls will finance the whole thing?" he said.

The snows of winter had begun to melt, the oaks had put out their buds, and Vercingetorix too felt the sap of approaching spring rising through him as the latest round in his dance of the swords with Rhia ended with both of them panting and sweaty, close enough to feel each other's heat, faces inches apart.

He leaned closer still, seeking her lips with his own—

Rhia backed away, hooking his left ankle with her foot in the same deft motion, sending him sprawling.

"You still have much to learn," she said without laughing.

"I have already learned more than I care to," Vercingetorix said sourly as he scrambled to his feet.

He had learned the annals of the tribes of Gaul. He had learned the laws of the druids. He had learned to read the heavens. He had learned the uses of the herbs and roots of the meadows and woodlands. He had learned secrets of the human body.

And he had learned the way of the sword from Rhia. He had learned moves and figures foreign to the fighting style of Gaul. He had learned to make his sword one with his body, to stop the thought that slowed the mind and give himself over to the dance. He was confident that he had learned enough to best any warrior in Gaul save his teacher.

But Rhia he could never best, and he doubted he ever would take his precious drop of her blood. And so his nights were filled with lustful dreams of the body he could see but not touch, and these warriors' dances became a tantalization so painful it became sweet, so sweet that it became agony to his flesh.

"Why do we not end this foolish game?" he demanded.

"This is not a game," Rhia said coldly, even though he could see the passion in her eyes, all but smell the desire on her breath.

"This is torture for both of us!"

"This is *power* for both of us."

"You burn for me as I burn for you. Can you deny it?"

Rhia would not answer with words, but her averted gaze made its meaning plain.

"There is a great magic in such a fire as long as it burns unconsumed, a weapon greater than any sword," said Rhia. "And this you have still not learned."

"This I *would not* learn!" said Vercingetorix, and he turned his back on her and stalked away.

Peering through the open tent flap, Caesar saw that all was in order. Despite the drizzle oozing down from the low, leaden, overcast sky, the legionnaires stood firm and still in their orderly ranks, even with the moisture dribbling down from their helmets onto their foreheads and noses. Their standard was planted before the formation in the sodden turf of the plain; his own eagle, a careful two heads higher, had been erected before the tent; and the trumpeters were ready. It was an impressive martial show, but it made Caesar feel as if he were part of some troop of gladiators touring run-down arenas in minor cities in Italy, attempting to impress the locals with pomp and polish.

"Really, Labienus, why don't *you* finally give the speech this time?" Caesar said only half jestingly. "You've certainly heard *me* regurgitate it often enough to know it by heart."

Gisstus suppressed a laugh. Titus Labienus, not noted for a finely honed sense of irony, regarded Caesar uneasily.

"I'm a soldier, not an . . . orator like you, Caesar," he said.

Caesar had more than a suspicion that "politician" was the word he had thought and masked. Labienus did not so much abhor politicians as regard them as a different species of creature, much as many poets could not comprehend why anyone would be interested in the arcana of engineering.

Which was just as well. Tall, built like Apollo with a luxurious mane of black hair that the balding Caesar could only gaze on with envy, Labienus was a charismatic leader and a brilliant general on a tactical level. He would have been a dangerous rival if he had had any political ambitions. Even the Gauls admired this perfect warrior.

That was why Caesar had chosen to tour with Labienus and five cohorts from his legion. It had made the task of winning the Gauls over to his scheme easier. He had also hoped that Labienus would relieve him of some of the drudgery of delivering the same speech over and over again. But no, the fearless soldier, who would face a pride of lions single-handedly before lunch and take on a herd of elephants afterward, turned craven at the prospect of delivering an oration.

But, then, nothing turns out to be as easy as it first seems in this barbaric country, Caesar thought sourly. Five cohorts of Roman infantry were not welcome within the walls of any of these Gallic hilltop redoubts, not even here at Bibracte, the Eduen capital. Not only were the men constrained to sleep in the open, within sight of the comforts and pleasures of these rude cities; he himself was constrained to deliver the speech in the open as well. Even, as now, in the rain.

This last performance shouldn't even have been necessary. One would have thought Diviacx could have done the recruiting, being the brother of their vergobret and a druid as well. But no, as a druid, Diviacx could take no part in warfare, not even to the extent of standing by Caesar's side with his mouth shut. And as Caesar had learned, the vergobrets were "tribal chieftains" in name only when it came to mustering troops. Each noble had his own collection of warriors, and the vergobret was powerless to raise an "army" except by force of charisma or oratory art.

Speaking of which, you had better stick out your chin, and paint a smile on your lips and a gleam in your eyes, Caesar told himself.

He nodded to Labienus, Labienus nodded to a centurion within the tent with no little relief, the centurion stepped outside and signaled to the trumpeters, who blew a fanfare, and Labienus marched out of the tent to take his place beneath his legion's standard at the head of his troops, facing the assembled Edui.

The trumpeters blew a louder, longer, and grander fanfare, and Caesar himself strutted out into the light rain, taking care to hold his crimson cloak away from his body with his upraised elbows and rotate his shoulders once, twice, thrice, to give it a proper dramatic swirl as he strode up to the map hanging from a lance plunged into the ground, and turned smartly to face the Gauls.

Gisstus emerged quietly to take his usual place beside the map, from where, in the guise of a lackey helping to display it, he could whisper to Caesar anything he might need to hear.

"Hail, Caesar!" shouted Labienus, snapping his arm out in a smart salute.

"Hail, Caesar!" five cohorts of legionnaires roared, saluting in perfect unison.

The Gauls, as usual, boorishly failed to join in the salutation.

There they stood, no more than a hundred of them, with their hilltop city gloomily visible through the mist, a rabble of some hundred warriors confronting five cohorts of a Roman legion. Which was more or less Caesar's point.

"People of Gaul, I salute you!" Caesar began.

This at least elicited a scattering of polite "Hail, Caesar"s, which would be described as an enthusiastic ovation in his next dispatch to Rome.

"Rome has rid you of the scourge of the Teutons, built roads, aqueducts, and bridges, conferred upon you the benefits of commerce with the greatest civilization on earth," Caesar declaimed.

This was greeted by sullen mutterings, for even the Edui, who had made out better than any of the other tribes, were not dim enough to fail to comprehend that not only did all roads lead to Rome but most of the profit flowed along them in that direction as well.

It was an old rhetorical trick. Caesar had used it so many times by now that he could do it in his sleep.

"And now Rome will bring you riches and glory!"

This never failed to pique their interest. Caesar then suddenly drew his sword, producing a mass intake of breath.

With a flourish, Gisstus unfurled the map behind him, which depicted the northern coast of Gaul and the isle of Britain beyond in a manner designed to maximize the size of the prize and minimize the width of the channel that must be crossed to get to it. Caesar planted the point of his sword in the center of Britain as if it were a succulent fig on the end of a dining knife.

"Britain, my friends, rich beyond measure, yet inhabited by people so primitive they think it the height of civilized fashion to paint themselves blue!" he declared.

This brought rude, superior laughter. It always did.

"Gold, silver, jewels, vast treasures, guarded not by great armies or mighty warriors, but by mere savages, a hundred of whom would be no match for a single Gaul!"

This brought the usual cheers and banging of swords and daggers on shields.

"I propose to bring the benefits of Roman civilization to these benighted savages—"

Hoots of derision. "And take their riches from them!" someone shouted. Someone always did shout something like that. You could count on it.

"Indeed, my friends! And share both those riches and the glory of triumph with *you*!"

Utter silence. You could perhaps hear a few greedy drops of drool fall.

"Rome is the most terrible of enemies, as the Teutons and a few misguided Gauls have learned to their sorrow, but Rome is also the greatest of friends, as you will now learn to your profit and glory and joy! We will invade Britain together, my friends, the noble warriors of Gaul—"

Caesar half turned and pointed with his sword to the cohorts massed on his right hand, who, on the signal, drew their swords as one, held them high in the air.

"—and the invincible legions of Rome!"

"Hail, Caesar!" the legionnaires shouted. Some of the Gauls replied, and since his men had been drilled to repeat the salutation as they did, the illusion was created that everyone now repeated it in unison.

"Hail, Caesar!"

The illusion in turn created the reality, as such illusions tended to do, and the salutation was repeated spontaneously.

"I like it not!" shouted a bluff blond fellow with an enormous unkempt mustache near the front.

There was at least one in every crowd.

"Dumnorix," Gisstus reminded Caesar in a whisper. "Diviacx's brother, but no particular friend of Rome."

"What is the great warrior Dumnorix afraid of, a horde of half-naked savages?" Caesar taunted, taking care to say it with a smile, so that the mockery drew laughter from all but Dumnorix, who glowered back at him, his fair skin blushing red.

"I fear no man!" he shouted.

"What, then, causes you to hold back from easy wealth and noble glory, O fearless Dumnorix?"

Though the rage thus evoked in him was visible, Dumnorix apparently was clever enough to know he had best choke it back and escape with a jest. "We are no race of sailors, and that channel gets stormy," he said. "We might find ourselves heaving our guts out before we got there, to say nothing of what the horses might do!"

Modest laughter at this.

"What, is the great warrior Dumnorix afraid of a little seasickness?" Caesar said good-naturedly, allowing him his escape. "Are there others here unwilling to sacrifice a bellyful of vomit for a mountain of gold and a paean of glory?"

Louder and more derisive laughter.

"Well, if there are, there are plenty of others in Gaul eager to take your share," Caesar said with a shrug, and, turning on his heel, pretended to stalk off.

But only for one, two, three paces. Then he stopped suddenly, snapped his fingers as if at his own forgetfulness, and turned back to face the Gauls.

"Oh," he said, "did I forget to tell you that half the booty we take will be yours?"

The cheers and "Hail, Caesar"s were louder and more prolonged this time, and Caesar took care to make his exit into the tent before they had fully died out.

"Another good performance, Caesar," Gisstus said when Labienus had gone off to bivouac his troops, and wine had been brought to soothe Caesar's throat. "Fortunately, the last."

Caesar sighed. "It *did* get boring," he said.

"But it was effective. Few of them are able to resist their greed, and the few that are clever enough to suspect our generosity are shamed into coming along for fear of appearing cowards."

"Except for that mound of lard, Gobanit," said Caesar. "Nothing shames him."

The Arverni tended to oppose whatever the Edui favored, and the closer the Edui had come to alliance with Rome, the more restive they had become. So replacing the biggest troublemaker, that Keltill, with his greedy and pliant brother, and getting him to create an "Arverne Republic" whose "Senate" could then keep electing him vergobret, had been a good idea at the time.

But Gobanit had outlived his usefulness. He had grown so fat and lazy that the thought of him leading the Arverni into battle was ludicrous. He had dutifully supported the invasion of Britain, but made it clear that he himself would not cross the water. Meaning that he had not the charisma to persuade the hotbloods among the Arverni, who had practically made a god of Keltill, to come along against their distaste for Rome. And these were precisely the sort of elements the whole thing was designed to eliminate.

Worse, if the restive leadership of the other tribes were to be eliminated without doing likewise to the Arverni, the effect would be to increase the relative strength of Rome's bitterest enemy among the Gauls.

"Something must be done about the Arverne situation before we embark, Gisstus," Caesar said.

Gisstus drew a forefinger across his throat.

Caesar shook his head. "If Gobanit were simply eliminated right now, half of the Arverne nobles would suspect us, and all of them would be contending to take his place. It would be chaos."

"So we *replace* him with someone both more popular and more pliant."

"Indeed . . ."

"The question is, with whom?" said Gisstus.

"Find someone," said Caesar.

"And where do you suggest such a mythical creature might be found?"

Caesar shrugged. "If one cannot find a unicorn," he said, "one must make do with an antelope horn glued to the forehead of a white goat."

The spring sun warmed the land, the crocuses bloomed in the meadows, and the birds beginning their mating songs seemed to be calling upon Vercingetorix to be gone from this cowardly refuge, to cease learning, to go, to be, to *do*.

And so Vercingetorix listened sullenly to the druid teachers drone on and waited for he knew not what. He practiced the figures of the way of the sword alone into exhaustion, and he waited. He dreamed each night of Rhia's body, and he waited. He burned with impatience, and he waited.

Only when Guttuatr finally appeared once more at the druid school did he realize what—or, rather, whom—he had been waiting for.

The Arch Druid had brought him here. The Arch Druid had commanded him to remain. The Arch Druid could not be disobeyed. Therefore, only Guttuatr could free him from his captivity in this place.

Guttuatr avoided him for two days, eyeing him from a distance, falling into conversation with other druids on his approach, shying away from him like a skittish colt or a teasing maiden. But, at length, Guttuatr finally allowed himself to be approached, walking near the edge of the forest.

"How much longer must I remain here?" Vercingetorix demanded forthrightly.

"Until you leave."

"That is not an answer!"

"Ask a better question."

Vercingetorix sought to contain his ire. "May I go whenever I want?" he asked.

"No man will stop you."

"May I go wherever I want?"

"No man may do that," the Arch Druid told him.

Vercingetorix refused to let his exasperation overwhelm him, and spoke instead from the honest confusion in his heart.

"Please, Guttuatr, speak to me plain, as the father I do not have. What am I to do? Who am I to become?"

"You believe you are ready to seek such knowledge?" Guttuatr asked. "You believe you are ready to pay the price?"

"Would I ask if I were not?"

"You do not know what the price is," Guttuatr said ominously.

"It cannot be worse than the price I am already paying for my ignorance!" Vercingetorix exclaimed.

"Walk with me," said the Arch Druid, and he led Vercingetorix into the forest.

Nothing more was said until the works of men were lost from sight, and the sounds of the druid school faded away into the chirpings of the birds and the whispering of the wind through the treetops, and even the loamy tang of the forest must have been as it was before men walked here and as it would be when they were gone.

"Have you never thought to ask why you were brought here to safety?" Guttuatr then asked.

"Does one question kindness?" Vercingetorix answered insincerely.

"Was it kindness to make you watch your father's burning in silence?"

"Certainly not! It was very cruel!"

"But a necessary cruelty," said Guttuatr.

"How can you call such cruelty necessary?"

"Why were you taught the way of the sword by Rhia?"

"That is not an answer!" Vercingetorix told the Arch Druid angrily.

"But it is," said Guttuatr. "For the two questions have the same answer. An answer that is also a question."

"Can you speak *nothing* plain?" Vercingetorix shouted.

"Destiny is both the answer and the question," Guttuatr told him calmly. "And more often than not speaks far less plainly than I."

"Destiny? Whose destiny?"

"Yours, of course. That of Gaul . . . perhaps. There was a sign in the heavens—"

"A comet declaring the coming of a king, everyone knows—"

"So everyone wants to believe," said Guttuatr. "But there was no comet."

"There was no sign?"

"I did not say that, Vercingetorix. There was no comet, but there *was* a sign, a true sign, and a far greater one, the knowledge of whose meaning few possess."

They were approaching a small clearing in the forest. From within its shadows and between its tree trunks, Vercingetorix could see a mighty lone oak in a sunlit circle.

"The sign of a Great Turning," said Guttuatr, "of the death of the Age in which we live and the coming birth of the next. And . . ."

"And?"

Guttuatr turned to regard Vercingetorix most strangely.

"When the Crown of Brenn tumbled from the brow of Keltill, and your hand plucked it from the air before it could fall . . ."

Guttuatr hesitated for a long moment.

"Yes? *Yes?*"

"I saw that sign again."

And before Vercingetorix could speak, the Arch Druid stayed him by raising his hand. "Do not ask me what it means," he said. "I do not know, I cannot know, for it was the sign of *your* destiny, not mine, Vercingetorix. You may choose to follow it blindly, or you may choose . . . to know."

They entered the clearing. The earth within it was covered with dark-green moss. And in the center was a single ancient oak. And growing from the bare ground sheltered by its gnarly roots were scores of white-speckled brown mushrooms.

"What is this tree . . . ?" Vercingetorix said softly. But he knew, for there was a magic here that he could feel.

"Have you not been told that 'druid' means 'man of knowledge,' but the inner meaning is—"

"Knowledge of the oak . . . This is . . . ?"

"*That* oak," said Guttuatr. He laid the palm of his hand on the bark of the mighty oak. "This is the Tree of Knowledge."

"The Tree of Knowledge?"

"Some call it the Tree of Life, for they are one and the same. Here a man becomes a Druid of the Inner Way. If he so chooses."

"If he so chooses?"

"Few are the druids who choose to walk the Inner Way. For to do so is to know your own destiny."

"Who would not wish to know—"

The Arch Druid silenced Vercingetorix with an upraised hand and a baleful stare. "What knowledge is the heaviest to bear?" he asked.

Vercingetorix remained silent, for he did not know.

"The knowledge of your own destiny," the Arch Druid said.

"Why should that be so heavy to bear?"

"What destiny do all men share?" said the Arch Druid.

And Vercingetorix knew. And though the heavy green leaves of the ancient oak moved not at all, he felt a chill wind blowing through the clearing, through his soul.

"Yes, all men's destiny is death," said the Arch Druid. "To eat of the fruit of the Tree of Knowledge is to step outside the dream men call time and know that our lives do not proceed moment by moment, like beads on a string. It is to stand upon a hill above a mist-shrouded forest, looking down on what will be. That hill is your death, and the fore-knowledge of its meaning is the greatest power a man can attain. *If* he has the courage to encompass it while he yet lives."

He reached down, plucked a mushroom, held it up to Vercingetorix.

"I offer you the gift of that knowledge now," said the Arch Druid. "But I warn you, bitter or sweet, it is the one gift that can never be returned."

Vercingetorix reached out and took it.

"Are you afraid?" asked Guttuatr.

"Yes," said Vercingetorix.

"Good," said Guttuatr. "He who would not be afraid to bear this knowledge is a fool, and thus unworthy. You may eat."

Vercingetorix found himself biting into the mushroom. It was bitter. He choked the rest of it down as fast as he could to avoid the taste, and then sat down between the roots of the Tree of Knowledge, leaned back against its ancient rough trunk, and waited to discover if what he would learn would be more bitter still.

Vercingetorix awakens into a white mist so dense he cannot see his own body. The only sound is the susurrus of a distant wordless song of seduction.

The mist begins to glow.

And there is light.

A single silver point of it above him.

A star.

A star that waxes brighter, and brighter, and brighter. It becomes the sun burning away the mist above him, and Vercingetorix stands upon the pinnacle of a fog-shrouded mountain. And now he can hear the chanting of an unseen multitude like a lover's whisper crooning in his ear:

"Vercingetorix . . . Vercingetorix . . ."

The hill beneath his feet begins to turn, or the mist swirls round it, and all the world now revolves about the place where he stands, the unmoving hub of a great wheel turning the dance of life through time.

He is once more an innocently happy boy riding on the road to Gergovia beside his father. "Can you keep a secret?" says Keltill.

Keltill anoints a dusty old crown with beer until it shines, then lowers it onto the brow of Vercingetorix. "Whatever the price may be, you must pay it," he says, bursting into flame, "for there is no one to pay it in your stead."

Keltill burns in a wicker cage as Vercingetorix watches helplessly, the sweet odor of roasting flesh assailing his nostrils, choking his throat, tearing his eyes.

"In fire shall you remember me!" his father proclaims, and he disappears into the flames, his eyes glaring from the face of a giant of fire.

The burning giant strides through green meadows and golden grain, in his wake ashes and fields burned black and the smoldering skeletons of trees.

Vercingetorix hears the voice of a far-off suffering multitude summoning him to battle.

"Vercingetorix! Vercingetorix!"

And he becomes the flaming giant.

And he stands once more atop the hill above the dance of life. Through the swirling mists below he beholds a great army of Gauls, warriors of every tribe beneath the standards of the boar and the hawk, the owl and the horse, the wolf, the stag, and the lynx.

And he rides at the head of this, his army, his heart joyously beating to the battle rhythm of the pounding hooves. Beside him rides Rhia, holding aloft the bear standard of the Arverni.

But Vercingetorix carries the eagle standard of Rome. And he rides a white horse bedecked with the gold-and-red trappings of a Roman general and wears a cloak of brilliant crimson.

Louder still becomes the chanting:

"Vercingetorix! Vercingetorix!"

He rides through the main plaza of Gergovia through a cheering multitude, up the stairs of the Great Hall itself into a Roman encampment, into an enormous tent draped in tapestries fringed with threads of gold, lit by golden lamps, the bare earth hidden beneath colorful carpets.

He luxuriates upon a soft couch, sipping heady red wine from a golden goblet. On a couch beside him reclines a stocky balding Roman wearing a crimson cloak. The Roman offers him a crown of prickly green laurel leaves.

"Vercingetorix? King of Gaul?"

Vercingetorix rejects the crown of laurel.

The Roman offers him the Crown of Brenn.

Vercingetorix hesitates.

The Roman becomes the Arch Druid Guttuatr.

"The greater the price to be paid, the greater the magic," says the Arch Druid. And he presses the Crown of Brenn down upon the head of Vercingetorix.

Guttuatr's robe becomes a gown of white mist, swirling, swirling, the gown of a woman without a face, with the face of his mother, Gaela, with the face of Epona, with the face of a golden-haired woman Vercingetorix knows from somewhere, with the faces, or so it seems, of all the women who were and are and will be flowing through time.

In the crook of her right arm she cradles a baby. In her left hand she holds a dagger.

She offers Vercingetorix the dagger. Vercingetorix takes it.

And plunges it into his own heart.

The golden-haired woman stands naked and beautiful before him. She kisses him. "Take that with you into the Land of Legend, Vercingetorix, king of Gaul," she tells him as she places the Crown of Brenn upon his head.

And Vercingetorix rides in a gilded chariot beside the crimson-cloaked Roman who wears a wreath of laurel. The Roman waves in triumph to the cheering crowds thronging a wide avenue through an endless canyon of great white buildings of ornately worked marble in the heart of a city that can only be Rome.

And Vercingetorix receives the accolade of all Rome as he marches afoot through the triumphal aisle wearing the Crown of Brenn.

"Vercingetorix, king of Gaul! Vercingetorix, king of Gaul!"

His heart brims with pride. His spirit soars with joy. It bursts out of his body and takes wing.

But the bird he becomes is the black carrion raven of death.

He swoops down, down, down, to alight on the sill of a barred window and peer into a dank stone cell.

Vercingetorix the raven beholds Vercingetorix the man lying dead in a pool of his own blood.

"Vercingetorix, king of Gaul!"

The raven croaks, and hops into the cell. It hops through the blood, cawing. It hops up onto the dead man's breast. Cackling, it hops onto Vercingetorix's face. It pecks at the corpse's eye—

As it does, the raven is thereby transformed into an eagle.

The bars of the cell window melt away. Brilliant sunlight pours through. The eagle flies up out of the cell, up, up, up, into the sky above Rome.

"Vercingetorix, king of Gaul! Vercingetorix, king of Gaul!"

Up through the swirling white mist of a cloud the eagle soars. Beyond is another time. Beyond is a starless night sky.

A star is born in the perfect blackness.

It waxes brighter and brighter and brighter. It becomes a brilliant golden sun burning away the night to reveal a blue noonday sky above.

Burning away the mists below to reveal a great city.

Which can only be a city in the Land of Legend. For it is a magical city.

A magical river flows through it; the great boats upon it, made not of wood but of gleaming metal, glide downstream and up without sail or oar.

Multitudes of wagons move through the streets of the city, drawn by magic alone, for there is not a horse or an ox to be seen.

Although it is bright noon, here and there magical torches have been set up on poles. These torches are capped not with pitch-soaked hay giving forth smoky orange flame, but with giant jewels—rubies, emeralds, amber—shining star-bright from within as if they have been hollowed out and filled with fireflies.

Close by the river rises a wickerwork tower tall as a mountain. But magic has transformed the wicker into metal.

Above the tower, above the eagle circling its pointed pinnacle, a silver bird flies at impossible speed, scribing a magic cloud across the blue sky, thin and straight as an arrow, white as chalk.

Vercingetorix's spirit folds its eagle wings and stoops down, down, down, out of the magic of the skies, to the magic of the city below.

He alights on the head of a stone statue.

The statue of a warrior of the Arverni mounted on a noble steed, sword held high.

And an unseen multitude chants with the mighty voices of the gods: *"Vercingetorix, king of Gaul! Vercingetorix, king of Gaul!"*

The face of stone becomes a face of flesh.

And it is Vercingetorix's own.

And the living arms of the Tree of Knowledge, gentle as those of a mother with her babe, lower him to the earth between its ancient roots.

Where he awakens into the dream called time.

VII

D ID YOU FIND that which you sought?"

"That which I sought?" Vercingetorix muttered, scarcely able to comprehend where he was, or who was this white-robed gray-haired man staring down at him so intently.

"The meaning of your death! Your destiny!"

Slowly his spirit began to return to his body. It was a waning afternoon, to judge by the deepness of the sky's blue and the length of the shadows of the trees surrounding the clearing upon whose mossy ground he sat, with his back up against the trunk of a mighty oak. He could feel the rough texture of the tree's bark as if he wore no tunic. He could see motes of dust floating glittering in the air, and tiny midges flying among them. He could hear the leaves of the trees rustling in a gentle breeze and distinguish the song of a far-off merle from the gabbling of a nearby tribe of starlings. He could smell the resin of the trees and the warmth of sunlight on living wood.

Vercingetorix took a deep draft of the cooling afternoon air, redolent with the loamy fragrance of the forest floor, held it in his lungs, stilled the confusion that roiled his mind, let it fill him, then exhaled it, and remembered.

"Oh yes, I saw my destiny, Guttuatr," he said. "I was . . . I am . . . My destiny is to become . . . king of Gaul!"

"King of Gaul!" cried the Arch Druid, deep dismay in his voice.

"What troubles you?" Vercingetorix asked. "You yourself placed . . . will place the Crown of Brenn on my head."

"Never will I crown a king of Gaul!"

"That is what I saw, Guttuatr," Vercingetorix told him calmly. "But . . ."

"But?"

Vercingetorix struggled to clear his thoughts. There was much to remember—or much to forget?—before the dead king of Gaul in a stone cell in Rome could once more fully become this living boy leaning up against an oak.

"But I was proclaimed king of Gaul in *Rome*!" Vercingetorix exclaimed, remembering only as he spoke. "And there will I die!"

And then he was the student again, at least for the moment, humbly seeking understanding from the man of knowledge. But this moment passed when Guttuatr shook his head, for it was the slow, heavy gesture of a troubled old man, not that of an all-knowing Arch Druid. Nor was there enlightenment in his words.

"This was *your* vision, Vercingetorix, not mine," Guttuatr said. "Do not expect anyone else to explain your destiny. The magic of your death, for better or for worse, belongs to you alone."

"But what of the magic I saw after my death, Guttuatr? Can you not—"

"You saw beyond your own death?" Guttuatr exclaimed. "No one ever has seen beyond his death before!"

There was a long silent moment in which nothing could be heard but the birds in the trees. The very breezes of the air seemed to stop still as Guttuatr's gaze turned inward.

"No one in this Age that is passing . . ." Guttuatr muttered softly. "Tell me what you saw."

"When I died, my spirit entered a raven—"

"The bird of death—"

"But I rose into the sky as an *eagle*—"

"The bird of power—"

"—above the city, and I beheld a statue of a triumphant hero such as the Romans are said to erect to boast of their mightiest victories. . . . But . . ."

"But?"

"But the face on the statue was my own! And the city was a magic city, not Rome! Magic beyond anything I have words to describe or wit to understand," he said, throwing up his hands in frustration.

And, so saying, it seemed to him that the boy who had entered the Land of Legend spoke as the man he had now become. Was he not the boy and the man, the raven and the eagle, the corpse on the stone floor and the king of Gaul? For would they not live together in his memory in this world while he yet lived and in the Land of Legend when he died?

Vercingetorix sat up straighter, feeling strength return to his flesh, clarity to his mind, power to his spirit.

"Indeed," he declared, "the magic of this vision is mine alone!"

"And can you tell me what it means?" asked the Arch Druid.

Vercingetorix was silent, for he found that he could not. It seemed that the meaning hovered just beyond his grasp, like a floating midge that seemed so slow but could somehow just not be caught.

"Very well, then, *I'll* tell you what the magic of your death truly means," the Arch Druid said in a gentler voice, extending a hand to help Vercingetorix to his feet.

"But I thought you could not!"

"It means what you *make* it mean, *druid,* for that is what you have now become," Guttuatr said when they stood facing each other, eye to eye, as equals. "Such visions in the Land of Legend are not plain-spoken, for if they were, we would be no more than slaves of the gods, our lives entirely controlled by what is written in the heavens."

"Are we not?"

"If we are, the gods do not wish us to know," Guttuatr said somberly. "Or perhaps it is we who give visions their true meaning when we make them come to pass."

"We make our own destinies, then?"

"Who knows?" said the Arch Druid. "Who can? When I as a youth ate of the mushroom, I saw myself taken up by the living arms of the Tree of Knowledge and placed on its highest branches. A great white bird descended from the sky and became a cloud. The cloud draped itself around my shoulders and became a robe of white. . . ."

Guttuatr shrugged. "I did not know that this meant I was destined to become Arch Druid until it came to pass. Perhaps, if it had not come to pass, the vision might just as truly have come to mean something else."

"And your death . . . ?" Vercingetorix presumed to ask.

"A huge millstone rolls over the land crushing all beneath it, yet I ride untouched atop it," Guttuatr said softly, his eyes meeting Vercingetorix's own, but gazing far, far away, as if he were seeing it all now. "It approaches the mouth of a cave, or perhaps a tunnel, for the cave is not an opening into the earth but into the sky. The millstone enters the cave with my Arch Druid's robe still riding it. I can see that the robe is empty as I lie on the ground and am crushed beneath it."

"But what does this mean?"

"I never knew until I saw the birth of the new star. And then I knew that I was destined to die as the last Arch Druid of the Great Age that is. And must seek out the one to lead us into the Great Age to come."

Now Vercingetorix knew why Guttuatr would not speak plain. *He* was the one of whom the Arch Druid's vision had spoken.

Vercingetorix, king of Gaul.

Lying dead in a stone cell.

In Rome.

And then the true meaning of his own vision struck him, sent his spirit soaring like the eagle it was destined to become.

"If I must die as king of Gaul in Rome, I must first become king of Gaul, and therefore cannot be slain before I do!" he exclaimed triumphantly. "And I cannot be slain in Gaul! And, armed with that knowledge, I need fear no man, no battle, the daring of no deed! I need not fear to face those who slew my father even if I must face them alone! Even if I must face an army alone!"

"You are not a god, Vercingetorix!"

"But I am destined to be a king! And so neither can I be slain before I fulfill my destiny to wear the Crown of Brenn!"

"And die!"

"I die as a king in Rome. *That* is the magic of my death. I have paid the price, and now it is mine."

"To do what?"

"To avenge my father's death," Vercingetorix declared. "To complete the great work that he died fighting for. To unite all Gaul under a king who will reclaim its honor."

"This is not a man of knowledge speaking! This is a boy given drink too strong for him to command!"

Vercingetorix regarded the Arch Druid with an unwavering eye. He saw a man of knowledge as he himself had now become. But he saw also an old man past his prime who had schooled him for purposes which even he had never truly understood.

The visions of the Land of Legend are not plainspoken, Guttuatr had said. Perhaps not to an old man destined to die with the Great Age that is. But it seemed they spoke clearly enough to a young man destined to be the king bringing in the new Great Age. Surely that was why he alone had seen beyond his own death and been granted a vision of the Great Age to come.

"No, Guttuatr," said Vercingetorix, "this *is* a man of knowledge who now speaks, not a boy. A man young and strong enough to wield the magic of that knowledge as his invincible sword."

The Arch Druid Guttuatr shakes his head as he stands beside the school's temple watching Vercingetorix disappear from sight into the forest. Vercingetorix wears a tunic and pantaloons of Arverne orange. From his belt hangs a sword. He does not look back.

"What have I created?" Guttuatr mutters.

"Have we the power to create anyone?" the druid Nividio says soothingly, summoned here not so much by command of the Arch Druid as by the need of Guttuatr, for Nividio is the closest thing that he has to a friend.

Guttuatr sighs. "Of course you are right, Nividio," he says. "But all of us have the power to make mistakes."

"The signs seemed clear, did they not?" says Nividio.

Nividio's robe bears no tribal color, though he was born a Santon. Nividio is not a magistrate. Nividio does not teach. Nividio is one of the Druids of the Inner Way, from whose small self-selected company Arch Druids are chosen. But Nividio has no desire to become an Arch Druid. He would so serve if called upon, but he knows he will be spared, for he has eaten of the fruit of the Tree of Knowledge, and the life he sees before him is the life he sees behind, that of a wandering druid of the woods, a creature whose purpose is to have no purpose, not a singer but the song.

And the death he has seen is that of a very old man lying down to rest alone beneath an oak deep in the forest, his flesh slowly and sweetly melting into the soft damp earth to feed the roots of the tree, to rise with the sap into its branches, to become its leaves, and then to blow away on the autumn wind.

"Are the signs ever clear?" says Guttuatr. "The sign of the Great Turning was plain, and so too did it point to that boy, but . . ." His eyes become furtive. "I say this to you, Nividio, because I would say it to no one else and I must say it to someone," he says in a voice scarcely louder than a whisper. "I would not have stopped Keltill's execution even if I could have. Because I wanted . . . I did not want . . ."

"You did not want the coming of a king," Nividio says. "And in that you were right, Guttuatr."

"But when the signs pointed to Vercingetorix as he who would bring the new Great Age, I feared what such an Age might become," Guttuatr says angrily. "And so I sought to raise him up as my successor, as the Arch Druid bringing in the new Great Age, and instead I may have made a terrible mistake. I gave Vercingetorix the fruit of the Tree of Knowledge so that he might enter the Land of Legend and return as a man of knowledge and a druid of the Inner Way. But he returned with the vision that his destiny is to be a man of action and a king."

Nividio knows that druids must not meddle in the world of strife. And that this is what Guttuatr has unwittingly done.

He would lift Guttuatr's burden if he could.

"You are too severe with yourself, Guttuatr," he says softly, presuming to lay a friendly hand upon the Arch Druid's shoulder. "There was no evil in your heart. You but followed your destiny. As do we all."

Guttuatr nods, he sighs, he reaches up to clasp the hand of Nividio on his shoulder. "But in so doing, I have brought into the world a man of knowledge pursuing the hot-blooded path of the man of action," he says. "A druid who would be king. Something that has never walked the earth before."

Considering that he did not know how long it would take him to reach Gergovia or what he would do when he got there, Vercingetorix felt strangely at peace as he made his way eastward through the forest. For the first time in his life, he was quite alone, and he took great pleasure in it. The forest was entirely empty of the sight and sound and smell of men; there was nothing but the sunlight dappling the tree crowns as the breezes whooshed through them, the songs and cries of the birds, the rustles and thumps of nearby or distant unseen animals.

Yet Vercingetorix did not feel an intruder in this realm. Carrying little but a sword, making his way where there were no paths by following the movement of the sun across the sky, the angles of the shadows, the position of the moss on the rocks and tree trunks, he felt himself a creature of it.

Here there was no school, no strife of tribe against tribe, man against man, Gaul against Rome, duty against desire, the way of knowledge against the way of action. No signs in the heavens, no vision of destiny. Here he was free. And he realized, to his surprise and consternation, that this was something he had never felt before.

He amused himself with the idea of simply remaining in the forest forever. He knew how to find roots and plants and fruits and berries, which might be eaten, and which not. He knew how to make snares to trap small animals and pits to catch larger ones. He had a sword, and flint to make fire. He knew how to find healing herbs should he fall ill, and build huts for shelter in foul weather if he found no cave. What more do I need? he teased himself by asking.

But he knew full well that he could not really remain a denizen of the forest for the rest of his life. A slain father, a destiny he could not forever deny, the world of strife would soon enough intrude.

"I still do not understand why I am here," groaned Diviacx, bouncing along on his saddle inexpertly, giving himself, or so Caesar hoped, as grievous an ache in his own testicles as the druid was giving *him* in his posterior.

"Surely, as what passes for a local sage, you have noticed that this is a chronic human condition," Caesar told him dryly, bringing his own horse up to a trot so as either to increase the druid's discomfort or to escape from his whinings.

Labienus remained behind, at the head of his troops, but Gisstus, riding beside Caesar, gave a small coughing laugh and sped up to keep pace. The four Eduen bodyguards Diviacx had insisted on bringing did likewise. In a few moments, the six of them had literally left the five cohorts of foot soldiers marching up the road in their dust. But Diviacx, grimacing and wincing, doggedly refused to be left behind, leaving Caesar to wonder what, if anything, these druids wore under their robes, whether they had the sense to gird their loins when embarking on long journeys on horseback or not.

Contemplating the unbidden image, Caesar decided that he really did not want to know. He was beginning to regret burdening himself with this druid. Like so much else in Gaul that had later turned out to be vexatious, dragging Diviacx along on this expedition had seemed like a good idea at the time.

Warriors of many tribes would be sequestered together in the camp he was going to set up at Portus Itius, on the channel coast, so having a druid at hand to adjudicate disputes would, he hoped, keep them from killing each other before the real slaughter had properly begun. Diviacx, being the only druid who would allow himself even to be caught within sight of a Roman, had been the only possible choice.

And perhaps that, as much as his complaints about the food, and the dust, and the horses, and the long hours of the march, is why I am coming to detest the man, Caesar thought sourly. Diviacx has been and will be a useful instrument, one who has enriched himself thereby and grown spoiled and querulous; a greedy fool at best, and, not to mince words, a traitor from a certain Gallic perspective. A man, in short, lacking in wit, and even more so in honor. How is one to like such a man even if he is one's own creature?

One cannot, Caesar decided. Enduring his company is bad enough. And, cruelly, he brought his horse up into an easy loping gallop.

Vercingetorix heard distant clatterings that must be the movements of animals. Then, as his way eastward took him ever closer to the source, these unwelcome noises became louder than the song of the forest, and finally they became the rumble of cart and wagon wheels, the babble of human voices, and then there it was. He emerged from the trees to confront a Roman road.

He had never seen one before, but he knew that was what it had to be, for no Gaul would build a road like this. It was as wide as eight horses riding abreast, raised an arm's length above the natural level of the earth on a platform of rocks and cement, and flanked by two muddy ditches dug into the ground. Its surface was paved with flat stones set in cement and was as flat as that of a well-used wooden table. And rather than embracing the landscape and becoming one with it, like a proper Gallic road, it was arrow-straight from horizon to horizon, thrust through hill and valley and forest like a sword of stone.

Upon it moved the carts of peasants heaped with grain, the wagon of a Roman trader bearing amphorae of what was probably wine, a herder of swine with his animals, peasants afoot, and—

—horsemen approaching at a gallop from the west, sending the road traffic scattering to the sides to get clear of their passage.

Without thought, Vercingetorix found himself mounting the side of the road as the riders approached, but when they drew close enough for him truly to make them out, he gasped.

There were seven of them riding abreast. Four were blue-cloaked Eduen warriors. One was a man in the bronzed armor and helmet of a Roman warrior whom Vercingetorix seemed to remember having seen before.

But the other two!

Flanked on either side by two Eduen warriors rode Diviacx, the druid who had presided over the burning of his father.

In the center position, mounted on a fine roan stallion draped with a reddish saddle blanket trimmed in yellow braid, wearing Roman armor but bareheaded, a cape of a brilliant crimson flowing behind him, was a man whom Vercingetorix had never in this world seen. But he knew he had met him in the Land of Legend. This was the Roman who would offer him first the crown of laurel and then the Crown of Brenn. This was the Roman general upon whose gilded chariot he would ride in triumph. This was the man who was destined to acclaim him king of Gaul in Rome itself.

This could only be Gaius Julius Caesar.

Vercingetorix drew his sword, held it above his head, and stepped out into the middle of the roadway.

What mad apparition is this? wondered Caesar.

Up ahead, a man in orange tunic and pantaloons had stepped out into the middle of the road and raised a sword as if to impede the passage of six armed horsemen, and the five cohorts of Roman legionnaires behind them.

Caesar's curiosity got the best of him, and, rather than ride down this ridiculous would-be bandit, he reined in his horse, raised his hand for his companions to do likewise, and halted before the man. Or boy.

For that was what he was, a boy on the cusp of manhood: man-tall and attempting a mustache to match his long, unkempt blond hair, perhaps in an attempt to appear older; he was well muscled and had the upright stance of a schooled soldier, but he could not have been more than eighteen.

Except for those strange blue pools of eyes, which, though mounted in the unwrinkled visage of youth, seemed to have depths that went back to the beginning of time.

As Vercingetorix felt the force of Caesar's gaze upon him, he knew that he would have recognized this as no ordinary man even had he not met him already in the Land of Legend.

Caesar was not tall, but his build was robust, and his dark hair, worn short, receded up his crown. This somehow made his head appear larger than it really was, as if the contents thereof far exceeded those of ordinary skulls. Perhaps his eyes enhanced this effect, for through them gazed a spirit whose confidence seemed utter. A man who commanded legions. And a man who believed he would somehow manage to prevail *against* legions, armed only with his sword and his destiny.

But it was not Caesar to whom Vercingetorix first spoke.

"Greetings, Diviacx," he said instead, brandishing his sword, and with as much threat in his voice as he could muster.

"You know me, Arverne?" said the druid.

"You'd be a hard man to forget . . . for the son of Keltill."

At this, Diviacx blanched, and his guards drew their swords.

"What have we here, Diviacx?" said Caesar in a voice both contemptuous and commanding. "Another of your petty feuds?"

"This is Vercingetorix, Caesar, the lost son of Keltill of the Averni, presumed by some to be dead," he said, motioning his men forward.

"And soon to fulfill the prophecy, if you have your way?" Caesar said sneeringly, to mask his pleasant surprise at this unexpected turn of events.

Gisstus and his spies had been searching for some pliant yet popular Arverne with whom to replace Gobanit. Now the gods had dropped none other than the son of Keltill into his palm!

"We'll have none of that, Diviacx," Caesar said. "This is a Roman road, and this young man, like all those who travel upon it, is under my protection."

He shot the druid a scornful sideways glance, then found his eyes drawn back to this Vercingetorix, who had not moved, who had not flinched, who looked back at him fearlessly and unwaveringly.

"Though, from the look of him, it may be *you* who need my protection, Diviacx," he said. "And you look at me as if you know me," he told Vercingetorix.

"Who does not know of Gaius Julius Caesar?" Vercingetorix said in an ironic tone that made it impossible for Caesar to continue to think of him as a boy.

"Have we met?"

"Only in the Land of Legend."

This is getting stranger and stranger, Caesar thought. But also more and more promising. This boy—no, this *man*—has . . . something. And he *is* the son of Keltill.

"Where have you been hiding?" Caesar said.

Vercingetorix pointed toward the surrounding forest with his sword. "In plain sight."

"And where are you going?"

"To Gergovia, to claim my father's legacy."

If the politician's trade did not require skill in the actor's art, Caesar would have been hard put to conceal his elation. This was almost too good to be true. Certainly too good not to be used.

"Your father's legacy?" he managed to say ingenuously. "But Gobanit is vergobret again this year, is he not, and that does not pass from father to son. . . ."

"My father's lands, his horses, his cattle, his gold, and his . . . honor. Such things do not pass from hand to hand from year to year."

"Well, then, our paths converge for a while, for I am riding to the channel coast to begin a great adventure," said Caesar. "So put up your sword, and we'll travel together for a time."

"For a time, Caesar," said Vercingetorix, sheathing his sword. Caesar gave the Eduen warriors a scowl, commanding them to do likewise. Diviacx looked as if he had bitten into a turd. Better and better!

"But you are without horse," Caesar said. "Allow me to lend you one."

"Allow me to purchase one from you, Caesar. It strikes me that you are not a man in whose debt it is wise to be."

"You don't seem to be carrying much money."

"In truth, I have none. But my father was a rich man, and I can pay you as soon as I reclaim my legacy," said Vercingetorix. "Or . . ."

"Or?"

Vercingetorix gave Caesar a strange crooked smile. "Or we can follow the old Gallic custom, and I will pay you back ten times what I owe in the Land of Legend, after both of us are dead," he said.

"What a marvelous custom!" exclaimed Caesar. "If only I could persuade my creditors in Rome to adopt it!" He burst out laughing.

Vercingetorix did not.

"Get him one of my own horses," Caesar said, turning to Gisstus. "The white stallion, I think."

Gisstus bent over to whisper in Caesar's ear before riding back to the approaching troops and supply train.

"Should I see if I can find a glue pot and an antelope's horn as well?" he said.

Caesar brought his horse up to a full exuberant gallop, and Vercingetorix followed. Only when they had put the Roman infantry, Diviacx and his bodyguards, and the rest of the entourage well behind did Caesar slow his mount to a walk suitable for conversation.

They rode side by side like two comrades along a road to Gergovia thronged with peasants and their produce, merchants and their wares. Or, Vercingetorix realized with a shock that was sad and sweet and bitter and strange, as he had ridden to Gergovia with his father when he was a boy in the long ago. Yet now his companion was the very man whose cunning and stealthy conquest Keltill had died opposing.

"What keeps you here all these years, so far from your own land?" Vercingetorix asked Caesar. What he truly wanted to ask was why he had given him this fine white horse decorated with the red and gold of a Roman general to ride, why he was being so kind and generous to the son of a man who had been his enemy.

"The same thing that sets you on the road to Gergovia," said Caesar. "Destiny."

"Destiny . . . ?" Vercingetorix said as blandly as he could to mask his shock. For this man seemed either to be hearing his thoughts or had somehow shared his vision in the Land of Legend.

"You can't fool me, my young friend, you know just what I mean," said Caesar. "Most men live lives with no more meaning than those of the beasts in the field. A few live lives that become legend. Not because they choose to, but because destiny chooses them."

To his bemusement and horror, Vercingetorix found himself drawn to Caesar. No man had ever acknowledged such thoughts to him so boldly, so frankly, and, moreover, granted him the assumed equality of sharing them. Not his druid teachers. Not Guttuatr. Not even his father. Once more, Vercingetorix had the uncanny feeling that Caesar had shared his vision. This was the man destined to acclaim him king of Gaul in Rome. How was this possible? But Caesar spoke as if he knew.

Dare I ask? Vercingetorix wondered. But it seemed like a question far ahead of its proper time. "Spoken like a druid . . ." he said cautiously instead.

"Oh, I was indeed once a pontifex, a performer of priestly rites—a druid of sorts, you might say," Caesar replied blithely. "But I found a higher cause to serve than our pantheon of petty godlings."

"A cause higher than the gods?" Vercingetorix exclaimed. "What can that possibly be?"

"In a word, *Rome*."

"You hold the cause of Rome above that of the gods!"

"Indeed I do!" Caesar avowed. "For the cause of the gods is merely the past, but the cause of Rome is the future, the cause of civilization itself. And far more profitable for those who serve it too. Roads like this one, bridges, aqueducts, cities with baths and sewers and arenas. Art and commerce and engineering. A rule of law and a secure public order that will one day encompass the world!"

"So the selfless Caesar comes to Gaul to bring civilization to us poor barbarians!"

Caesar laughed, but only briefly, as if to draw out the sting, then grew quite earnest. "Ah, but the genius of the Republic of Rome, that which sets it above and apart from all other nations and which is destined to make it the master of the world, is that you may be born a Greek or a Scythian or a Gaul and *earn* the right to be a citizen of Rome!"

"You don't have to be born a Roman . . . ?"

Caesar laughed again. "I'll not deny that it's an advantage!" he admitted. "Winning Roman citizenship, like winning any great prize, may not be easy to accomplish, but it is within the grasp of any man of ability and courage. Men of many peoples and all standings have achieved it. Scholars. Statesmen. Soldiers. Even gladiators and slaves! Nor must you forswear the people of your birth to accept it."

"How is this possible?" asked Vercingetorix, unable to quite wrap his mind around this strange concept.

"One emblem of Rome is the fasces," Caesar told him. "This is simply a bundle of sticks strapped together. Each stick is a people of the provinces of Rome, still possessed of its own individuality, but bound with all the others in the fasces that is Rome. The individual sticks may be snapped over a weak man's knee. But, bonded together, the collectivity is invincible. So you see, one may be a Gaul and a Roman at the same time as easily as an Arverne and a Gaul. Indeed, from what I've seen here, much more easily! Your father, in his way, understood. He saw that Arverni could remain Arverni and Edui Edui, yet at the same time be bound together in the fasces of Gaul. In this, he thought like a Roman, though he knew it not. His tragedy was that the tribes of Gaul were not civilized enough to comprehend this, and so they slew him for it."

"You mourn the death of a man who proclaimed you his enemy?"

Caesar needed only a quick look at the young man's face to know that he was about to snare him.

"A man may be judged by the quality of his enemies, Vercingetorix;

therefore, it is right to honor enemies of quality in their passing," he said. "For, by so doing, you honor yourself."

Caesar realized that this piece of sophistry might be a bit too Greek for him. Something simpler and closer to home was required.

"Your father never knew me," he said, "and so he and I never conversed together as we do now. If we had, perhaps things might have gone better for him; perhaps I could have shown him that we shared the same goal. He sought to unite the tribes of Gaul under himself to drive me out. I will unite the tribes of Gaul under the Republic of Rome."

Vercingetorix turned to glance back at the cohorts of infantry, now slowly bridging the gap they had opened and coming up behind them.

"Conquer us with your legions, you mean," he said.

"Perhaps, my young friend, but not necessarily in the manner that you mean . . ."

Caesar halted his horse and reared it up on its hind legs while bringing it around to face the oncoming Roman foot soldiers in one continuous motion, a fine piece of horsemanship that Vercingetorix sought to emulate but accomplished with a good deal less grace.

"Look at them, Vercingetorix!" he said. "Be honest with yourself—a fearsome enemy to confront, are they not?"

Vercingetorix certainly had to admit that they were.

Shields strapped to their backs, helmets and short swords across their armored chests, the Roman infantry marched a dozen abreast and scores of ranks deep. Each helmet, each breastplate, each shield and sword were identical, as if forged by the same smith at the same moment. The effect was to make each legionnaire appear identical to every other. There was something not quite natural about it. Facing such an army in battle would be like facing an army of huge metal-clad ants.

Caesar wheeled his horse around again and proceeded up the road very slowly, and Vercingetorix followed suit.

"Now imagine the legions of Rome as your allies," said Caesar. "As your shield. Imagine yourself not confronting them but riding before them into battle at the side of their commander, as you are doing now."

Vercingetorix heard the clattering thunder of thousands of marching feet slapping the stone roadway behind him in a regular pounding rhythm. As they drew closer, he breathed the dust they kicked up and smelled sweat on leather. This was but the smallest fragment of the vast forces that Caesar commanded, and yet their passage seemed to shake the world.

"Rather than conquer Gaul by grinding its warriors into the dust with my legions," said Caesar, "I will use them to conquer the hearts of the Gauls."

"You are a sorcerer as well as a general and a sometime priest?" Vercingetorix said dryly.

"And a lawyer too!" said Caesar. He laughed. "Not to mention a writer of no little skill, if I do say so myself. But none of these arts are required to win the noble warriors of Gaul to the venture I am proposing, only the politician's craft. For I know that the surest way to convert enemies to allies is to make your best interest their own."

Vercingetorix had never met a man who spoke like Caesar, who in one moment made him feel a barbarian and in the next clarified his understanding in a way that raised him up above himself. He sensed that this man was an accomplished liar, and yet also capable of using the most profound truths to his own ends too.

And he also sensed that the might of Rome was rooted in more than its legions, that Caesar wielded another, greater power, whose true nature presently eluded his understanding.

"And what is this venture of yours that will accomplish the seemingly impossible?" he asked.

And now I have you, Caesar thought. "I will lead an invasion of Britain, my young friend," he said, "a land rich beyond dreams of avarice, yet defended only by primitive barbarians. My invincible infantry and the best cavalry in the world—that of all the tribes of Gaul—fighting side by side to earn fame, glory, and riches. And the Gauls will have half of everything our joint forces seize!"

"You would have us join you in pillaging Britain as you pillage Gaul?"

"Such an ugly word!" said Caesar. "Nor is it just. Think of it, rather, as an orderly system of tribute. The Britons pay a certain amount to Gaul, Gaul pays a certain amount to Rome, in return for which our legions keep the peace, do the collecting, build the roads that make commerce possible, introduce the benefits of our medicine, our arts, our schools. And so is civilization spread, and so does Rome help its friends to help themselves."

Caesar was pleased to note that Vercingetorix, though clearly intrigued, moderated his enthusiasm with a suspicious stare, for were he a big enough fool to swallow it all whole, his usefulness would surely be limited.

"But at a price, Caesar?" Vercingetorix said. "The Gauls will no doubt be expected to bear the cost of the forces we are invited to raise to support your legions?"

Caesar laughed. "Spoken like a Roman!" he said. "Rome may be many things, but a dispenser of alms isn't one of them!"

He then summoned up a great sigh. "What a pity!" he moaned.

"Pity . . . ?"

"I like you, Vercingetorix, son of Keltill, I sense you would be worthy of being the son that, alas, I do not have. It vexes me that you cannot take part in our grand and glorious adventure."

"And why not?" demanded Vercingetorix.

"In a word, Gobanit," said Caesar.

"Gobanit?" said Vercingetorix.

"The vergobrets of all the major tribes of Gaul, and most of the minor ones, have eagerly agreed to join us. All save the slothful and cowardly Gobanit, who would deny the warriors of the Arverni their fair share of the riches and glory."

"I have no love for Gobanit!" snapped Vercingetorix. "He will not tell *me* what I may do or not!"

"Indeed?" said Caesar in the manner of a purring cat, feigning a surprise so obviously false that his equally feline grin acknowledged that he knew that Vercingetorix knew it. "My sentiments exactly."

The chill that pierced Vercingetorix's heart at these last words was like a knife of ice, for, though he remembered not where or when, he knew that his father had spoken them. Could it be possible that in this moment the spirit of Keltill was using the mouth of Caesar to speak to him?

"Gobanit lit the fire that burned my father," said Vercingetorix, sensing that he was telling Caesar something he already knew.

"So I have heard," said Caesar. "And so you ride to Gergovia to avenge your father's foul murder and regain your birthright. As a loyal son must do. But how?"

Vercingetorix touched the hilt of his sword.

"You intend to ride into Gergovia alone and through the city and plunge your sword through the fat and into the black and cowardly heart of the vergobret of the Arverni?"

Vercingetorix nodded.

"Will you now?" said Caesar.

"It is my destiny, and I have seen it in the Land of Legend," said Vercingetorix. "I cannot—"

Vercingetorix stayed himself, for he had been about to say, *I cannot be slain on the soil of Gaul.* And this was surely more than Caesar should know. "I will stop the thought that slows the mind," he said instead.

"And *you* called *me* a sorcerer?" said Caesar.

They were now approaching a crossroads where the dusty and winding earthen Gallic road to Gergovia intersected the arrow-straight Roman road of stone.

"Our paths diverge now," said Caesar. "But I think not for long. I sense in you a man of destiny."

"Like yourself, Caesar?"

Caesar laughed. "Indeed," he said. "And so, as one man of destiny to another, as one sorcerer to another, allow me to arm you with a bit of *my* magic."

And his mien became earnest. He reared his horse, whirling it around, once, twice, thrice, with his right hand upraised.

Behind them, for as far down the road as the eye could see and perhaps more, the ranks of Roman legionnaires ceased their thunderous marching, one rank after another like a wave magically moving backward out to sea, and, in their thousands, were in a few moments standing still and silent, flesh-and-metal trees in a human forest.

Then Caesar took off his bright crimson cloak and draped it around Vercingetorix's shoulders.

"Wear my crimson cape as you ride my horse into Gergovia," he said, "for no other Roman in all my legions may wear one of this hue, and so all will know that the young man in Arverne orange riding the white horse of a Roman general is cloaked in the mantle of Gaius Julius Caesar. They must either believe that you have taken them from me, or that you stand very high in my favor indeed."

Caesar laughed, but his eyes were as hard and cold as polished metal. "No one is likely to move against you without knowing *which.* That should be enough to . . . raise the thoughts that slow the mind, and perhaps open the way for you to work your own sorcery, my young friend."

He clasped forearms with Vercingetorix in the Roman manner.

"If you succeed, you may return the cloak to me when you arrive at the head of an army of Arverne warriors," he said. "If not, you can give it back to me in your Land of Legend when we are both dead. For, one way or the other, I am sure we will both get there."

"As am I," Vercingetorix told him. "But who is to say what part each of us will play in the other's legend?"

And he reared his horse and rode away alone toward Gergovia.

Caesar sat there on his horse, watching the boy he had cloaked in his own colors disappear up the primitive Gallic road, and wondering exactly what he had just done, wondering who was using whom for what purpose.

Wondering whether King Philip of Macedon might have had a moment like this regarding the boy Alexander riding off into his own destiny. There was something in this youth's eyes, in his illogical certainty in himself and his destiny, that Philip must have seen in the son who would so surpass him.

And, ludicrous as it seemed, Caesar felt a pang of jealousy.

"The cloak too, Caesar? What next, your standard?"

Gisstus had ridden up behind him to interrupt his reverie as no one else would have dared, and just as well.

"I have others," Caesar told him. "And other horses. A horse and a cloak wagered against the replacement of Gobanit with a leader with good reason to be loyal to me . . ." He shrugged. "The odds may be long, but the stakes are favorable. I want you to find out everything there is to know about this boy. I do not want an unbroken, wild horse among us. Find me his bridle."

"Do you *really* believe he can just ride alone into Gergovia and capture the city?" asked Gisstus.

"By force, of course not, Gisstus. But by . . . a certain kind of sorcery . . . ? Somehow, I believe I do!"

VIII

THE CLOSER HE GOT to Gergovia, the more crowded the road became, but even when it passed through lands that were once his father's, no one hailed Vercingetorix as the son of Keltill. That no one recognized him was hardly magic, but that no one dared meet his eye must be the mantle of the spell cast upon him by Gaius Julius Caesar.

He could well understand their unease, their fear, and their hope as they beheld a youth in Arverne orange, wearing neither armor nor helmet and armed with an ordinary sword, but riding a white horse festooned with the trappings of a Roman general, and a crimson cloak of the hue reserved for Caesar himself.

Though no one would speak to him, Vercingetorix heard the murmuring voices; though no one would meet his own eye, he felt the weight of a multitude of eyes upon him. He knew a procession was forming behind him, for, even when he slowed his horse to a pace slower than that of a heavily laden cart, no one would pass him.

And as the road began to mount the hill, he quickened the pace of his horse to a fast walk, so that the carts and wagons and peasants afoot behind him followed at a clattering, rattling, dust-raising pace, approaching the city like the vision of his future army.

Baravax, captain of Gergovia's city guard, customarily assigned only two warriors on the ground to guard the gates by day, when they were opened, but stationed six more, armed with lances, atop the ramparts between the two towers flanking them, where they could easily cut down any troublemakers attempting to enter.

Though this might seem excessive, Baravax was the third son of a poor shepherd family who had become a guard to escape a grinding life of poverty, and he was determined to guard his position as carefully as he guarded the city.

Baravax was surprised and dismayed when Milgar shouted down from the wall that a mob, or perhaps even an army, was approaching the city. He scrambled up the nearest ladder to the walkway atop the wall, where Milgar was pointing down the road with his lance.

Baravax shaded his eyes against the bright sun with his hand, but still had to squint to see clearly. At first, all he could make out was a cloud of dust approaching the city gates at an unusually rapid pace. Then he was able to discern that Milgar's "army" consisted of a crowd of the usual wagons and carts, but moving so rapidly, for some reason, that the crowd of people afoot had to trot to keep up. Then he saw a man riding a white horse leading them. And more people, arriving in dribs and drabs across the open plain, falling in behind him, joining his procession.

Still, this was certainly no "army," or even a "mob," just what one would expect on the way to market, except for the man on the white horse. But then he brought his horse up to a gallop and quickly outdistanced his followers, and as he galloped up to the gates, Baravax saw that his horse was draped in the red and gold of a Roman general.

The rider was a youth of no more than twenty years in a plain tunic of Arverne orange. He had a sword, but wore neither armor nor helmet, and bore no shield or standard. Around his shoulders swirled the crimson cloak of Gaius Julius Caesar.

At the approach of this disquieting apparition, Baravax's men did as they were schooled to do: the guards on the ground stepped toward each other and crossed their lances to bar his way, and those on the wall above their gates raised theirs threateningly, announcing their readiness to hurl them down if need be.

Baravax scrambled back down the ladder to confront the horseman on the ground.

"Who are you?" he demanded.

The blond youth on the white horse sat still and silent as a statue.

"Who are you?" Baravax demanded again.

He did not like this at all. His duties had become more complex since Gobanit had replaced Keltill. In Keltill's day, it was simple enough: his duty was to keep the peace, see to it that fights were broken up before serious harm was done, apprehend thieves, or, better yet, keep them from entering the city. Now, though, there were factions among the Arverni. Gobanit's supporters. Young bloods who hated Gobanit for burning Keltill. Enemies of Rome. Friends of Rome. Old Critognat and his comrades, who knew not what they liked, but knew they did not like things as they were now. A captain of the guard was hard put not to be drawn into the swirl and eddies of these dangerous currents, but Baravax knew that if he could not stay clear he could be swept away.

The man on the white horse did not speak or move until the people and wagons and carts rumbling and rushing up the hill had spread out expectantly behind him.

"Who are you?" Baravax said again. "Speak, depart, or be slain!"

The Arverne wearing Caesar's cloak reared his horse. "I am Vercingetorix, son of Keltill!" he shouted. "I have returned to claim my birthright! And I come offering riches and glory!"

The crowd behind him gasped in surprise.

It was all that Baravax could do to stifle his moan of dismay. Surely he had no right to bar entry to the son of Keltill. Surely if he did there would be trouble from these people. But, just as surely, Gobanit, who was even now meeting with his "Senate" in the Great Hall, would not be pleased. But surest of all was that Baravax had to act now. And act cautiously.

So he signaled to the gate guards to lift their lances and allow Vercingetorix to ride into the city. But as he did, and the people poured in behind him, Baravax summoned Milgar down from the wall and ordered him to gather a squad of guards from within with which to follow close behind Vercingetorix.

Vercingetorix had not ridden far into Gergovia when he noticed that the guard captain and about a dozen warriors were following him at a discreet distance. The market was under way, and the avenue leading into the main plaza was crowded, so he was forced to walk his horse very slowly, and forced thereby to observe the changes wrought by time since he had last been in Gergovia. By time and by Rome.

Here and there, white-painted wooden columns supported porticoes that ludicrously embellished the fronts of ordinary dwellings of graying wood and brownish wattle. Many roofs of thatch had retained their conical shapes while the reeds had been replaced by reddish tile. There were a few new buildings crafted entirely of square reddish-brown bricks. He saw women in flowing Roman robes with elaborately coiffed hair held up by tiaras and combs of silver or some iridescent gray stuff with a rainbow sheen. There were warriors wearing Roman helmets, breastplates, bearing Roman swords, and men whom he took for merchants wearing white Roman togas—one, ridiculously enough, wearing his over orange Arverne pantaloons.

When he reached the plaza, he saw that it was now paved with stones set in cement. There was a stone fountain in the center, where water sprayed from the mouths of four crudely carved bears standing on a round pedestal facing the quarters of the wind.

Stalls offered the usual local goods—dressed carcasses of boar and sheep, live fowl, turnips and carrots, barrels and jars of beer, orange-and-gray plaid cloth, silver jewelry in the good old style, ironwork, whole hides and crafted leathers, herbs and roots and mushrooms from the forest. But some stalls, overhung with colorful fringed awnings, purveyed goods that could only have come from afar—amphorae and casks of wine, cloths in colors never seen in Gaul, Roman clothing, dried brown fruits on strings, stools of carved wood, little thrones of wood and leather, wondrous translucent goblets, leather cylinders containing rolls of white cloth, and stranger things Vercingetorix's eye could not identify. All of the merchants presiding over these stalls wore Roman garb, and most of them, by their short stature and dark hair and complexions, seemed to be Romans. And they were assisted by slaves, a few of whom had skin darker than heavily tanned ox hide.

There were the usual bards and jugglers and musicians, but some of the musicians played harps of unfamiliar design, some produced piercing and haunting sounds by blowing through sets of reeds of different lengths. There were new odors in the air: some savory, some florally sweet, some sickeningly so.

Gergovia had been touched by Caesar's "civilization," and though Vercingetorix found much of it distasteful, it would be impossible to contend that *all* of the changes were for the worse, for the city seemed cleaner, and the stink of the sewage gutters was notable for its absence.

But the manner in which the Great Hall at the far end of the plaza now sought to mimic that "civilization" was truly a desecration. The sand-colored stone and the gray wood facings had been painted white, obliterating the venerable floral carvings. Stone columns flanked the entrance now, supporting a white-painted wooden roof over a low flight of broad stone stairs.

A fitting lair for the likes of Gobanit.

Vercingetorix rode very slowly through the crowded market, spiraling inward toward the fountain, making three full circuits before he got there, saying nothing, meeting no eye, gazing steadfastly straight ahead, drawing the crowd of the curious with him. And all the while, he heard his name whispered and murmured and passed among the people. By the time he reached the fountain, the area around it was thronged, and trading in the surrounding market had all but ceased.

As Vercingetorix halted, the warriors who had been tracking him emerged from the crowd to form a circle around him—whether to hold back the crowd to protect him or in preparation for seizing him, he could not tell. Perhaps they did not know either, for their swords remained undrawn, and some of them faced outward like guards, others faced inward, and still others craned their necks and twisted their bodies in indecision. An expectant silence fell upon the plaza, and all eyes were upon him as everyone waited to hear the words of the silver-tongued Vercingetorix.

But the only public speech the silver-tongued Vercingetorix had ever delivered had been a few simple words in praise of his father, and then he had been quite drunk. For the first time since he had ridden into the city, Vercingetorix knew fear.

Still . . .

"I am Vercingetorix, son of Keltill! You know my name but you do not know *me*, for I was forced as a boy to flee when Gobanit violated the sanctity of the Great Hall of the Arverni to seize my father and steal all that Keltill had save that which he held most dear, his name and his honor!"

At this there were scattered shouts of "Keltill!" but also much low, guttural murmuring. The Arverne warriors surrounding Vercingetorix moved their hands to the hilts of their swords.

"See what the man who set the torch to the pyre that burned Keltill has done to the heart of our people and our city," Vercingetorix declaimed, indicating the Romanized façade of the Great Hall with a wave of his arm. "Gobanit feigns the glory of Rome with white paint and stone fakery, but it is all a sham, for he has not the stomach to emulate Caesar's singular virtue and ride at the head of the warriors of the Arverni into battle!"

The cries and shouts became ugly now. The captain of the guard nodded and drew his sword, and his men followed suit. When he made a signal with his hand, they all turned to confront Vercingetorix with a fence of pointed steel.

"This horse I ride was given to me as a token by Caesar himself," Vercingetorix declared. "A token of his promise that all Gauls who join in his invasion of Britain will divide half of the spoils among them. This you already know. Gobanit will not lead you in joining this grand adventure, and this too you know already."

He grabbed onto the edges of the crimson cloak and spread his arms wide to display it like the wings of an eagle.

"But know this too! This is Caesar's own cloak! This you know to be true because all others are forbidden to wear a cloak of this color. But Caesar has given it to me to wear. To be returned to him when I exchange it for a cloak of Arverne orange and ride to his encampment at the head of an Arverne army! I was forced to flee as a boy, but now I am returned as a man to recapture the birthright which was stolen from me! To lead all who would follow me to glory and fortune and slay the slayer of my father!"

"That's enough!" cried the guard captain. "Seize him!"

The warriors rushed inward at Vercingetorix. As they did, turning their backs on the crowd, the front ranks of that crowd surged forward amidst shouts, curses, shoving, the outbreak of chaotic empty-handed fighting.

Vercingetorix drew his sword and reared his horse, whirling his mount round and round in a bounding hind-legged circle, its front hooves pawing the air, causing the warriors to fall back in disarray as he swiped at them with his sword. He felt destiny smile on him, allowing him to control the horse with a skill that had eluded him on the Roman road.

Vercingetorix leapt from his horse onto the back of the guard captain, knocking him to the stone-paved ground. He then pulled him back to his feet with one hand and laid the edge of his sword across his throat with the other.

No more than a few moments had passed. No killing or maiming blows had yet been struck. Four of the warriors had been disarmed by the crowd and were being held with their arms twisted behind their backs while their comrades threatened their captors with their own swords uncertainly.

"Stop!" Vercingetorix shouted as loudly as was able. *"As I would not slay this brother Arverne, so let no other Arverne here harm another!"*

But the thuds and shouts of fistfights within the body of the crowd could still be heard along with screams and shouts of fear and rage and confusion.

Vercingetorix saw that words were not enough.

Sword to his neck, he marched the guard captain backward to the fountain, up over its rounded stone lip, into the shallow water, to its center, where streams of water flowed from the mouths of the stone bears, and forced him up on their round pedestal beside him.

Then he withdrew his sword from the throat of the guard captain and handed it to him.

The guard captain stood there, holding the sword loosely, utterly dumbfounded. The silence was sudden and profound, and Vercingetorix spoke into it.

"Slay me if you will," he said. "Slay honor and glory in the service of dishonor and scorn! Slay riches in the service of cowardice!"

The guard captain stood there frozen, his head slightly cocked to one side, his shrewd eyes measuring Vercingetorix, glancing at the crowd to measure *its* mood, then back at Vercingetorix. He gave him the subtlest of nods.

Vercingetorix offered an outstretched hand to the guard captain and addressed the crowd. "Or give me back my sword, and I will enter that nest of spiders alone, and I will challenge Gobanit to fair and honorable battle. Let the gods decide! Let them choose our destiny!"

At this there was a great roar of approval, as Vercingetorix had known there must be, for no Arverne, no Gaul, wherever his loyalty might lie, could deny another's honorable appeal to the will of the gods as expressed in such a challenge to combat.

"Well and fairly spoken," said the guard captain, and handed Vercingetorix back his sword to a thunderous ovation.

Vercingetorix climbed out of the fountain and turned to regard the entrance to the Great Hall. A squad of guards had emerged from the building. Six of them, swords drawn, stood shoulder to shoulder atop the stairs, barring entry. Six more had descended to the foot of the stairs and had advanced a dozen or so paces before them.

He ran to his horse, mounted as quickly as he could, and, with sword still drawn, charged at the Great Hall at a full gallop.

The guards before the stairs froze for the briefest of moments. Then some raised their swords threateningly, while others dashed to escape, and all was confusion as they stumbled and tumbled into each other.

Vercingetorix did not wait for a gap to open up; rather, he jumped

his horse over and through the melee, and in the next leap, he was riding up the low flight of stairs straight for the guards blocking the
entrance.

Two of the guards fled to the side, two of them hesitated, the other
two bravely stood their ground, swords leveled at the horse's chest,
blocking the entrance with their bodies and pointed steel.

Vercingetorix wheeled his horse right, brought the flat of his sword
down hard on the blade of one guard's weapon close by the hilt, sending it clattering, and then, as the other guard circled round to his left
hand, kicked him square in the jaw, sending him tumbling off balance
down the stairs. He then reared his horse again before the door—
causing it to come down with its full weight on its front hooves as they
hit the door, smashing it inward—and rode into the building.

The Great Hall of the Arverni had been transformed.

The chests that held the gold and silver, the gems and jewelry—and
there were many more of them—were now tightly shut, and lined up in
neat rows. The grease and soot had been cleaned from the ancient
paintings that covered the walls, but in many places the paint had come
off with it, and the damage had been "repaired" with fresh and over-
bright colors. The imposition of the new Roman style on the venerable
Gallic mode was outrageous.

A semicircle of white-painted wooden benches, five rows deep and
rising toward the rear, half enclosed a large central well where the long
oaken banquet table had been replaced by a smaller, lower one painted
shiny black, with curved and gilded legs in the likeness of clawed eagles'
feet, surrounded by soft-backed upholstered couches. Upon the table
were silver plates heaped with fruit and cheeses, platters painted in
woodland scenes bearing baked confections, platters decorated with
ocean waves offering displays of small fishes.

Reclining on the couches, eating this fare as three serving wenches
filled their glass goblets from small amphorae, were eight men, no
doubt members of Gobanit's self-serving "Arverne Senate." Four of
them wore tunics and orange Arverne pantaloons. Two of them were
dressed as Romans in white togas with orange piping. Another two
wore togas over pantaloons. Vercingetorix was gratified to see that
Critognat was not among them.

The only person whom Vercingetorix recognized was Gobanit. His
uncle, to judge from his soft and jowly face, had put on considerable
weight, though how much was hard to tell with a toga draped over his
body as he lolled on his couch.

Vercingetorix rode right up to him, sword drawn, terrorizing the serving wenches, causing them to stumble backward in their haste to escape the hooves of his horse.

"Guards!" Gobanit shouted. "How did this barbarian get in here?"

When he saw that the guards were not to be seen, he turned his ire on Vercingetorix. "How dare you intrude upon the deliberations of the vergobret of the Arverni and his senators in this brutish manner!"

"To serve the will of the gods and the people," Vercingetorix told him.

"To serve—! Who, by the gods, are you?"

"I am Vercingetorix, son of Keltill, come to claim my birthright!"

By now the senators were sitting upright.

"What do you want from me?" demanded Gobanit.

"What is rightfully mine, Gobanit!"

Gobanit's attitude changed abruptly. "Well, of course," he said, favoring Vercingetorix with an unctuous smile. "There was no need to ride in here like some Teuton barbarian, nephew. As his only lawful heir, or so it was supposed, I inherited your father's lands and treasure, but now that I see you're alive and well, of course—"

"What about my mother?"

"You haven't heard . . . ?" said Gobanit.

"Heard what?"

"Your mother has . . . joined Keltill in the Land of Legend, Vercingetorix," Gobanit said, not quite meeting Vercingetorix's eyes as he spoke. "Gaela died a most noble death. She was seen to have thrust a dagger into her own heart when captured by Teuton raiders in order to avoid dishonorable slavery . . . or worse. You should be most proud of her. . . ."

Gobanit's eyes darted evasively to the right and behind Vercingetorix, and, turning his head, Vercingetorix saw that the dozen guards he had ridden through had entered the Great Hall and were tentatively advancing on his rear with their swords drawn.

He leapt off his horse, and stuck the point of his sword under Gobanit's chin, where his jaw met his throat.

"I don't believe you for one moment, Gobanit!" he said, prying him up off his couch at sword point. "You slew her or had her slain as surely as you killed my father!"

Gobanit's eyes bulged with terror.

"Whoever told you that is a liar! As surely as I did not kill your father, I did not kill your mother!"

"You're the liar! You lit the fire! I was there! I saw it!"

Beads of sweat broke out on Gobanit's cheeks and brow. "I had no choice!" he whined. "If you were there, you know that the druid Diviacx commanded me!"

"You could have refused!"

"At what gain? Some Eduen would have done the deed, and I would have been slain myself for defying a druid."

"You would have preserved your honor! Draw your sword, Gobanit, for I would preserve *my* honor by granting you the honorable death in fair combat you withheld from my father."

And he withdrew his sword from under Gobanit's throat.

Gobanit staggered backward, screaming, "Kill him! *Kill him!*"

Thought stopped as Vercingetorix whirled around, his sword before him, blade parallel to the floor, in a sweeping circle, and saw that it was not the guards who had come up behind him, but three of the Arverne senators who had risen from their couches and were rushing toward him, swords thrust out to skewer him.

Continuing his whirling turn but sidestepping as he did, he allowed their motion to carry them past him, then, still smoothly turning, sliced one deeply across the buttocks, and confronted the other two as they clumsily reversed direction, slashing one's throat, ducking sidewise, and spearing the other under the sternum.

Withdrawing his sword with another whirling, dancing turn, Vercingetorix found himself facing Gobanit in the process of clumsily drawing his sword from beneath his toga, and without pause twisted his wrist as he plunged his sword deep into his uncle's belly, so that he could rip upward, toward Gobanit's heart.

Gobanit fell screaming and was already dead when Vercingetorix pulled out his bloody sword, and thought returned. And if what the man of action had done seemed to have happened in an instant, the next moment seemed to last an eternity, as the man of knowledge beheld the results.

One man lay screaming and blubbering on his stomach in a growing pool of blood. Another lay supine and unmoving. A third was on his back, his head lying at an impossible angle, the gaping wound in his neck gushing blood as a mountain spring gushes water. Gobanit lay facedown in yet another lake of gore.

Without thought, Vercingetorix had slain not merely his first man but his first three, and though he had done it like a dance, with his own blood hot and his sword singing, now he only felt his heart sinking and his gorge rising, and his spirit was hard put to find the glory in it.

But Vercingetorix forced himself to choke back his nausea, for there was no time for vomiting or contemplation. Gobanit's five remaining "senators" had scrambled to their feet, though none had summoned up the courage to draw a sword. The dozen guards had come up behind them, and were surveying the carnage in numb stupefaction, glancing uncertainly at their captain, and Vercingetorix knew that he must immediately assume their command.

"You . . . you killed not just the vergobret but two senators!" Baravax stammered. "That was no fair and honorable combat. . . ."

What was he to do now? Whose orders must he obey? Surely not a dead man? The remaining senators? But they seemed as reluctant to speak as he was to act.

"Surely not," said Vercingetorix. "I offered Gobanit honorable combat, did I not? Yet he refused the challenge and instead sought to have these cowards cut me down from behind. I therefore slew no man of honor. I slew no man worthy of being a leader of the Arverni!"

"You . . . would claim Gobanit's place by right of arms!" whined one of the senators.

"Never has that been done!"

"We must hold an election!"

"I do not seek to proclaim myself vergobret by force of arms, for that is not our way," Vercingetorix declared. "I claim only my father's lands and property and the loyalty of those nobles and warriors who owed loyalty to him. All who wish to follow me I will lead to join Caesar's invasion of Britain. I invite all who would become vergobret to gather their warriors and do the same. Let us hold the election upon our return, and let our deeds in battle speak for us."

"Well spoken!" cried Baravax, sealing his decision by raising his sword high in salutation, then nodding to his men, who, after a moment's hesitation, did likewise. Clearly Vercingetorix was the only one in the Great Hall *worthy* of his loyalty. And, after all, by far the most likely to emerge as the man with the power to appoint the guard captain of his choosing.

IX

JUNIUS GALLIUS' ENGINEERS had erected the camp palisade, enclosed it in the usual entrenchment, and finished the docks in less than a week. Two hundred ships had already made the journey from the Mediterranean without serious mishap.

Caesar had his four legions bivouacked snugly inside the fortifications, with the tribal encampments of the Gauls being set up safely outside, and even Dumnorix, who Caesar suspected was a lot more cunning than the oaf he took pains to pretend to be, had been seduced away from his well-justified suspicions when shown to the sybaritic quarters laid on for the favored few Gallic leaders within the Roman walls.

Moreover, it was a fine sunny day on the northern coast of Gaul, a region not famed for such weather, and even the customarily saturnine Gisstus was grinning broadly when he caught up to Caesar outside his tent, bearing a mysterious sack.

"Good news, better news, and amusing news, Caesar. Vercingetorix is only two or three days away, and as for bridling your young unicorn, we already have the means among the Carnute hostages. You knew her yourself. Intimately."

"I did?" Caesar shrugged. The memories of the amatory lessons he had delivered in the hostage grammaticus last winter were sweet, but there had been so many pretty young faces and ripening nubile bodies that they all seemed to blur together in a pleasant rosy haze. "A Carnute girl? What was her name?"

"Marah," said Gisstus.

"You are saying that Vercingetorix will remember her, and fondly?"

"Oh yes. He met her only once or twice, but there was a plan to seal an alliance between the Arverni and the Carnutes by marrying them. Then too, he's been at a druid school since he fled Gergovia, where, I am told, the boys' opportunities for amatory experience are limited to each other, and the Gauls take a grimly dour view of such sexual recourse. So somehow I doubt that Vercingetorix would have forgotten a girl tasty enough to have appealed to *your* sophisticated palate, Caesar. Indeed, I would say he might still be a virgin."

"A virgin!" exclaimed Caesar.

"We're not in Rome, Caesar. Perhaps you've noticed?"

Caesar had indeed noticed that the sexual practices of this part of the world were peculiar. The Teutons even mocked warriors who availed themselves of natural sexual pleasures before their twenty-fifth year or so, believing it made them less fierce.

"Here's another little surprise for him," said Gisstus. He reached into the sack and pulled out a crown. "The legendary Crown of Brenn!"

It was a rather crudely fashioned crown, but apparently crafted of gold.

"Is it real?" asked Caesar.

"Well, it's gold all right," Gisstus told him, "but I had the thing made. I saw the real one myself, if you will remember. Assuming it was the real one, and not something Keltill had made up for the occasion. I hear from certain cynical sources that more than one petty Gallic chieftain claims to hide the real thing."

"You really think it would fool Vercingetorix?"

"Is he a jeweler?"

"But didn't he have the real thing when he fled? How could he be made to believe that I—"

Gisstus made a dramatic pass over the crown with his free hand. "Druid magic!" he said. "The Crown of Brenn has a will of its own and journeys to meet its appointed darling of destiny!"

Caesar laughed. "What *would* I do without you, Gisstus?" he said.

Critognat, who had slain more men in combat than he could count and had an abundance of honorable battle scars to prove it, found himself riding as second-in-command beside a war leader of the Arverni less than half his age and with no battle experience at all.

And willingly!

Of the four thousand Arverne warriors riding behind them, about half had inherited their loyalty to Vercingetorix through their loyalty to his father. Most of the rest were followers of Critognat, or of experienced warriors like Cavan, Blosun, and Rackelanar, who looked to him as their senior. Critognat knew full well that he could have claimed leadership of the Arverne forces, just as he could have demanded an immediate election of a new vergobret and probably won it.

But he had done neither of these things. There was something magic about the young son of Keltill that made an old warrior not only love him but trust in his leadership against all common sense and experience—the magic of how Vercingetorix had seized this leadership. Or how he had not.

When Critognat learned that Vercingetorix proposed to postpone the election until all who might seek to be elected vergobret had the chance to prove their worthiness on the field of battle, he had wept with joy. Unblooded in battle or not, here was a man with the heart of a true Gaul! Here at last was a leader who loved honor above power and understood that the loyalty of warriors must be won with the sword.

If Vercingetorix held him under a magical spell, it was the right sort of magic. The magic of honor and the sword. The kind of magic that had brought Brenn's army to victory at Rome itself.

To the northeast, by the shore of the gray rolling sea, was a Roman stockade. And before it Critognat could see tens of thousands of warriors setting up an enormous encampment. Gauls of many tribes, to judge by the standards and pennants set out above them.

"Never have I seen such a gathering of the tribes," said Critognat. "Never had I thought to see one."

"Never has there *been* one since the time of Brenn," said Vercingetorix.

"But gathered together not by a Gaul, but by a Roman," Critognat muttered, shaking his head ruefully.

"What do we do now?" grunted Critognat.

It was a good question for which Vercingetorix had no good answer, for they were approaching the edge of the Gallic encampment outside the Roman palisade, and there seemed no place to go; indeed, they confronted a scene of pandemonium.

Though standards staking out tribal territories had been planted widely, thousands of warriors were clustered around each of them, leaving only ragged random aisles between the tribal encampments. These might be wide enough for the parade of camp followers and tradesmen offering their wares, but far too narrow for the Arverne troops to pass, assuming there was any territory closer to the palisade where Vercingetorix could quarter his troops.

Nor were the troops of the tribes who had already claimed their territory properly quartered. Some tents had been pitched. Here and there, enterprising peasants had set up large cookfires and were roasting pigs and sheep and chickens for sale. There was an abundance of bread loaves, but no ovens to be seen. There were brewers selling beer out of barrels or whole casks, but the briskness of their trade seemed to be moderated by the amphorae of Roman wine that were everywhere.

Horses were tethered and did their shitting and pissing where their masters sat gambling, eating, but mostly drinking, and likewise befouling the nearby ground. The boisterous encampment sent up a stench that had Critognat wrinkling his nose.

"I've seen better-organized pigsties," he grumbled. "Smelled them too. Where are we supposed to quarter our troops? Where are the vergobrets? Who is in charge of this mess?"

"Keep the men mounted for now," Vercingetorix told him, "and I'll try to find out."

He summoned Baravax, and had him assemble a dozen warriors before riding into this unruly encampment, for he didn't like the smell of it, and not just that of the steaming urine and fly-speckled dung. Then, flanked by his guards, he rode in a zigzag fashion up the disorderly paths between the tribes in the direction of the palisade gates.

He had exchanged Caesar's crimson cloak for one of Arverne orange, but he was still riding the horse Caesar had given him, with its red-and-gold saddle blanket, an unpopular combination of colors here, to judge by the sour looks he got, by the mutterings that seemed to be stopped just short of coherent curses by the presence of his escorts.

So he was pleased to see the familiar face of Litivak as he approached the boar standard.

"Litivak!"

"Vercingetorix! I hear you've become a great general," Litivak said. His tone of voice did not allow Vercingetorix to tell whether this was sincere congratulation or wry jest.

"Those who followed my father now follow me, if that's what you mean," Vercingetorix said carefully. "Perhaps *you* can tell me what is going on here? I see no Romans. I see no vergobrets. No one seems to be in charge of anything."

"Caesar keeps his legions inside the wall, where the vergobrets, and whoever else he seeks to seduce, are favored with luxurious quarters. The rest of us are at liberty to fend for ourselves."

"Well, I can see the wisdom in keeping Romans and Gauls apart . . ." said Vercingetorix.

"It may help to keep the peace now," said Litivak. "But once we find ourselves fighting alongside each other . . ." He shrugged.

"Under whose command?"

"Caesar's, who else?"

"I mean all these tribal armies."

"I am given to understand that Caesar has assigned command of the Gallic auxiliaries to his favorite lieutenant, Titus Labienus."

"A *Roman*?"

"Can you imagine all these tribes accepting a *Gaul* as their commander?" Litivak scoffed.

"So Labienus is in charge of the bivouacking arrangements?"

Litivak shrugged. "Does it look like *anyone* is in charge of *anything* out here?"

"What should I do, then?"

Litivak looked his horse up and down. "That's a Roman general's horse you're riding, isn't it?" he said suspiciously.

"It's Caesar's," Vercingetorix told him.

"*Caesar's!* How in the world did you ever come by it?"

"He lent it to me . . . or sold it to me . . ." said Vercingetorix. "It's a strange story. . . ."

"Well, Caesar's horse should at least be enough to get you inside Caesar's fortress," Litivak told him.

Vercingetorix rode on toward the palisade gates. They were open, but the way was barred by four Roman legionnaires, who appeared more bored than hostile.

"You are?" said the one who seemed to be in charge, an older man with a long scar on his cheek and more gray than black in his hair.

"Vercingetorix of the Arverni."

"Ah, the famous son of Keltill," said another snidely. "Is it true that you slew a hundred men single-handedly in Gergovia, serviced their widows in a single night, and then started in on their horses?"

The gray-haired legionnaire silenced him with a poisonous look.

"No one gets in without someone who knows him by sight on hand inside to identify him," he told Vercingetorix apologetically. "You could be anyone, after all. No offense intended."

"None taken," said Vercingetorix.

"Announce him, Claudius," the squad leader ordered, and the legionnaire who had spoken trudged inside.

Claudius returned from within looking dazed.

"Well?" demanded the squad leader.

Claudius regarded Vercingetorix with much more respect than before.

"We let him pass," he said. "But without his escort. Himself himself awaits him."

"*In Latin that we can understand,* please, Claudius."

"Himself, Marius," Claudius said. "Gaius Julius Caesar."

"Hail, Vercingetorix," said Caesar.

He was amused to note that, though Vercingetorix had exchanged the crimson cape for one of orange, the animal still bore the livery of a Roman general. Caesar had deemed it politic to be attended by Labienus when greeting arriving tribal leaders and was even more amused to observe Labienus' outrage at this sight. Not that Labienus was the most difficult officer in his army to scandalize.

Vercingetorix sat there on horseback silently for a long awkward moment, apparently unwilling to return the salutation in like Roman manner, lest it be taken as a gesture of fealty. The boy had good political instincts.

"Greetings, Caesar," he said instead.

"Uh, hail, Vercingetorix," said Labienus.

"My chief lieutenant, Titus Labienus," said Caesar.

"Greetings, Labienus," said Vercingetorix. "I have heard much about you."

"Have you?"

"It is said by your enemies—your former enemies—that you are the worthiest of foes, a clever general and brave as a lion," said Vercingetorix. Labienus seemed close to blushing, and it seemed to Caesar that Vercingetorix was subtle enough to catch it. "Almost as brave as a Gaul," he added with a little grin that turned into a chuckle in which Labienus could join, thus allowing this truly modest man to escape from his embarrassment.

Vercingetorix then untied a large cloth pouch from his saddle and dismounted with it. Reaching into it, he withdrew Caesar's cloak, neatly folded. "Thank you for the loan of your mantle," he said, handing it to him. "It shielded me well, but I do prefer orange."

Vercingetorix took a small leather bag out of his pouch and handed that to Caesar. When Caesar opened the drawstring, he saw that it contained five gold coins with Vercingetorix's own image graven on them.

"What's this?" he asked.

"Payment for the horse," Vercingetorix told him. "I told you you would have it when I regained my birthright, and now I have."

"Oh no," said Caesar, handing the money back to him, "you'll not get off as easy as that, my young friend! I intend to hold you to the Gallic version of our bargain," he told him. "*Fifty* gold coins when we both are dead and meet again in the Land of Legend!"

He and Vercingetorix laughed.

The befuddled look on Labienus' face was choice.

"Come, my young friend," said Caesar, clasping Vercingetorix's arm like that of an old comrade, "allow me to show you to your quarters."

In stark contrast to the situation outside the palisade, all that Vercingetorix saw inside was well ordered and clean. There were cookfires, baking ovens, thick porridge bubbling in great black iron kettles, amphorae of wine and barrels of water set out at regular intervals. There were dung ditches dug at a decent distance away from the legionnaires, and the Roman horses, far fewer than those of the Gauls, were likewise corralled well away from the men.

The legionnaires themselves were bivouacked in neat rows of identical eight-man leather tents separated by dirt avenues as straight as a Roman road, and thousands of them sat outside enjoying the sunshine, eating porridge, drinking wine, mending armor, sharpening swords and javelins.

Caesar led him past a much smaller group of tents isolated from the main Roman troop encampments that, strangely, were under guard. Stranger still, Vercingetorix was surprised to see Diviacx passing from one to another.

"The students from the grammaticus are quartered within," said Caesar.

"The hostages, you mean."

"They *are*, after all, receiving the benefits of a Roman education," Caesar insisted mildly.

"Diviacx is teaching Gauls how to be Romans?"

"Here we have students from many of your tribes, and who would the leaders thereof trust to supervise them inside a Roman encampment but a druid?"

"And the only druid you could find who would so serve is Diviacx," Vercingetorix said sourly.

"I sense you love him not."

"How could I love the man who condemned my father to death?"

"How indeed?" said Caesar. He gave Vercingetorix a sidelong speculative look. "As one man of destiny to another, I find him impossible to love myself. Though he is an ally of sorts, there is something about him I find rather despicable."

"Then why do you use him?"

"Why don't *you* kill him?" Caesar asked slyly.

"Kill a druid?" exclaimed Vercingetorix. "If I did such a thing, even the Arverni . . ." He stayed himself, realizing that Caesar's question had been rhetorical.

Caesar nodded. "Even men of destiny are slaves of necessity," he said. "Some tools—a well-made sword, a good knife, a nicely crafted stylus even—one may come to love. Others—an ordinary mallet, a plain pot, a peasant's scythe—may lack all charm but still serve necessity. And when there is no other at hand . . ." He shrugged.

They reached a section of tents pitched close by the eastern wall, well away from both the legionnaires' bivouacs and the hostage tents. There were a score of them, set more widely apart than those of the legionnaires, and a Gallic tribal standard was set up before each of them. Caesar halted before an Arverne bear.

"Your quarters," he said, drawing aside the flap and ushering Vercingetorix into a scene more like the bedchamber of a Roman harlot than an officer's field quarters.

There was a Roman-style bed raised up off the ground on curved and carved wooden legs and piled with the pelts of bear and lynx. There were wooden tables, small and large, all painted in red and black, the largest and most elaborate ornamented with fittings of brass. There were brass and bronze serving plates and goblets embellished with silver. Overfragrant oil burned in brass lamps, giving off a sickeningly sweet odor of lavender. Above the bed hung a tapestry depicting three creatures that seemed half man and half goat performing sexual acts with naked women, one of which Vercingetorix would not have believed

possible. Fierce desire rose unbidden in his loins, and a burning blush
bloomed on his cheeks.

"Admittedly a bit on the Spartan side," said Caesar, "but I hope
you'll find it hospitable enough for a military camp. And at least you
won't have to worry about being cold and lonely at night."

He clapped his hands, once, twice, thrice, and two women entered
the tent, one red-haired and draped in a loose black robe, the other
black-haired and wearing a robe of red. Both were in the first flower of
youth and stunningly beautiful. Vercingetorix found himself bending
forward at the hips in an attempt to hide the state of his arousal. Caesar
nodded, and the black-haired woman fetched them goblets while the
other took up a small amphora and poured wine.

"Your body servants," said Caesar, "and never fear, they have been
well schooled to serve your body."

He nodded again, and both women doffed their robes with simulta-
neous flourishes and openly lubricious smiles. Underneath they wore
tiny breechclouts, black for the black-haired one, red for the red, and
nothing more.

Vercingetorix had never in his life seen two women in such a near-
naked state at the same time, had never seen any woman as perfectly
formed as these, had never beheld a single woman willing to slake his
lust at all. But he sensed danger here, some kind of sweet trap, in which
these two women and all that surrounded them were the bait.

Then too, there were his men to consider, not just in terms of the
injustice of their relative discomfort, but of how they would regard a
leader who luxuriated here while they camped outside with their
horses.

It appears to be true! Caesar marveled as he observed Vercingetorix's
reaction to the sudden revelation of nubile feminine flesh. His eyes were
practically popping out of his head, his priapic state was amusingly
obvious, and more amusing still were his embarrassed attempts to conceal it. Either the boy *is* a virgin, or at the least his experience must be
severely limited.

Vercingetorix nodded toward the two body servants in a manner
that he no doubt deemed covert, and leaned closer to Caesar. "A word
in private. . . ?" he whispered.

Caesar led him over to a far corner of the tent.

"It's not that I don't appreciate your hospitality, Caesar," Vercingetorix said, "but I do not deem it wise to enjoy such luxuries while my men sleep outside in the open. A commander should share not only the dangers but the conditions of his troops, not set himself above and apart. And so I will sleep outside with them, if it does not offend you."

"No offense taken," Caesar told him. "This tent will remain yours whenever you wish to use it, for as long as you like." He nodded in the direction of the body servants, now donning their robes. "For whatever you like."

Did the boy blush? Be that as it may, Vercingetorix gave Caesar a cool, measuring look with those eyes that seemed decades older than the rest of him. "I do find it peculiar that you offer to quarter the Gallic commanders here together. . . ."

"How so?" said Caesar, taking care to keep his voice and visage neutral.

"Why separate commanders from their troops?" asked Vercingetorix. "Why quarter rival commanders close by each other instead?"

What a strange youth this Vercingetorix was, one moment an embarrassed boy, the next a cunning general in danger of perceiving the true situation all too clearly.

"Your second question is the answer to your first, my young friend. It is my hope that quartering the commanders of the individual tribal forces close together may cause them to develop a camaraderie and come to see themselves as the leaders of a united Gallic auxiliary army." Caesar gave Vercingetorix an ingenuous smile. "Did not your father seek something similar?" he said.

"To drive you out of Gaul," said Vercingetorix. "And they killed him for it," he added perplexedly. "And I still do not quite understand why you are so willing to see Gaul united—"

"Under Rome, not against us," Caesar told him. "Your father failed because the vergobrets of Gaul saw no advantage in being united against me under him. But I will show the advantage of uniting under a Roman proconsul for profit and civilization."

Caesar could see that, virgin or not, Vercingetorix was not naïve enough to swallow this whole, even though there was more truth than falsehood in it.

"Dine with me in my tent tonight," he said, "and much will be made clear."

But not everything, my young friend.

If the tent that Caesar had offered him seemed to Vercingetorix fit for a Roman bordello, Caesar's own would have been fit for a king if the Romans had one. It was four times the size of the ordinary tents and divided into separate chambers by hanging tapestries depicting landscapes from various countries that must be Roman provinces, and the cloth borders framing them were interwoven with threads of gold. Instead of a bare earthen floor, there were carpets. The oil lamps illumining the tent were of gold, and the perfume they gave off was subtle. Two musicians sat in a far corner of the dining chamber, one strumming a stringed instrument, the other playing a set of wooden pipes. There was a large, low dining table set with silver platters and small golden plates offering fruits, nutmeats, olives, pastes of various strange kinds and colors, fishes in sauces, golden goblets, a small amphora of wine.

Three low plushly padded couches were set up around the table. One was empty. Caesar reclined on another, wearing a white toga trimmed in crimson. Reclining on the other couch was a stunningly beautiful young woman, blonde and fair-skinned like a Gaul, but wearing a diaphanous flowing white dress cut low in the Roman style, with her hair likewise elaborately done up in ribbons and a silver tiara trimmed with some shiny grayish gems that did not seem to be minerals.

The smile with which she greeted him was radiant.

Caesar rose and escorted him to the third couch with a hostly gesture which he hardly noticed, and if this was accompanied by words of greeting, Vercingetorix didn't hear them. His attention was captured by the woman, not just by her beauty, but by the way her eyes tracked his every movement. Even when Caesar kissed her lightly on the lips before returning to his own couch, her eyes remained on him.

It was arousing, intriguing, but also embarrassing, for she must know him, and therefore they must have met. But how could he have possibly failed to remember meeting a woman like this?

"This lovely creature is one of the prize pupils of our Roman grammaticus," said Caesar, "and, uh, a protégée of mine. Her name is—"

"Marah," she said.

"Marah!"

"You two know each other?" said Caesar. "What an amazing coincidence!"

Too amazing to *be* coincidence, Vercingetorix realized. "We . . . met as children," he said carefully.

"He offered to make me his queen," said Marah with a little laugh that, though gently mocking, seemed affectionate as well.

"His queen?" said Caesar.

"It's a long story," Vercingetorix said dismissively, blushing at the memory of his boyhood braggadocio, but also rendered wary by this confluence of his old boast, the girl he had made it to, and the man who his vision had told him was destined to turn it into reality.

But Marah had no such compunction.

"It was on the day his father sought to make himself king," she said. "He just couldn't quite keep the secret, and I was a little provincial girl impressed by the son of a local chieftain who was even more impressed with himself. . . ."

"And what have you now become?" Vercingetorix snapped, chagrined by the memory and more than a little vexed by her speaking the truth of it.

"A civilized and educated lady—"

"Impressed by a *Roman general* who is even more impressed with himself!"

Caesar broke the moment of tension with a laugh. "Can you blame her? Can you blame me? I am, after all, a most impressive fellow!" He laughed again. "In fact, the three of us are most impressive people!"

He poured three goblets of wine with his own hand, lifted his own in toast. "Surely we can drink to that!"

Thus far, the little play he had set up was going quite nicely, but it was best not to rush things. So, as servants brought course after course and he poured goblet after goblet, Caesar contented himself with pretending to drink more than he really was, cozening Vercingetorix into drinking more wine than your beer-guzzling Gaul would be used to, and listening to the hopefully future lovers catch up on their brief childhood memories and banter about their divergent paths into adulthood.

Romans did water their wine to diminish its intoxicating effect when they were struck by an attack of abstemiousness, but it was more often done to ameliorate the harshness of a mediocre vintage, such as what was usually palmed off on the Gauls. Caesar had, however, laid on an excellent vintage, the watering of which would have been an outrage to Bacchus—not because he imagined that Vercingetorix could be a connoisseur, but so that it would glide down his throat smoothly and rapidly at full strength.

He had not written Marah's part in the drama beyond telling her who the third party at the feast would be and letting her know that he knew of their youthful connection, playing the avuncular older lover stepping aside to become matchmaker to the young couple. For, as any practical sophist knew, the best dissimulations were those that cut closest to the truth.

And so he ate, and he drank sparingly, and he listened to Vercingetorix tell Marah the brief story of his life, and he listened to Marah extolling the virtues of a Roman education and Roman civilization. He didn't move to channel the proceedings in the chosen direction until Vercingetorix was somewhat drunk and their conversation was approaching the edge of acrimony.

"You sound as if you are *glad* to have been taken hostage by Rome, Marah."

"And indeed I am! Had I not been, knowing what I know now, I would have volunteered!"

"Volunteered to be a hostage!"

"Gladly, if that were the price of a Roman education. Without it, what would I be?"

"The wife of an Arverne vergobret?"

"A girl given in marriage to seal an alliance between the Arverni and the Carnutes."

"And what would have been so bad about that?"

"Between a boy and a girl there should be something more."

"And there was not?"

"I didn't say that . . . but were we not both to be used to help Keltill become king of Gaul? A plan foredoomed to failure."

"The wrong man with the right idea," said Caesar, seizing his opportunity.

"The right idea? To drive your legions into the sea?"

"That was the foredoomed part. But giving Gaul a king . . ."

For the first time in a long while, Vercingetorix's gaze was drawn away from Marah. His eyes were bloodshot and somewhat glazed, and what Caesar beheld was an inexperienced youth seeking a way out of an argument with a woman his lust sought to woo, but behind the boy was a man, and that was whom Caesar sought to address now.

With a negligent wave of his hand, he ordered the servants and musicians to leave.

"I've been in Gaul long enough to know that the political system here just doesn't work," he said when the three of them were alone.

"For *you* perhaps, Caesar," said Vercingetorix. "It has served *us* well enough since the time of Brenn."

"You believe your own father was wrong, then?" Caesar said slyly. This silenced and befuddled the boy utterly. "I have studied the histories and governments of many lands, and the most important lesson that I have learned is that peoples must adapt their forms of government to the needs of the times. Rome too was once a chaos of fractious tribes. Then a kingdom. Now a republic. Later . . . whatever destiny may require . . ."

He raised his goblet.

"This much Keltill understood, and for that I salute him!"

Vercingetorix seemed properly moved by this gesture.

"It was all very well for each of your tribes to be ruled by its own vergobret, and those rotating from year to year, as long as you could afford petty feuds and the occasional battle as sport and entertainment," Caesar told him. "But, confronted by the need to wage war against a common enemy like the Teutons, it just didn't work. And so you were constrained to seek the aid of Rome."

"*Diviacx* sought the aid of Rome!"

"And was right to do so. Had he not, the Teutons would have ruined Gaul."

"And instead we now confront Rome!"

"And I have come to believe that, to succeed in doing that, Gaul needs a king," said Caesar.

Vercingetorix needed another swallow of wine to aid in his digestion of that one. "Caesar offers Gaul advice on how to fight his legions!" he exclaimed.

"No," Caesar told him. "Gaul can never prevail against the legions of Rome. I offer advice on how Gaul may *confront* Rome and survive. Your people need a king to lead them into a fruitful relationship with the civilization destined to rule the world."

Strangely enough, Vercingetorix seemed to take no great umbrage at this. "But Rome has no king!" he said instead.

"Rome had kings once, but we grew beyond them and established a republic," Caesar told him, gliding blithely over a century or two of bloody and turbulent strife.

"And now Rome is ruled by a Senate of educated and enlightened men acting in harmonious concert under a system of written law," Marah gushed with the convert's enthusiasm, a description of the Senate that Caesar himself needed a drink of wine to wash down.

"Not that our system of government is perfect either," he managed to say with a straight face. "Rome too suffers from lack of a single strong ruler able to hold office long enough to really get things done—"

"—but Roman law provides for the election of a kind of king called a dictator when needed," said Marah, "and Caesar—"

"Gaul is hardly ready for such politically sophisticated solutions at this stage," Caesar said, cutting her off hastily. "Why, it's not even fully a province of Rome yet."

"And never will be!" Vercingetorix exclaimed fervently. "How can you speak of our need for a king and turning Gaul into a Roman province at the same time?"

"And why not?" Caesar said spontaneously, and as he did, a grand vista opened up. Until this moment, he had simply sought to crown the boy his puppet king and use him to unite the fractious tribes long enough to declare Gaul a conquered province and return to Rome in triumph. But now he realized he had stumbled on a system that would serve him well when he became dictator, and indeed well serve the new Rome he would create even after he was gone.

"Every Roman province is ruled by a proconsul elected by the Senate," Caesar said, thinking aloud. "Almost always a Roman politician sent to rule a conquered people. But if a local king agreed to his country's becoming a province of Rome in return for being elected proconsul for life, Gaul, for current example, could indeed become a Roman province and be ruled by its own king at the same time! And so might the circle be squared!"

He fixed Vercingetorix with a seductive stare.

"What do you think of that, my young friend?"

Though the boy's eyes remained bloodshot, something behind them suddenly seemed to clarify as he gazed unwaveringly back, like mist evaporating from the surface of twin pools to reveal bottomless blue depths.

"You seek not to become proconsul of Gaul for life yourself," he said. It was not a question.

"Your gods and mine forbid!" Caesar told him with total honesty. "I tell you plainly, my destiny is to rule Rome, not Gaul, and since Gaul will then need another proconsul, why not a local king?"

"You sound as if you have someone in mind . . ." said Vercingetorix, in the strangest tone of voice, as if the wine had transported him elsewhere, as if he were speaking from within a dream.

"It would have to be someone rich enough so we wouldn't have to worry about him skimming more than his fair share of the taxes. . . ."

"Someone with a Roman education," said Marah. "Or at least . . . with a queen who had one . . ."

"Can you think of anyone who fits that description, Vercingetorix?"

"You could not simply appoint a king of your own choosing, Caesar," said Vercingetorix. "Gauls will only follow a hero who has proved himself so. A . . . man of destiny."

"Heroes are made, not born, my young friend, or, rather, they can make themselves, with a little help from their friends. And our campaign in Britain is a chance for many Gauls to earn themselves crowns of laurel. If the gods so will it." Caesar shrugged. "On the other hand, Mars is a capricious god, and may decide that one hero is quite enough to wear the laurels. Or . . . if political necessity so dictates, I could always decide so myself. . . ."

"You offer me a crown of laurel?" said Vercingetorix.

And once more he seemed to be speaking from within a dream.

"I cannot accept a hero's crown that I haven't earned, Caesar," Vercingetorix tells the Roman general, just as he rejected the crown of laurel in the Land of Legend. Indeed, he seems to have entered the Land of Legend, outside the dream called time. He knows what Caesar will do next because he has seen him do it, and he has seen him do it because he has stood upon the hill of his own death looking down on all that was, and is, and will be, and his life does not proceed from the past into the future moment by moment like beads on a string.

And so, even though he remembers that he has entrusted it to Guttuatr, he is not surprised when Caesar reaches into a leather sack behind him and withdraws the Crown of Brenn—or a Crown of Brenn—and holds it up before him, for he has seen this moment before. The only surprise is Caesar's, at his lack thereof.

But Caesar masks this quickly and proceeds as if he too is in the Land of Legend. "And would you accept *this* crown from my hand, Vercingetorix?"

"Nor can I accept the Crown of Brenn from your hand," he tells Caesar. "But that does not mean it is not my destiny to wear it."

And as he speaks these words, Vercingetorix realizes he has said too much, and the spell is broken, and he comes back down from the Land of Legend into the world of strife.

Where he now knew in all-too-practical detail how his vision in the Land of Legend would be fulfilled; how, and perhaps why, it would be Gaius Julius Caesar who would make him king of Gaul, and how it would be possible for him to be acclaimed as such in Rome.

The man of action was exhilarated by this revelation and more elated still by the rapt and eager gaze of the woman he had promised to make his queen. But the man of knowledge was troubled. For, although the vision he had seen in the Land of Legend had told him that it was his destiny to be acclaimed king of Gaul by Rome and Caesar, it had not told him whether accepting such a destiny would be to serve Gaul and the memory of his father or to betray them.

More disquieting still, if a man's life did not proceed through time from moment to moment like beads on a string, if he had stood upon the hilltop of his own death and seen his destiny entire, did he *have* the choice to accept or reject it?

Vercingetorix had more to digest than the copious Roman food soaked in strange sauces, and so spent an uneasy night sleeping in the open with his men. Who would not be tempted by the offer of a crown and the appearance of the girl he had lusted after as a boy as a beautiful and sophisticated woman eager to become his queen? Would I betray Gaul by accepting such an offer? How so, if Gaul would be united and ruled by a Gaul, and Caesar's legions would return to Italy?

These thoughts troubled Vercingetorix's sleep far more than the abundant snores of the men around him; while his mind could find no reason to reject what Caesar offered, his heart would not agree.

The next morning, Vercingetorix breakfasted with his troops, ordered Critognat to see to their more orderly disposition, and then returned to the Roman fortress to meet with the other Gallic leaders. It would seem that word that the Arverne leader had passed the night with his men rather than luxuriating in a Roman pleasure tent had spread among the warriors of the other tribes: for as he passed each of their encampments on the way, many warriors greeted him with smiles and nods and even the scattered thumping of swords on shields, no doubt as much in rebuke of their own leaders as in his praise.

The manner in which he was greeted by the Gallic leaders who had spent the night inside the Roman stockade, however, was another matter. These were gathering in the open near the tents that Caesar had provided for them. Some were already seated on Roman stools, others were still in the bleary process of emerging from the previous night's revelries. There were about a score of them, among whom Vercingetorix recognized by face or reputation Epirod of the Santons, Comm of the Atrebates, Luctor of the Cadurques, Cottos of the Carnutes . . . and Dumnorix, a man whose face and reputation the son of Keltill was not likely to forget.

Dumnorix was seated on a stool near the center of the rough semicircle, and complaining.

"Rusty old junk that's seen more campaigning than a hundred-year-old whore!"

"The wooden swords we played with as children were better," a Sequane whom Vercingetorix did not know agreed.

"What troubles you?" Vercingetorix asked the Sequane, pointedly avoiding speaking to the brother of the man who had condemned his father.

"The quality of the weapons the Roman merchants sold us to equip our warriors has proved even lower than the price."

"You brought your armies here unarmed?"

"Not completely. But most of us did not have all the weapons we needed for our men—"

"—or the time to forge them—"

"—and the Roman merchants offered to supply what we needed immediately at half what it would have cost—"

"You bought weapons you hadn't even seen?" exclaimed Vercingetorix. "What did you expect?"

"We're not all as rich as . . . the son of Keltill!"

"Nor do we all dine alone with Caesar," sneered Dumnorix.

"They weren't alone! Caesar's paramour was with them."

"A real beauty!"

Vercingetorix's ears burned; whether from the urge to defend Marah's honor or from chagrin at hearing the plain truth, he did not know, but he found his hand moving to the hilt of his sword.

"A Carnute girl dressed up as a Roman harlot," said Comm.

"Hold your tongue!" Vercingetorix shouted.

"The three of them?" said one of the Parisii. "I have heard that Caesar cares not which hole he plants his standard in. Or whose. Perhaps Vercingetorix was in . . . a position to tell us whether this is true?"

At this, Vercingetorix's sword leapt forth. But Dumnorix stood up and shouted, "The man who draws the blood of another Gaul inside this Roman trap will answer to me with his own!"

Vercingetorix was not the only one dumbfounded by this. All fell silent. No one moved.

"Fools!" said Dumnorix. "You think Caesar truly plans to enrich us all with half the booty? The same Caesar whose merchants have already cheated us? He'll put us all in the forefront of battle to take the casualties, and then—"

"If you have so little stomach for battle, why are you here?" demanded Comm.

Dumnorix shrugged. "Because I'm a Gaul," he said. He laughed. "Because I fear death in battle less than I fear being deemed a coward by the likes of you!"

The general laughter broke the black mood. Vercingetorix sheathed his sword, but he could not quite allow Dumnorix to escape verbally unscathed.

"Or perhaps, like the moth drawn to the flame, you could not resist the bait within yonder tent even though you believe it a trap, Dumnorix?"

Vercingetorix said this in a light tone, but there was no bantering spirit in the looks he and Dumnorix exchanged.

"Strange talk from the man who passed the night in Caesar's tent," said Dumnorix.

"I passed the night sleeping outside among my men, and all who slept outside the palisade know it," said Vercingetorix. He raked the nobles with a disdainful eye. "And so would you, had you shared the hardships of your men!"

This produced some shamed faces, but more ugly murmurs, and Vercingetorix sensed that, like it or not, it was his turn to make peace.

"I begrudge you not the pleasures offered here by Caesar," he said. "I chose to sleep outside because otherwise the envious among you might have believed I curried special favor by accepting Caesar's offer to dine with him."

And thus have I taken my first step toward kingship in alliance with Rome by telling my first silver-tongued lie, he realized.

"If you so feared our contempt, why didn't you refuse?" demanded Comm.

"And gravely insult the leader of this whole expedition before we even left Gaul?"

He then compounded the dissimulation by concocting what he hoped was a sufficiently lustful leer.

"Rest assured, I shall not always so deny myself," he said, vowing to himself that he would spend alternate nights in the tent provided by Caesar, but vowing also that he would not avail himself of the carnal services of his "body servants," without quite understanding why.

He then approached Dumnorix and forced himself, against his rising gorge, to lock arms with the Eduen.

"Like Dumnorix, I too pledge that any Gaul who draws the blood of another Gaul within this Roman fortress will answer to me with his own!" he declared. "Here we must show the Romans that we are united as Gauls and will fight together as brothers!"

There were general shouts of approval, and then the banging of daggers and swords on stools in the absence of shields. Dumnorix seemed genuinely moved.

Vercingetorix avoided being seen with Caesar after their dinner so as to not create any further impression that he was Caesar's favorite.

The Arverni and the Edui being the strongest tribes and old rivals, it was inevitable that he and Dumnorix would be seen by the vergobrets of the other tribes as rivals for leadership of the Gallic forces. But it seemed there would never be a leader of a united Gallic army, for the Arverni would never accept the leadership of an Eduen, and the Edui would not accept the leadership of an Arverne. And whichever of them most appeared to be *seeking* such command would lose favor among the other tribal leaders.

So he and Dumnorix kept up the brotherly charade they had begun, serving as both the rallying points of differing factions and peacemakers between them. Dumnorix voiced his skepticism of Caesar's intentions, whereas Vercingetorix professed hot-blooded eagerness for battle. Thus Dumnorix, leader of the tribe most closely allied to Rome, found himself in the uncomfortable position of looking askance at the Roman whom his own brother had brought to Gaul, and the son of the man who had sought to eject the Romans by force found himself something like the champion of Caesar.

Vercingetorix suspected that Caesar had somehow arranged for things to fall this way, for no one had more credibility as his supporter than the son of Keltill, no one less as his detractor than the brother of Diviacx, and if the invasion was successful, Dumnorix would look the fool, and he would emerge as a king acceptable to the Edui. He was coming to think like a future proconsul of Gaul already, like a Roman, as if Caesar were a lodestone and he but an iron nail.

Nor was his suspicion that Caesar had been using Marah for his own purposes lessened when he finally "chanced" to encounter her again.

The sun was sinking through a broken overcast of low clouds, turning the sand of the rocky beach upon which Vercingetorix strolled the color of copper, the sea the color of iron, and the sky a streaky and mottled orange and blue. He had wandered far from the docks and anchorages where the ever-growing Roman invasion fleet was being marshaled, and the only sounds were the rush of the waves breaking on the rocks and the raucous cries of seabirds. Looking out to sea lost in thought, Vercingetorix did not notice the figure approaching him along the strand until she was close enough for him to see that it was Marah.

She wore a simple brown dress that fell just below her knees, she was barefoot, and her long blond hair blew freely in the sea breeze. She was a vision of an honest and natural Gallic girl, and therefore even more enticing than the sophisticatedly garbed half-Roman he had met in Caesar's tent. But Vercingetorix found himself wondering whether this innocent effect had been just as artfully crafted. And rebuking himself in the next moment for so mean-spirited a thought.

"And what are you pondering so deeply as you gaze out to sea, Vercingetorix?" she said softly. "Britain? The glories of battle to come?"

"Destiny," Vercingetorix found himself blurting, and then was instantly chagrined at how ponderous and self-important it sounded.

"Destiny . . . ?" Marah said, and then she laughed. "*Whose* destiny, Your Future Majesty?"

His ears burned at the memory of how crudely he had made a fool of himself when they were children. Nor had he improved much since. The uncomfortable truth was that, though he might be silver-tongued in discussing the affairs of men, he was entirely innocent of the art of bantering with women.

"Mine, and yours, and Caesar's," he ventured. "He has sent you to me, has he not? Else it would not be allowed."

Marah gave him a look that seemed older than her years. Or at least older than *his*. "Nothing happens here that Caesar does not allow," she admitted.

How much more would she admit? Vercingetorix wondered. How much more do I really want to know? "And you are his . . . special favorite?"

"Believe me, Caesar has no . . . special favorite," said Marah, and she laughed.

"What are you laughing at?"

Marah laughed again. "At you, Vercingetorix," she said teasingly. "That is not the question you really wanted to ask—now, is it?"

Vercingetorix's ears burned, and a bubble of emptiness blossomed in the pit of his stomach.

"You and Caesar have been . . . ?"

"Go on, spit it out!"

"Lovers," Vercingetorix managed to say, feeling quadruply the fool: at the tone in which he voiced it, at his embarrassment, at his callowness, at something else he cared not to confront.

"For a time," Marah said easily, and her ease only made his unease worse.

"For how long?"

"You're jealous!" Marah exclaimed. "As if you expected me to save myself for you!" She gave him a sardonic leer which suddenly made her seem utterly Roman. "Next will you declare that *you* have saved yourself for *me*!"

Vercingetorix found that it took more courage to meet her eyes in that moment than anything else he could remember having to do in his whole life. It was not made easier when she laughed, then reached out and took his hand.

"It's all right," she said gaily. "It's charming. It's a good sign."

"A good sign?" Vercingetorix all but stammered.

"You have no cause to worry," Marah told him. "Julius Caesar is a great man, and a season as his occasional companion has taught me more of the world than you can imagine. But he is also twice my age, married, and a man whose destiny lies not in the provinces with me, but in the center of the world in Rome. . . ."

"What . . . what . . . are you saying?"

"Caesar was my mentor in the amatory arts as he was in other things Roman, but that was all," Marah told him. "And he had many other such students."

"And you weren't jealous?"

"Of what? Is every chicken jealous of every other who enjoys the services of the cock? Do you imagine that I am jealous of every girl you have lain with?"

Vercingetorix found himself blushing with shame, not for what he *had* done, but for what he hadn't.

"Spoken like a Roman," he managed to say.

"And why not? You had better start learning a little Roman sophistication yourself, Vercingetorix, future king and proconsul of Gaul!"

"You really believe Caesar's offer was serious?" Vercingetorix said, eager to retreat to safer ground.

"If it were not, would he have made me part of it?" Marah said banteringly.

"So you admit it, then?" Vercingetorix replied in kind.

"He uses me for his own purposes as he uses everyone, if that's what you mean," said Marah. "But as I am his willing instrument, so he is also mine."

"What do you mean by that?"

"This," said Marah, and she suddenly kissed him fleetingly but openmouthed on the lips. Vercingetorix, his lust instantly inflamed, sought to clasp her to him, but, with yet another laugh, she danced away.

"You know Caesar . . . intimately, Marah," Vercingetorix said to cover yet another callow moment of embarrassment. "Do you trust him?"

"Completely," she said.

"Completely?"

"I trust him to be Julius Caesar! I trust him as much as I trust you."

"What's that supposed to mean?"

"It means you're both men of destiny," said Marah. "And such men can only be trusted to follow their own stars."

She gazed deeply into Vercingetorix's eyes, then clasped him behind the neck with both hands and drew him into a longer, deeper kiss, her tongue touching his and sending a bolt of lightning to his groin.

Then she broke the embrace.

"That's what makes them so exciting!" she said, and ran back up the beach.

There was perhaps a hint of gray in the bellies of some of the larger clouds fleecing the sky, and the usual foamy chop on the grayish-green waters of the Oceanus Britannicus, but the weather was holding, the last of the ships had arrived from the Mediterranean, the hulls that Gallius had built here were completed, the masts installed, and construction crews were even now putting up the rigging. Five hundred ships rode the rolling waves of the channel, as many as the sardines that a good fisherman might pull up in a successful cast of his net.

Caesar stood on the shore regarding his enormous fleet with satisfaction as Gisstus approached him. His legions would sail aboard the war galleys and the equally seaworthy merchant ships he had commandeered for the purpose, as would Vercingetorix and his Arverni, perhaps the forces of a few other tribes for appearances' sake. The rest of the Gauls could cross to Britain aboard the troopships Gallius had thrown together here. These were little more than sharp-prowed barges fitted with oars and sails, but the channel was not wide, and it was not exactly vital that they be sturdy enough to make more than a one-way crossing.

"Three more days and we're off to Britain," he said when Gisstus reached him.

"Or off the land and onto the water anyway," said Gisstus.

Caesar laughed. "Don't tell me you're afraid of seasickness like our suspicious friend Dumnorix?" he said.

"Oh, a little puking for the greater good and glory of Rome is not beyond my courage, Caesar," said Gisstus. "But the gods of this piece of sea have an odious reputation for serving up sudden capricious changes in weather. Perhaps we should sacrifice a bullock or two to Neptune, in the Greek manner, just to be on the safe side."

"*Must* you always worry about the worst possibilities, Gisstus?"

"It's what you pay me to do, Caesar," Gisstus reminded him, and of course it was true. An optimist would make a poor spymaster. Moreover, Caesar knew that his own sanguine temperament needed the balance of such a man whispering in his ear.

Tomorrow they could begin loading supplies; then the legions would board, followed by the Gauls, who, being incapable of choosing an overall commander for a unified auxiliary army, had no choice but to accept the overall command of a Roman general; they had been mollified by his choice of the Roman general they most admired, Labienus.

They would not be told that Labienus was to be replaced by Tulius until they were landed in Britain. Labienus was the last man Caesar wanted in command of such an admittedly dirty piece of business, whereas Tulius was unencumbered by an excessive lust for glory or an overdeveloped conscience. Tulius would have no compunction about sending those Gallic leaders whom Caesar did not wish to survive and their troops into well-chosen fiascoes. Vercingetorix and his Arverni would be given the easiest roles in the heroic drama. After a few battles in which the leaders of minor tribes were slain leading their forces into bloody disaster, it would be easy to get the remnants to accept integration into Vercingetorix's army.

And when Dumnorix met his unfortunate end, the same could be done with the Eduen survivors, leaving Vercingetorix in command of a de-facto army of Gaul fighting at the side of Rome's legions. When the dust had cleared, it would be easy enough to get the Gauls to accept a well-made hero like Vercingetorix as their king and the Senate to elect him proconsul of Gaul.

"Any more dark thoughts save the weather, Gisstus?" Caesar asked in fine good humor.

"Well, there's always the Britons," Gisstus replied. "It's hard to imagine this armada sneaking up on them. Maybe they have mighty magicians. Maybe they have secret weapons. And in any case, I am reliably informed that the food there is horrible."

Caesar laughed heartily. "You never fail me, do you, Gisstus?" he said, clapping him on the shoulder. "I *knew* you'd think of something!"

"An army is a war engine, and keeping it well armed and supplied is at least half the battle," Caesar told Vercingetorix as they walked along the docks and jetties lining the shore.

Caesar had summoned him to watch the loading of the ships, no doubt to impress him, and impressed Vercingetorix was. There were more ships than Vercingetorix would have imagined existed being rowed in from anchor to be loaded, then rowed out again to anchor to make room for more. Some of the things Vercingetorix saw being loaded amazed him, and surely would have daunted him were he a Briton and civilized enough to comprehend what he saw. Swords, shields, armor, arrows, and javelins in profusion, but also wagons disassembled for more efficient storage, and parts of things Caesar called siege towers, catapults, and ballistae, which, he claimed, could launch clouds of arrows longer than a man and stones three times as heavy. And there were all manner of tools and implements to manufacture more in the field.

Assuming that the Romans would feed their army primarily by foraging, Vercingetorix was surprised to see the huge amounts of grain being loaded, and more surprised still when Caesar told him that his legions could fight on such stuff, without meat, without their energy or spirits flagging. They were even loading wine, because, Caesar told him, Britain was likely to have none, or at any rate none that would be drinkable, and when Vercingetorix jocularly demanded a supply of beer for the Gauls as well, Caesar quite seriously ordered his quartermasters to see to it.

"Rome has turned war from an art into a science," Caesar told him as they reached the last dock in the line, where tents, stools, furniture, wax tablets, scrolls, maps, rugs, adzes, saws, hammers, and kegs of nails were being loaded. "It's the difference between a band of warriors, however large, and an army."

"But where is the glory in overwhelming your enemy with great engines that hurl huge stones and arrows?" Vercingetorix demanded. "Who among you will then be able to truly boast of victory in courageous battle?"

"Fear not, my young friend," said Caesar, "I am quite good enough with words to take care of that!" And he laughed at Vercingetorix's befuddlement. "Gaining victory by whatever means is the task of an army," he went on in a much more serious vein. "You Gauls fight for glory. The legions of Rome fight to win. Better inglorious victory than glorious defeat."

"Is winning everything?"

"Perhaps not," said Caesar, "for even victory is properly only a means to a political end. There is even that which we call 'Pyrrhic victory,' after a Greek king who won so many great and glorious battles at such cost in men and treasure that he destroyed his armies and impoverished his kingdom."

Vercingetorix found himself pondering this conundrum in silence. When they were quite alone, Caesar's demeanor became almost furtive, hesitant, a mood Vercingetorix had never seen afflicting him before.

"I sense you wish to discuss something other than military matters," Vercingetorix finally said.

Caesar nodded, but would not meet his eye, and, entirely uncharacteristically, he seemed reluctant to speak.

"What is it?" Vercingetorix said softly. "You can speak your heart to me."

"Can I?" said Caesar, looking out to sea.

"This is not at all like you. . . ."

"No, it isn't," said Caesar, still avoiding his gaze. "This is a delicate matter . . . and, well, I am not the most delicate of men. . . ."

"Speak plainly, then. Man to man."

Caesar shrugged, and now he did at last look Vercingetorix squarely in the eye.

"It's about Marah," he said.

"Marah . . . ?"

"How shall I put this . . . ? I have a wife I love back in Rome, I'm old enough to be Marah's father, while you . . ."

"What are you trying to tell me, Caesar?"

"For me, she was a companion for my lonely nights far from home. But for you . . . much more. . . ."

"It was a long time ago. . . ."

"Would you believe I didn't know?" said Caesar.

"No," said Vercingetorix.

"Good," said Caesar, managing a little smile. "I would not speak thusly to a man who was a fool. Yes, I knew, but that was before you and I met. And what I am trying to tell you, my young friend . . ."

He paused. He looked away again.

"You know, even as you have no father, I have no son, and, well . . ."

Once more Caesar's eloquence seemed to fail him.

"What I am saying is that, if it should come to pass that Marah becomes your—"

"*Queen?*"

Caesar laughed, and a certain tension seemed to be broken. "*Consort,* queen or not," he said. "I want you to know that that need not be something that comes between you and me. And were it possible for me to choose a son . . ."

He fell silent once more, then clasped Vercingetorix's right arm.

The man who had taken the first flower of the woman he would wed had told him there would be no blame if he stole her away. His father's enemy had told him he would be proud to have him as a son. He knew not what he truly felt, only that it brought tears close to his eyes.

All Vercingetorix could do was return the embrace.

X

A S THE LAST WAN SUNLIGHT sank beneath the invisible horizon, the hard wind continued to howl in off the Oceanus Britannicus, driving a heavy rain inland and whipping the slate-black sea into an evil cauldron of towering waves and foamy breakers. The ships fully laden with Roman legionnaires rolled sickeningly, and the lighter and more fragile ships, meant for the Gauls but not yet loaded, slammed against their docks.

Roman sailors and engineers, soaked and cursing, struggled to keep the docksides padded with whatever they could—bales of hay, sacks of grain, coils of rope—to prevent the storm from cracking the planking of the empty boats against them. Roman troops, who had boarded before the storm, lined the railings of the galleys, puking over the sides or sucking lungfuls of air in an effort to avoid doing so. These were the lucky ones who had reached the railings first and held back their comrades on the decks with knees, elbows, and fists. The unlucky ones were constrained to do their vomiting on the crowded deck, on each other, amidst sporadic fistfights, while those who had failed to gain deck space fared even worse.

The Roman encampment was empty, save for the hostage huts and the tent of Caesar, which had not been struck before the storm broke, and a disconsolate rearguard cohort manning the gate and patrolling a sea of mud in the pelting rain.

Outside the palisade, it was impossible to keep fires going, and the majority of the Gauls did not have tents. From time to time, singly or in small groups, warriors slunk off homeward, to the unconvincing derision of their fellows.

No lightning flashed, no thunder rumbled. It was a dull, plodding storm of the sort that could drag on for hours or days, nor was there presently a sign of its breaking.

The rain beat a drumroll against Caesar's tent, and the wind flapping and snapping the canvas made the oil lamps flicker. All but the essentials had been packed away and loaded, and the atmosphere inside matched his iresome gloom. Nor was Caesar the only one in a foul humor. All of his generals who would go to Britain save Tulius were already aboard the boats with their legions, and no doubt wishing they were here in the tent.

Caesar had told Labienus that he was to be left behind to serve as "acting proconsul of all Gaul," making it sound like a boon. But Labienus was not fooled, and kept glaring sullenly at Tulius. Nor was his mood improved by Caesar's order that the change in command was to be kept secret from the Gauls until they were safely on their way across to Britain and there was nothing they could do about it.

Tulius himself, dutiful pragmatist that he was, knew full well that what might seem to the innocent Labienus to be a promotion over him was far from a sweet plum. It was in fact a nasty assignment to eliminate those Gauls who must be eliminated, and who were going to be outraged and distrustful in the extreme when they were informed of the mysterious change of command.

Caesar had confined the leaders of the Gallic auxiliaries to the encampment as soon as his legions starting boarding the boats, according to plan, but he had made what in retrospect was the mistake of taking down their tents before the storm blew in. Now they had been huddled here in his tent for long hours, muttering and bickering among themselves. Caesar had spent more time outside in the mud and rain with his rearguard than was necessary, preferring the foul weather to the foul mood of these Gauls, half of whom demanded he give up and re-establish the comforts of the camp, while the other half groused that the gods were cursing the whole enterprise and it should therefore be abandoned.

Caesar certainly didn't want to unload everyone and re-establish the camp, at which point, no doubt, the sun would come out, and Apollo, having overcome Neptune, would have a good laugh at his expense. But putting to sea in the teeth of a storm would no doubt further tempt Neptune's wrath, and abandoning the whole enterprise was out of the question.

Unload, wait for better weather, and start all over again?

Load the Gauls and their horses, set sail, and hope that the weather would improve or the fleet would make it across to Britain in the storm?

The decision was Caesar's to make, his chances of making the right one equaled that of making the wrong one, and he could not procrastinate forever, so he had sent Gisstus to fetch Demetrius, the Greek soothsayer. Caesar did not place much faith in soothsaying as a predictive art, but there were times when it had its other uses. As a sometime pontifex, he had learned the craft of making the bones and guts say what he wanted them to. But since he didn't know *what* he wanted them to say, that was not going to work this time. Now he had to make an arbitrary decision that could determine the outcome of the whole venture. The oracle of a soothsayer might be no better than the toss of a coin, but it was no worse either. And if someone was going to take the blame for a wrong guess, better Demetrius than Gaius Julius Caesar.

Gisstus arrived, soaking wet, with a gray-haired old man in a white robe vaguely resembling that of a druid and embroidered with a profusion of stars, comets, constellations, and other astrological arcana. The mystical effect was considerably marred by the fact that the rain had rendered it translucent and clinging, revealing the resemblance between the corpus it contained and one of the sacrificial tools of his trade, a scrawny chicken.

"Well, when will the storm end, Demetrius?" demanded Caesar.

"The omens are not clear, noble Caesar—"

I needed you to tell me this? Caesar thought peevishly, though he could sympathize with Demetrius, who, like any accomplished soothsayer, plied the trade mostly by telling his clientele what they wished to hear and discerning what that was by reading them, not the omens.

"Then allow me to help you clarify them," Caesar said. "Speak! When will the storm end? If you are proved right, I'll make you a rich man. If you're wrong, I'll nail you to a cross and feed you to the fishes!"

Demetrius gave him a half-quizzical, half-terrified look. Caesar, without altering the sternness of his visage, shot a sidelong glance at the semicircle of Gauls, who were taking this farce quite earnestly.

"Great Caesar, the skies are hidden, and the gods of this land are not ours," Demetrius intoned, "but this storm will end within the week if a bullock is sacrificed to Neptune."

Remembering that Gisstus had ironically suggested much the same thing, Caesar could barely keep from grinning, despite the dire situation. Gisstus himself had an even harder time choking back his laughter.

"And how long if we sacrifice two bullocks?" Caesar said. "How many will it take to end the storm by morning?"

Demetrius shrugged.

"Perhaps," said Caesar, his anger rapidly becoming genuine, "*one Greek soothsayer* might do the trick?"

At this Demetrius paled. "Let the gods themselves speak," he said, producing a coin from within his robe and holding it aloft like a talisman. "And not through such a poor creature as myself, but through a man of destiny—yourself, Caesar." He handed Caesar the coin. It was old. It was Greek. One side bore a portrait of Alexander the Great.

"Toss it in the air, let it fall. If it lands with Great Alexander upright, the storm will end by dawn."

"And if not?" Caesar demanded.

"If not," said Demetrius, staring him full in the face, "the gods refuse to speak, and not even you can command them."

Caesar found himself laughing inwardly, even though the joke was on him. All this to avoid choosing by tossing a coin, and Demetrius had weaseled out of it by bringing it down to a coin toss anyway.

He tossed the coin in the air and let it fall to the dirt floor of the tent. The Gauls clustered round, leaning over the portent.

"Face upward!" cried Comm of the Atrebates, whose appetite for loot and glory apparently remained keener than his fear of the stormy sea.

Gisstus reached down, picked up the coin, tossed it to Caesar. "Alexander has spoken," he said.

"You had better be right," Caesar said, flipping the coin in the direction of Demetrius, who plucked it skillfully out of the air like a trained monkey. And so had I, Caesar thought. "We load the boats now."

"On the toss of a coin!" groaned Dumnorix.

"Seasick again, Dumnorix?" said Comm, to derisive laughter.

"It's the will of the gods," said Luctor.

"What if the storm lasts for *days*?" demanded Dumnorix.

"You don't trust the word of the gods?" said Caesar.

"*Your* gods, not mine," Dumnorix told him.

"And not even *yours* at that," said Epirod. "It's not even a Roman coin. Alexander's not even a Roman hero."

"They have a point, Caesar," said Tulius.

"*What?*" exclaimed Caesar.

"Far be it from me to challenge the words of the gods speaking through coin tosses or chicken guts," Tulius said sardonically, "but if we load our friends here on the boats, and it turns out that whosoever gods spoke through the coin toss are playing tricks on we mere mortals . . ." Tulius shrugged eloquently, glancing at the Gauls with a sympathetic eye.

Caesar's immediate reaction was anger at a subordinate's presuming to argue with his order in the presence of others, but then he realized that the clever Tulius was using this situation to begin to win the favor of the Gauls, which would well serve his mission later.

Besides, Tulius *did* have a point.

Still . . .

"What do *you* say?" he asked Vercingetorix, certainly his firmest supporter among the Gauls. "Would a few days waiting out a storm aboard ship turn your warriors into sniveling cowards unable to hold their own against savages?"

"Gauls will fight bravely under the worst circumstances!"

More than half of the Gauls cheered at this, if not exactly whole-heartedly.

But not Dumnorix. "Well spoken, silver-tongued Vercingetorix," he said sarcastically. "But days spent aboard ship in port during a storm puking our guts out and trying to control terrified horses, followed by a voyage across the Oceanus Britannicus, *would* be the worst circumstances."

"You speak like a man with a better idea," said Vercingetorix.

"Alas, I speak only as a man with a less terrible idea, if not by much," said Dumnorix.

"Or a coward," muttered Comm.

"Coward, am I?" shouted Dumnorix, rounding on him. "I'll show you who's a coward!" He turned to Caesar. "Here is my challenge, Caesar, if you dare accept it! Load us and our horses on your boats. But at dawn, we set sail for Britain, storm or no storm, even in the face of rains as heavy as waterfalls and waves as high as mountains!"

There was a moment of stunned silence in which all that could be heard was the flapping and snapping of the tent fabric in the wind and the drumming of the rain upon it.

Dumnorix ran his eyes slowly around the assembled tribal leaders, and Caesar saw that he had captured them. And then he sealed it, and by so doing, captured the situation, and Caesar as well.

"Accept this challenge from a seasick coward," he said, "and I myself will be the first to lead my men aboard!"

The Gauls, being Gauls, could only roar their approval.

"Well spoken yourself, silver-tongued Dumnorix!" said Vercingetorix, and gave a Gallic arm-embrace to his erstwhile rival. "And I myself will be the second!"

"So be it!" said Caesar, and Dumnorix gave him an ironic Roman salute and stalked dramatically out of the tent, into the teeth of the storm.

And so, in the end, the gods had smiled upon him through the darkness of this stormy night, for the Gauls had led themselves exactly where he wanted them to go, had they not?

Dumnorix, flanked by two Roman legionnaires and trailed by a centurion, trudged through the sucking mud to the palisade gate, thoroughly soaked, his long hair plastered to his forehead, his mustache dripping rain. He had never doubted that this invasion of Britain was a trap, and not a subtle one. But it was a powerful trap, for any leader of Gauls who failed to fall into it would be deemed a coward, and any Gaul deemed a coward would soon have no warriors to command.

Dumnorix was certain that the storm had been sent by one of his gods, not Caesar's, probably by the war god Teutates, and not as a curse but as a blessing. For he had seen no escape from the Roman trap until it came.

The gate to the palisade was barred shut and guarded by four sour-faced and sodden legionnaires. "Open the gate!" said Dumnorix. "Dumnorix, vergobret of the Edui, would address his men and give them their orders!"

The gate guards neither moved nor spoke.

"It's all right," said the centurion. "It's Caesar's orders he'll be giving. We're finally going to board the Gauls. And when that's done, we can close down this place for good, and get in out of the slop ourselves!"

The guards slipped the bar and opened the gate.

Dumnorix strode through with his Roman escort, through the muck and rain, and into the Eduen camp, where his men hunkered miserably in the mud and rain under cloaks and blankets pressed into pathetic service as makeshift tents. He sought out his standard-bearer, had the boar standard planted in the middle of the encampment, ordered a trumpeter to blow a summons, and stood there beside it in the pouring rain until as many of his warriors as possible had gathered within earshot.

It was a sullen and grumblesome gathering that Dumnorix found himself facing, and not without justice. Had he not led them into this disaster, however unwillingly? And now here their vergobret stood, facing them in muck and rain, guarded, or so it appeared, by three Romans. Were I one of you, I would not have much use for the vergobret of the Edui either, Dumnorix thought bitterly. Well, I led you into it, and honor demands I lead you out of it. Even at the cost of honor.

"I have been ordered by Caesar to lead you out of this storm and onto the boats," he began, gesturing floridly with his left arm to mask the manner in which he let his right hang loose at his side, close by the pommel of his sword.

This was greeted with just the groans of dismay and mutters of anger he had anticipated. He raised his left hand high, palm outward, in a demand for silence, and his right caressed the sword pommel in a natural completion of the gesture. This did little to silence the protests. But it was not supposed to.

"I know what you are thinking," Dumnorix shouted over the tumult in a disparaging tone. "You believe that the Romans would only have us board their boats in the teeth of this howling storm to put to sea and drown us in the maelstrom."

At this there was a roar of outrage, albeit a confused one, for there was agreement with his words but not at all with the sardonic tone in which he had delivered them.

Dumnorix took a deep breath.

"Well, you are right!" he roared, drawing his sword and plunging it into the neck of the Roman to his right before the man even had time to be surprised. "It's a trap! Scatter to the four winds! Return to our own lands, where we belong!"

"Who will board his men after Vercingetorix?" demanded Caesar. "Don't all speak at—"

He stopped in mid-sentence, suddenly staring toward the tent entrance. Vercingetorix whirled around to see a Roman centurion, bleeding profusely from wounds on his right arm and left thigh, half staggering, half falling into the tent.

"The Edui . . . Dumnorix . . . Caesar . . ."

Caesar rushed to his side and cradled him in his arms, heedless of the blood. "Go to the ships and fetch a surgeon!" he ordered Tulius, and only when the general had departed on an ordinary servant's errand did he speak to the centurion, displaying a sense of priorities that left Vercingetorix quite touched.

"Easy, man, help is on the way," Caesar then said gently. "Now, do you think you can tell us what happened?"

"Dumnorix . . . he . . . tricked us. . . . When he spoke to his men . . ."

The centurion hesitated, wincing in pain; then forced himself to continue. "The Romans would drown us in this storm, he shouted . . . and he drew his sword and cut down one of the guards before . . . before I could . . . draw my own . . . and by the time I did, Edui were rushing forward to aid him, he was shouting at them to scatter and flee. . . . It was all swords and confusion. . . ."

Caesar's face had been darkening with anger and flushing red as he listened to this. "I am shamed to have failed you, Caesar . . . but there were only three of us . . . they took us by surprise . . ." the centurion said.

Now purple veins in Caesar's temple throbbed with rage, yet he managed to lay the wounded centurion gently on the ground. "No blame," he said. "For your bravery against hopeless odds, you shall be promoted to primus pilius."

But when he rounded on the Gauls, his fury was uncontained. "I'll crucify the cowardly bastard when I catch him, and all who fled!" he roared. "And if this man dies, I'll execute the Eduen hostages too! I'll . . . I'll . . ."

"Calm yourself, Caesar," said his man Gisstus, "you know—"

"I'll . . . I'll . . ."

Caesar's tongue seemed to turn to wood in his mouth, his body began to shake, his knees crumpled, his eyes rolled upward, showing only whites; the Gauls shrank backward as he began to foam at the mouth like a mad dog—

—all but Vercingetorix, who had learned of this malady in the druid school and knew what it was before Gisstus spoke its Roman name.

"The falling sickness!"

"Touched by the gods!" cried Comm.

Vercingetorix had already dropped to his knees at Caesar's side, and as he had been taught, he jammed the heel of his left hand into Caesar's mouth to prevent him from biting his tongue, wincing at the pain of the bite as he kept Caesar's teeth pried open. He pressed the thumb of his right hand hard into the back of Caesar's neck, rotating it rhythmically.

"What are you—"

"Druid magic!" said Epirod. "I have seen this before."

Caesar emerged from the blinding white light of the fit to find himself supine on the ground with a hand in his mouth and a not unpleasant pressure at the back of his neck.

He looked up and saw the face of Vercingetorix looking down on him, then realized the hand was his. And Caesar's teeth were biting cruelly into it, his mouth tasting blood.

Hastily, he spit out the hand, pried himself upright, saw that the blood was Vercingetorix's, not his own.

"Your hand . . ."

"It is nothing, Caesar; I've had worse from playing too roughly with dogs. . . ."

"Still . . ."

As his wits returned to full clarity, he saw that the Gauls were staring down at him with expressions of fear tinged with awe, and then he remembered that many of the superstitious believed that victims of the falling sickness—among them, some said, Great Alexander himself—were favored by the gods. Indeed, there were times he believed it himself, times when he had returned from wherever his spirit went with visions.

But this was not one of them.

On the other hand . . .

"What are you staring at?" he shouted. "Have you never seen the gods speak thusly to a man before?"

The Gauls shrank back fearfully, as well the treacherous, lying bastards should. All save Vercingetorix, who offered him his uninjured hand instead.

Just as Caesar was rising shakily to his feet with this aid, Tulius returned to the tent with the surgeon.

"Caesar—"

"I'm all right, Tulius," Caesar told him brusquely. Then, to the surgeon, "Tend to the wounded man, while I tend to *these*."

He glared at the Gauls. "It would appear that Dumnorix and the Edui have robbed us all of glory and fortune—"

"What?" exclaimed Tulius.

"Dumnorix has fled with an unknown number of his troops," Labienus told him. "So much for your chance to lead an army of Gauls to glory, Tulius. The invasion can hardly go ahead now that—"

"That's for *me* to decide," Caesar snapped peremptorily.

"I only—"

"Never mind that now, Labienus. I put *you* in charge of order here. Restore it. Take however many men you need off the boats and do it! And have whatever so-called leaders of the Edui still remain here brought to me. Including that lying dog's brother, Diviacx!"

Few words were spoken among the Gauls while the Romans rounded up the Eduen prisoners, and Vercingetorix himself was at a loss for words. Caesar huddled in a corner of the tent in hushed conversation with his man Gisstus, whose face always seemed familiar to Vercingetorix somehow, and who, though no Roman noble or general, always seemed to have Caesar's ear.

It was Decimus Brutus, a Roman officer not much older than himself, who finally brought in half a dozen sodden Edui under the guard of an equal number of legionnaires, among them a fearful Diviacx and a defiant-looking Litivak.

"As you can see, Caesar, *I* did not betray you," Diviacx whined, "I'm still here—"

"Silence!" roared Caesar. "Dumnorix is your brother, you treacherous swine!"

"Am I responsible for that? I'll have Litivak—"

"Another unbidden word and I'll rip your tongue out myself!" Caesar said. "Brutus, what's the situation out there?"

"Utter confusion, Caesar. Perhaps two-thirds of the Edui scattered when Dumnorix fled." Brutus nodded at Litivak. "But this man rallied the rest to him and kept them from leaving."

"This is true?"

"Someone had to uphold the honor of the Edui," Litivak said. "We are not all oath-breakers, Caesar."

"We shall see about the *honor* of the Edui when we have Dumnorix before us," said Caesar. "Brutus, take as many men as you need, and track him—"

"You can't do that, Caesar!" cried Diviacx.

"*You* are telling *me* what I can't do?" Caesar roared. "And when did I give you permission to speak?"

"I crave your pardon for misspeaking myself," Diviacx said in a groveling tone that curdled Vercingetorix's stomach. "But allow me to explain, Caesar."

Caesar gave Diviacx a curt, contemptuous nod, clearly as disgusted with him as Vercingetorix was.

"This is a matter of Eduen honor, to be—"

"Eduen honor?" shouted Caesar. "About as real as the teeth of chickens!"

"Something that my brother has stolen from us and that must be returned," Diviacx told him. "He must be condemned by a druid enforcing the law of—"

"Congratulations, Diviacx," said Caesar, "you have just volunteered. And the verdict and punishment had better not be in doubt."

"So be it," Diviacx said softly. "But if Dumnorix is captured and held by your men, no Gaul will see this as other than an act of Rome."

"He's right!" cried Comm.

"No Gaul must be seized by Rome!" said Litivak.

"It is true," Vercingetorix told Caesar. "Dumnorix has disgraced the Edui, but if your men seize him, it will rob the Edui of the chance to redeem their honor, and his punishment will be seen not as druid justice but as your vengeance."

"He is right," said Litivak. "Do this thing, Caesar, and what remains of the Eduen army will no longer heed me unless I denounce you."

Caesar grew more thoughtful at this. "Point taken," he muttered sourly, "but—"

"Send Litivak after him," said Diviacx, "a man who has proved his loyalty."

"I'll not trust another Eduen with anything until Dumnorix is captured and disposed of."

"Then send Vercingetorix," said Litivak.

"*Vercingetorix?*" cried both Caesar and Diviacx. Vercingetorix himself was taken aback.

"He's an Arverne who has won the admiration of many of the Edui," said Litivak. He gazed at Vercingetorix with more warmth than Vercingetorix had ever expected to see on an Eduen face.

"Vercingetorix . . . ?" said Caesar in quite another tone, his fury apparently slaked by this suggestion for some reason Vercingetorix himself did not understand.

"Let him take a mixed party of Arverni and Edui," suggested Litivak.

"Oh no!" said Caesar. "I'll permit no more Edui out of my sight until Dumnorix is captured, condemned, and executed."

There was a long moment of silence as Caesar and the Gauls glared at each other.

Then Caesar smiled at them.

"I will send either Brutus with a force of Romans after him, or Vercingetorix with his Arverni," he said with the poisonous sweetness of a dose of hemlock in a cup of honey. "But let it not be said that Caesar is not a reasonable man. You get to choose."

There was another long silence.

"Do I hear any votes for Brutus?" said Caesar.

When there were none, he turned to Vercingetorix, cocking an inquisitive eyebrow at him. Gisstus seemed to be attempting to gain his attention, but Caesar paid him no heed.

"I cannot order you to do this, my friend," Caesar told him, "nor would I if I could. But would you volunteer?"

"I cannot refuse such a request," Vercingetorix told Caesar, then cast a black look at Diviacx. "Nor will I pretend that it displeases me to do it."

"Get rid of them," Gisstus hissed urgently in Caesar's ear when Vercingetorix had departed. "We must speak privately at once."

It sounded like an order, and Caesar would have taken umbrage at being addressed thusly by any other man.

"Tulius, take these *noble Gauls* to their men and have them see to it that there are no further defections," he ordered. "And make sure they're securely guarded while they do it. Brutus, take Diviacx back to his tent, and guard him well against loneliness."

"You've made a mistake, Caesar," Gisstus told him as soon as they were alone in the tent.

"How so?" asked Caesar irritably. He did not at all like being told he was wrong by anyone, even Gisstus. But any commander who trusted no one to tell him such things was courting disaster.

"Dumnorix may know too much," Gisstus told him.

"He does . . . ? For whom to know?"

"Vercingetorix."

"Keltill!" Caesar groaned, realizing that Gisstus was right. The minor matter of eliminating that troublemaker now threatened major problems.

Diviacx had condemned Keltill under druid law, but Caesar had encouraged—or, to be blunt about it, ordered—the druid to get it done if the situation turned out to warrant it. No one else knew this, save Gobanit, who was dead, and of course Gisstus.

As far as Caesar knew . . .

But Dumnorix was Diviacx's brother.

And however much Diviacx had or had not told him, he knew that Gisstus had been there when Keltill was seized, disguised as a simple Eduen warrior. . . .

"You really think he knows?" asked Caesar.

Gisstus shrugged. "We certainly can't be sure he doesn't."

"But if so, why would he have held his silence so long?"

"If he knows, Dumnorix would have held his silence to protect his brother and to avoid Arverne retribution against the Edui. But now that half the Edui disown him, and Diviacx is ready to condemn him to death—"

"He has no reason to remain silent and every reason to speak and take vengeance before he dies . . ." groaned Caesar. "Take care of it yourself, Gisstus. But use a Teuton weapon. It won't do to have our hand visible behind this one either."

It was still raining hard when Vercingetorix reached the Arverne encampment. There were neither stars nor moon to see by, and Dumnorix's defectors had broken up into small bands and scattered. But Vercingetorix realized that Dumnorix's choices were limited. To the northwest was the sea, to the east were the lands of Teuton tribes, so surely the Eduen vergobret would be trying to make his way back south, to the lands of the Edui, within a wedge-shaped territory between the coast and the Rhine. And he was less than an hour ahead.

Leaving Critognat in charge of the rest of his men, Vercingetorix dispersed a thousand of his warriors into small groups, and sent them south along an ever-widening front with orders not only to seek out Dumnorix directly but to question everyone in their paths, for surely *someone* would have seen Dumnorix and his men.

Taking Baravax and a dozen guards, Vercingetorix rode out several leagues behind the center of this widening front. Rather than trying to capture Dumnorix themselves, any party picking up the trail was to follow it cautiously at a distance and send a messenger back to him.

. . .

Hunched over on their horses against the rain, two men in rough brown peasants' cloaks but with Teuton javelins lashed to their saddles rode a mile or so behind Vercingetorix's party, hidden from them by the rain, the distance, and the darkness, but tracking them easily enough by the noise of their horses and the churned-up mud of their passage.

"What are they *doing*, Gisstus?" muttered his companion, a chunky balding man with a befuddled and grim demeanor. "And why are we following them? I thought we were supposed to be after Dumnorix."

"We *are*, Marius, and so are they," Gisstus told him. "That's why we're following Vercingetorix. He's got hundreds of men, and he's using them like a pack of hounds. The hounds find the trail, then the hunters run down the prey. . . ."

"But the jackals following them move in—"

"*Wolves*, please, Marius, *wolves*!" said Gisstus. "A much more honorable predator! The very one, in fact, whose teats suckled our noble ancestors Romulus and Remus."

The storm was easing, though the rain had not yet ceased, and Vercingetorix could detect a hint of gray lightening the blackness of the sky at the horizon when a rider came galloping up to his party out of the southwest. The horse, a roan mare, was drenched with rain and its own foam, and wheezing with exhaustion. The rider was a wiry blond man a few years older than himself, helmetless, but with a sodden orange Arverne cloak pulled up over his head against the rain, and was breathless with excitement when he reported.

"We've found Dumnorix! My men are following him as we speak!"

"Where is he?"

The man seemed to catch his breath, or perhaps to rein himself in as he had his horse. "Well, actually, Vercingetorix," he admitted in a somewhat more subdued voice, "we've found his *trail*."

"You've not actually seen Dumnorix?"

The man shook his head.

"Well, then, how do you know—"

"A village. A half-dozen or so Edui practically rode through it, they said—"

"But how—"

"One of them had a vergobret's standard. It was lashed to his saddle, not held aloft, but a boy saw the boar."

"But if you never saw them, how—"

"I am *Oranix,*" the fellow declared, as if that was supposed to settle things. Then, when Vercingetorix showed no sign of reacting to what he clearly had intended as a boast: "You haven't heard of me? I am the greatest tracker among the Arverni, and my men are experienced hunters all. Once we find tracks, we never lose the trail. I myself once tracked a wounded stag for six days across the passage of whole herds of deer before I slew it."

There was something about this fellow that had Vercingetorix grinning. "Where are they heading?" he asked.

"Southwest."

Vercingetorix turned to Baravax. "Have one of your men exchange horses with the great Oranix," he ordered. "You *can* lead us to wherever your friends went?"

"Of course!" said Oranix indignantly. "They blaze a trail behind for us to follow, that's the way it's done, you know! Or did you imagine we grew to manhood within the walls of Gergovia?"

Oranix's hunters had indeed blazed a trail that Oranix could easily follow, though Vercingetorix could not see how, and, moving as fast as the muddy ground would allow, they caught up with the hunters within the hour. All four bore bows, and all were helmetless and shieldless and garbed as woodsmen.

They were no more than a mile from the coastal marshes. Dawn was breaking, the rain had dwindled to a foul misty drizzle, the ground here was viscous brown muck, and Vercingetorix did not need Oranix or his men to tell him that the trail of churned-up mud and trampled turf they were following led straight into the swamp.

"Six of them."

"Could be eight."

"No more than a half hour ago."

"Maybe less."

The spirits of Vercingetorix's men became as sodden as the terrain as he led them toward the marshes, for Dumnorix had made a cunning choice. These bogs were crisscrossed by innumerable creeks and rivulets, and what so-called dry land there was would be watery ooze where hoofprints or footprints would disappear as soon as they were made. Once inside, Dumnorix could choose any point at which to emerge, and one would either need to surround the entire marshland with an army, or be favored by the gods with fantastic luck, to intercept him emerging.

Not even Oranix and his hunters showed any enthusiasm for entering when they reached the margin of this dank and forbidding tangle of moss-greened trees, tall moisture-laden grasses, pools of stagnant water, clinging and reeking mud. A thick layer of fog lay heavily over it, from which emerged mournful cries of unseen birds, the guttural croaks of frogs.

"*Can* you track them in there, Oranix?" Vercingetorix asked the self-styled great hunter.

Oranix shook his head. "Not possible. We'll have to use *your* technique, Vercingetorix—search out and flush our prey, not track it, the way we hunt pheasant with dogs. We separate into groups of two and—"

"Separate!" moaned Baravax.

"In there?"

Vercingetorix's warriors were unashamed to show each other their fears. Oranix and his hunters regarded them with contempt.

"You are afraid?" shouted Vercingetorix. "Of frogs and birds and mud? I myself will go alone. And we will all stay within voice range by making the calls of birds from time to time—"

"The merle," suggested one of the hunters.

"A bird that shuns marshlands—good choice," agreed another.

"We'll always know it's us, and I doubt this Dumnorix is woodsman enough to know the difference," explained Oranix.

"In any event, I doubt he and his men will be paying much attention to birdcalls," said the hunter who had suggested the merle. "Goes like this." And he demonstrated a sweet, harmonic, warbling whistle.

"Anyone who encounters more of them than he can deal with, makes the cry of the wolf to attract aid," said Vercingetorix.

"He'll attract a whole wolf pack instead!" exclaimed Baravax.

All the hunters laughed. "Fear not," said Oranix, "wolves no more favor such environs than we do."

"Well, they're entering the marshes," said Gisstus, lying prone in the tall, muddy grass of a hillock. "And so must we."

"On horseback?" groaned Marius.

Gisstus shook his head. "You're right," he said. "You can hear a horse stumbling around for miles in there. Dumnorix and those with him are trying to evade detection, so they'll end up on foot if they haven't dismounted already. And so must we."

"I like it not, Gisstus; it's a filthy mess in there."

Gisstus stood up, the front of his tunic caked with mud. "Our calling has always been a dirty one, Marius," he said, "or hadn't you noticed?"

As he waded knee-deep in slimy water, leading his horse, long since rendered useless and worse by the treacherous terrain, it seemed to Vercingetorix that he had been slogging aimlessly through this swamp forever, even though the position of a wan sun dimly visible from time to time through the slowly evaporating fog told him it was not yet noon.

Far-distant cries and clashes of metal on metal and three inept wolf calls told him that some of his men had encountered Dumnorix's. But not Dumnorix, Vercingetorix hoped, for he wanted Dumnorix for himself; even though Caesar wished him brought back alive to be tried and condemned by Diviacx, if he resisted—

There was another wolf call, this one much closer, then shouts and screams, the sounds of battle, another wolf call, and another, and another, more cries, and clashes of weapons.

Vercingetorix waded heavily through the swamp toward the battle sounds, but he could not have gone a quarter of a league before they died away into silence—

Then he heard a sodden sucking sound.

Vercingetorix made himself as still and silent as a tree of the marshland.

Yes, those were footfalls, and too heavy to be other than human, unless those of a horse.

And no horse could be making those guttural cursing sounds.

The footfalls seemed to be moving in his direction, but with the tall grass, the undergrowth, and the muffling tricks of the fog, it was difficult to tell exactly—

His horse whinnied.

The footfalls stopped.

Vercingetorix pondered this ill luck for a moment, then realized it could be turned to good fortune. He dropped the reins, drew his sword, and slapped the horse hard on the rump with the flat of it.

The horse whinnied again, this time in protest, as it plodded clumsily and noisily away through the swamp grass, and Vercingetorix, moving from tree to tree, bush to bush, shadow to shadow, followed at a discreet distance, making himself invisible in plain sight.

"I tell you, Marius, not even one famished wolf would venture into this swamp, let alone a whole pack," Gisstus said in a hushed tone as the two Romans crouched in the tall grass. "And even if they did, they certainly could do a better job of howling than *that*."

"And how, may I ask, do you intend to find anyone in here, Gisstus?"

"I don't. I'll let them find us."

"But they don't even know we're here."

"They're signaling each other with these wolf calls. Haven't you heard the clashes of arms before and after? So I'll just call them to us."

Marius frowned unhappily. "But how do you know whether it's Vercingetorix's party or Dumnorix's you'll be calling?"

"I don't. It doesn't matter. The one is seeking the other. We keep them all coming toward us, stay hidden as they stumble into each other, and wait for Dumnorix to make his appearance."

So saying, Gisstus raised his mouth to the sky and his hands to his mouth, and made the sound of a human inexpertly imitating the cry of a wolf.

That howl seemed close, but Vercingetorix refrained from moving toward it, intent on following the horse that was the bait in his moving trap, for the animal was making a lot of noise as it struggled through the swamp, and beyond he could hear the footfalls moving tentatively in its direction.

"What's that?" hissed Marius nervously, dropping down on his belly in the mud at the sound of something heavy thumping and crashing toward them. Gisstus took cover below the tops of the swamp grass too, then groaned as he saw a riderless horse emerge from a copse of trees a tenth of a league or so away and begin listlessly cropping the vegetation.

Vercingetorix stood still and silent behind the moss-covered bole of an old tree, watching his horse grazing, and listening to the footsteps moving through the trees on the other side of the marsh-grass meadow, this way, that way, circling, observing.

At length, Dumnorix—shieldless, on foot, caked with brown mud and green smears of vegetation as well as the blood of battle—peered out at the horse from between two trees.

Vercingetorix dropped to his hands and knees and began crawling invisibly and silently through the tall grass toward the horse as Dumnorix, in a crouch but clearly visible, began to edge toward it.

By the time Dumnorix was nearly upon the horse, so was Vercingetorix. He drew his sword, leapt to his feet, and ran at him, shouting, "Dumnorix! Defend yourself, you cowardly Eduen bastard!"

The horse bolted and ran.

Dumnorix whirled to face him, drawing his own sword, and parried the blow with a loud sideways clang of steel on steel.

"I should've known that Caesar would send his catamite!" he shouted, aiming a wild, swinging blow, which Vercingetorix easily enough parried.

Containing his rage was another matter. "This isn't for Caesar!" he shouted, with a sweep of his sword that Dumnorix countered with ease. "This is for my father!"

"You hear that?" asked Marius.

Gisstus covered Marius' mouth with his hand, raised himself up high enough above the top of the swamp grass to see the two men clanging steel against steel and shouting at each other, then dropped down again and began crawling toward them through the cover of the grass, clutching his Teuton javelin.

"Your father?" said Dumnorix, seemingly with enough genuine perplexity to let his sword droop along with his expression. Honor forbade Vercingetorix to take lethal advantage of this, even against a man such as Dumnorix.

"You think I don't know?" he cried instead. "You killed my father!"

"I did what?" Dumnorix exclaimed, now slowly bringing up his sword and circling backward, away from Vercingetorix.

Vercingetorix began a slow, deliberate circling dance toward him, but his mind was clogged with black thoughts, and his heart burned with the memory, and the blood pounded through him, and he could not strike without first spewing it all forth.

"Gobanit set the flame, but your foul brother condemned him, and *you* were there, you commanded the guard! Your plot! Your treachery! Your orders! *You killed my father!*"

"You fool! You idiot!"

With a wordless shout, Vercingetorix leapt forward and stabbed at Dumnorix's stomach. Dumnorix parried the thrust, but clumsily, and Vercingetorix was able to slide his blade along Dumnorix's sword and plunge a finger's length of it into Dumnorix's gut below his buckler. He was about to lean into it to turn it into a killing stroke when—

—a javelin pierced Dumnorix's back, the point emerging from his chest, as he screamed in outrage and agony:

"It was Caesar!"

"Caesar . . . ?" whispered Vercingetorix, as the dying Dumnorix staggered backward and collapsed into the mud. "*Caesar . . . ?*"

"With my dying breath, I swear it," said Dumnorix, raising his head in a final effort, speaking thickly, blood bubbling out of his mouth. "Who else could make Gobanit and Diviacx act together? Who else was Keltill's declared enemy? Who else would set Arverni against Edui? Who else but—"

"*Caesar?*"

Something was up and moving in the grass, in the direction from which the javelin must have come—

Vercingetorix whirled to see a running man. His spirit filled with fury and agony but empty now of the thought that slows the mind, Vercingetorix flung his sword like a spear and skewered the running man through the back.

As that man had skewered Dumnorix, who now lay unmoving in a growing pool of his own blood.

Vercingetorix ran to the man he had slain, who lay facedown in the muddy grass, pulled out his sword, kicked the corpse over on its back. The dead man was Gisstus.

Caesar's man Gisstus.

Not wearing his customary Roman vestments but disguised by the simple brown cloak and tunic of a Gallic peasant.

Time seemed to stop as Vercingetorix regarded just the dead face and not the latest disguise. The dark hair. The olive-tinged complexion. Time crawled backward into the long ago, into the plaza of Gergovia, to the day of Keltill's burning. And now Vercingetorix knew why the face of Gisstus had always seemed familiar.

For, as he regarded that face in death, he saw it cloaked in the blue of an Eduen warrior at his father's last feast, whispering orders in the ear of a fearfully reluctant Gobanit. *Commanding* the druid Diviacx. And only one man commanded Gisstus.

"Caesar!" Vercingetorix shouted in soul-deep agony. *"Caesar!"*

And then yet another of Caesar's cowardly assassins was up and running for his wretched life through the swamp grass.

This one Vercingetorix knew he wanted alive. The man was no woodsman, nor was he in the prime strength of youth, and it took but a short chase for Vercingetorix to exhaust and corner him against a thick tangle of undergrowth and trees.

The Roman in peasant disguise had no sword, only a javelin and a dagger, and these he tossed away.

"I yield!" he said fearfully.

"You yield? So what!"

"You'd kill a disarmed man? Where is your honor, barbarian?"

"Where is yours, Roman, as you beg for your worthless life?"

But then it was that Vercingetorix realized why he needed this man alive. "Perhaps not entirely worthless," he told the Roman coldly.

Prodding him in the small of his back with the point of his sword hard enough to draw blood but not to do serious injury, he marched the Roman back to the body of Gisstus.

"You want your life, you shall have it," he said. "It is of only one use to me. . . ."

He reached down with his left hand, grabbed the head of Gisstus by the hair, and lifted it out of the mud. Then he sliced it from its neck with a one-handed stroke of his sword and threw it, still gushing blood and dripping gore, at the stomach of the Roman, who caught it reflexively.

"*Someone* must bear my tribute to Caesar," he said.

And then, as the Roman ran off in terror, Vercingetorix raised his eyes to the sky, where the fog had given way to blue, and gave free vent to the rage he now allowed to course through him and fill his spirit. He howled at the heavens, at the gods, at Gaius Julius Caesar, at his own stupidity, at destiny itself, full-throated, at the top of his lungs, like a wolf.

Only Tulius and Labienus had chanced to be in the tent with Caesar when this Marius had unceremoniously dumped the severed head of

Gisstus on the camp table, where it now stared up at him, blue-skinned, blind-eyed, but somehow having retained that sardonic expression even in death, as if bidding him a final bilious farewell.

"Tribute, he called it!" Caesar cried. *"Tribute!"*

"That's what he said, Caesar," Marius said fearfully. "And when I escaped, he was howling like a mad dog."

Tears welled up in Caesar's eyes, tears that surprised him, for not until this dreadful moment had he realized how much he had loved this sour, unlovable man. Yet somehow he could not bring himself to display those tears before his lieutenants, let alone a stranger.

The rage in his heart, however, was another matter. Rage at the man whom he would have made king, whom he might have come to love as a son, who had now turned this entire British venture into a pointless farce, and who had deprived him of the one man in all Gaul with whom he could share his secret thoughts—to *that* he could give full and free vent.

"*Tribute,* he called it?" he roared like a lion in outraged agony. "I will enrich the man who brings me the head of *Vercingetorix* as tribute! And anyone who gives him sanctuary will find his own impaled on a Roman lance!"

"Is that wise, Caesar?" asked Tulius.

"What would you have me do, Tulius, award him a laurel wreath for slaughtering my friend?"

Tulius shot a fleeting sidelong glance at Marius.

"Go," Caesar ordered Marius.

"Well, Tulius?" he demanded when the man had gone. Tulius fidgeted nervously, apparently equally leery of spitting out whatever it was in front of Labienus.

"How will you explain such a decree to the Gauls?"

"How will I—? Oh."

Caesar caught himself short. The sunlight streaming in through the tent flap was beginning to sparkle with the beginnings of an aura, turning purple around the edges of the beam. He was thinking with his guts, not his brain, and his rage was bringing the falling sickness near. He took four long, deep breaths and forced himself to think coldly in this most hot-blooded of moments.

Tulius, who knew all, had managed to say enough, without saying more than Labienus needed to hear.

I *can't* outlaw Vercingetorix for slaying Gisstus, he realized, for the Gauls must never know that my agent had even been present at the death of Dumnorix, any more than that my hand was behind the elimination of Keltill. Still . . .

"Against my orders, against the will of the druids, Vercingetorix slew Dumnorix for being behind the plot to kill Keltill," Caesar declared. "And you heard him make this foul accusation, Labienus."

"I most certainly did not!" Labienus exclaimed in scandalized outrage.

"Oh yes, you did."

"I heard no such thing!"

"I *order* you to have heard it, Labienus."

"You are ordering me to *lie*?" Labienus said in an astonished tone, as if ordering a general to do that which politicians were constrained to do almost every day as part of their craft was somehow akin to ordering him to slay his own mother.

"Think of it as a military necessity, Labienus," Caesar told him, to ease his punctilious conscience. "It will make your command of the Gauls a lot easier—"

"My what?"

"Back to the status quo ante, Labienus. Vercingetorix's treachery will not be allowed to stop the invasion of Britain. I order you to announce this version of events to what Gauls remain here, and take command of the Gallic auxiliaries after all."

"You do?" exclaimed Labienus.

"And as a gesture of my good faith and magnanimity, you can tell them that I am freeing all the hostages, so that all who choose to follow you do so of their own free will. Enjoy yourself, my friend. The storm is over. Off to glory. Hail, Titus Labienus!"

"Hail, Caesar!" Labienus shouted happily, and replied with a salute so heartfelt that it almost seemed he would disjoint his arm with the force with which he raised it.

"What was that all about?" a befuddled Tulius asked as soon as Labienus had departed.

"Giving my noblest general his heart's desire."

"But now most of the Edui will turn on the Arverni because Vercingetorix killed Dumnorix, and most of the Arverni will turn on the Edui because they will believe the Edui plotted to kill Keltill."

"Exactly," said Caesar.

"But you're releasing the hostages, so most of the Edui and Arverni will probably just go home now."

"Especially the most suspicious ones and the worst troublemakers," said Caesar.

"But that means your plan—"

"—has changed. Which is why I'm sending Labienus on this futile adventure in your place. I have other work for you here. I'll go along to Britain for a while, for appearances' sake. You will take command of the legions remaining in Gaul and hunt down Vercingetorix—"

"Four legions to hunt down one man?"

"We have made an enemy it would be much better to have had as an ally, but a good enemy can be put to use too," Caesar told him. "Vercingetorix is going to be very difficult to capture. It's going to take a long time. There will be Arverne resistance to crush. Make sure there is. You're going to have to conquer and occupy their territory, and those of any of the minor tribes allied with them, I'm afraid."

"And, Vercingetorix having killed Dumnorix, the Edui will do nothing. . . ."

"Except, perhaps, applaud," said Caesar. "And the remaining Arverni will not aid the Edui when we turn our full attention to conquering *them* afterward."

"Utterly ruthless and cynical," Tulius said approvingly.

Caesar nodded. "Which is why I could hardly entrust such a task to Labienus. Gisstus once suggested that we slay all the leaders and troublemakers and any Gaul presuming to replace them, lay as much waste as necessary to declare Gaul a conquered province, and go home in triumph. And that is what we are now going to do."

Caesar laid a tender hand atop the bloody head of his dead friend and forced himself to gaze on his face one last time. Only now did he allow himself tears.

"Had I listened to him in the first place," he muttered, "this utterly ruthless and cynical man might be alive today."

And I would not be here so all alone.

XI

IN THE HOT BLOOD of his lupine madness, with the Arverni whom he had led into the marshes scattering in terror and so too the Arverne army he had left in the Roman encampment, Vercingetorix retrieved his horse and began a frothing gallop across the countryside toward Gergovia. It took him four days to reach the Gallic road to the city, and along the way, he saw Roman infantry cohorts fanning out through the countryside, accompanied by small detachments of cavalry and many empty wagons, behaving nothing like serious search parties, and everything like serious sackers. Several times, he believed he had been spotted, but, strangely, they never gave chase.

The road itself was clogged with people fleeing the growing terror of the countryside and eyeing him as if he were a wolf from the forest, but no one sought to impede or seize him until he reached the foot of the hill upon which the city stood. There the road was blocked by a dozen Arverne guards led by Baravax. They were armed with swords, but none were drawn, and so Vercingetorix did not draw his as he reined up before them.

"Vercingetorix!" cried Baravax. "Are you mad? There's a Roman garrison in Gergovia. There's a price on your head. You can't go there!"

"I see they've given you your old job back, Baravax," Vercingetorix said bitterly. "I also see that you've taken it."

Baravax moved closer, and spoke softly for his ears only, for the people backed up on the road were forming an ever-growing crowd behind them. "Be glad that I did, else another might have come here to capture you rather than warn you." Then, in a whisper: "And even so, I must not be seen to do so. I'm going to create a distraction. You use it to be gone."

And behind his back, he made a signal with his hand to his men.

"There's a fat price on his head!" one of them shouted.

"Why don't we collect it?"

Three of the guards moved slowly forward and even more hesitantly drew their swords.

"Sell one of our own to the stinking Romans!" some shouted from the crowd.

"He's the son of *Keltill*!"

Few were the voices raised against him in what was swiftly turning into a mob whose ire was being turned against the guards, and as they shrank back in fear, Vercingetorix realized that this had been Baravax's intent.

"Draw your swords!" Baravax ordered. "Disperse this crowd!"

The Arverne guards drew their swords but showed little interest in advancing with them on their own people.

Baravax rounded on Vercingetorix in a great mock fury. "See what you bring! I'll not have my men slay Arverni in the service of Rome or be slain by their own people! Be gone, before the blood of Arverni shed by Arverni is on your head!"

And he whacked Vercingetorix's horse on the rump with the flat of his sword. The horse reared and bolted, and Vercingetorix encouraged it to ride off in a fair imitation of an out-of-control gallop.

In the valley below, smoldering fires glowed blood-red in the darkness, revealing the flickering black silhouettes of ruined homesteads and ruined lives, mourned by the lonely bleat of orphaned cattle. Vercingetorix reined in his horse as he rode along the overlooking ridgeline, forcing himself to behold the desolation before slinking back into the safety of the forest. This was surely the darkest of the many such nights he had known since he brought the wrath of Caesar down on his own people.

If wrath it truly was, and not something worse. For the Romans did not burn crops, they forced the peasants to harvest them and hauled them off. They did not slaughter sheep and goats and pigs, they herded them away. They even rounded up and stole the geese and the ducks and the chickens. They did not kill the men they captured, they shackled the able-bodied and led them away into slavery. Only when all this had been done did they burn the buildings and set fire to the stubble in the fields, leaving those too old or too young or too feeble to be of value as slaves to fend for themselves in a blackened and smoking wasteland.

Caesar had not even been in Gaul when it had begun. He had given his orders, departed for Britain, and left them to his lieutenant Tulius to carry out.

Such could not be hot-blooded vengeance. It was being done in an orderly manner by disciplined troops for some purpose. Caesar had put a price on his head, and Tulius had declared that the lands of the Arverni would be occupied by Rome until he was either slain or captured. Yet the actions of the Romans made it seem that this was the last thing they wanted to happen.

In the days that followed his shameful flight from Gergovia, he had at first wandered aimlessly, keeping to the forest, eating well enough off what he could forage, sleeping under the trees, trying with no success to formulate a plan to redress the wrong he had done both to the innocent Dumnorix and to his own people.

All because of a vision.

And if that vision were false?

At length, he decided that there was only one way to test the truth of his vision of his own destiny. He could not test whether or not he would one day be acclaimed king in Rome, but it would be easy enough to see if he could not be slain on the soil of Gaul.

All he had to do was court death.

If he was slain, he had followed a false vision into disaster for his people, and death would be just punishment.

So he had ridden out of the safety of the forest a dozen times, appearing openly on roads, in villages not yet sacked, inviting the desperate and the greedy to seek to claim the price Caesar had put on his head. None succeeded—singly, in pairs, in threes and fours—and his sword took more lives than he cared to count; enough, it would seem, for the legend of his invincibility to spread, for finally no Arverne would dare challenge him.

But this could all be laid to the teachings of Rhia, who had made him a swordsman no one in the land could best save herself. So next he attacked the rearmost wagon of a Roman train, heavily laden with grain, decapitating the legionnaire driving it, setting it ablaze with a torch, and easily outrunning the cavalry guards.

Perhaps *too* easily.

Perhaps he indeed could not be slain on the soil of Gaul. Or perhaps, to judge by the ease with which he escaped the feckless pursuit of the Romans, Caesar did not *want* him slain or captured. Either way, it was an invitation to boldness.

This afternoon he had observed from a safe distance a cohort of Roman infantry, with a small detachment of cavalry and a large train of empty wagons, moving toward a farmstead. At the pace at which they were moving, they would be there within the hour.

There might be no way to prevent the Romans from sacking the farmstead, but he decided to try to save its people from slavery. For, if he could not be slain in battle, might not he and those he led prove invincible?

And so Vercingetorix had galloped ahead and reached the farmstead in advance of the Romans. A palisade so new that its logs were still half green had recently been thrown up around the large round thatch-roofed manse of its master and the courtyard of his holdings; a barn, a pigsty, sheds of ducks, chickens, and geese, a smithy, a bake house. Beyond the enclosure, and surrounding it as far as the eye could see, were fields of golden grain ready for the harvesting.

The palisade gate was open, and when Vercingetorix rode unopposed through it, he almost passed unnoticed into the pandemonium in the courtyard. The courtyard boiled with panicked people. Half a dozen women were loading carts with household goods while adolescent boys attempted to hitch them to balky horses. Peasants were frantically butchering two freshly slaughtered pigs and a cow. Small boys and girls were chasing down chickens and ducks and trying to stuff them into wicker baskets.

A large, beefy man mounted on a black stallion—helmetless, shieldless, armorless, but wearing a sword—seemed to be presiding, and it was he who first noticed Vercingetorix and challenged him.

"Who in the name of the gods of shit and piss are you?" he demanded. "What are you doing here? Don't you know the Romans are coming?"

"I would lead you against them," Vercingetorix told him.

"*Lead us against them?* All we can do is flee with whatever we can, and perhaps thereby escape slavery."

"Fleeing is useless. They're close behind me, their cavalry will run you down easily, and their infantry will do the rest."

"What do you suggest, then, *great leader?*" the man on the black stallion snarled sarcastically. "Are you mad? Who do you think you are?"

"I am Vercingetorix, son of Keltill."

Then there was a sudden silence as they all ceased what they were doing and all eyes turned to regard him.

Dracovax, son of Marnil, did not think of himself as a rich man or a poor one. He held no slaves, though some seventy-three Arverni owed him their allegiance, working his fields, tending to his livestock, and otherwise living their lives and earning their sustenance under his aegis. Though he had fought in a few small battles when he was a hot-blooded young man eager to prove his manhood, he was no warrior. Dracovax was a successful farmer approaching the end of his middle years and content with the life he was living.

Or, rather, had been living. Now he and his people were about to lose everything they had, everything generations of his ancestors had so painstakingly won from the soil. And for causes comprehensible only to the likes of Caesar and the nobles and warriors who followed or fought him. And they had nothing to do with sowing and reaping crops to feed the seventy-three mouths that followed *him*—not for glory or conquest, but to fill their stomachs.

"Vercingetorix . . ."

"They say he has slain a hundred Romans."

Dracovax had heard that this boy was the cause of his misfortune. He had slain an important Eduen, had somehow enraged Caesar against not only himself but all Arverni and those weaker tribes who had previously considered themselves under Arverne protection.

"It is said he cannot be defeated in battle."

This too Dracovax had heard, and also that the Romans offered a handsome price for his capture or death. But what Arverne would betray another to these Roman thieves and slavers for slaying some Eduen who no doubt had it coming?

Fighting the Romans seemed madness, but Dracovax could see no other hope for himself or his people. He might be getting too old for battle, but he was yet too young for slavery. And still would be when the last tooth had fallen from his gums, and the last white hair from his skull.

"I am Dracovax, son of Marnil; this is my homestead, and I would save my people from slavery if I can," said the man on the black stallion. "Is it really true that the Romans cannot defeat you?"

"This I do not know," Vercingetorix admitted.

He hesitated. Then he said something he had never presumed to proclaim before, not knowing whether he spoke truth or a silver-tongued lie, but knowing that he must say it to learn whether it was the one or the other.

"But I *do* know that I cannot be slain on the soil of Gaul," he said. "This the gods have granted me in a vision."

The intakes of breath around him made a sound like the sighing of the wind through the tree crowns of a forest.

"Druid magic . . ." said a woman's voice.

"You are a druid?" asked Dracovax.

Am I? wondered Vercingetorix. Just what have I become?

"I am a man of knowledge," he said. "But I am also a man of action."

"But druids never join in battle," said Dracovax.

"Never have we faced such an enemy as the legions of Caesar," said Vercingetorix. "When the Wheel makes such a turning from one Great Age into another, even druids must turn with it or be crushed beneath it."

"Well spoken!"

"The words of a druid indeed . . ."

"But of a warrior also!" cried Vercingetorix, drawing his sword.

And thus did he commit himself and the people of Dracovax's farmstead to seemingly hopeless battle.

There were nearly four hundred men in a Roman cohort. Vercingetorix now commanded fewer than four dozen: peasants, bakers, smiths, stablehands, and a third of those half-grown boys. There were swords and spears for a dozen of them; the rest had only scythes, woodsman's axes, and butchering knives. There were half a dozen horses, none of which had ever faced battle.

"Accept that you cannot save your fields or your property, Dracovax," Vercingetorix said when he had this pathetic force assembled. "So do not leave them for the Romans. Forget the carts. Move your people out of here now, and set this place on fire. Let all flee on foot through the fields, firing the grain behind them. All save you, and me, and these other five horsemen. When the Romans see the flames, they will send their cavalry ahead. We will ride to meet them and delay them until your people have time to retreat from their infantry into the forest behind a wall of fire."

Dracovax regarded him with a mixture of awe and terror. "Seven of us against a Roman cavalry detachment!" he exclaimed.

"I have seen their cavalry, and there cannot be much more than a score of them."

"Three or four to one! Hopeless odds!"

"You are right," declared Vercingetorix. "For they are mere Romans and we are Gauls! Perhaps we should leave half our number behind to make the fight a fair one!"

The brave cheer that went up set Vercingetorix's blood afire and his spirit soaring, and so, sword held high and flames of destruction behind him, he galloped forth to meet the cavalry of Caesar at the head of his tiny army of peasants and stableboys.

The Roman cavalry were galloping two abreast down the narrow earthen road approaching the burning farmstead, but as soon as their commander saw Vercingetorix's little force riding up toward him, he had his trumpeter blow a short series of notes, and the Romans spread out across the road and on either side of it in a wide skirmish line.

Vercingetorix led his horsemen off the road to the left, as if attempting to pass them on the flank, but since his goal was to delay the Romans, not escape them, this was a feint, and when the two forces were but half a dozen horse-lengths apart, he wheeled his mount and made straight for the center of the Roman line, hoping to break through, create chaos, attack the right flank from behind.

He slashed the Roman trooper on his right across the throat with a sweep of his sword, ducked under a sword thrust from the one on his left, and was through, and attacking him from behind. His sword clanged harmlessly off the back of the Roman's helmet, the Roman trooper wheeled his horse smartly to face Vercingetorix, but the gap in the Roman line was open, and Vercingetorix's men rode through it.

Or some of them did.

Vercingetorix was too busy fending off sword thrusts to see what had happened, but somehow, within moments, two of his men were dead on the ground, and instead of being behind a shattered line of Roman cavalry, he and the remaining four were within a circle of Roman horsemen.

He reared his horse and slashed down on the hand of one attacker, sending his sword falling to the ground; thrust straight forward, piercing another through the eye.

He whirled his mount to see one more of his men on the ground, being trampled by panicked riderless horses as a javelin was hurled right at him. Vercingetorix flicked it away with his sword, saw another of his men take a javelin in the stomach. He reared his horse again, saw a beardless boy pierced screaming through the neck, put his head down against his horse's neck, tucked his sword against his body, and made for the encircling line of Romans.

Javelins whizzed past his head—one bounced off his helm—then he reared his horse, whipped out his sword, slashed at the Roman on his right, and saw—

—Dracovax take javelins, one, two, three, chest, back, stomach. No Roman javelin was sharper than the look of astonishment, pain, fury, and betrayal that Dracovax threw him as their eyes met in the briefest of instants before he too fell.

Then Vercingetorix was through the encircling Romans, and the remaining Roman cavalry was once more galloping two abreast down the road in good order toward the flaming fields, behind which the friends and families of the men he had led into this swift and useless slaughter were attempting to flee.

"Bastards! Cowards! Come back and fight!" Vercingetorix shouted after the Romans. "I am Vercingetorix, son of Keltill! Come back and fight! Kill me if you dare!"

He galloped behind them for a while, shouting and waving his sword, but it was as futile as the deaths he had brought to the brave men who had followed him, for he gained no ground on the Romans, nor did they deign to take up his challenge.

The last he saw of the Roman cavalry, they were riding straight into the flames, and he never knew what became of the Gauls running for their freedom beyond them.

Now Vercingetorix endured one last look at the embers of their lives dying to cinders down there, where the night hid the blackened fields that only hours ago had been rich golden croplands, where an unseen dog howled its anguish at the stars and gave voice to his own.

Whether the remnants of Dracovax's people had escaped or died or been enslaved he might never know, but never could he forget them. For never could he forget the bitter lesson he had learned at their expense.

Perhaps Caesar did not want him slain or captured.

Perhaps *he* could not be slain on the soil of Gaul.

But certainly those who followed him could be killed, as easily as a husbandman might wring the neck of a chicken.

For two nights and two days, Vercingetorix lurked in the forest, his spirit shrouded in mists like the fogs that lay upon the woodland, and no less heavy and dampened than the sodden branches. Finally, he decided to return to the place from which he had left the way of the man of knowledge in the wan hope of finding wiser counsel than his own.

The sun was beginning to set through the tree crowns when he reached the druid school, casting long wavering shadows on an eerie scene of orderly destruction. The thatched huts had been burned to the ground but with care, for neither the grass of the clearing nor a single tree had been singed, and the stone temple still stood untouched. Not a person was present, but neither were there corpses or any sign of a struggle.

Vercingetorix dismounted, examined the ashes of the huts, paced around the periphery of the clearing, peered into the deepening shadows of the forest. No one. No sound but the day birds returning to roost and the night birds tentatively beginning their songs.

There was only one other place to go, only one other's counsel that he could think to seek, and so Vercingetorix remounted and rode back through the trees, back to the cave of Rhia.

A bloody red twilight had enveloped the forest by the time Vercingetorix got there, and firelight glowed somberly within the opening in the rock face.

Vercingetorix dismounted and entered. Though he had taken many lessons outside, never had he been invited into the cave or sought entry, so he made his way cautiously along a dark and narrow passage toward the firelight at the far end.

He emerged into a rough-hewn circular chamber where a fire burned in a large brass brazier. Before the fire, back to him, was a warrior in armor and helmet with a sword held in both hands, its point grounded upon the rocky floor.

Rhia whirled around at some slight sound made by his approach, her sword held high over one shoulder, and Vercingetorix found that, without thought, he had drawn his own sword and assumed the same position.

Rhia smiled mirthlessly. "Well learned," she said.

"Well taught," said Vercingetorix. "But where is everybody? The druids of the school—"

"Gone into the forest to hide in plain sight."

"And you remained to face the wrath of Caesar alone?"

"I remained to wait for you," said Rhia. "For now begins the destiny for which my life was crafted."

"Crafted . . . ?"

"Are not all our lives crafted for destinies we do not know, by gods or forces or magics we never see or understand?"

"Some of us see our destinies before they arrive," Vercingetorix said somberly. "But whether boon or curse . . ." He could only shrug.

"Does it matter?" said Rhia. "Can we resist destiny? When I was a wild creature of the forest and lived without words in which to think, I saw without thought, and so was one with both this world and the Land of Legend, and I saw . . . I saw . . ." Her brow wrinkled, as she struggled to find words to bind that which could not be bound by words.

"I saw *you*, Vercingetorix," she finally said. "And likewise I saw myself . . . my life to come . . . my death. . . ."

"As I saw my destiny under the Tree of Knowledge . . ."

"Perhaps," said Rhia, "but as an animal might." Sword still held high above her shoulder, she yet trembled like a fawn, and Vercingetorix felt the desire, the need, to comfort her.

"Let us not speak of such things," she said in a whispery voice. "Let me just say that, as this sword was crafted by men to be my weapon, so was I crafted by the gods to be yours."

Rhia strode forward. But not to embrace him. Instead, she reached down one-handed with her sword, put the tip of it under his, and raised both up so that the two warriors were separated by crossed swords held high between them.

"I am your weapon to wield to the last drop of my blood," she said. "Nothing more and nothing less. Your sister of the sword. You must accept our destiny, for in this there is no choice. Swear this oath with me!"

She reached up with her free hand and ran the palm of it along the cutting edge of her sword, drawing a thin line of blood.

She kissed the palm, smearing her own blood upon her lips.

Vercingetorix stared at her, stunned and transfixed for a long moment, before he understood. Then he too ran his palm down the edge of his sword, and kissed the blood he had drawn onto his lips.

Swords still crossed, they kissed, closed-mouth but long, without erotic ardor, but with a fiercer passion.

"Brother and sister of the sword!" he declared.

"Until death parts us in this world," said Rhia, "and forever in the Land of Legend."

Am I vexed or am I content? Caesar asked himself, and the question was its own answer, for in this season of his life, each of these humors seemed to contain the seed of the other. The foray into Britain had proved as pointless as he had known it would, but upon his return he had found that Tulius had done well in subjugating the Arverni and their tributary tribes, so well that what he had extracted from them in goods and slaves exceeded the whole cost of the British expedition.

Now, as he rode under a blue stormless sky, the Alpine peaks were capped with snow only at their heights, the grass was still green in these valleys, and the passage south to Gallia Narbonensis for the winter was proving a sweet and soft one. Beside him rode Brutus, as he had in Britain—a poor substitute for Gisstus as a mirror for his inner thoughts perhaps, but one whose youth and naïveté encouraged his brighter aspects.

Behind them, his legions marched in good order, and among the formations of infantry and cavalry, there were long lines of slaves, herds of sheep and horses, and many wagons bearing not only foodstuffs, leathers, and cloth, but sacks of dyes known only to the Gauls, gems, excellent metalwork, and more gold than Caesar had even hoped for. The men were in a fine humor, and why should they not be, marching south for the usual winter of rest after an unusually successful and lucrative campaigning season.

"They wouldn't dare!" cried Brutus.

Four cavalrymen were galloping down the mountain slope toward them with hands full of snowballs that they were throwing at each other in wild good spirits.

Brutus laughed as they approached.

"Or would they?"

But when two of the troopers reached them, each holding a snowball, another produced a wineskin and poured wine on them.

"Taste this!" he cried in delight, as Caesar and Brutus were each handed a snowball.

Brutus bit gingerly into his. "Delicious!" he exclaimed.

Caesar, constrained to do likewise, tasted his snowball. It was indeed delicious, and unexpectedly so; if anyone could work out a way to create such a cool treat in the heat of the Roman summer, his fortune would surely be made.

"Wonderful!" said Caesar, and plastered a happy grin across his face. But his heart just wasn't in it, and Brutus sensed this.

"The men are in a happy mood," he said when the troopers had departed. "Why is *your* mood not light, Caesar?"

"Because we'll be marching the other way in the spring, Brutus," said Caesar. "After leaving the Gauls to their own devices all winter . . ."

"But with the Arverni all but conquered, we'll be ready to turn our attention to the Edui. . . ."

"True," said Caesar.

"Then why do you worry?"

"In a word, Vercingetorix," said Caesar. "Still at large." I can't tell him that this is by my own order, can I? And certainly not that it's turned into a mistake.

"A fugitive in the forest, detested by all save the Arverni for the slaying of Dumnorix," Brutus said scornfully.

"True again, my young friend. But the Arverni are turning him into a legend."

"A mythic hero with no army. What can one man do?"

"Am *I* not one man, Brutus?" Caesar said sardonically.

The first light snow of winter had dusted the boughs of the trees. Vercingetorix sat close by Rhia as they warmed themselves around a campfire that sent sparks up into the crystalline night. The savory smoke of the rabbit they had spitted and roasted clung to his nostrils as they hunkered there, picking off morsels.

Here we are, thought Vercingetorix sourly, camped alone on a chilly early winter eve, smacking our lips over crackled meat around a cozy fire, soon to turn to doing likewise over each other, were we any natural man and woman. But brother and sister of the sword did not have the right to think such things, though for two turnings of the moon, he had spent all his days and all his nights with Rhia.

Caesar had taken his main force south for the winter, leaving only garrisons to hold Gergovia and the larger villages. But Vercingetorix knew that the Romans would return in full force in the spring. Now was the time to raise an army, overwhelm the garrisons Caesar had left behind, and be prepared to confront the Romans when the snows in the mountain passes melted.

So he carved a crude bear out of oak, affixed it to a pole, gave it to Rhia, and anointed her "standard-bearer of the army of the Arverni," hoping that the legend of his invincibility, the presence at his side of such an arcane bearer, and the outrageousness of raising the bear standard at all would rally the Arverni to it.

But all he could rally at any one time were a few real warriors and a score or two of starving peasants to raid small villages garrisoned by no more than a handful of legionnaires. This had resulted in half a dozen easy and pathetic "victories" by "the army of the Arverni." These makeshift bands would slay the Romans and all they deemed collaborators, drink all there was to drink, eat what they could stuff into their bellies, and then disappear with what was left before Roman reinforcements could arrive.

A week ago, though, this frustrating routine of what amounted to little more than banditry had produced disaster.

The village they attacked had a large supply of Roman wine; the "army of the Arvernes" had gotten drunker than usual and passed into oblivion for the night. A Roman or two must have escaped in the confusion, for the revelers awoke to find the village surrounded by half a cohort of Roman infantry.

With the first rays of the sun, the Romans moved in from all directions like a fist slowly closing on a peach. Vercingetorix, Rhia, and the half dozen Arverni who had horses found themselves fighting to escape with their lives. Since the Romans had no cavalry, slashing their way through the thinly spread infantry line was not difficult for those who were mounted, nor did the Romans seriously seek to impede them, intent as they were on the less risky task of massacring those without horses.

It would have been easy enough to flee, for infantry could hardly pursue horsemen, but Vercingetorix could not honorably leave the rest of his men to perish. So, once the Roman infantry had turned their backs on his tiny escaping cavalry band, Vercingetorix wheeled his horse around and reared it. Rhia, seeing this, did likewise, raising his standard as high as she could.

"Attack!" shouted Vercingetorix, waving his sword, and charged toward the rear of the Roman infantry.

He had hardly brought his horse up into a full gallop when Rhia cut in front of him and barred his way with his own standard.

"What are you—"

"Look behind you!" Rhia shouted.

When Vercingetorix did, he saw that, rather than riding with him in an attempt to attack the Romans from the rear and rescue their fellows, his six "cavalrymen" were disappearing into the distance.

"Cowards! Bastards!" he shouted after them in a fury.

He wheeled again, and would have charged the Romans alone had not Rhia seized the reins of his horse and restrained him at sword point until reason returned.

When the Romans captured the village, they took care to slice ankle tendons, pierce thighs, cut off feet, and otherwise disable without killing, and to take as many prisoners as they could. These they took to a prominent place on the road to Gergovia and crucified. It was said the prisoners took days to die. Longer than it took the carrion birds to pick their bones clean.

Vercingetorix had not had the heart to raise his standard since. Who would have been willing to rally to it if he had?

An owl hooted. A distant wolf howled. Another answered. Something small scurried through the forest. Something somewhat larger pursued. There was a shrill little scream, a thrashing, then silence.

Vercingetorix found that, in the midst of these grim and frustrating memories, he was huddling closer to Rhia. His "war" on Caesar had ended in ignominy before it began, and she was his entire "army." What further purpose was there to blood oaths, or their brotherhood and sisterhood of the sword?

Perhaps the nights really *were* worse than the days, sleeping close beside her for the warmth, worse still lying awake while she muttered and writhed in her sleep, dreaming amorous thoughts of him, he dared to hope. What reason remained not to fulfill them?

"Our time as brother and sister of the sword would seem to be over, Rhia," he ventured.

"You must not acknowledge defeat."

"As I must not acknowledge that the sun will rise in the morning whether I will it or not?" Vercingetorix said bitterly.

"You have seen your destiny in a vision. . . ."

"Cannot visions lie?"

"Their truths may not be spoken plain, but they do not lie."

"Neither do they point to the path to their fulfillment. What are we to do now?"

Rhia was silent, nor would she meet his gaze. Somehow this emboldened Vercingetorix to move closer to her. She in turn seemed to lean closer to him. Vercingetorix dared to put a hand upon her thigh—

—and she pulled back from his touch as if his hand were afire. "No, Vercingetorix," she said softly, still unwilling or unable to look him in the eye. "We must not. Destiny has brought us together not for pleasure but to serve a purpose—"

"Destiny or not, Rhia, we are a man and a woman."

"I have my vow, and you—"

"Vows must be kept!"

It was the voice of Guttuatr, as he emerged like a spirit from the darkness, but he became very much a creature of flesh when he strode to the campfire, squatted down, and immediately and without invitation ripped a haunch off the spitted rabbit.

"Those who would be lovers must leave flesh untouched," he managed to say between greedy mouthfuls. "Sacrifices must be made."

"I don't notice *you* leaving flesh untouched or making any sacrifices," Vercingetorix snapped petulantly.

Guttuatr froze. He took the rabbit leg from his mouth and tossed it away into the forest. His craggy face, reddened and deeply etched by the firelight, was a mask of deadly earnest as he stared at Vercingetorix.

"What sacrifice would you have me make . . . druid?" he said.

Vercingetorix let his desperation and ire speak for him.

"Command the tribes of Gaul to unite against Rome!"

Guttuatr shrank back as if confronted with the unspeakable. "I cannot do such a thing!" he exclaimed.

"Oh yes, you can!"

"You know not what you ask!"

"Oh yes, I do!" said Vercingetorix, and though these were the iresome words of the man of action, as he spoke them they became truth, his spirit became calm, and it was the man of knowledge who now spoke to his fellow druid.

"I call upon you to descend from the world of knowledge into the world of action. I call upon you to make the sacrifice of that which you hold most dear—the purity of your own spirit."

"You call upon me to do what no druid must do," Guttuatr said softly, "what no Arch Druid has ever done." It seemed to Vercingetorix that, for the first time since he had known him, he saw Guttuatr afraid.

"You must, Guttuatr, or the way of the druids itself will surely perish. If you do not, Caesar will find us as we are now when he returns in the spring, and crush us all. Gaul will become but a name for a conquered province of Rome, and you will trade the precious purity of your druid's robe for a toga!"

"Who dares ask me to do such a terrible thing?" said Guttuatr, regarding him as if seeing a demon.

"Who dares ask?" Vercingetorix roared at him. "I do, Vercingetorix, son of Keltill, who died in fire to save our people! I do, the boy you trained as your instrument because the heavens commanded you! I do, Vercingetorix, denied all the pleasures of an ordinary man! I do, Vercingetorix, whose hands are steeped in blood! I chose none of this! If I am a monster, you have made me so!"

"To break my vow and use the druid's art to bend the worldly destiny of men . . ." Guttuatr muttered hesitantly.

But his very hesitancy was answer enough. Vercingetorix saw that his words had conquered the Arch Druid, and held his silence.

Guttuatr sighed. "It is a terrible magic you ask me to make, and the price will be terrible."

"The greater the magic, the greater the price that must be paid, as someone has told me often enough."

"I must have a human life with which to work this art," said Guttuatr.

"It has been done before . . ." Vercingetorix said coldly. "And I have already sacrificed countless lives to accomplish nothing."

Was it illusion, or had the night sounds ceased? All at once, Guttuatr's visage transformed from that of an old man whose will he had tamed into that of the fiercest of Arch Druids from the legends of long ago.

"Never have the druids made magic such as this," he said. "And so the life that must be paid must be unlike that of any that have been sacrificed to the gods before. The life of a *druid* . . . and not taken, but freely given."

The crowns of the surrounding trees are still frosted with snow, but the sun rising toward its zenith has melted it away from the circular clearing, revealing the bleak brownish remnants of grass and rocks tinged the dirty purple of old bloodstains by the dying moss and more tenacious lichen.

The Arch Druid Guttuatr stands in the center of the circle, his breath rendered visible by the frost, bearing the great oaken staff of his office, crowned with its fallen star.

Once, twice, thrice, he raps the nether end upon a rock, and from the four quarters of the wind, druids emerge from the forest. There are many of them, perhaps as many as two hundred, an unnatural number for the size of the clearing, which fills completely. Their white robes are trimmed with the colors of all the tribes of Gaul. The mood is sullen rather than solemn as they wait for the Arch Druid to speak.

"I have summoned you all here from the far corners of Gaul to bear witness to a sacred circle of judgment such as has never been held before. . . ."

Murmurs sweep through the assembled druids.

"For it is a druid who is to be judged."

The massed intake of breath is like a wind through the trees, and the white exhalations drape the druids in a momentary fog.

"And more. Much more. I call upon the druid Diviacx of the Edui to come forward."

There is a commotion in the middle of the crowded clearing, and then the way parts for Diviacx, who strides forward in his blue-trimmed white robe. His face is impassive; only his eyes, darting this way and that, betray his fearful unease.

"I am to be judged by the druids?"

"Far crueler than that, Diviacx. You must judge yourself."

"Myself?"

"Who better to judge the story of your life in this world and what it will mean in the next?"

"You ask a hard thing, Arch Druid."

"Have you not done hard things before, Diviacx?" shouts a voice from the assembly. It is Vercingetorix, coming forward in a druid's robe, pure white like Guttuatr's, unmarked by tribal emblem.

"Or was it easy to conspire to bring the Romans here for your own profit?" he says as he approaches.

Diviacx turns away from Guttuatr to confront Vercingetorix and his fellow druids. "I did it to save us all from the Teutons! And they are gone, are they not?"

"You did it for the Edui!"

"I did it for all Gaul!"

"Then will you now prove it?" Vercingetorix asks insinuatingly. "Will you now save us from the Romans? Even the Arverni, *Eduen*?"

"I am a druid before I am an Eduen!" Diviacx declares. "I would save us from the Romans if I could," he says more weakly, and perhaps with genuine sorrow, "but I know not how."

"You begin by swearing to speak nothing but truth within this sacred circle," Guttuatr tells him. "No matter where its path may lead."

Diviacx withdraws a dagger from beneath his robe. "With an open heart and the last drop of my blood, Arch Druid," he says softly, and he slashes his palm, raises his hand aloft, and allows a few red drops to stain the whiteness of his robe.

"Did you not conspire with Caesar to murder my father?" Vercingetorix demands.

"Did your father not conspire to make himself king of the Gauls against all law and tradition?" cries Diviacx. "And did *you* not murder Dumnorix, my brother?"

"No, I did not."

"What?"

"I swear to speak nothing but the truth within this sacred circle, no matter where its path may lead," says Vercingetorix, and from beneath his druid's robe he withdraws not a dagger but a warrior's sword. "With an open heart and the last drop of my blood." And he slashes not his palm but his forearm, and allows his blood to flow down his white robe's sleeve.

"The truth is, I did *wish* to slay your brother, Diviacx, and this sword did pierce his innocent flesh, for I believed he conspired with you and Caesar to kill Keltill. For this I ask his spirit to forgive me. And for this that spirit's brother may take my life if he so wishes."

Vercingetorix hands the dumbfounded Diviacx his sword.

"But before you do, Diviacx, know that it was *Caesar's* hand that slew your brother, not my own."

"Caesar . . . ?" whispers Diviacx as the sword hangs limply in his hand. "*Caesar?*"

"Through the instrumentality of his assassin Gisstus," says Vercingetorix, "who slew him with a javelin from hiding like the serpent he was."

"*Gisstus!*" exclaims Diviacx.

"Whom I then slew, and whose head I threw at Caesar as a token of my outrage and a declaration of war between him and myself."

"You knew this man?" asks the Arch Druid.

Diviacx's head droops deeper than the sword hanging from his hand. "He was Caesar's secret emissary at . . . at . . ."

"At Gergovia!" cries Vercingetorix. "At the seizing and burning of my father!"

"Why should I believe he slew my brother?" Diviacx demands.

"You have just admitted that you conspired in secret with him to burn my father."

"I admitted no such thing," Diviacx insists, albeit weakly, and with an evasive look in his eyes.

"Do you deny it under an oath sworn in blood?" says the Arch Druid.

"I . . . I cannot," Diviacx replies miserably in a voice barely above a whisper. Then, plaintively: "It's true? Gisstus slew my brother? From hiding? Without honor?"

"I swear it under blood oath as the man who saw it and avenged Dumnorix," Vercingetorix tells him in a tone not devoid of sympathy.

"Under orders from Caesar?"

"Who else could order Gisstus?"

Diviacx sighs. His eyes grow misty. His lower lip trembles. "Caesar betrayed me!" he cries. "And tricked me into betraying my own people! And killed my brother!"

The assembled druids, who have maintained a rapt silence, now mutter and cry among themselves. The Arch Druid lets this continue a while before raising his staff to command a silence in which to speak.

"Behold the work of Rome, which has not only set tribe against tribe, but Eduen against Eduen, Arverne against Arverne, brother against brother, *druid against druid*!"

"What I did, I did for Gaul, or so I truly believed," insists Diviacx. "I was the unwitting tool of treacherous Caesar. And yet . . ."

"And yet?" says Vercingetorix.

"And yet my own brother, full of honor, has paid with his life for what *I* have done!" Diviacx cries out in anguish.

"And would you now be the tool of Gaul, Diviacx?" says Guttuatr.

A light dusting of snow begins to fall. The druids sigh as if they have been given a sign. But of what, they do not know. Nor does Diviacx.

"I don't understand. . . ."

"You say you conspired to bring the Romans to save Gaul from the Teutons. You said you conspired to slay Keltill to preserve our people and our way. . . ."

"I swear this to be true!"

"Would you now do as much to preserve Gaul and its way from the *Romans*?"

"With the last drop of my—"

Diviacx stops short as a terrible comprehension dawns in his eyes. The druids gasp, then murmur, then fall so silent that it seems the fall of the snowflakes upon their robes can almost be heard.

"With the last drop of my blood," he says softly, and humbly hangs his head.

Guttuatr takes a step forward. There is something hesitant about it, and so too in his voice as he begins to speak.

"It is not our way to fight as one people under a single leader. Our diversity has long been our strength and our freedom. It has preserved the tribes of Gaul from those who lust for power. The druids have always been the guardians of the things of the spirit, and never intervene in the worldly destiny of Gaul. And yet . . . and yet now, if we do not intervene, the destiny of Gaul will be for its very spirit to perish. . . ."

"No!"

"It cannot be!"

"Silence!" roars the Arch Druid, and, with one hand, he holds his staff aloft. "Hear my words, and spread the tale of what occurs here today to every corner of this land, and let it enter the Land of Legend! I, Guttuatr, Arch Druid of Gaul, take it upon my own spirit to commit a lesser evil in order to prevent a greater one. I command—yes, *command*—an unnatural pact among us, among all the tribes of Gaul!"

He turns to regard Diviacx, whose eyes have remained downcast and averted. "And there is only one way to seal it," he says in a much quieter voice.

Diviacx looks up slowly to meet the gaze of the Arch Druid.

"And you know what that way is, do you not, Diviacx?"

"In blood sacrifice . . ."

"Freely given, Diviacx, freely given."

"Is there no other way?" asks Diviacx, looking slowly around the gathering of druids, but his voice betrays the knowledge that there can be none.

No one speaks, no one moves.

"So be it . . ." Diviacx declares.

"Speak your judgment, Diviacx!"

Diviacx hesitates, then raises his head high and speaks in a loud, proud voice:

"Before the tribes of Gaul, I accept this sacrifice as a fitting end to my story in this world and a worthy beginning to my story in the Land of Legend!"

"And at whose hand, Diviacx? *You* must choose."

Slowly Diviacx turns to regard Vercingetorix.

"To seal this pact among the tribes in Eduen blood, I choose an Arverne. In the name of justice, I choose the man whose father I now see served the same destiny and made the same sacrifice for it. To unite the Gaul to which I brought the scourge of Rome, and which I now must give my life to save, I give it to the man the heavens have declared must lead us."

He hands Vercingetorix back his sword.

"I choose Vercingetorix, son of Keltill!"

Vercingetorix looks deeply into his eyes, and his expression is tender. "Noble words, Diviacx," he says softly.

Then he turns to address the druids.

"Behold, it is not the son of Keltill who sends Diviacx from this world and into the next in the name of vengeance, nor an Arverne in the name of his tribe's honor, but a *druid* in the name of the people and the spirit of Gaul!"

Diviacx spreads his arms and offers up his chest.

"I offer up my life with an open heart that that spirit not perish!"

Vercingetorix places the point of his sword upon Diviacx's breast. He pauses. He takes Diviacx's right hand in his own, and places it upon the hilt of the sword, then the left, so that their four hands are clasped together around it.

And together they plunge the sword into Diviacx's heart.

XII

C AN YOU SEE the clouds moving?" asked Rhia.
Vercingetorix gazed up at a leaden ceiling of dirty grayish
clouds, the sort from which snow or rain might come down,
but not the sort likely to produce a short storm that would clear the
heavens.

He shook his head.

"Neither can I," said Rhia.

"I believe this weather will hold. . . ."

"And there will be no moon. . . ."

Gergovia perched atop a hill that rose out of a broad meadow, both
logged clear in the long ago, but the stream meandering through the
meadow nurtured a string of copses along its banks. A makeshift village
had grown up under the shelter of these trees: crude huts of wicker and
wattle with conical thatched roofs thrown up by impoverished peasants
whose winter stores and livestock had been stolen by the Romans, and
who hoped to survive until spring by fishing the stream and hunting the
small game that gathered round the water source.

Or that was what the Roman garrison occupying Gergovia was supposed to think.

Vercingetorix and Rhia stood on the stream bank farthest from the
city, just far enough out of the trees to be able to study the late-
afternoon sky.

"So be it," said Vercingetorix. "We do it tonight."

Most of the inhabitants of the village *were* starveling peasant families, and huntsmen with their wives and children as well, for among the

early arrivals were some dozen of them, led by Oranix, the "great hunter," whose lives and livelihoods had been imperiled by pillaging Romans turning hunters into prey.

Vercingetorix had immediately put them to work winkling out the scattered warriors who had, singly or in small groups, escaped Caesar's legions and hidden in the forest. Now there were about half a hundred of them in the village. Many had arrived lacking arms, but smiths had fled into the haven of the forest too, and deep within the woods they had forged new swords and axes.

The seemingly pathetic refugee village was now a hunting blind from which Vercingetorix intended to take Gergovia from the Roman cohort holding it.

Gergovia, like all such Gallic redoubts, was designed to be easy to hold and difficult to take. An approaching army would be visible from long distances, giving the defenders ample time to prepare a warm reception of arrows. The Roman general Tulius had obviously reckoned that a few hundred men would be enough to hold the city through the winter against whatever the scattered Arverni could muster.

Vercingetorix had hoped that the druids would gather him an army from the other tribes, particularly the intact forces of the Edui, to overwhelm by sheer numbers the six hundred or so Romans holding the city.

But the druids had failed.

The same word came back from all the tribes. Take your own city back, Vercingetorix, and then we shall consider joining your army of Gauls. Even Litivak, who now commanded enough Edui himself to make the difference, informed Vercingetorix that he would not endanger his own position by attempting to lead his warriors where he knew they would refuse to follow.

And so Vercingetorix had been reduced to assembling about half a hundred actual warriors and about three hundred peasants and hunters, and hiding them here in plain sight of the Romans. It would be suicidal folly to attempt to storm the city and scale the walls or ram in the gates with such a force, and he had assembled and held this "army" together only by swearing a blood oath that they would not be called upon to try.

"The gates will open themselves for you," he promised whenever wills had wavered. "If they do not, you will know I have been slain. And I cannot be slain on the soil of Gaul."

Only his death could render the vision false and his boast vain. No matter how many times he defied death and prevailed, he could never truly know that the next time might not be the last.

And tonight he was going to have to do it again.

The only magic that he truly had was the magic he must make.

Under other conditions, Vercingetorix would hardly have considered a cold, misty rain a favorable omen, but on this moonless night under a starless sky, it was a gift of the gods, further cloaking their approach to Gergovia.

Vercingetorix and Rhia climbed the hill under cloth blankets smeared with mud from the stream and then coated with the brownish remains of winter grass. They crawled quickly for a bit, stopping still for longer intervals, so that only by unfortunate chance might the Romans on the wall catch sight of these little knolls in motion.

Theirs was a slow, soggy, miserable progress, but in the end worth the discomfort, for they reached the base of the wall without causing the alarm to be sounded. Here, pressed against the foot of the wall, they were invisible to those upon it, and made their way to a section of the wall midway between two of the towers.

Vercingetorix made certain that both his sword and the trumpet he carried were firmly fastened to his belt and well baffled with the rope coiled about his waist, then nodded to Rhia. From her sack, Rhia withdrew two daggers and handed them to him. The daggers had been purpose-crafted by the most skilled of the smiths. Their blades were short and stout and sharpened for only half their lengths. The handles, forged of a piece with the blades, were overlarge, and their broad, flattened sides formed a cross with the blade edges.

Gergovia's wall was constructed of large rough stones held in a kind of log cage rather than simply mortared together. The logs were arranged in no rigid order, their placing complementing and reinforcing the piling of the stones, and there were plentiful chinks and small gaps between rock and wood.

Vercingetorix drove the first dagger into such a chink at knee height, then the second into a chink at waist height. Rhia handed him a third dagger, which he drove in at head height above the first. He put his right foot on the handle of the first dagger, then, using the third as a handhold, put his other foot on the second, so that he was now standing on both dagger handles, using them as steps.

Rhia handed him a fourth dagger, which he placed an arm's length above the third; then he withdrew the first, placed it an arm's length above the fourth, and, using the highest dagger as his next handhold, climbed a step farther up the wall.

Slowly, painstakingly, quietly, Vercingetorix scaled the wall on a movable ladder of daggers. It was arduous, muscle-straining going, and when he finally reached the top of the wall, he was panting, his arms and legs ached, and he was sweating even in the wintry night. But even now he could not ease his limbs' fatigue. He hung by the knives just below the lip of the parapet, uncoiled his rope, and dropped the end down to Rhia.

He then raised his head cautiously to peer up over the lip of the parapet. A single legionnaire, armed with a lance and patrolling the section of the walkway between the nearest two towers, was approaching. Vercingetorix ducked back down until he heard him pass, reach the right-hand tower, turn, pace back to the left-hand tower, turn again, and return. He clung there, timing the guard's movements, as the Roman repeated the cycle twice.

When the guard's footfalls dwindled away to the left a third time, Vercingetorix waved to Rhia, pulled himself up onto the walkway, drove two daggers into the top of the wall, and secured his end of the rope to their handles, allowing Rhia to scramble quickly up the wall behind him.

As the guard reached the left-hand tower and turned, they both dropped to their bellies in the shadows. Rhia handed Vercingetorix her sword and its belt and doffed her cloak.

Beneath it she was entirely naked.

She crawled toward the approaching Roman until they were only a body's length apart, then suddenly stood up.

Startled, the Roman brought his lance down to bear on her, but then, in the next instant, he froze.

"Where . . . where did *you* come from?" he stammered.

"From a cold and lonely bed," purred Rhia, striding forward with arms opening wide to embrace him.

Transfixed, the Roman lowered his lance, no doubt without thinking, as Vercingetorix could well understand, for, inappropriate to the occasion though it might be, *his* brain was powerless to prevent his own manhood from rising.

Rhia pressed her naked breast hard against the unprotesting Roman's chest, reached up behind his neck with both hands to draw his face down into a kiss.

There was a dull crack and a low grunt as she snapped it.

Quietly, almost tenderly, Rhia slid the dead legionnaire to the walk-way as Vercingetorix ran toward her. She buckled on her sword and threw her cloak around her shoulders, hiding very little, as they dashed to the ladder by the tower and scrambled down it.

They were inside the city.

Rhia had done her magic.

Now, thought Vercingetorix, I must dare to do my own once more.

The streets of Gergovia were largely deserted and quiet, for no one would be abroad in the depth of this rainy night without pressing purpose. Vercingetorix's memory served him well as he led Rhia away from the wall to approach the gates in it stealthily through a maze of back streets and alleys where unseen footfalls gave easy warning of the few patrols.

They emerged from an alley into the main avenue between the plaza and the city gates, close by the gates themselves. The avenue was deserted at this hour, and they were able to move from portal to portal, shadow to shadow, until the gates were visible where the avenue ended in a small open area.

Now the easy part was over.

Two low stone towers flanked the gates, and two legionnaires armed with lances were positioned on either side of each tower atop the parapet, gazing outward. Two more lance-armed legionnaires guarded the gates on the ground inside the city.

"Six to two, not bad odds," Vercingetorix whispered.

"And those lances are better at intimidating unarmed townspeople or dealing with horses," said Rhia. "Foolish of them not to arm the guards with swords."

"They could hardly expect an attack by swordsmen from *inside* the city . . ." said Vercingetorix.

He gazed into Rhia's eyes. She gazed back steadily into his. Never more than in this moment, which might be their last, had he wanted to kiss her. He was certain that his desire was shared, but he knew that it could not be.

"Still the thought that slows the mind . . ." Vercingetorix whispered instead. And found that she was whispering the same thing to him. And then—

—they were running silently, swords in hand, toward the Romans guarding the gate.

The Romans shouted wordlessly, one foolishly threw his lance,

Vercingetorix slapped it out of the air with his sword, there were more shouts from the wall above, and then they were upon the gate guards.

Rhia slashed the neck of the Roman who had thrown his lance, nearly decapitating him; Vercingetorix ducked aside from the other Roman's first thrust, dived to the ground, rolling under his second thrust, and came up with his sword plunging into the Roman's gut.

The guard screamed in dying agony, screamed even louder as Vercingetorix yanked his sword out, pulling a slimy green loop of intestine with it. He and Rhia dashed to the gates, unbarred them, flung them open. Vercingetorix grabbed the lance from the blubbering Roman's flaccid hand and rammed it into the lower right-hand gate hinge, jamming the gate open. Rhia, looking around frantically for something to secure the left-hand gate and finding nothing close to hand, shrugged, took off her cloak and belt, and stuffed them into the upper and lower hinges.

Vercingetorix blew a long, loud, warbling, and inexpert note on his trumpet, and then he and Rhia, who was naked once more save for her sword, were standing side by side just inside the gateway passage as planned, while Romans clattered down the ladders from the gate towers.

They must now hold the gates open for perhaps five minutes. Unless their courage had failed them, Vercingetorix's little makeshift army would now be running toward the open gates, and once inside would be a match for the Romans, most of whom would be waking unprepared from sleep.

The gateway was wide enough to accommodate the passage of two wagons, which was a disadvantage, but the passage through it was as deep as the width of the city wall, and the last thing the Romans would have anticipated was to have to take it from defenders already inside the city.

As half a dozen and more legionnaires clambered in confusion toward the open gates, Vercingetorix and Rhia took up positions facing each other with their backs close to the passage's walls and their swords held out at arm's length to block it.

This still left a wagon width's gap, and after only a moment's hesitation, three Roman lancers and two swordsmen spontaneously dashed into it.

Once again, a Roman foolishly tried to spear Vercingetorix by throwing his lance like a javelin, and once more Vercingetorix slapped it aside with his sword. The now defenseless Roman wisely sought to flee, but was trapped in the passageway by the crush of his fellows.

Vercingetorix took a long, quick stride toward him, swinging his sword high, sideways, and two-handed, severing his head from his neck with a single blow, then kicking the headless body toward the center of the passage as it fell, jerking and twitching and spewing blood.

Rhia had already somehow slain one of the Roman swordsmen and likewise thrown the corpse to the center of the passage, where the body of the decapitated Roman fell upon it even as Rhia gutted the other swordsman, whipped him around screaming with her sword to shield her from a thrown lance, then threw him, not yet dead but unable to do more than howl in agony, upon the two corpses.

Having seen their fellows slain in moments and turned into a barricade of flesh, the two remaining Romans recoiled in horror and fear and fled backward, leaving Vercingetorix grinning ferally at Rhia. She grinned back at him, naked and panting, and spattered with blood, and unspeakably desirable.

But such a bizarre thought was driven from his mind in the next moment when a fresh press of Romans jammed into the passageway, all swordsmen now, and Vercingetorix became one with his weapon.

Swords flashed and clanged, men shouted and screamed, blood flew through the air in drops and gouts, and bodies piled up in the center of the passageway, the dying blubbering and groaning in a growing pool of red.

Vercingetorix lost all track of time, which now seemed to crawl as slowly as a snail across a stone as attackers came at him, and now seemed as rapid as his sword strokes slicing their limbs, piercing their stomachs, spearing their hearts. He was aware of the sharp slicing pains of his own wounds, not as agony but as goads. His heart pounded, his breath came freely and deeply, and there was a terrible pleasure in it all.

The more Romans appeared, the deeper and wider the barricade of their bodies became, and the easier the gateway passage to defend, for now Vercingetorix found himself fighting side by side with Rhia from behind it, close enough to smell the intoxicating aroma of her battle sweat, close enough to touch.

The shouts of pain and surprise and agony, of her battle cries and his own, the pounding of his blood, melded into a roaring torrent of sound upon which his spirit rose up. The sword in his hands seemed alive with a will of its own, wielding him as its instrument, as he gave himself over to an awful but exhilarating abandon.

"They're here! They're here!"

First Vercingetorix came to the awareness that Rhia was shouting at him. Then he realized that the roaring in his ears had become the exultant shouts and battle cries of a multitude advancing rapidly toward him.

Turning, he saw twoscore and more Arverne warriors waving their swords and screaming as they rushed up the last yards of the roadway leading to the open gates, and he thought he glimpsed Oranix among them. Behind them were hundreds of peasants, huntsmen, smiths, half-grown boys, even women, brandishing spears, scythes, hoes, torches, knives, tree limbs.

He had one moment to regard Rhia—naked save for a veil of blood; scratched, stinking, panting, and exhausted, but with her lips creased in a triumphant smile and her eyes blazing with lustful glory as they met his own.

Then the Arverne warriors surged between them, kicking and shoving aside the barricade of Roman corpses. And Vercingetorix found himself hard-pressed to make his way through his own forces to the front of the battle, to lead the Arverni pouring into Gergovia to take back what was rightfully their own.

For Vercingetorix, most of the night passed like a time passed in a Land of Legend aflame with blood-pounding visions of glorious and vengeful death and destruction.

The commotion at the gate quickly aroused the townspeople from their slumber, and they poured into the streets in shock and confusion that turned to vindictive elation when they realized what was happening. Those who were not armed returned to their dwellings only to snatch up what fell to hand—a sword, a knife, an ax, a mallet—before returning to the streets to join in the sanguinary search for Roman legionnaires.

Most of the Romans were awoken into a chaos in which they found themselves outnumbered by angry mobs consisting of the entire population of the city. It quickly turned into a bloody blur of a rout without order or strategy or the need therefor.

Once most of the Romans had been cut to pieces or beaten to death, and the remaining few score taken prisoner, the ire of the mobs turned on those who were deemed collaborators. Wineshops and other merchant establishments purveying Roman goods were looted and sacked, buildings that had been Romanized with wooden imitations of columns or merely an excess of white paint were set ablaze, and anyone caught in the street wearing an item of Roman attire was fortunate to escape with a beating.

Vercingetorix drifted through this night of retribution not as the leader who had called it into being, but as one more Arverne giving free vent to unfettered rage, joining in the slicing and mauling and stomping of Romans, smashing open amphorae with his feet, standing in the midst of a crowd setting a merchant's goods ablaze, though careful not to harm a fellow Gaul, however Romanized.

But then he found himself in the plaza, crowded with joyfully irate Arverni. Scores of them had climbed into the Roman fountain and were ineffectually attacking the crudely carved stone bears with mattocks and hoes and wooden mallets. To judge from the hooting and cheering and torch-waving and debris-tossing, not all the Roman wine had been poured onto the stones of the plaza rather than down gullets.

Across the plaza, another such drunken and ecstatically vengeful mob had gathered in front of the Great Hall, working up their courage to storm it and no doubt attempt to destroy the Roman entrance portico that had been added to it. But standing at the foot of the steps and bravely trying to defend the Great Hall from the mob's outrage were Baravax and a score of Arverne warriors armed with axes and javelins.

The sight of Baravax about to be torn down by the mob whose actions *he* had incited abruptly awoke the man of knowledge within the unthinking man of action.

The press of shouting people paid no heed to his presence among them as he shouldered through them, and for a moment Baravax menaced him with his javelin when Vercingetorix confronted him at the foot of the stairs.

Then he recognized him.

"Vercingetorix!"

"Death to the Romans!" a drunken voice shouted.

"Death to collaborators!"

Rocks and bits of rubble began to fly from the anonymous safety of the midst of the mob.

"You saved *my* head—now it's time for me to save *yours*," Vercingetorix told Baravax, and he mounted the stairs. From this vantage he could be clearly seen, and slowly recognized by a score of people, and then, as the word spread, by everyone. The shouts and cries of the crowd guttered away into silence, and then a foot-stomping chanting began.

"Vercingetorix! Vercingetorix!"

King of Gaul! King of Gaul!

In his mind's ear, unheard voices added the refrain. Vercingetorix basked in this song to himself longer than was needful, for there was an intoxication to it headier than even the blood-hot thrill of battle.

And perhaps more dangerous.

"The Romans have been defeated and Gergovia is free!" he shouted to quell the chanting and his own sweet delirium. "Today Gergovia is free of Rome, tomorrow the lands of the Arverni, and after that all Gaul!"

"Vercingetorix! Vercingetorix! *Vercingetorix! Vercingetorix!*"

Was it a phantom of his desire, or *were* there now scattered voices out there indeed adding "King of Gaul"?

"The battle is won and the enemy is defeated! Go to your homes now, and let no Arverne's hand be set against any other!"

This was greeted not with adulatory chanting but with hoots and jeers. Taken aback, Vercingetorix realized that they would not be calmed until they were fed with meat they wanted to eat, until they were given something they wanted to hear.

"The enemy is Rome! The enemy is Caesar! From this day forward, let no Arverne's hand be set against any other, and let no Gaul set his hand against any other Gaul! Harm not the Great Hall of the Arverni, for from this day forward it belongs to *you*, to all of you, from the loftiest noble to the bastard child of the tiller of the smallest plot of land! Sleep well on the memory of glorious victory won, for tomorrow you will taste the sweet fruit thereof. Tomorrow we will hold council here to choose a new vergobret—not elected by a lackey Senate, as in the days of Gobanit, or even by an assembly of nobles, as in my father's day, but by *all of us*! A vergobret chosen by *you*, the brave Arverne people who have thrown off the yoke of Rome with your own hands!"

For the first time, Vercingetorix beheld a great multitude obeying his words as if he were a king as the crowd did indeed disperse toward sleep.

Shortly before noon the next day, Vercingetorix entered the Great Hall to the sound of his name's being shouted, being chanted, being sung, by a throng such as had never been seen there before. Warriors. Peasants. Townspeople. Artisans. Even beggars and whores. The Great Hall of the Arverni was packed with Arverni, blood-spattered, wild-eyed, drunk with beer, and triumph, and glory.

The great old wooden table from Keltill's day had been brought back into the center of the hall, and there stood the great old warrior Critognat presiding over a dozen warriors of similar vintage to keep it clear.

Critognat waved him to the table. This was hardly necessary, since it was the only possible place for him to stand and be seen by all; even so, Rhia, Baravax, and half a dozen guards had to clear a way for him through his own cheering and riotous people. The chanting broke up into a wordless cheer as he was seen to make his way toward it and then mounted it.

"The Arverni are without a vergobret, and I would—"

The chanting of "Vercingetorix! *Vercingetorix!*" resumed, accompanied now by the rhythmic beating of swords and daggers on shields, of feet on the stones of the floor. The sound was thunderous. And heady.

But Vercingetorix's blood had cooled during the night, and now he sought to do more than bask in this adulation—he meant to shape and to use it.

"Hear me before you elect me!" he cried, after he had raised both arms above his head for a silence in which to speak. "As the Arverni are without a vergobret, so is Gaul without a leader, and I tell you truly, I would be both!"

A wordless roar, and then they were chanting again, but this time words of a kind surely not heard since the time of Brenn.

"Vercingetorix! King of Gaul! *Vercingetorix! King of Gaul!*"

"*No!*" Vercingetorix shouted. When the chanting and banging of shields and stomping of feet still went on, he shouted even louder: "*NO!*"

"No, Arverni," he went on when the crowded Great Hall had been reduced to silent mystification. "You have the power and the right to acclaim me vergobret, but no single tribe may proclaim me king of Gaul. Only *Gaul* may do that! Nor would I wear the Crown of Brenn until I have earned it in battle! I would lead an army of Gaul to victory, but not as king, for I will not rule in Gaul until there is truly a Gaul in which to rule! And I have seen it in a vision that this *shall be*! A king of Gaul shall parade in triumph through Rome itself!"

"Vercingetorix! King of Gaul! *Vercingetorix! King of Gaul!*"

Now Vercingetorix let it go on, until at length it died away of its own accord.

"Our vergobret had long been chosen by the council of nobles, and then by Gobanit's Senate of traitors. But now the Great Wheel is turning, and we must all become great to turn with it. And so I would be proclaimed vergobret by *all* of the people!"

"Ver-cin-getorix! Ver-go-bret!" someone shouted out, and then someone else, and then it became a kind of chanting song, the words sung by voices, the rhythm beaten out by stomping feet, clapping hands, swords and daggers upon shields.

"So be it!" Vercingetorix finally declared when he was granted silence in which to speak. "And these are my first words as your vergobret: I, Vercingetorix, vergobret of the Arverni, outlawed by Caesar, now outlaw *Gaius Julius Caesar*! I declare his life forfeit should he dare once more to set foot in Gaul! So too do I outlaw all Romans in Gaul! I declare all their goods the property of the first loyal Gaul to seize them! Take what you want and destroy the rest! Let us sweep all things Roman from our hearts and our land! Let us begin this happy task here and now!"

At this a tremendous cheer went up, as Vercingetorix had known it would, and what was supposed to happen next was what he had given them leave to do, pour out of the Great Hall and begin the cleansing of all things Roman from the lands of the Arverni, and, he hoped, inspire the other tribes of Gaul to follow their lead.

But this plan went awry.

"Death to Caesar!" someone shouted. "Death to Rome!"

This was met with full-throated roaring enthusiasm, and instead of emptying out, the Great Hall was filled with a chanting of *"Death to Caesar! Death to Rome!"* that swiftly proceeded to ferocious cries of fury.

And to Vercingetorix's horror, he found himself beholding a gathering whose mood had changed with the suddenness of a summer thunderstorm from victorious elation into bloodthirsty rage. Fists shook in the air, daggers and swords were brandished. He found it a fearsome and ugly sight—the face of the madness of the night before exposed in the full light of day, made no more bearable by the knowledge that he had taken part in it himself.

His people, like famished wolves, were howling for something to tear apart, something to kill; he could see it, he could hear it, he could smell it on their breath and sweat, and he could not deny that he felt it himself.

"Death to Caesar! Death to Rome!"

And then the prey was tossed into their midst.

"Death to these Romans!" shouted a grizzled old warrior at the back of the hall near the entrance.

Their hands tied behind them, their armor and helmets gone, stripped to their breechclouts, their bodies scratched bloody, their faces bruised purple by beatings, a score or so of Roman legionnaires, prodded by spears, swords, broom handles, pitchforks, staggered inside.

This stilled the chanting and caused a surge of people to rush at the helpless Romans, kicking, pummeling with fists, some armed with swords and daggers.

"Stop!" Vercingetorix shouted as loud as he knew how. *"Stop before you dishonor yourselves before the gods and all Gaul!"*

This stayed the impending murderous vengeance for a moment Vercingetorix knew would not last.

"Are we to become the barbarians the Romans say we are?" he added quickly. "Is it our way to rip our enemies to pieces like a pack of mad dogs, or are we Gauls?"

"Is it our way to let *these mad dogs* live?" demanded the old warrior who had first called for their blood.

"All Romans in Gaul are outlawed!"

"By our vergobret himself!"

"Kill them!"

"Tear them apart!"

"No!" declared Vercingetorix.

"Would you spare them, Vercingetorix, vergobret of the Arverni?"

"No," said Vercingetorix, "I would not spare them."

And he gazed out at his people, red-faced, blood-lusted, their fury stayed by his words for what could only be moments. The silver-tongued Vercingetorix knew not what to say next. And so he allowed whatever might come forth to speak through him.

"No, I would spare the life of no Roman, but I would not waste their deaths either," he said. As these words escaped his lips, he knew what he was going to say, he knew what he was going to do, and he trembled with the knowledge.

"I would use their deaths to make magic," he declared, and that brought utter stillness, the rapt attention of all eyes upon him, upon this warrior, this vergobret, who all knew had worn the robe of a druid when he had taken the sacrifice of the life of Diviacx.

And Vercingetorix knew what they were thinking:

What magic would he make with a score of lives?

"I will use their deaths to make a great magic," he said. "As Caesar and Rome caused the burning of my father, so will I burn these Romans. I will burn them not only as your vergobret, but before all the tribes of Gaul as a druid, with the Arch Druid by my side. We will seal the pact we made with the life of Diviacx once more. This time with the lives of the enemies of Gaul! As is only just!"

As is only just, Guttuatr, Vercingetorix thought grimly. As you commanded me to watch my father burn and do nothing but endure, so must you now pay the price of enduring your collaboration in this terrible magic that the destiny you called upon me to fulfill commands me to make.

The vast crowd spread out across the meadow and halfway up the hill on which Gergovia stood. The entire population of the city and more had turned out for the spectacle: Arverni from the countryside, leaders of most of the other tribes, and even their curious followers, bards, druids, musicians. The late-winter day was cool, but the sky was a cloudless blue and the sun rising to its zenith warmed the blood and the spirit, as did the beer being passed around; a gay festival atmosphere prevailed.

"This is *wrong*, Vercingetorix," said Guttuatr as the Roman prisoners, their arms bound behind them, were marched through the jeering, hooting, laughing throng to the wicker man.

"Wrong to execute by burning?" Vercingetorix said bitterly. "Tell that to the spirit of Keltill!"

"Your father would never have done this thing, even had he made himself king," said the Arch Druid.

"Would not have sacrificed captured enemies? Would not have burned them in a wicker man, as was so often done in the long ago?"

The Romans had been given much wine before being brought forth, leaving them just barely able to walk, and now more was being poured down their throats as they were prodded, thrust, and stuffed into the wicker man, for Vercingetorix had no desire to see them suffer more than this ceremony required. Many might take pleasure in what was about to come, but for him it was grim necessity.

The wicker man was a cage in the rough shape of a man. It took a large one to hold a score of Romans. Its head stood half as high as the top of a full-grown oak, and it was a fat fellow, its unseemly girth crammed with the prisoners, even trussed as they were, and piled atop each other in two layers.

"Your father would not have presumed to don a druid's robe before a gathering such as this," said Guttuatr.

Vercingetorix and Guttuatr stood together before the wicker man, alone save for Baravax and his guards, who were loading the Romans into it and piling up logs and kindling at its feet. Guttuatr, as always, wore his white robe, and carried his staff of office.

Vercingetorix wore the garb of an Arverne warrior—sword and helmet included—but carried a folded druid's robe, pure white and untrimmed by tribal colors, over his left arm.

"You object more to the garment I intend to wear than to the burning of these Romans or the words I would have you speak," Vercingetorix ventured in an attempt to lighten the tension between them.

"I am not a fool, Vercingetorix," Guttuatr said coldly. "You intend to use it to make a magic that has never been made before. But I do not pretend to know where it will lead if it succeeds."

"Nor do I," admitted Vercingetorix. "But we both know that Gaul will fall to Caesar if it fails."

The Arch Druid sighed. "That," he said with no enthusiasm, "is why I am here."

Vercingetorix had prevailed on Guttuatr not only to attend himself but to summon vergobrets, leaders, and nobles of all the tribes of Gaul to bear witness to the burning of the Romans.

The Arch Druid had at first refused to collaborate in such an atrocity.

"You must, even as must I," Vercingetorix had told him. "Exactly *because* it is such a terrible atrocity. All who witness it will know that it will so outrage Caesar that no further collaboration is possible. Thus will it bind together the tribes of Gaul in adversity. There will be no turning back."

Most of the vergobrets had come. Vercingetorix could make out their standards staked in the ground among the crowd at wide intervals, but the boar of the Eduen vergobret was not among them. Liscos had developed a convenient illness and sent Litivak in his stead, or, rather, had not forbidden Litivak to attend with twoscore of his own warriors.

When they met, Litivak had been distant, and his unease apparent. "Why are you doing this, Vercingetorix?" he had demanded. "Surely you know it will bring down the wrath of Caesar on all of us."

"The wrath of Caesar has already fallen on the Arverni," Vercingetorix told him. "Now the wrath of the Gauls will fall on Rome."

"The wrath of the *Arverni,* you mean. And do not suppose I don't know why you're doing this. You *mean* to bring down the wrath of Rome upon all Gaul."

"If you believe that, then why are you here?"

Litivak had shrugged, and sighed. "Because, though Liscos still believes Caesar, I doubt not that Caesar will turn on the Edui as soon as he finishes off the Arverni. So we must fight or die."

"Spoken like a true Gaul!" Vercingetorix had ventured warmly.

"Spoken like a man who knows his choice has been taken from him," Litivak had said as he turned his back and walked away.

Worse was waiting when the Carnutes arrived. Cottos, their vergobret, greeted Vercingetorix warmly, as did Epona, who was with their party, but Marah was with her, and obviously only under her mother's duress, for while she would meet his eyes, it was with an angry glare and a curled lip.

Only when her mother angrily thrust her upon him would she speak, and then her words were like a dagger in his heart.

"You at least owe it to him to tell him what you told me," Epona had said.

"I owe this barbarian nothing."

"Then why are you here?" said Vercingetorix.

"Because my mother demands that I witness this disgusting and hideous spectacle," said Marah, glaring now at Epona and not at him.

"She understands nothing of the necessities of—"

"I understand the difference between barbarism and civilization as you so obviously do not!" Marah shouted at both of them. "Caesar released hostages when we no longer served his . . . necessities, rather than kill us in a childish petulant rage. Which is more than can be said for this . . . this . . . boy who would make me his Queen of Gaul."

And she too had turned her back and stalked away.

Vercingetorix takes a step forward, raises his left hand.

The door to the wicker cage is tied shut, and the guards withdraw into the watching crowd, still and silent now with expectancy, and the only sounds to be heard are the cries of terror and angry curses of the drunken Romans.

"You have told me, Retake your own city from the Romans, and then we will see about doing what you have done in our own lands," he says.

He gestures at the Romans in the cage. "Behold, this I have done, and Gergovia is free. Here are Caesar's men in a good Gallic cage, and as they burn, so will the lands of the Arverni be burned free of the pillage and death and desecration that they have brought!"

A cheer goes up, but almost entirely from Arverne throats. The vergobrets and nobles of the other tribes stand stone-faced beneath their tribal emblems, some with their arms folded across their chests.

"When Caesar returns with his mighty legions, you will wish you had never been born, you cowardly Arverne turd!" a Roman shouts boldly from the cage.

Vercingetorix smiles as if the Roman has spoken at his bidding.

"When Caesar returns with his mighty legions, he will be met by the mightier army of *Gaul!*" he roars.

And the assembled Arverni in their thousands pound daggers and swords upon shields, feet upon the earth, a rhythmic thunder to accompany the chanting:

"Vercingetorix! King of Gaul! Vercingetorix! King of Gaul!"

The Bituriges and the Santons, the Turons and the Parisii, the Atrebates and the Belovaques, far outnumbered by the chanting multitude, stand silent. Some glance around fearfully, some stare in guarded outrage, realizing that Vercingetorix is about to bring Rome down upon them all, like it or not. Litivak narrows his eyes like a commander coldly and speculatively studying a field of battle.

"Yes, I intend to lead all Gauls who will follow me in driving the Romans from our land," Vercingetorix declares. "For I am Vercingetorix; my name may mean 'great leader of warriors,' but it can also be taken to mean 'leader of great warriors.' And that is you, Edui; that is you, Carnutes; that is you, Santons, Atrebates, Bituriges, Parisii; that is you, my fellow *Gauls,* for that is what we all must become if we are to survive!"

The Arverni roar their approval. Here and there, warriors of other tribes begin to join in. Even a few vergobrets—Epirod of the Santons, Comm of the Atrebates, Cottos of the Carnutes—beside whom Epona gives full voice. Marah regards Vercingetorix with frosty disgust.

The chanting begins again:

"Vercingetorix! King of Gaul! Vercingetorix! King of Gaul!"

But now the Arch Druid, Guttuatr, raises his staff high above his head. *"Silence!"* he commands.

And silence he receives.

"Vercingetorix speaks the truth. This is the time of a Great Turning, and the peoples of Gaul must turn with it or perish from the earth. This has been written in the heavens, and . . ."

The Arch Druid seems to hesitate for a moment before going on. "And it has also been written . . . that all Gaul must unite . . . under one war leader, and that must be Vercingetorix, son of Keltill."

"Vercingetorix! King—"

But before the chant can fully rise, the Arch Druid pounds the end of his staff hard upon the earth.

"But not as king!" he roars.

"So be it!" Vercingetorix shouts, and unfolds the pure white druid's robe and dons it, over his warrior's garb and arms.

"So be it," repeats the druid that the warrior has become. "I swear to you an oath as a druid and as war leader of Gaul. For behold, now they are one and the same. Never shall I be king in Gaul while a Roman soldier remains on the soil of our land. May my life be taken and my honor forfeit if ever I seek to violate this oath."

A stillness descends on the crowd.

Critognat emerges from the crowd and hands Vercingetorix a torch.

"As war leader of the armies of Gaul, I say that, from this moment forth, we are all *Gauls* or traitorous lackeys of Rome!" Vercingetorix declares. "All who are not with us are against us! And all who are against us must die!" He half turns, and backs up to the pile of logs and kindling at the foot of the wicker man.

"As the son of Keltill, who died in fire, I now fulfill my father's failed destiny and seal in fire the alliance among us against Rome. By this fire, every Roman will know that every Gaul is his enemy, and by this fire, every Gaul will know that Caesar can give him no quarter."

And he throws the torch upon the pyre.

Vercingetorix watches in silence as the kindling ignites, then the logs, and then the wicker man itself. His eyes are drawn to the blazing giant, a sketch of a man drawn in flame, towering above him, burning bright.

Within that flaming spirit, men writhe and scream and cry out in their agony, and from that spirit out of the Land of Legend there comes the savory aroma of roasting meat and the sweet, foul stench of burning flesh, and they are one and the same.

Somehow both are the smell of Keltill.

Vercingetorix would look away, but he cannot. He cannot move. For

there are eyes looking into his from within the man-shaped fire, and
they capture his own. And he falls down into them, and through them,
and into the Land of Legend.

Here he can still see the flame and hear the screams and cries. But it
is a corpse on a funeral pyre burning in the flame as warriors solemnly
pound out a dirge on their shields with their swords. And the screams
and cries arise from the throats of famished wretches, children, dod-
dards, crones, grubbing for roots and worms on a treeless and unfor-
giving earth.

Yet Vercingetorix finds himself wearing the Crown of Brenn as he
rides a white horse triumphantly through an honor guard of Roman
centurions toward Caesar, seated humbly before him.

And he hears the familiar chanting.

"Vercingetorix! King of Gaul! Vercingetorix, King of Gaul!"

Then he is upon a horse in the midst of a ferocious battle, surrounded by Romans and Gauls. He spies Caesar, fighting afoot.

Caesar's sword goes flying through the air; Vercingetorix rears his
horse.

And snatches the tumbling sword out of the air as he did the Crown
of Brenn as a boy. And the sword becomes the crown, and he places it
upon his head, riding in the center of a great army of Gauls.

Like the shadow of a dark front of clouds moving at magical speed,
Vercingetorix's army rides across fair, sunny Gaul, plains rich with
ripening grain, lush green valleys thronged with fat sheep, orchards
laden with fruit, farmsteads with bursting granaries.

But as the army of Gaul passes, a wall of flame follows in their wake,
and the grain burns in the fields, and the sheep become rotting skeletal
corpses, and the trees fall in fire, and the farmsteads are smoldering
ruins, and the skies are black with evil roiling smoke.

A vast Roman army pursues them across this desolate landscape.
But it is an army of stoop-shouldered cavalrymen leading skeletal
horses, of ranks of legionnaires afoot, too weak to bear armor, their ribs
showing through threadbare tunics. There is only one rider among
them, and he is wearing the crimson cloak of Caesar. But the horse is a
bleach-boned skeleton, and so too the man.

And Vercingetorix hears the voice of Keltill. Out of the long ago.

"In fire do I become the tale the bards will sing.
In fire, I enter the Land of Legend as a king!"

And Vercingetorix is declaiming with him.

"As the fire sets my spirit free . . ."

And then he stands before a burning man-shaped cage of wicker already beginning to crumble into embers, wrapped in the oily and obscenely savory smoke of the roasting corpses within. And, turning to gaze at the multitude who have witnessed the terrible magic he has made, leaves the Land of Legend, chanting the last words of his father's death ode:

"So in fire will you remember me."

XIII

C AESAR WAS CHILLED even wrapped in his heavy winter cloak, and once more, snow avalanched down from the mountain slopes onto the valley floor had forced him to dismount and lead his horse through the treacherous terrain of hidden rocks, sodden soil, and melt pools.

But he was mindful only of the larger logistical problem. Cavalrymen reduced to leading their horses. Wagons endlessly mired in snow and mud. Cracked wheels. Broken axles. Snow and misty rain. The infantry were most used to the hardship and grumbled the least. The infantry were the heart of his legions and highest in Caesar's affections, and, were it not unseemly for their commander to do so, he would have given over his horse entirely and marched the whole way afoot with them.

At the moment, he was effectively doing it anyway, for the only men in front of him were trailblazers on foot, testing the way ahead with poles.

Young Brutus led his horse and slogged in the forefront with him, but Labienus, Antony, Trebonius, Galba, and the rest of his generals stayed back within the main body of the troops, so that they could ride through the passes on paths well trodden by thousands of foot soldiers.

Perhaps I should *order* all of them to lead from the front as I do, Caesar mused half seriously. It would serve them right.

They had all blanched at the prospect of crossing the Alps from the south with an army in early March.

"Never been done before," Galba had grunted.

"Hannibal crossed the Alps with *elephants*," Caesar had told him. "And that had never been done before either."

"You're sure you want to risk such a venture?" asked Labienus.

"Even you are afraid, Labienus?"

"I fear no danger in battle," Labienus replied with proper indignation. "But who can fight the weather? Valor will avail us nothing if there's a late blizzard in the high passes."

"Are you more afraid of a little snow and ice than of the Gauls?" Caesar had roared at the lot of them. "Are you going to let a little bad weather keep you from taking vengeance against the savages who burned Roman soldiers alive?"

Caesar picked up his pace, deciding to join the trailblazers at the very point of his huge army, eager to make himself physically useful, eager do his part to reach the other side of the mountains all the sooner.

Brutus puffed and groaned a step behind him, keeping up. "Who would have thought it possible to cross the mountains this early in the year?"

"No one, Brutus, least of all the Gauls, who believe Romans softer men than themselves!" Caesar told him. "And that is why we are doing it. To crush this barbarian horde before Vercingetorix can form it into a real army."

This was no stripling barbarian chieftain. This was a clever and ruthless leader.

First he had heard travelers' tales filtering back over the mountains which had seemed like fantasies crafted to horrify the credulous on dark and stormy nights.

Vercingetorix, accompanied only by a naked amazon, had used magic to force the gates of Gergovia. A wrathful mob had then poured through them, torn the Roman garrison to pieces with their bare hands, and roasted and eaten them. Vercingetorix had erected a giant wooden cage in the form of a man and burned a hundred legionnaires to death inside it. He had done this robed as a druid and holding the Arch Druid at sword point. According to yet another lurid tale, Vercingetorix was now himself Arch Druid, having come by the office via some hideous magical rite wherein Diviacx had been offered up as a human sacrifice to Pluto.

Then Tulius managed to send a messenger back to Gallia Narbonensis, and the report he delivered, though less florid, was grimmer still from a practical point of view.

Diviacx was indeed dead. He *had* been a human sacrifice at some grisly druid ceremony. Vercingetorix had not become Arch Druid, but the druids were now doing his bidding and calling all the tribes of Gaul to war against Rome under his command.

It was also true that the entire garrison of Gergovia had been slain, save for some score or so of legionnaires whom Vercingetorix *had* burned alive to seal some barbaric blood oath among the tribes at which most of the vergobrets had been present. After which he had placed all Romans in Gaul under sentence of death, to be conveniently carried out by any Gaul who wished to loot their property.

Many of the tribes had risen against the isolated Roman garrisons. No prisoners were being taken. Tulius had managed to concentrate the survivors in a single force near Bourges, large enough to keep the Bituriges from joining in and, for the moment at least, intimidating enough to keep Vercingetorix's army from attacking.

This baleful news had enraged Caesar to the point where he suffered a bout of the falling sickness. If his spirit had had a vision wherever it had gone, he returned with no memory of it, but he had emerged calmer, in which state he had to admire Vercingetorix's ruthless cleverness.

How Vercingetorix had turned the druids into his instrument might be a mystery, but the burning of the Romans in the presence of the vergobrets had been a demonic stroke of genius, implicating them all in a hideous outrage against Rome.

Vercingetorix was clever. Vercingetorix was ruthless. Perhaps he was even a master of druid magic, as the superstitious Gauls believed. But he was a Gaul commanding Gallic barbarians, facing Gaius Julius Caesar commanding the legions of Rome.

Caesar caught up to the trailblazers, and they greeted him like a comrade, pleased to see him among them, and by now no longer surprised.

"I thought I'd give you a hand again," said Caesar, drawing his sword. "The more help you have, the faster you can blaze the trail, the faster our army can move, the sooner we can get there, and the sooner we can take our vengeance on the bastard swine who burned our comrades alive!"

He poked his sword into a snowbank, using it as they used their poles, but as he proceeded along the wall of whiteness, he began thrusting it with a vigor more appropriate to the skewering of enemies, for he saw images emerging from the glare, drawing him into it: burning men, burning fields, a burning city, walls of flame so hot and bright they were burning white, the white of desert-bleached bones, of the salted soil of what had once been Carthage, a lifeless wasteland and his legions marching across it, through white sand, white ash, under a pitiless sun burning out of a silvery-white shimmering sky, the taste of burning copper and thin, sour blood. . . .

And a giant afire, striding toward him across this desolate landscape, crushing his legions to dust in his wake, and his face was that of Vercingetorix, and upon his head he wore the false Crown of Brenn that Gisstus had crafted, and he laughed and threw the severed head of Caesar's dead friend at him, shouting, "Here is your tribute, Caesar! Take your triumph back to Rome!"

"You shall see who is the harder man, Vercingetorix!" Caesar cried, thrusting his sword through the flaming heart of the giant. "You shall see what happens to a people who dare to pillage what is Rome's! How Caesar deals with a man who so spurns friendship offered freely as if by a father to a son!"

"Caesar? Caesar?"

Caesar came blinking up from whiteness into whiteness.

He was lying on his back in a snowbank with the coppery taste of his own blood in his mouth from having bitten his tongue.

The falling sickness. And a vision therein.

One that he did remember but did not understand.

"Caesar? Are you all right?"

Brutus was standing over him, holding out a hand to help him up. The trailblazers had ceased their labor and gathered around him in a circle of concern.

Spurning the helping hand, Caesar rose unaided to his feet, forced a laugh. "Just the falling sickness, my friends," he said. "They say it is the gift of the gods, though if I had my choice I'd prefer a pot of gold, or even wine."

Brutus' face was a carefully composed blank, but the simple and honest legionnaires eyed their commander with an unmasked nervousness tinged by a certain superstitious awe.

"But sometimes the gods grant me a vision with it," said Caesar, "and they have done so today."

"And what did you see, Caesar?" one of the trailblazers ventured uneasily.

"I saw the Gauls, my friends, as they are even now, drunkenly cele-brating their atrocities and squabbling over the plunder, never dreaming that a Roman army is about to fall upon them. And do you know why?"

"Because no Roman army has ever crossed the mountains in winter before?"

"Indeed!" said Caesar. "Because they are barbarians and we are Romans! Because barbarians believe that what has never been done before is impossible. They will never understand that, for Romans like us, *nothing* is impossible. And that is why we will defeat them."

This little speech seemed to satisfy the trailblazers, for they returned to their task with even more vigor and will than before. Caesar allowed himself to fall about a score of paces behind, to the apparent relief of Brutus.

"A noble speech, Caesar," Brutus said.

"And true, as far as it goes," Caesar told him. "But there is another and greater reason why we shall surely defeat Vercingetorix and his Gauls."

Brutus gave him a quizzical look.

Caesar nodded in the direction of the trailblazers, then turned to point back at his army: horsemen, wagons, men marching in good order, filling the width of the Alpine valley, stretching back as far as the eye could see and farther, into the winding and narrowing pass leading beyond the far horizon.

"There is the other reason, Brutus!" he declared, and the pride he heard in his own voice was entirely unfeigned. "While the quarrelsome tribesmen of Vercingetorix spend the winter celebrating their cheap victories, my loyal legions trudge dutifully up these snowy mountains! He commands a Gallic rabble while I command a Roman army! His men fight for loot and their own glory. My men fight to win."

"You see?" said Oranix. "There they are!"

"It's true!" exclaimed Litivak.

When Oranix had reported that his scouts had seen Roman troops moving through the Alpine passes before the winter snows had melted, Vercingetorix had assumed that this must be merely a scouting party. But Oranix insisted that his men had seen a Roman army on the march, and this Vercingetorix had found impossible to credit, so he decided to ride east to see for himself.

Rhia, who now never left his side, rode with them. Critognat, bored with the desultory looting, came along too. Likewise Litivak, who had been on the verge of withdrawing his Eduen warriors from the army of Gaul when the report arrived, for his men were growing restive and sullen lurking in the lands of the Arverni with little to do, and the Eduen vergobret was strongly suggesting he withdraw.

"Liscos still believes Caesar will content himself with destroying the Arverni," Litivak had told Vercingetorix.

"And you . . . ?"

"I'd best see for myself," Litivak had replied.

Now the five of them sat on their horses just within the cover of a tongue of forest atop a foothill a safe distance northwest of the pass, watching the Roman army arrive in Gaul.

An army it indeed was. Formation after orderly formation emerged in narrow file from the pass, then spread out across the plain like honey pouring from the lip of a jug onto a tabletop. First came a screen of cavalry, then five ranks of infantry, then supply wagons, then another five ranks of infantry, then more cavalry leading another formation, and another, and another, like an endless succession of orderly waves rolling in across a sea of melting white snow and frozen brown mud.

"The gods favor us!" Critognat exclaimed enthusiastically.

Oranix and Rhia regarded him as if he had gone mad.

"More Romans to kill than we ever could've hoped for!"

Vercingetorix would have laughed were the situation not so grave. Here was a fearless Gaul such as might have ridden with Brenn, and he doubted that Critognat was jesting.

"Enough of a threat to rouse the fighting spirit of the Edui, Litivak?" he said dryly.

"This is indeed an army meaning to conquer all Gaul," Litivak said. He shook his head. "But we are not prepared to confront an army like *this*."

And we never will be, Vercingetorix knew full well.

"That is no doubt why Caesar has returned so unexpectedly early in the year," he said instead. "To catch us unprepared and dare us to attack him with what we have."

Which was no more than a force of some twelve thousand Arverne warriors Vercingetorix knew he could count on, about half that number of Litivak's Edui, and a disorganized assortment of troops from the smaller tribes whose size and composition varied from day to day.

"A worthy enough challenge," declared Critognat. "I say we should thank Caesar for offering us such glory by allowing him an honorable death in combat when we defeat him instead of burning him alive."

"You're getting soft in your dotage," Vercingetorix told him with a laugh.

Only Critognat laughed with him, for in truth there was not much to laugh about. The sole glory to be gained by accepting Caesar's challenge and attacking such an army would be a glorious defeat.

So that must be what Caesar is counting on, Vercingetorix realized. A full-force attack by an unprepared and outnumbered army of Gauls like Critognat: fearless of death, fighting for glory and honor, unable to obey any orders but those of their own stout and noble hearts.

Why *else* risk the mountain passes in winter? And arrive when there were no crops ripening in the fields or fresh grass for horses? Was it not Caesar himself who had declared that keeping an army well supplied was at least half the battle?

"Surprise may be on Caesar's side," Vercingetorix said, "but time is on our side if we make it our ally."

"How so?" asked Litivak. "You sound as if you have a plan."

"Perhaps I do . . ." Vercingetorix muttered, thinking aloud. "It is the end of winter, and our forces are far fewer than Caesar's. . . ."

"You sound as if this is an advantage!" exclaimed Litivak.

"And why not, if we make it so?" Vercingetorix told him as the strategy took full form in his mind. "We have stored up what we could of food and fodder, and we are among our own people. Down there is a vast army marching through a winter-barren hostile land that must survive with what it has brought with it. Caesar therefore must count on a quick series of great battles."

"Perhaps only one!" said Critognat. "All the warriors of Gaul against all his legions! Night and day! Without respite or sleep! Gauls can stand up to that! These Romans certainly won't! We'll fight till they drop from exhaustion, or surrender in despair, whichever comes first!"

"No, Critognat," Vercingetorix told him. "Why give the enemy what he hopes for? Instead, we will fight Caesar's legions as the ants overcome the beetle that invades their nest, with a multitude of tiny bites that harry it and exhaust it and force it to be gone."

"*Ants!*" roared Critognat. "We are not ants!"

"As a pack of wolves brings down a great stag, then, by ripping out its belly."

"I like the sound of that better. But I still do not know what it means."

"We starve them," Vercingetorix told him. "Quick concentrated attacks on their supplies. Ride in, destroy, ride out—do it over and over again."

"Where is the glory in that?" demanded Critognat.

"In victory, Critognat, in victory!"

"Who would wish to boast of such a victory without honor?"

"He has a point," said Litivak. "Few Gauls would have their fighting spirits roused by a call to such inglorious battle, and many would deem it craven, and not without justice."

In his heart, Vercingetorix knew this to be true, but the man of knowledge knew that all other paths would lead to defeat, to a Gaul conquered by Rome. And where would be the honor or glory in that?

And so he must dissemble.

Perhaps even to himself.

"Once the Romans are out of food and weakened by starvation, *then* we destroy them in one grand, glorious battle."

"It *might* work," muttered Litivak. "And in truth, I can see nothing else that might."

"Still," said Critognat, "it seems cowardly. I have no love for the Romans, but even they should not be forced to fight with their ribs showing through their skin."

The valley was broad, the hills to the east were low and sparsely wooded, but to the west there was forest, and the Roman road that ran arrow-straight through the valley was no more than a mile from the edge of it in places. Roman infantry, twenty ranks wide and ten ranks deep, marched with brisk assurance through the valley behind a screen of cavalry. Scores of heavily laden supply wagons rumbled along the road behind them in a long, narrow, vulnerable line, but the supply train was guarded along its entire length by infantry five ranks deep, in turn flanked by cavalry outriders.

Brandishing lances before them, a wild and unruly horde of nearly a thousand Gauls came galloping out of the forest along a wide front, howling and screaming toward the western flank of the Roman supply train.

The Roman cavalry guarding the wagons wheeled smartly to confront them, and the infantry behind them began to form turtles: the front ranks with their shields before them, the rest with their shields above their heads to form a protective roof.

The Gauls held on to their lances rather than throwing them like javelins as they clashed with the Roman cavalry, creating a terrifying and thunderous bang and clatter that was more noisy than effective, for most of the lances were blocked by shields. Even so, the shock and momentum of the charge knocked many Romans off their horses, to be trampled in the melee.

But the Roman line held, the Romans drew their swords, and in such close combat, swords were much more effective than unwieldy lances, and the Romans quickly broke the Gallic line roughly in the center—

—or so at least it seemed, as half the Gauls wheeled north, the other half south, fleeing along the roadside with the Roman cavalry in pursuit and other Roman cavalry units swinging out in broad arcs to cut off their escape.

But behind the first wave of Gauls had been a tighter, narrower formation of Gallic cavalry. Its front ranks were armed with swords and axes, and led by Vercingetorix himself; behind them galloped several hundred Gauls bearing flaming torches.

Vercingetorix led his warriors through the gap in the Roman cavalry, swords and axes smashing at the shields of the turtles. The Gauls behind flung scores of torches over the turtled Roman infantry. Most of them fell short, bouncing off shields, causing little more than confusion among their rear ranks.

But some of them reached wagons heavily laden with sacks of grain, ten of which smoldered, caught, burst into flame.

Their shields might protect them from the Gallic steel before them, but not from the searing heat of the roaring fires behind, and many of the Romans panicked and sought to flee, and their orderly formation broke. This in turn created chaos in the infantry lines to either side of the breach as Romans collided with Romans.

The Gallic cavalry formation now divided in two. Half of them followed Vercingetorix through the gap in the infantry line, came up *behind* the ranks of turtles, then wheeled up onto the roadway among the wagons headed north. The other half rode through the breach, executed the same maneuver, and reached the road headed in the opposite direction.

The Gauls galloped along the road in both directions through the narrow path between the wagons and the turtles, swordsmen and axmen shielding the torchbearers, who flung their torches into wagon after wagon at close range.

As these wagons caught fire, the drovers lost control of their terrified horses, who pulled flaming wagons this way and that, smashing into other wagons, adding to the panic, spreading the fires.

Both wings of the first wave of Gauls had meanwhile made for the forest with much of the Roman cavalry that had sought to cut them off now in pursuit. The rest of the Roman cavalry broke off to ride back in confusion toward the conflagration, where the infantry that had been guarding the supply train scattered in disarray as they sought to escape the swiftly moving fire.

The whole battle lasted less than ten minutes, from the time the first wave of Gauls burst from cover until Vercingetorix blew a signal on a trumpet and the remaining Gauls wheeled off the roadway, rode through the rear of the broken Roman formations, and disappeared back into the depths of the forest whence they came.

The slopes of the defile were steep and rock-strewn, but not so steep that nothing would grow on them, and the cleft between them, green with an abundance of fresh spring grass, was not quite narrow enough to be called a gorge, and not quite wide enough to be truly deemed an alpine meadow.

Vercingetorix crouched behind a seemingly natural jumble of boulders piled up by his men atop the ridgeline, watching the Roman supply train approaching. This was not one of the more direct routes through the Alps, but the pass was wide enough to allow an infantry guard to march on either side of the wagons.

"Clever prey," said Oranix, crouching beside him. "They never stumble into the same snare twice."

"You sound like you approve."

"Of course I approve," said Oranix, watching the Romans approach with the keen and concentrated gaze of the hunter. "Dull prey makes for a boring hunt."

Dull prey, Caesar's army was not. The first attack on a Roman supply train had been the easiest one, for Caesar had probably never seen such tactics before, but never again did he group his supply wagons together on a road. Each of his legions then moved with its own supply train in the center of a large infantry formation. They did not rely on roads. They kept far away from the forest.

This had freed Caesar to group his cavalry into several large scouting forces, seeking to hunt down the "army of Gaul."

Vercingetorix had then divided his forces into three main parts: Arverni led by himself, Edui led by Litivak, and a force composed of warriors from a collection of the smaller tribes led by the Atrebate vergobret Comm. The Gallic leaders knew the terrain far better than the Romans, and each commanded many more men than the roving Roman cavalry units, so it was easy to lead them into disastrous ambushes.

But Caesar regrouped his forces once more, this time into legion-sized units with the cavalry never far in advance of the infantry, and sent *them* roving independently around the countryside.

Once the snows melted and sowing began, the Romans gave over hunting for the elusive army of Gaul and instead took to harrying the peasants in their fields and sacking villages, trying to provoke the army to attack and tie it down in battle long enough for reinforcements to arrive.

Vercingetorix did attack, but not as Caesar had intended. He brought together only enough forces to attack single legions, and fought only long enough to destroy food supplies, never allowing a battle to last more than half an hour. Ride in, break through to the supply wagons, fire as many as possible, ride out, disperse, do it again. And again. And again.

Yet again Caesar regrouped his army, this time into three main forces, each with the supply wagons clustered in the center, each far too large to attack and penetrate. But these impregnable formations were too cumbersome to hunt down anything. All they could do was attempt to provoke suicidal attack by slaughtering villages, taking slaves, sacking towns. Several contingents of warriors from the smaller tribes deserted to return to their lands when Vercingetorix refused to take the bait and these lands Caesar cunningly gave over despoiling.

Vercingetorix had been constrained to call a council of his main lieutenants when even Litivak openly considered defecting. This was held over a roasting boar and a barrel of beer deep in the forest and away from other ears, for Vercingetorix knew full well what he was going to hear.

"There's no honor in this!" Critognat complained.

"Even the Arverni are calling you a coward!" said Comm. "And I'm beginning to agree with them!"

"Why fight if we're not even protecting our own people?" demanded Luctor of the Cadurques. "What are we supposed to tell our men to keep them from leaving?"

"Caesar attacks the farmsteads of those tribes who have troops in this army of yours and leaves the others be," said Litivak.

"Thus does he seek to divide us," said Vercingetorix.

"Thus is he succeeding," Litivak told him. "Liscos is now *demanding* that I withdraw my men. Unless I obey, *I* take the blame if Caesar *does* turn on the Edui once he has finished with you, not him."

"But if you don't," Vercingetorix told him, "the glory will be yours, not his."

"*Glory?* What glory?"

"The glory of winning the war."

"Winning the war!" growled Critognat. "We haven't even won a single real battle!"

"No glory!"

"No victory!"

"But no defeats either," Vercingetorix told them, "and if any among you can point one out, I now invite him to speak."

There was only sullen silence.

"We are winning the war," Vercingetorix insisted. "We are defeating the greatest power in the world. Caesar brought his army here in winter knowing it would have to live off what it brought with it until grain was ripe in the fields and grass in the meadows. Yet crops are only beginning to grow, and we have destroyed half of what the Romans brought to see them through to summer. They will be starving before then. Caesar must either retreat over the mountains or fight us with an army whose horses are dead or dying, whose legionnaires' knees have been rendered too weak to keep them standing, and *then* shall Gaul know the most glorious victory in the history of the world, for then shall we have done what no other people have done—not the Greeks, not Carthage with Hannibal and all his mighty elephants—we shall have defeated and humbled Rome!"

This silver-tongued speech had been enough to hold the army together, but Vercingetorix knew that, to bring that victory, sooner or later he would have to force down their unwilling throats a strategy far more bitter still.

But for the moment . . .

As the head of the Roman supply train began to move past his position, Vercingetorix saw that this one was guarded by infantry alone. "No cavalry at all this time . . ." he muttered.

"Clever prey," Oranix said again. "They've learned that we're choosing slopes too steep for horses to climb."

Behind the boulders piled up on the ridgeline and screened from sight were bales of hay wrapped around smaller boulders for weight, and soaked in sticky pitch. Vercingetorix's men were positioned all along the ridge on the other side of the crestline—like the hay bales, invisible from below.

Vercingetorix peered down into the valley, back at the line of boulders poised atop the ridge, down again. The center of the Roman supply train was now directly below him.

He raised his trumpet to his lips and blew the first signal.

All along the ridgeline, his men prized the piles of boulders free with stout tree branches, and hundreds of them, large and small, tumbled and bounced down the slope, kicking up clods of earth, dislodging more boulders, stones, and pebbles, rumbling and roaring toward the Romans within a fearsome cloud of dust.

Even from this distance, Vercingetorix could hear the cries of "Avalanche!" from below, as the front ranks of the Roman infantry guard knelt down with their shields before them in a futile attempt to block the mighty wave of rock and dust—

—which picked up speed as it reached the bottom of the slope, crossed the narrow valley floor, and broke upon them, smashing them backward into their fellows, crushing, pulverizing men, reaching the wagons, shattering wheels, cracking axles, panicking horses, as—

—Vercingetorix blew the second signal, and his men lit the hay bales and sent a second avalanche, this one of fire, rolling down the slope.

The flaming hay bales, even with their stone centers, formed a lighter avalanche than the boulders, and moved more slowly, causing the fresh green mountain grass to smolder in their wake. They had just enough speed when they arrived at the valley floor to roll through the decimated Roman infantry to reach the chaotic disarray of overturned and shattered wagons, and set them ablaze.

"We must last out until the grain in the field is ready for harvest, and that is all there is to it," said Caesar. "We will just have to reduce the rations again."

"Again?" moaned Tulius, holding up his bowl, which contained but a handful of porridge that had been boiled with grass to eke out the dwindling grain supply. "The men are eyeing the horses hungrily, and I must admit they're beginning to look good to me too."

"Surely you're not serious!" exclaimed Labienus. "We've got no chance at all without cavalry."

"Surely not," Caesar said peevishly. "We've lost enough of them already, and now at least there's enough new grass to sustain what we have left."

"Too bad it won't sustain *us*," said Galba.

"If it comes to that, perhaps it will," said Caesar.

Caesar choked down the last gluey and tasteless morsel of his own ration of gruel, which did little to assuage the dull ache in his gut.

A spring shower was descending, and behind was his bundled tent, but Caesar insisted that he and his commanders share every hardship of the men and be clearly seen to do so. If the ordinary legionnaires squatted outside in the rain to eat their midday meal, so would they. And if the men must make do with two handfuls of this grim green slop a day, the generals, and he himself, must enjoy no better. Morale was bad enough without having tales get around of fabulous luxuries—such as extra handfuls of gruel—being secretly enjoyed by high officers.

"Why don't we capture some of the more important cities?" suggested Labienus. "Nothing like a few one-sided major victories to improve morale. If Vercingetorix fights us for them, we'll have him where we want him."

"And find ourselves tying down large garrison forces in each city we hold to keep down hostile populaces, with our troops still on very short rations. Were I Vercingetorix, I would be most pleased to allow us to occupy as many such cities as we like."

"Perhaps, then, we should retreat south and try again when the situation is more favorable . . . ?" suggested Trebonius.

"And what, may I ask, are we to eat along such a long retreat, grass and worms and marmots?" Caesar said scathingly. "And what do you suppose we will find when we return, save a larger army of Gauls emboldened by our disgrace?"

He did not deem it politic to say "*if* we return," which, given the fatuous public hand-wringing of the Senate over the situation, and the private glee of his ever-more-numerous enemies therein, did not seem likely if he dragged the remnants of a starving army back over the Alps with its tail between its legs.

Which, Caesar had no doubt, was exactly what Vercingetorix was trying to force him to do. I should never have been so open with him. I should certainly never have told him that keeping an army supplied is half the battle. Worse still, thanks to my own folly, Vercingetorix knows that conquering Gaul is only a necessary military prelude to the conquest of Rome by political means.

Caesar had certainly not been forthcoming with his own generals about *that!*

Labienus, with his overdeveloped sense of honor, would report it to the Senate. Most of the rest of them probably would betray me out of ambition. No, there has been no man with whom I can fully share such thoughts since Gisstus was slain.

"Send out more foragers," he told his commanders. "Hunt down deer, hunt down boar, hunt down *rabbits,* fish every stream with nets, winkle every last mouse and vole out of its burrow. Strip the bark from the trees and scrape the moss from the rocks and boil it all into bitter soup. We need only survive until there are crops ripening in the fields, and *then* we shall attack every city in Gaul one by one if need be, not to hold but to sack, until we *force* the Gauls to fight to defend them. *Then* shall we crush them, and *then* shall the Gauls eat a defeat far more bitter than what they force us to swallow now."

If I have to eat grass, grass will I eat. If it comes down to dung, I will eat dung too. For there are morsels even less nourishing than grass, destinies far less possible to choke down than shit, and these I will *never* swallow.

Vercingetorix looked back down the valley at what he had wrought. The blue skies of summer above this rich farmland were fouled with a pall of sooty smoke; there were fires burning everywhere the grain in the fields had not yet been reduced to ash; the smoldering skeletons of orchards glowed an ugly orange against the blackened landscape.

Vercingetorix and Rhia rode a horse's length ahead of a squad of fifty warriors. He had divided the force with which he had entered this valley into a score of such squads, each with a druid whose authority would, he hoped, preclude the use of force by Gauls against Gauls.

Before him, the valley was a golden sea of ripe grain alternating with the stubble of that which had already been harvested, dotted with small groves of apple trees heavy with reddening fruit. Sheep grazed in the lush green fields around farmsteads, their granaries beginning to fill with the harvest, their sties filled with fat sows suckling new litters of piglets, the chickens and ducks and geese leading the season's hatchlings, a vision of bounty and well-being.

Vercingetorix raised his right arm and made a circling signal as his squad approached a little village of wood and wattle-and-thatch houses and granaries, surrounded by pigsties, duck ponds, and grassy fields where grazed the sheep. Thirty of his warriors fanned out to encircle the buildings in the center of the village where the peasants had already gathered. The rest accompanied Vercingetorix to guard him against their expected and not unjustified ire.

Dagavar, wife of Pithrin, mother of Comak, Belandra, Frisa, and Dirnor, watched the great hero ride into her village with an angry and uncomprehending heart. She knew this was Vercingetorix himself, for beside him rode his warrior woman carrying the bear standard. It almost shamed her to hate this boy, who could not be six years older than her own eldest son. But hate this vergobret of her own tribe, this sorcerer, this ravager of the land, Dagavar did.

She knew that Caesar and his Romans were the enemy, for so the druids proclaimed. Certainly she had no love for them; for she understood that if they had remained in their own country, where they belonged, this blond boy would not now be leading his warriors into her village to destroy the life she and Pithrin had built here for their children.

But how could anyone in her village not hate and fear Vercingetorix when all they had to do was look out into the distance and see the boiling black pillars of smoke to know that he and his warriors had already destroyed half the crops and livelihoods of the valley?

And for what? So that one clan of leeches would rule over them and extract unfair tribute, rather than another? So that a portion of their crops would be stolen in the name of "Gaul" rather than "Rome"?

War should be left to the nobles and warriors, and the folk of the land should be left alone to bring in the crops and tend the livestock as long as those who ruled were allowed to steal their unfair share.

What sort of war was this that turned farmers into beggars and destroyed the land in the name of saving it?

Vercingetorix rode into the dusty little square, where a score or so men had gathered with their wives and their children. He halted before them, warriors on either side of him. He did not dismount.

"I am Vercingetorix, commander of—"

"The great hero of Gaul!" a burly gray-haired fellow shouted scornfully, to hoots and jeers. Some of the men held scythes and hoes and pitchforks and meat knives.

"Why do you ruin the lands and destroy the crops of your own people?" demanded the portly woman of like age standing at his side with a raging glare in her eyes.

"To prevent a greater despoliation by Caesar's legions," Vercingetorix replied, as he always did. "The Romans would steal anything left behind for them to steal in any case."

"Stolen by the Romans, destroyed by you—what difference does it make to us? We are still left with nothing!"

And as he always did, Vercingetorix reached into the large leather sack affixed to his saddle, withdrew a handful of gold coins, and tossed them into the peasants' midst. "Do you suppose Caesar will pay in gold for what he takes?"

There was a scramble for the coins, but the adults seemed less avid than the children.

"Do you suppose we can eat your gold?"

"Enough!" shouted Vercingetorix, exasperated not with them but with himself, with having to repeat this dishonorable act over and over. But as the peasants must make the bitter sacrifice of their goods in this world that Gaul be free, so must he make bitter sacrifice in the Land of Legend, that of his own honor.

For there he had seen what would be the sweet fruit of such sacrifice, his and theirs—the legions of Rome, stoop-shouldered cavalrymen leading skeletal horses, legionnaires afoot too weak to bear armor plodding across a lifeless landscape. He had seen Caesar, a skeleton riding the skeleton of a horse. A cruel and mysterious vision burned into his brain. Crueler still, now that he knew what it meant.

"Every sheaf of grain, every scrawny chicken, every blade of grass!" he declared, drawing his sword. "Flee with what you can carry, and destroy *everything else!*"

The howls and protests were enough to have his guards drawing their swords, moving closer to him, and brandishing them menacingly.

"You do it or we will! No food or fodder must be left behind for the Romans. They would seize everything they find, so you lose nothing you would not lose anyway!"

"And what are we to do when what we can carry is gone?" shouted out an old man.

"What we all must do for Gaul, sacrifice and suffer."

It was Guttuatr who spoke these words, from behind the peasants;

they turned and saw a druid in a pure white robe bearing a staff with a fallen star atop it.

"The Arch Druid himself!"

Guttuatr slowly made his way to Vercingetorix's side, and turned to deliver the speech that he had now delivered scores of times. It had aged him. There were more lines in his face. His nose now seemed less that of a proud raptor and more that of an old man. His eyes no longer showed the same strength nor the line of his mouth the same resolution. Something had gone out of the man holding the staff of the Arch Druid's office. Perhaps some power had left the staff itself.

"It has never been for druids to take a hand in the affairs of war—"

"Nor honest farmers either!"

"Let warriors slaughter each other and let us be!"

"Will the Romans let any of us be?" said Guttuatr. "The Romans wage war on the very soul of Gaul, and *all* Gauls must sacrifice to save it! Warriors must sacrifice their lives, farmers their crops and livestock. . . ."

He faltered for a moment, and looked back at Vercingetorix with accusation in his eyes, and when he turned and spoke again, there was an inner message in his words that Vercingetorix knew was meant for him.

"And druids most of all," he said.

"Oh, and what do *you* sacrifice, Arch Druid?"

"More than you can know . . ." Guttuatr said somberly. His lower lip trembled like that of a doddard. "Perhaps more than even *I* can know . . . Perhaps, in the end, the very thing I seek to save . . ."

"He mocks me, Brutus," said Caesar.

And so, he thought, does the landscape of this accursed country, even the weather.

He rode a dozen or so horse-lengths ahead of the vanguard of his starving army, accompanied only by the young officer, whom he allowed more and more to follow at his side like a favorite hound.

The clear blue sky, fleeced with but a few pure white clouds, and the summer sun warming his skin mocked him with memories of better times in sweeter climes. On the northwestern horizon, the hills were green with grass, and forest climbed their slopes.

But he rode through the landscape of his terrible falling-sickness vision: burnt fields and meadows where the only signs of life were the

occasional green shoots peeping up through the endless ashes, and carrion crows squabbling over what little flesh remained on the charred
corpses of farm animals.

And to the northeast, in the direction in which they were presently
marching, there were already black clouds of smoke on the horizon.
They were always marching through these wastelands toward those
black clouds, for the army of Vercingetorix, grouped all together now as
a juicy bait, always remained just within range of his advance scouts,
but always beyond reach, firing the land as they retreated before him.

"How long can this go on, Caesar?" asked Brutus.

"Until we catch them and destroy them," said Caesar. "However
long it takes."

"But that could be forever," Brutus muttered disconsolately.

"Vercingetorix is a clever general," said Caesar. "He does what I
would do in his place. Faced with a superior force, he lures his stronger
enemy into endless pursuit, destroying everything as he retreats before
us, so that we are forced to march through a desert."

"A cowardly strategy," Brutus said primly.

"But an effective one."

"As long as he can maintain it," said Brutus.

"*What?*" cried Caesar. Suddenly he began to see the beginning of
hope. "You are absolutely right, my clever young friend!"

"I am . . . ?" said Brutus, with such a choice look of befuddlement
that Caesar almost laughed aloud.

"These Gauls prize honor and glory above all else, and that will be
their downfall!" And then Caesar *did* laugh, not at Brutus, but at his
own folly.

"What *is* it, Caesar? What have you found to laugh about?"

"Myself, Brutus, myself! I have been a fool. Here is a lesson for
you—a general should never trap himself in outdated wisdom. A strategy that once would have been futile may later prove wise."

"I don't understand. . . ."

Caesar gazed at the black smoke rising before him in the far distance. "Then perhaps neither will *he*," he said.

"You have lost me completely, Caesar," said Brutus.

"Worse still, I lost myself," said Caesar. "But no more. In the winter,
in the spring, taking a city bereft of supplies would have been a disaster,
but now there are a city or two whose tribes are minor ones which
wisely sought to keep out of Vercingetorix's ruinous war—"

"Like the Bituriges?"

"Exactly, my young friend, exactly! Vercingetorix has thus far kept out of their territory, for fear of accumulating new enemies."

He wheeled his horse around.

"But now we will force *him* to follow *us*! To Bourges! Where the Bituriges will surely have stored away the harvest within its walls against the general chaos outside."

"But surely Vercingetorix will realize where we are going and, with his well-fed horses and us moving mostly afoot, will be able to get there before us."

"Exactly!" said Caesar. "Pray to the gods that he does!" He laughed again, this time more heartily. "On second thought, why bother them with beggarly entreaties? He will have no choice! We have him, Brutus, we have him!"

And he set off at a full gallop to give the order.

Vercingetorix had called Critognat, Litivak, Comm, Luctor, and Cottos into council in a small forest clearing some distance from their troops. The night sky was moonless but star-bright, yet empty of omens that might aid him in comprehending the mind of Caesar. Even though a young boar was roasting on its spit above the fire around which they hunkered, Vercingetorix could summon up no visions from the flames. Nor did the barrel of beer into which they dipped drinking horns from time to time provide any.

For five days, Caesar's army had ceased its futile pursuit and instead marched away through lands already burned black. And today he had even refused the bait when Vercingetorix had shown his assembled forces atop a ridge to his southeast, continuing relentlessly to the northwest.

"He is going somewhere," said Vercingetorix. "That much is obvious."

"You do not have to be the Great Leader of Warriors to figure that out," snapped Comm.

"But where?" said Luctor. "And why?"

"Why should we care?" said Critognat. "Wherever he's going, we can move faster than he can, so let *us* finally chase *him,* catch him, and finish him off."

Vercingetorix knew that Critognat was speaking for most of the Gauls. Morale had been low since this strategy of despoiling and burning Gaul before the Romans had begun, but now that Caesar had seized an initiative that Vercingetorix could not explain, it was getting worse. Even Litivak was, in his darker moments, openly skeptical of his leadership.

"It is not yet time," Vercingetorix told them nevertheless.

"You always say that!" said Critognat. "Why *not* now?"

"Because we must have patience. Because time is on our side. Because the Romans only become weaker day by day."

"You always say that too!"

"Because it is always true."

"Arrgh!" growled Critognat, throwing up his arms in disgust. "We act like cowards who have shot arrows into a lion and slink back waiting for him to bleed to death, lacking the courage to do what honor demands!"

Litivak had said little, but now Critognat had spoken what his warriors, restive with disgust, were telling him. Surely the time had come for him to be forthright himself.

"Time is *not* on our side," said Litivak. "The Romans' bodies may be weak with hunger, but our spirits are weakened by this craven retreating, this destruction we wreak in our own land, which makes us hated by our own people—"

"—which makes us hate ourselves!"

"Well spoken, Cottos!" declared Critognat. "I say it is time to remember what it means to be Gauls, and attack now before our troops lose *all* heart!"

"That is what he's inviting us to do," said Vercingetorix, "and only a fool accepts an enemy's invitation."

"He is desperate," said Luctor. "All the more reason to fall upon him now."

"He is both desperate *and* cunning," said Vercingetorix.

"So what does the cunning Vercingetorix suggest we do?" Litivak asked, somewhat taken aback by the edge he heard in his own voice.

"Continue the strategy that has made him so desperate, and in the end victory will be ours."

"In the end, we will all be old men with beards down to our belly buttons!" roared Critognat. "In the end, we all end up in the Land of Legend! In the end, what tale of glory will we have to boast of to the heroes we will meet there?"

"I tell you, Vercingetorix, your 'army of Gaul' will not survive much more of this," said Litivak.

"Meaning what, Litivak?"

Litivak paused to take a deep draft of beer, or, rather, took a long drink of beer to allow him a pause. But when he had swallowed it all, there was still nothing else for it.

"Meaning *I* cannot keep my warriors under your command much longer," he said.

"*Cannot* or *will not*?" demanded Vercingetorix.

"I will not lose the loyalty of my own men in the service of a strategy in which neither they nor I believe, and I *cannot* disobey my own vergobret when Liscos finally summons up the courage to order me to withdraw—"

"For fear of losing your chance to succeed him, Litivak?"

"Who are *you* to chide *me* for such modest ambition, Great Leader of Warriors and would-be king of Gaul?"

"Well spoken, Litivak," Vercingetorix admitted softly, touching Litivak's heart. Still. . . .

"I tell you, no matter what *I* will or do not will, my Edui will no longer follow a leader who takes them where they do not want to go."

"You speak of me or yourself?"

Litivak sighed. He calmed himself with another swallow of beer before he spoke again. "Both," he said. "My men will not follow me if I follow an Arverne who leads us only into dishonor. They're at the point where they will follow whoever will lead them where they want to go."

"Which is where?"

"Either home, or in an attack on the Roman army on its desperate march to wherever—"

Litivak stopped in midstream as the revelation struck him.

Of course!

"Or find out *where* the Romans are going and get there first!"

"Yes!" exclaimed Vercingetorix.

"Yes, what?"

"Yes, I know how to get there first." For Vercingetorix had now remembered the first time he had seen a Roman road, arrow-straight from horizon to horizon, thrust through the landscape like a sword of stone. Caesar was on no such road now. But his army was marching as if one were there. That was his Roman nature. And that was his Roman mistake.

He picked up a twig from the ground and began making purposeful marks with it in the dirt.

"Look! *Here* is where Caesar broke off pursuing us," he said, marking an X in the dirt. "And *here* is where he was the second day, and *here* the third, and the *fourth*, and the *fifth*."

He drew a line connecting the five position markers.

"Straight as an arrow!" said Comm.

"And to where does the arrow point . . . ?"

"By the gods, of course!" exclaimed Luctor. "To the lands of the Bituriges!"

"Who have held aloof from the war," said Litivak.

"And whose lands neither we nor the Romans have entered," said Cottos.

"And who therefore have been able to bring in the harvest!"

"And no doubt stored it *here*!" Vercingetorix said, jabbing the point of his stick into the earth. "In Bourges!"

"Of course! *That's* what they're after!"

Vercingetorix nodded. "The Romans' last hope of resupply," he said. "And, knowing where they are marching, we can easily ride there first."

"And then," cried Critognat, "when he arrives, we destroy him!"

"No," said Vercingetorix. "We burn the granaries of Bourges. Every bit of food for man or horse in the city."

There was a brief moment of silence, during which nothing could be heard but the distant hoot of an owl and the death scream of some small creature nearby in the woods.

"What!" howled Litivak, bolting to his feet. "You've gone mad!"

Have I? Vercingetorix wondered. But the logic of it was as cold and clear and hard as a sword of ice. They must slay Caesar not here in Gaul, but where he must be slain if another Caesar was not to come to avenge him.

In Rome.

Vercingetorix rose slowly and deliberately to his feet, then turned, took a step backward toward the fire. He let it heat his back just short of pain, knowing that this was going to be the hardest thing he had ever had to tell them. Knowing that this was not at all how Gauls thought of war. Knowing that the one man in all Gaul who would understand it completely, who would even admire it, was the man he was going to destroy, Gaius Julius Caesar.

"Here is the great and final victory I promised you," he said. "Greater even than victory in this one war. By destroying Caesar's last hope of supply and sending him crawling back over the Alps to disgrace in Rome, at such a terrible price to ourselves, we teach any Roman general who would seek vengeance or glory in Gaul just how dearly we hold our liberty, just how impossible it is to break our spirit, just what will happen to any fool who tries. Thus do we defeat Rome not only for our time or the time of our children or our children's children but for all the ages to come."

"We can't do this!" cried Litivak.

"We can easily reach Bourges before Caesar's army," Vercingetorix said evenly.

"You would not burn the granaries of Bourges and leave its people to starve were it an *Arverne* city!" Litivak shouted at him in a fury.

"I would do it to Gergovia itself if that was what it took!" Vercingetorix shouted back just as hotly.

He now saw something worse than anger or even hatred in Litivak's eyes: a pity so deeply regretful, so sorrowful, that hatred would have come as boon in its place. Vercingetorix found that pity stealing into his own heart, pity for himself, pity for what he must become. But he was Vercingetorix, was he not, chosen by destiny to become king of Gaul? Who had stood outside of time and seen in a vision his life entire. Therefore, where was his choice? He must harden his heart, and his will must be forged in cold, hard steel. Only thereby could Gaul be saved and destiny fulfilled.

"We must win this war at any price," he said, "or the very soul of Gaul will perish. There is no choice."

"At the price of your own honor?" demanded Litivak.

"If need be."

Litivak took two long steps away from Vercingetorix before he turned to address the others. "The worst of it is that this vile plan will work, and you all know it will work too!" he said.

Comm, grim-faced, nodded in reluctant agreement. Cottos and Luctor looked away from both Litivak and Vercingetorix.

"The Bituriges have never sent a single man to support us," said Critognat. "They bought their safety from the Romans with their cowardice. Let the bastards pay for our victory! It is only just!"

Hearing such words spoken by this simple-hearted old warrior,

Vercingetorix knew he would retain the forces to do this necessary and terrible deed. If Critognat understood, so would the like-minded warriors of the Arverni. And to do this thing, the forces of the Arverni alone would suffice.

"Oh yes, your plan will work, *Great Leader of Warriors,*" Litivak told him scornfully, "but you can no longer style yourself Leader of Great Warriors, Vercingetorix, son of Keltill. For no great warrior would buy victory at such a price. Your plan will work in *this* world, but it is without honor. It is wrong! You've spent so much time fighting Caesar, you're beginning to think like a Roman!"

"The Romans fight to win," said Vercingetorix. "And if we are to defeat them, so must we."

"The Edui will not fight at the side of a man who would do such a thing!"

"Nor will the Cadurques," said Luctor.

"In order to defeat the enemy, we must become the enemy?" said Litivak, and spat into the fire as if it were Vercingetorix's face. And, followed by Luctor, he stalked out of the circle of firelight and into the darkness of the forest night.

XIV

WELL, another two days' march and we will be there," said Tulius, "but Vercingetorix's army is arriving already."

"Excellent," said Caesar, in high spirits despite the reduction in the ration to *one* handful of gruel a day.

"What's so excellent about it?" asked Labienus. "It means he'll have time to bring his army into Bourges before we can catch him outside the walls. It means a siege."

"Exactly," said Caesar.

Caesar, Labienus, Tulius, and Gallius sat outside Caesar's tent, slurping down their meager share of the tasteless slop in full view of the surrounding troops. It seemed more watery today, and more noticeably tinged with green from the added grass.

Dionysus protect me! Caesar thought. I'm beginning to become a *connoisseur* of this stuff! His rumbling gut, however, was not in agreement. Patience, he told it as he licked the last of the gruel off his spoon, soon you will eat your fill.

"You *want* a siege?" Labienus said in no little perplexity.

"Why attack a pack of wolves in the process of entering a trap?" Caesar told him. "Why not wait till they're inside and have barred the exit behind them?"

"You're assuming he'll make the mistake of accepting a siege," Labienus said dubiously.

"Why do the Gauls build fortified cities on hilltops?"

"Because they know that fighting from inside them is an advantage . . . ?" Labienus muttered, his perplexity now complete.

Caesar laughed. Labienus was a great tactician, an inspiring leader of men, a soldier's soldier, and perhaps *because* of that he had difficulty with the concept of winning battles with means other than swords and valor.

"Explain it to him, Gallius," he said.

"It is an advantage when one tribe of Gauls is being besieged by another," the chief engineer told Labienus, "but they've never seen *Roman* siegecraft. They'll piss themselves when they see the battering ram I've constructed!"

He gave Caesar an imploring look. "I wish you'd let me deploy the catapults. I do believe I've perfected the formula for Greek fire, and I'm anxious to try it out."

"The point is to cook the grain supplies in Bourges *in our pots,* Gallius," Caesar told him dryly, "not inside the city's granaries."

"Couldn't we at least heave dead horses over the walls? Or cows or dogs—it doesn't really matter—you half cover them with water, leave them in the sun till they're good and maggoty, then—"

"Something strange is going on, Caesar!"

Brutus came running up to the tent in a dither. Had he been a horse, he would have been in a lather.

"When is it not, in this strange land?" Caesar said, still in a fine humor.

"There's been some disagreement between the Arverni and the Edui—"

"Next you will surprise us with tales of cats falling out with dogs," said Tulius.

"The scouts have seen the Gauls making encampment outside Bourges, but they've also seen Litivak's Eduen cavalry riding away!"

"Well, well, well . . ." crooned Caesar.

Vercingetorix's alliance with this Litivak's personal army of Eduen warriors *had* always been about as natural as an alliance between cats and dogs, which was why Caesar had not yet attacked the Edui on their home grounds, calculating that the implied threat to do so would sooner or later persuade their vergobret to recall him. But Litivak's campaigning with Vercingetorix seemed also a campaign to succeed the spineless Liscos, and as long as the lands of the Edui were kept out of it, Liscos lacked the political authority to order him to defect.

Now Litivak had defected anyway.

But why? Caesar asked himself. Perhaps his own men forced it on him? Or perhaps he's finally realized his chances of succeeding Liscos will evaporate entirely if he's still supporting Vercingetorix when we destroy this so-called army of Gaul?

In any case . . .

"Bring Litivak to me, Brutus," Caesar ordered. "I must speak to him."

"How am I supposed to do that?" Brutus asked glumly.

"Use your imagination, Brutus! Show some initiative! Guarantee him safe passage. Offer him gold for his time. Tell him any lie you like. I don't care how you do it."

"Yes, Caesar," Brutus said without noticeable enthusiasm for this opportunity to prove his worth, and turned to depart.

"Hold!" cried Caesar, suddenly realizing that he had been paying too much attention to one part of the report. "You said the Gauls were camped *outside* the city? They haven't entered?"

"No, Caesar."

"But *why*?" asked Labienus.

"Why indeed?" muttered Caesar.

And then it struck his brain like the gift of a joyous vision from the gods.

"Of course!" he cried. "It's obvious!"

"It is?" said Tulius.

"It certainly is if you're the Bituriges in Bourges! You've managed to stay out of the war long enough to harvest your grain and store it up behind your walls. Now Vercingetorix arrives with an army to feed and us close behind. Would *you* invite a horde of rats into your granaries to protect them from an approaching cloud of locusts? Would the Bituriges invite his army in to devour their supplies and invite a Roman siege? This changes everything!"

"It does?"

"Vercingetorix is camped outside the walls because they won't let him in! Knowing the Gauls, they're still arguing about it! If we're lucky, he'll have to fight his way inside!"

Caesar leapt to his feet.

"Labienus! Tulius! Give the order to break camp at once! If we march all night, and into the morning, we can catch Vercingetorix out in the open with his back to the wall of a city still closed to him and crush him against it like a walnut!"

. . .

At first, the Bituriges had refused all entry to Bourges, but they could hardly bar the Arch Druid, so Vercingetorix had dispatched Guttuatr to treat with them. He emerged an hour later with an agreement from their vergobret, Jarak, to allow Vercingetorix into the city to parlay, but accompanied only by his standard-bearer, Guttuatr himself, and half a dozen guards, and only afoot.

And so a score of Biturige warriors surrounded Vercingetorix, Rhia, Guttuatr, Baravax, and five Arverne warriors as they made their way through the city to the Great Hall. The bear standard of the Arverni was greeted with hoots and curses.

Bourges was a smaller city than Gergovia, but it seemed a good deal richer. The proximity of Tulius' major garrison to their capital had given the Bituriges an excuse to keep out of the war during the winter, and the advent of Caesar's huge army likewise in the spring. A walk through the city made it clear to Vercingetorix that Bourges had profited well from its craven neutrality and commerce with Rome. The people looked well fed; there was meat, fruit, vegetables, and beer in the market stall, as well as amphorae of Roman wine and olive oil, baskets of spices, rolls of cloth, jewelry, even scrolls, which could only have been brought here by Roman merchants. No wonder the townspeople did not welcome the commander of the army of Gaul.

The exterior of the Great Hall of Bourges, ironically enough, was not defiled with any vain attempt to adopt Roman style. Inside, it was another matter. Roman tapestries depicting goatmen, naked women, impossibly lush forests, monstrous sea-beasts, gods and goddesses all but hid the stone and wood of the walls. The sunlight filtering in through the narrow window slits was augmented not by torches but by large brass oil lamps. A mosaic of many-colored small tiles covered the floor with a scene from a seacoast no one here could ever have seen. A semicircle of tiered marble seats in the Roman manner enclosed a well.

These seats were half filled with Biturige nobles, perhaps threescore of them, some wearing bits and pieces of Roman garb and jewelry, a few even wearing togas. Vercingetorix could see no arms-bearing warriors among them. Perhaps this was meant as a sign to him, or perhaps it was the true state of things.

Jarak stood alone in the well of this Biturige "Senate," and he at least was dressed entirely as a Gaul, in yellow-and-blue pantaloons, white linen shirt, and leather jerkin. But he wore no helmet and bore no arms. His blond hair had gone half gray, and his sun-leathered skin had its lines of age, but he was still a vigorous man, and Vercingetorix felt his strength when Jarak approached and embraced him in greeting.

Though his warrior woman bore the bear standard of the Arverni, surely the most detested tribal emblem in his city, Jarak found himself wishing that *he* were a bear, so that he might hug the life out of this arrogant young hero, who surely did not come here to confer any boons on his people.

But the sigil of the Bituriges was the owl, bird of wisdom, not the bear, and it was as the owl that Jarak had not only kept the Bituriges out of this war but allowed them to wax prosperous. So it was as the owl that he spoke, or, rather, like an owl pretending to the innocence of a duck to hide his wisdom.

"I welcome you to Bourges, Vercingetorix, son of Keltill, but I do not understand why you are here with your army."

"Caesar's legions are even now approaching your city; surely you know that."

"If your army were not here uninvited, they would not be coming here, so take it elsewhere and they will leave us in peace," he said.

"Not so," said Vercingetorix. "They are after your food supplies."

Everyone knew that the tactic of Vercingetorix was the famishment of the Roman army, and the Romans well knew that the granaries of Bourges held plenty of grain, thanks to their commerce with the Bituriges. Until now, this had seemed anything but a calamity. There was a good surplus, the Romans were rich in gold but poor in food, and, things being what they were, the exchange of the one for the other should have been on terms quite favorable to the Bituriges.

But Vercingetorix was obviously here to prevent such commerce from happening. Jarak suspected that the fat days of neutrality were over, that the war had come to the Bituriges and now they would be forced to take one side or the other. Or, rather, that Vercingetorix was here to force them to enlist in his cause whether it benefited them or not.

"So you have brought your army to Bourges to defend the city from the Romans?" he said, resigning himself to the inevitable.

"Not exactly," said Vercingetorix evasively, and Jarak did not at all like the furtiveness in his eyes.

"Explain yourself, then!" said Jarak.

.   .   .

"I would rather address myself to all of you at once," Vercingetorix told the Biturige vergobret nervously.

"That is your right," Jarak said coldly, and turned to address the assembled nobles.

"Vercingetorix . . . *son of Keltill* . . . wishes to explain to us why he has brought his army here." Jarak shrugged. "He is said to be silver-tongued, so perhaps he can make more sense of it than a speaker as unskilled as myself."

With this inauspicious introduction, Jarak took his place in the front row of seats, Rhia and Guttuatr did likewise along with Baravax and the guards, and Vercingetorix found himself facing the hostile attention of the assembly.

"Caesar is on his way here with his starving army, and his intent is plain," he began forthrightly, "to get his hands on the abundant food supply of this city—"

"Or is Caesar on his way to Bourges because your army is here unbidden?" someone shouted out from the back of the hall, to hoots and jeers.

"Caesar is desperate to feed his army with the harvest you have stored up here!" Vercingetorix shouted back. "The army of Gaul is here to prevent him."

"So you *have* come to defend our city?" said Jarak.

Vercingetorix hesitated. This was moving far faster and more bluntly than he had intended, but he could conjure up no words that would glide it down their throats without provoking their outrage.

"No," he said, "for that is what Caesar wants me to do."

"What, then?" Jarak demanded.

Vercingetorix sighed, took a deep breath, and said it:

"You must evacuate Bourges and take with you all you can carry, for the granaries of Bourges must be burned along with every scrap of food left in the city."

The outrage was fully what Vercingetorix had expected. The Bituriges were on their feet, red-faced with rage. The warriors who had escorted him inside drew their swords and looked to Jarak for orders.

Rhia had her sword out and had leapt to his side. Baravax and his men formed a protective circle around them a moment later. But Jarak stayed his men with an upraised hand.

"We are not oath-breakers here!" he shouted. "You came to our city under peace bond to parlay, Vercingetorix, and that oath shall be honored. Anyone who slays you within these walls shall answer to me. But you shall not burn our granaries or our city."

"You do it yourself, if you deem that more honorable. But anything edible in Bourges *will* burn."

"We will do no such thing!"

"You have no right!"

"The choice is yours!" Vercingetorix roared over the tumultuous shouting. "You will open the gates, or you will force me to smash them down and do it with your people still inside!"

"Spoken like a Roman!"

"The Romans themselves will be here soon enough, and they shall not have the granaries of Bourges!"

"The Romans might at least pay *something* for turning us into famished wretches," Jarak snarled. "You would turn us out into the countryside you yourself have made a wasteland both starving and destitute!"

"I will pay you ten times the worth of what is destroyed, in the Land of Legend when we are all dead, in the good old Gallic fashion," Vercingetorix blurted, and immediately wished he had bitten his tongue before the leaden jest rolled off it, for the jeers and howls of contemptuous rage with which it was greeted burned his ears with well-earned shame.

"Fight Caesar for the city if you must, and we will defend Bourges at your side!" someone shouted.

"I told you, that is the trap Caesar sets for us!" said Vercingetorix, his shame transforming into chagrin, and thence easily enough escaping into anger. "He would destroy us in open battle and snatch victory from the jaws of defeat, thanks to our stupidity!"

Jarak held up both hands for silence.

"You call it *stupidity* to die a hero rather than live a coward?" he demanded. "You would have victory at the price of honor?"

"*You* dare to question *my* honor, Jarak, vergobret of the Bituriges?" Vercingetorix shouted back in a blood-red fury. "You, whose people have profited from trade with the Romans while others have died and starved and sacrificed their all to drive them from Gaul?"

Veins stood out on Jarak's temples, but his words cut all the deeper for the coldness with which he wielded them:

"Where is this 'Gaul' of which you speak, Vercingetorix? In the wasteland left behind by your army? In what way is the Gaul of *your* desires better than the Gaul of Caesar's? He would rule Gaul as a province of his Rome. You would rule the lands of the Bituriges as a province of your Gaul. The only difference you offer us is that, whereas Caesar would purchase our grain, you would burn it. Is that what you would have us fight and die for? Or just your own glory?"

"You have until dawn to decide!"

Vercingetorix signaled to Baravax, and, with his guards before him and Rhia guarding his rear, he stormed out of the building, never looking back to confront the shouts and jeers and curses of the *fellow Gauls* of whom his vision had told him he would be king.

"Fighting you has made him think like you," said Litivak, "and thinking like you has turned him into something no better than you are."

"Many people might view that as a compliment," Caesar said dryly.

Brutus had been subtler than Caesar had expected. He had persuaded Litivak to parlay by telling him that Caesar was not only willing to reward him with gold for continuing to maintain his neutrality, but was now of the opinion that he might prefer *him* over the feckless Liscos as vergobret of the Edui and was interested in discussing how he might assist Litivak in achieving such a mutually advantageous outcome.

Like all the best lies, it cut close to the truth. Indeed, why not make it so?

Litivak had insisted that they meet far from either of their armies, each accompanied by ten men only—here, on this bare hilltop, where approaching forces of assassins or abductors would be visible from afar, and before the sun was down.

Caesar, knowing the store the Gauls set in oath-keeping, had agreed, and now here they were afoot, man to man on the pinnacle, while Brutus and nine Roman cavalrymen and ten equally suspicious Edui sat on their horses, glowering at each other a carefully equidistant measure back.

"May I presume to ask what atrocity Vercingetorix has committed that persuades you to abandon his noble cause?" Caesar asked.

"It is nobility and honor which he is about to abandon," said Litivak.

"Something which you, of course, would never do . . ."

"I would certainly not destroy my own people's city and see its inhabitants starve in order to keep it out of my enemy's hands!" Litivak declared self-righteously.

"You wouldn't?"

"Would even *you*?"

Caesar held his tongue, for of course, were he in Vercingetorix's position, that was exactly what he would do. Given the sound strategy Vercingetorix had been following from the beginning, it made perfect sense. He had already turned the countryside into a wasteland, so why not a city?

"Of course not," said Caesar. "Indeed, we both have a common interest in preventing such an atrocity."

"We do?"

"Of course we do," said Caesar. "Fight with me to save Bourges from the Arverni, and I will leave half the food supplies for the populace. You will become their hero, and I will pay you well besides. . . ."

"My men are no mercenaries to fight for Roman gold, and neither am I! You insult my honor with such an offer!"

"No such insult intended, I assure you," Caesar told Litivak. "I will pay in coin both more honorable and far more valuable than mere gold. You will ride back to Bibracte at the head of an army that has not only triumphed over your ancestral enemies, the Arverni, but won the Edui the friendship of Rome. My favor will pass from Liscos to you, you will be elected vergobret, and when Vercingetorix is defeated and Gaul is conquered—"

"—*if* Gaul is conquered!"

"—*when* Gaul is conquered, and I need a loyal proconsul to rule over it, it will only be natural for me to turn to my good friend the vergobret of the Edui, who, by our crushing of the Arverni, will stand alone as the most powerful tribe in the land. . . ."

"If Gaul is conquered . . ." Litivak said in a much less defiant tone.

"Come with me tomorrow, Litivak, and I promise you will see why there is no 'if' about it," said Caesar. "You need only observe, and commit your men if you choose to join the winning side. And there will be a chest of gold for you either way, not as a payment, but as a gift from a man who would be your friend."

Outside the Great Hall of the Bituriges, the sun was beginning to set in a fiery vision of the conflagration to come when Vercingetorix, Rhia, and Guttuatr, surrounded by Baravax and his little troop of guards, began to make their way back to the city gates, his life and theirs dependent on the honor of a people he had accused of having none.

The prosperous streets of Bourges bustled at this hour with wives going to and from the markets, men gathering in the taverns, merchants and artisans returning to their well-built houses, children playing and chasing each other home for the evening meal.

They all might as well be ghosts, or perhaps *we* are the ghosts, Vercingetorix mused somberly. For though none of the townspeople sought to harm them, no one would pay them heed either, looking away with curled lip as they passed, staring through them as if they were not there and no doubt wishing it were true.

"Spoken like a Roman, they said," Vercingetorix muttered. "Guttuatr, is this so? Are we—am I—becoming like them?"

"We have all had to make our sacrifices, warriors their lives, farmers their crops, druids our lofty stance above the battlefield of worldly strife, and you—"

"My honor!"

The Arch Druid sighed. "We each do what we must. . . ."

"Enough!" grunted Vercingetorix. "Go now, all of you; I would walk the streets of this city alone—"

"It's not safe!" said Baravax.

"If I die here, is it not meant to be? If I should fear to walk alone among my own people, what right do I have to call myself a leader of Gaul? Go, all of you!"

And then, when Baravax hesitated: "That is an order, Baravax."

At that the guards reluctantly turned to leave. "Go with them, Guttuatr," Vercingetorix said in a softer tone of voice. "You I cannot order, but you I ask to understand that this I must do."

Guttuatr nodded and left with the guards, but Rhia hung back.

"Let me come with you," she said.

Vercingetorix nodded at the standard she bore, the brazen bear upon its wooden pole. The standard of the Arverni. His standard.

"The people here hate the standard you bear, Rhia," he said. "Lower it and take it from the city. Less dangerous if you can find a sack within which to hide its ensign."

"Far more dangerous for you to wander these streets alone."

"For the future king of Gaul?" Vercingetorix said bitterly. "I have seen my death in a vision, and it will be in Rome, not here, remember?"

"And if that vision was false?"

"Was it not you who declared that such visions do not lie?"

"But I also said that they do not always speak plain."

"You fear for my life . . . as a woman," Vercingetorix said, presuming to lay a tender hand on her cheek. "But as a warrior of honor, you know full well this is something I must do."

"Perhaps . . ." said Rhia, gently touching his hand upon her own face.

"If I die here because my vision was unclear, then *that* is what was meant to be," Vercingetorix said, almost wishing it would be so. "And I will be released from the iron hand of destiny."

Rhia took his hand from her face.

"No one is ever released from the iron hand of destiny," she said, and with that she departed.

As night falls upon the city, the streets empty out and Vercingetorix wanders them in a bubble of solitude.

Soon the only light is the glow of hearth fires and torches and oil lamps leaking wanly out from the shadowy shapes of the houses. He seems to be the only one abroad, and as a fog descends from the heavens upon the city, enrobing all in a pearly whiteness tinted pale orange here and there, Vercingetorix begins to doubt his own existence, becoming a phantom moving through the ghost of an already bygone city dissolving into mist.

There is nothing to be seen in the swirling whiteness, and so Vercingetorix might imagine anything therein, might see any vision, as a man standing upon the mountaintop of his death outside of time might see his life entire, might walk the Land of Legend while he yet lives.

With a grin more radiant than any gold, Keltill tosses a shower of coins into the sparkling festive air. "Life is to be spent on the pleasures of living!"

"Not so bad for someone who's never kissed a girl before," says Marah teasingly, pulling away with a girlish laugh, which becomes the laugh of the sophisticate telling him: "Is every chicken jealous of every other who enjoys the services of the cock?"

"Brother and sister of the sword, Vercingetorix, that is all that we can ever be," Rhia tells him, and they share a chaste and bloody warrior's kiss.

Vercingetorix does not understand why such visions should fill him with heartrending sadness, but they do, and it becomes an even deeper shame when the voice of Marah mocks from within a flaming giant.

"I owe this barbarian nothing!"

Bright-orange flame rolls across fields of green grain like a wave across a sea, trees laden with ripe red apples crumble to ashy skeletons, and the wave of fire surges ever onward, leaving a blackened landscape in its wake as it breaks over the walls of a distant city.

"No great warrior would buy victory at such a price!" shouts the voice of Litivak.

A pall of black smoke hangs above the burnt-out city, walls breached and tumbled, buildings hollow shells, roasted and blackened corpses set up on wooden stakes in the wasteland like scarecrows against the carrion birds who circle above, whirling, creating a great cruel wind that blows up dust, the gray ash of bone, a swirling white fog. . . .

The moon sends down a silvery beam to pierce the fog and reveal a woman standing in a pool of light. She wears a flowing robe of the purest white like that of a druid, but it is open at her right breast so that the naked babe she holds in her arms may suckle.

Vercingetorix, with a warrior's reflex, has drawn his sword without even realizing he has done so.

"So quick to reach for your sword, Vercingetorix, man of action."

Chagrined, mortified, Vercingetorix sheaths his weapon.

Her face . . .

Is the face of Gaela, his mother. Of Marah. Of Marah's mother, Epona. Of a hundred women he has passed on a street, on the road, in a village he has burned. Of none of them. Of all of them.

"Who are you?" says Vercingetorix, but he knows, though he cannot put it into words or thoughts.

"Just an ordinary woman. A mother of Gaul. Come to offer a sacrifice to clarify the vision of Vercingetorix, man of knowledge."

"You offer me a sacrifice?"

"As did Diviacx, Vercingetorix, Druid King of Gaul."

The woman strides forward, taking the baby from her breast, and reaching beneath her robe to pull out a dagger. Cradling the baby against her, she holds the point of the dagger above its heart.

"I offer you the sacrifice of the innocent life of this child. Take it, if it should serve the cause of Gaul!"

"You know I would not do such a thing!" Vercingetorix exclaims in outrage.

"But you took the life of Diviacx to serve your just cause."

"Willingly given!"

"And you burned a score of Romans alive—"

"Enemies—"

"—and you would leave thousands of innocents to starve and destroy a city to serve *your just cause*. So why not the life of this babe?"

"Because that's different!"

"Tell me, then, silver-tongued Vercingetorix, how the lives of those unseen thousands are anything but the life of this single child before you, writ large."

And she holds out the knife to Vercingetorix.

"The courage to take the life of a city, the courage to take the life of a single child—it should be all the same to the hero of Gaul, *serving his just cause*."

And the fog seals itself over the moon once more, and the terrible apparition disappears into the mists from whence it came.

It was a gorgeous sunrise. The brilliant crescent of the sun peering up over the walls of Bourges painted golden glory across a perfect blue sky. Atop the walls, half the population of the city had gathered to bid farewell to the army of Gaul. Carnaxes sounded, trumpets blared, women waved, children cheered.

Fools, thought Vercingetorix as he rode at the head of his departing army. And I am one of them. Yet his heart felt as if a dagger had been withdrawn from it, and his spirit soared with the eagle rising high above the battlements.

"I don't understand you!" said Critognat. "First you won't fight! Then you plan to burn the granaries! Now you change your mind and ride away! Why?"

"It came to me in a vision," said Vercingetorix.

"In a vision? Now we follow visions?"

Vercingetorix laughed more freely than at any time he could remember in a dozen moons or more.

"When have we followed anything else?" he said gaily, and the old warrior laughed with him. "We are a people who hear the voices of our hearts, not slaves of cold logic, are we not? We are not Romans, after all—we are Gauls!"

XV

YOU DO NOT SEEM PLEASED, Caesar," said Tulius.

"I am not pleased," said Caesar.

"But you should be."

"*Should I?*" Caesar muttered.

Before him, as a banquet set out for his delectation upon a table, lay the city of Bourges atop its low hill—intact, and laden with grain, meat, and fruit. On the plain between the city and the higher hilltop where he, Brutus, and Tulius stood beside their horses was an army. But not the army of Vercingetorix.

It was *his own army,* blithely setting up its mobile siege towers, its catapults, its troop formations, its bivouacs, entirely unopposed.

"What troubles you?" said Brutus. "Vercingetorix has left us a fat, sweet plum for the picking!"

"Has he?" said Caesar. It was difficult to credit, since it made no sense. "Or has he secreted his forces inside the city?"

"Scouts *saw* his forces depart, and the plain down there was churned up with the hoofprints of thousands of horses clearly riding away from the city," Tulius told him.

"But *why. . .?* It makes no tactical sense! *I* would have *destroyed* Bourges rather than let it fall into my hands!"

"You would?"

"Of course I would, Tulius! He was a fool not to! I like it not!"

"The enemy's mistake saves us from an ignominious starving retreat, and *you don't like it,* Caesar?"

"I do not *understand* it," said Caesar, "and I do not like what I cannot understand."

"Perhaps things are about to become clarified," said Brutus, nodding in the direction of Bourges, where the city gates were opening to emit five horsemen riding out under a flag of truce.

"Why do I doubt it?" Caesar muttered as the gates closed behind them. "Nevertheless, I suppose we should hear whatever it is they have to say."

He started to mount his horse, then paused.

"You ride ahead, Brutus, and make sure our friend Litivak is otherwise occupied," he said. "Whatever these Bituriges have to say before we batter down their walls, I doubt it would do us any good to have him hear it."

Caesar's tent had been set up and his standard planted in the middle of the army, as was his custom, so that to reach it the emissaries from Bourges were constrained to ride between two great siege towers, and through the midst of thousands of jeering legionnaires.

By the time Caesar and Tulius had ridden back down to the plain, the Bituriges had already reached the tent and, from the looks on their faces, seemed to have been suitably daunted. A crowd of centurions and ordinary legionnaires had gathered around, and Caesar saw no reason to disperse this audience.

The five Gauls—some sort of tribal leader and a pro-forma escort—had not dismounted, and so Caesar did not dismount either, nor, since they did not greet him with a proper "Hail, Caesar," was he put in a mood for formalities himself.

"Well?" he demanded.

"I am Jarak, vergobret of the Bituriges," said the bluff fellow with long graying blond hair.

"And I am Gaius Julius Caesar, proconsul of all Gaul," Caesar said dryly, "and now that we have introduced ourselves, perhaps you will tell me what you want."

"The question is, what do *you* want, Caesar," said Jarak, "since it is *you* who have brought an uninvited army to the gates of *my* city?"

Caesar had to restrain his impulse to smile. There was something immediately likable about this Gaul, but that was a sentiment he could not afford to harbor.

"I think you know what I want," he said. "And I think you also know that you are powerless to deny me."

"You want food supplies from our city, and it is certainly true that your legions could easily enough overwhelm us," said Jarak.

"Exactly," said Caesar.

"Well, then," said Jarak, "there is no need for you to attack Bourges. The Bituriges have never wanted any part of this ruinous war, Vercingetorix's army has departed, and we have a surplus to sell; so all that remains is to settle on a fair price."

At this, the press of legionnaires hooted and laughed as Caesar studied Jarak carefully, wondering if even such a barbarian chieftain could truly be as naïve as his words made him seem. Surely not. The man was desperate and doing his best not to show it.

"You misunderstand," he said. "I have more men to feed than Bourges has citizens, they are near starvation, and so I must have *all of it*."

At this a great cheer went up from the troops, of the sort that might have emanated from a pack of famished wolves finally spying prey in the dead of winter, and Jarak could no longer hide his terror.

"What will become of my people?" he cried plaintively. "This is unjust!"

"This is *war*," Caesar reminded him, "and justice has nothing to do with it."

"I ask your mercy!"

Caesar ran his gaze slowly around the circle of gaunt faces surrounding them, playing to his own men rather than to the Gaul as he spoke in a scornful voice expressing what their eyes told him they felt, using the orator's inner art to invoke his own ire so he could give it full voice.

"You dare to snivel for mercy from an army that has been forced to march through a wasteland eating grass and bugs?" he roared. "You, Gaul, who burned Roman prisoners alive like the barbarians you are, instead of enslaving them like a civilized people?"

A great howl of fury went up from the legionnaires, and a few swords were even drawn; it was clear to Caesar, and to no one more than Jarak, that, flag of truce or not, they would tear these Gauls to pieces at a word from him. With that thought, an even darker one began to knock ghoulishly at the door to Caesar's mind.

"The Bituriges had no part in it!" Jarak whined.

"So you say," Caesar said coldly. "Why should we believe you?"

"I swear it upon my honor!"

Jeers and hoots and more swords drawn.

"A dog's honor!" someone yelled.

"A swine's!"

"A serpent's!"

"A *Gaul's!*"

"There is a difference?"

There was ominous laughter at this last, and it came to Caesar that now he knew what he was inciting, and to what bloody purpose.

He was going to do a terrible thing. He was going to do it *because* it was so terrible. Because terror was such a potent weapon.

Vercingetorix had not shrunk from using it in such a manner—now, had he? He had sacrificed the lives of Romans in a hideous but effective blood rite to bind the tribal leaders to his cause.

So I will counter with a blood rite of my own, and far grander, as befits a proconsul of Rome.

"We are not oath-breakers!" Jarak cried angrily, allowing his outrage to overcome his fear. "Our word is good! We are an honorable people!"

There was an inchoate roar at this, which Caesar immediately formed into words. "Not oath-breakers! An honorable people!" he shouted. "You Gauls would break your oath to your own mothers for a barrel of beer!"

The legionnaires cheered. Caesar was pleased to see Jarak's face purple with rage.

"Your word is good? You bugger your sons and lie to your wives about it!"

This was finally enough to goad Jarak into drawing his sword, just as Caesar had intended, and his guards followed their vergobret's foolish, hot-blooded lead.

"You would even draw sword under flag of truce!" Caesar roared in righteous indignation as a score or more legionnaires rushed forward to confront them.

"*Stop!*" shouted Caesar. "*We* do not dishonor a flag of truce, even if the barbarian dogs traveling under it do! We are Romans, not barbarians!"

The legionnaires froze. Jarak froze too, then regarded Caesar much more coldly, apparently realizing, but too late, that the whole thing had been a deliberate provocation. His men held their swords upright, uncertainly, as their horses bucked and reared.

"We do not slay emissaries, however treacherous," said Caesar.

"Surrender your swords and you shall return unharmed to your city. If you do not, we can always . . . burn you alive."

Jarak lowered his sword, hesitated, then handed it to Caesar. Seeing this, his men sullenly dropped theirs to the ground.

"Have these men tied backward on their horses and smeared with dung before they are sent back to Bourges," Caesar ordered Tulius in a voice loud enough for only him to hear, and then addressed himself to Jarak for the benefit of the legionnaires.

"You will open your gates or we will smash them open—it is a matter of indifference to me," he said. "But know this, Jarak, vergobret of the Bituriges, if I find so much as *one sack of grain* burned or otherwise withheld, I shall do to your city what Vercingetorix has done to the countryside of his own land. Only, being Gaius Julius Caesar, proconsul of all Gaul, and not a stripling savage chieftain, I will do a much more thorough job of it."

At this, there were not only cheers but a chanting of "Hail, Caesar!"

"Now take these creatures out of my sight!" Caesar ordered.

When the Bituriges had been removed, Tulius turned to Caesar with a befuddled expression.

"What was all that about?" he said. "Surely you realize that, when their vergobret returns to Bourges tied backward on his horse and covered with shit, there will be hotbloods who will take it as a something of an affront."

"Do you really think so?" Caesar crooned.

"They'll do exactly what you have warned them against doing."

"Well, then, they won't be able to say they weren't warned—now, will they?" said Caesar. "Assuming, for the sake of argument, that any of them will be left alive to say anything."

"You *want* to provoke a bloodbath? But why? We could've probably gotten what we wanted without a fight."

"Then we wouldn't have gotten what we wanted, Tulius," Caesar told him.

"Which is?"

"A demonstration of our credibility."

"Our credibility in doing *what*? A demonstration for whom?"

"For Vercingetorix. I will credibly demonstrate my will to commit atrocities even more horrendous than his own."

Tulius shook his head.

"I can see why you didn't want Litivak to witness any of this," was all he could say.

"Ah yes, Litivak!" said Caesar. "No, better that he not be troubled with the bothersome details of the arrangements. But not for all the world would I have him miss out on the entertainment."

Bourges had been surrounded by orderly formations of Roman infantry deployed out of arrow range of the walls. Eight mobile siege towers—two before each quarter of the city walls—were positioned within the front rank of the infantry. These were huge wooden ladders on wheels inside log frameworks clad with thick planking for protection. They were provided with parapeted platforms at their summits, slightly higher than the city palisade, and clad with wooden shields at their bases to protect the men poised to propel them forward.

To the east and far to the rear, eight catapults sat unmanned, and among them was a battering ram of logs bound together with iron hoops and faced with iron, so enormous that it was set on two wagons, one behind the other, with fifty men manning the poles jutting out from each, like so many galley slaves.

A man appeared atop the left-hand siege tower facing the gates. His armor and helmet were no different from those of his troops, but the bright crimson cloak blowing in the breeze behind him announced the presence of Gaius Julius Caesar. A cheer went up from his army. A few futile arrows were launched his way from the parapets of Bourges, but fell far short. Caesar raised his right arm high above his head, and held it there for a dramatic moment. Then he brought it down, trumpets blew, and it began.

The eight siege towers began to roll slowly toward Bourges, the Roman infantry advancing at a measured pace behind them. Archers on the city walls shot arrows at them as they came into range, and Roman archers crouched down behind the tower-platform parapets answered the Biturige volleys. Both were largely ineffective, which worked to the advantage of the Romans, since their archers were able to suppress the fire of the Bituriges well enough so that flaming arrows could not prove a significant counter to the siege towers.

When the siege towers were all but upon the walls, another signal was sounded. An aisle opened up in the eastern infantry formation, and the hundred legionnaires manning the poles of the battering-ram wagons began to push. They had to lean into it with all their strength and weight to get the ram to move at all, and when it began to move it rolled forward slower than the slowest walk of a very old man. But once in motion, it began to gather momentum.

The siege towers reached the walls, and legionnaires scrambled up their interior ladders. Where the summit platforms met the top of the walls, the leading Romans, fighting shoulder to shoulder from behind a wall of their shields, engaged the defenders in bloody close combat in restricted quarters, seeking not to slay as many Bituriges as possible but merely to push them back off the wall so that the troops behind them could pour into the city.

The battering ram, meanwhile, was gathering force, rolling toward the gates faster and faster, the pace of a man walking vigorously, trotting, beginning to run—

The Romans heavily outnumbered the Bituriges, and there was an endless line of replacements waiting to ascend the tower ladders. They were inexorably pushing the Bituriges back, and in several places were already fighting them atop the walls when—

With a tremendous rumble that shook the earth and a great cheer from the legionnaires, the huge battering ram, rolling at the speed of a trotting horse, and with the men on the poles hanging on now rather than pushing, struck the city gates head-on with a crash that shattered them completely and shook the walls themselves. The ram rolled through the flinders unaided for a few wagon lengths, and the Roman army began to pour into Bourges behind it.

The first waves of Romans made directly for the walls, running alongside them, dashing up the interior ladders and stairways to attack the defenders from below and behind, trapping them between themselves and the other Romans atop the wall and the siege towers. The Bituriges on the walls had no chance at all, nor did the Romans give them any quarter, cutting them to pieces with swords, spearing them with javelins, throwing them off the parapets, as more Romans dropped into the city via the towers, and formation after formation of legionnaires marched through the shattered gates.

Organized squads spread out through the city to seize and secure the granaries and storehouses, but these were only the smallest portion of the Roman troops entering Bourges. The rest were free to commence general looting, pillaging, destroying, and butchery.

The houses on one side of the street were all beginning to burn, and legionnaires were pouring from them like ants, bearing bits and pieces

of whatever they could carry. Most of the houses on the other side of
the street were already merrily aflame, but there was an island of temporary safety large enough for half a dozen legionnaires to continue
their ravishment of three screaming young girls.

Farther up the street, a score of legionnaires had found a few
Biturige warriors and were making a slow, gory game of cutting them to
pieces. Behind them, women, children, and old men were stumbling
out of burning buildings, some with their hair afire. Shrieks of pain, ter-
minal moanings, cracklings of fire, sharp reports of burnt-out timbers
collapsing, and drunken laughter filled the air, which stank of ash, fire,
roasting flesh, drunken piss, and spilled beer.

Caesar had been parading him under guard through the carnage for
perhaps half an hour now, and Litivak had no recourse but to allow
himself to be led through the horror like a dog on a leash, rendered
mute by the shock of the assault on his eyes and ears and nostrils, on his
spirit itself, unable to even find the words to express his uncomprehending disgust and outrage.

"Why are you showing me this . . . this . . . ?" he finally managed to
mutter.

"Atrocity?" Caesar suggested with a fatuous grin.

"Why subject me to it?" Litivak snarled at him.

"Why, to win you to my cause, of course. I've arranged this entertainment just for *you*, Litivak. Relax and enjoy it."

"Enjoy it! Win me to your cause! Are you are mad, or do you believe
I am?"

"Not at all," said Caesar with a mildness that somehow was more
chilling to Litivak than anything he had seen or heard or smelled. "I'm
the sanest man I know, and surely *you* are sane enough to be convinced
by cold, clear logic."

Litivak saw that Caesar had been leading him back toward the shattered gates through which they had entered the city. Now they were in
sight, giving him hope that this nightmare would soon be over.

A long train of wagons laden with sacks and barrels of grain, dressed
carcasses of cattle and swine, baskets of live chickens, geese, and ducks,
apples fresh and dried, vegetables, hams, was leaving the city. Bloodied
and bruised Bituriges were dragging timbers outside at sword point.
One of the more seriously wounded prisoners collapsed in the dirt, and

when he could not rise, a legionnaire stabbed him through the heart with his sword.

"You call this hideous butchery cold, clear logic?" Litivak cried in outrage.

"Indeed I do," Caesar told him as they slid past the timber-bearers and outside the city, where a long line of wooden crosses were being hammered together beside the wall. "Now Vercingetorix will have no doubt what will happen to any city I choose to attack and he fails to defend."

He favored Litivak with the warm, friendly smile of a serpent. "And so will you come to see the logic of serving my cause," he said. "Having witnessed the alternative."

"I'd die first!" cried Litivak, and never had he said anything more sincerely.

"Perhaps," said Caesar, "but there are worse things than death, are there not? Is not loss of honor one of them for a noble Gaul such as yourself?"

Caesar had Litivak escorted to a hilltop overlooking the city and left him there while he saw to the preparations for the final act of the drama he had prepared for the Eduen's benefit.

This took nearly three hours. Everything edible had to be removed from the city, and the troops withdrawn to a safe distance as Gallius brought up the catapults. Some two hundred Bituriges—mostly men, but a scattering of women and children to make the spectacle all the more hideous—had to be nailed to the crosses, and the crosses erected at regular intervals before the city walls.

The sun was beginning to set by the time all this was accomplished and Caesar returned to the hilltop where he had left Litivak. Brutus had arrived to keep him company. Both of their faces were pale, and it was difficult to determine whose eyes were the more haunted. When Caesar turned to observe the vista from their vantage, he had to admit that, for sheer dramatic horror, it put the legendary sack of Carthage to shame.

A pall of smoke hung over the city, acquiring a golden-orangish tint from the bloody sun beginning to sink behind it. Black thunderheads of fresh smoke from the larger fires boiled up through it, and bright flames could be seen through the smoke sustaining them. At this distance, the people trapped inside were too small to be seen, and only the roar of major blazes could be heard clearly, but their cries and screams merged into a thinly audible wail, like the buzz of a distant beehive. Before the city walls, Bituriges hung on crosses, but at this remove, their cries and writhings must be left to the imagination.

"Was . . . was . . . this brutal butchery really necessary, Caesar?" Brutus stammered.

"Oh, indeed, Brutus, and a masterstroke as well, for without this brutal butchery, Vercingetorix might harbor some illusions about what will happen to the next city we attack, and our friend here might even conceivably fail to join us in the siege of Gergovia."

"How can you possibly believe I would—"

"A moment, please, Litivak, and then you will understand all, I promise," said Caesar, raising his arm both to quiet the Gaul and to prepare the signal. "Poor Gallius has waited long to try this out, and it would be cruel to torment him further."

He dropped his arm, a trumpet blew, and the lever arms of the eight catapults were released from their tension, throwing large clay amphorae in high arcs toward the city.

Six of them cleared the walls nicely, and four of those burst into flame in proper explosions; the others simply released what from this distance looked like oozing puddles of fire. The remaining two fell short and hit the walls, releasing the burning ooze with a dull thud.

"The catapults need work, I'd say, wouldn't you, Litivak?" said Caesar, shaking his head as he turned to confront the Gaul. "But don't worry, my friend, I promise you they'll get it." He favored Litivak with a smarmy smile. "And *you* will have the honor of choosing where."

The catapults launched another fusillade as Litivak stared at him numbly, and Caesar was pleased to note that now they had gotten the range, for all eight amphorae cleared the walls to feed the conflagration consuming the city.

"Will it be Gergovia or Bibracte? What do you think, Litivak? *I* would prefer Gergovia, of course, since Vercingetorix could hardly remain vergobret of the Arverni if he allowed . . . such brutal butchery to befall his own capital, and I will destroy him if he defends it, and either way the war will be over before any such disaster should befall the Eduen capital."

Caesar shrugged. "But a promise is a promise, Litivak, and I *did* promise the choice would be yours. Perhaps you have some strange reason for preferring that I first destroy Bibracte? I can't imagine why, but still, if you wish . . ."

Litivak's mouth quivered as if he were struggling to form words, but what could they possibly be under the circumstances?

Caesar shrugged again, theatrically, quite enjoying his own performance.

"I'll tell you what, Litivak!" he said as if the idea had just come to him. "We will march southeast for five days, which will put us more or less equidistant from Gergovia and Bibracte when we reach the fork of the Allier River. We will camp there for a day and then move on. If your cavalry joins us, you receive a chest of gold, we march south on Gergovia together, conquer the Arverni together, and end this war, then back to an intact Bibracte we parade, where you will be hailed as a hero."

Caesar paused for suitable dramatic emphasis.

"If not . . ."

The light of comprehension, if not of approval, dawned in Brutus' eyes.

"If not," Caesar said, "at least you won't be able to complain that I left the consequences to your imagination." Another fusillade of Greek fire, if such it truly was, soared over the walls of Bourges. The walls themselves were beginning to burn in several places now.

"You bastard . . ." Litivak muttered.

XVI

THE SUN AROSE gorgeously through a rosy-golden morning mist, but it was an evil beauty, for the mist was a haze that perfumed the air with the tang of burning wood and things best left unthought, and on the far horizon a pillar of black smoke was still visible feeding it.

The army of Gaul gathered in rolling countryside where the leaders had mounted a small hill in order to be seen. But so many warriors were gathered that their words must be relayed from ear to mouth to ear to reach them all.

Comm of the Atrebates spoke first, no doubt speaking for a congress of the smaller tribes, all that was left of the "army of Gaul" save the Arverni after the defection of the Edui and the Cadurques.

"We obeyed the druids and joined this unnatural alliance because you promised to drive the Romans from Gaul, but instead you have laid waste to the countryside, time after time refused to give battle, and now—"

"Coward!" shouted Epirod of the Santons.

"—and now you let them massacre Bourges without even *trying* to defend the city!"

"Had we fought for the city, we would've lost the battle, and Caesar would have sacked it anyway," Vercingetorix said coldly.

"We should have fought!" Critognat shouted angrily. "Had we lost, we would have died with honor!"

The leaders shouted their agreement with this, and some banged their swords on their shields. As Critognat's words spread from ear to mouth to ear among the assembled warriors, waves of shouting and shield-pounding spread, like those made by a stone tossed into a pond. Vercingetorix found himself facing the open contempt of his own army.

"You are angry and so am I!" he shouted as loudly as he was able, so that as many as could would hear his words from his own mouth. "You are angry with me and I am angry with you, but I am even more angry with myself!"

He waited until these words had been relayed to the farthest reaches of the assembled army and the shield-banging and shouting had been silenced.

"I am angry with myself for listening, like you, to my heart and not to my head! We should have forced the evacuation of the city and burned the food supplies! Had I followed necessity instead of visions, thousands now dead would yet live, and Caesar's famished legions would be retreating back across the Alps! Take back the command you entrusted to me if you find me unworthy! Take it back because we have been fools! Take it back because I have been the biggest fool of all!"

No one within earshot knew how to greet these words. But as they were relayed throughout the army, a murmuring arose—sullen perhaps, but not enraged, or so to Vercingetorix it seemed.

And he knew that, although the words he had just spoken had arisen uncrafted from his heart and he believed every one of them, the bravado he must now utter would ring hollow in his own ears even as he declaimed it.

"Take heart!" he shouted. "Yes, I have been a fool! Yes, we have made a terrible mistake, and paid a terrible price! But Caesar has been an even bigger fool, and made a far more terrible mistake, and the price he will pay is certain defeat! For, after this monstrous massacre, every Gaul will now understand his true nature! No Gaul will stand by his side! No Gaul can remain neutral! By this evil and dishonorable atrocity, Gaius Julius Caesar has achieved what my father could not, what I could not, what no Gaul could accomplish—he has united all the tribes of Gaul, every man, woman, and child, against himself! As in the long ago, when Brenn was king and we made Rome tremble! And when all the tribes of Gaul are united, not the entire world can stand against us!"

At this they banged their shields, if with no great enthusiasm.

But Vercingetorix knew full well that it was a silver-tongued lie. The Gauls were more divided than ever. Without Litivak and his Edui, the "army of Gaul" amounted to his own Arverni and a few thousand auxiliaries from minor tribes. And Caesar had been far from a fool. The massacre he had committed was a plain message: Now *I* will lead and *you* must follow.

For *this* is what will happen to any city you fail to defend.

The cheeriness of the bright morning sunlight mocked Vercingetorix's mood as he and Rhia paced the walls of Gergovia, surveying the frantic activity below. The entire population of the city was working with a feverish will born of terror and desperation to finish the new outer fortifications before Caesar's army arrived.

Four ditches encircled the city, and a fifth was being completed. The three outermost ditches were lined with sharpened wooden stakes to impale charging cavalry. They should also be wide enough to prevent the Romans' fearsome catapults from coming within range, or their siege towers and battering rams from reaching the city walls. The inner two ditches were filled with hay steeped in pitch. Planks had been nailed to logs to form simple mobile bridges, and these were stored within the walls, so that if the Roman assault were not only stopped but broken the Gallic cavalry could emerge to harry their retreat.

"Caesar has forced me to lead the Arverni into his trap," Vercingetorix muttered somberly.

"Trap? We're turning Caesar's trap into our fortress."

"So it would seem," said Vercingetorix. "But Caesar *knew* that this was a trap I could not evade. After Bourges, if I failed to defend my own capital, I would be a general without an army. But by defending Gergovia, I am doing just what he wants me to do."

"You should not cloud the mind with such thoughts before a battle you *must not* lose. That you *cannot* lose."

"Cannot lose!" Vercingetorix exclaimed bitterly.

"Cannot lose," Rhia said softly. "You have seen the vision of your life entire, have you not, and it ends not here but as king of Gaul in Rome."

"Visions!"

"Such visions do not lie."

"Do they not?" Vercingetorix said angrily. "I followed a vision at Bourges. And it led to the deaths of thousands and into the jaws of Caesar's trap!"

"Did it lie? Did it show you anything that did not come to pass? Some visions tell us only what we already know in our own hearts. You followed such a vision at Bourges. Not because it revealed what was to come, but because it spoke to you of what you knew to be right. Visions may speak to us in riddles when they speak of the things of the world, but when they speak of the things of the *spirit,* they always speak plain."

There was a half-moon that night, and no cloud. Vercingetorix walked alone between the city wall and the innermost ditch, hoping for a sign to paint itself across the starry heavens, or perhaps fearing that one would appear.

Visions in the sky. Visions in the Land of Legend. Visions seen in fire. Visions seen in mist. These had he followed since he first surrendered to destiny under the Tree of Knowledge. He had trusted in that destiny. Like a good Gaul, he had listened to the voice of his spirit.

And it had robbed him of the life of a natural man. He had no wife. He had not even known a woman. Marah scorned him as a barbarian. Rhia was sworn to celibacy. He had sacrificed all to follow his visions of destiny.

But Caesar crafted his own destiny by following the ruthless logic of necessity, and his army was as united under his command as a flock of birds in the sky or a school of fish in a river.

Whereas I command Gauls, Vercingetorix thought peevishly. Ready to fight and die for glory alone. And that very strength is their weakness, for they are willing to die defeated for glory rather than triumph without it. And willing to follow a leader only when he leads them toward it.

Vercingetorix walked on, staring upward into the heavens, where nothing was written this night, and so almost stumbled into Guttuatr, who was circling the walls in the opposite direction.

"Seeking a sign?" he asked the Arch Druid sardonically.

Guttuatr looked unnaturally pale in the silvery moonlight, which seemed to grave the lines in his face ever deeper—a ghost of what he had been, or perhaps of what he would become.

"As are you?" he asked.

"I seek not another of the visions that have drawn me into Caesar's snare," Vercingetorix told him, "but a way out of it. How did I allow myself to fall into this trap, Guttuatr?"

"By doing what was right."

"What was right?" Vercingetorix said bitterly. "Then tell me who benefited! The people of Bourges who were slaughtered?"

When Guttuatr did not answer, Vercingetorix answered for him. "I'll tell you who benefited, Guttuatr—only Caesar!"

"Might contends with might on the world's battlefields," Guttuatr told him. "Right and wrong contend within each man's spirit. *You* benefited, Vercingetorix. The man of action found the man of knowledge he had lost."

"Perhaps," he told Guttuatr, "a man of knowledge must not shrink from doing a lesser evil to prevent a greater. There are times when we must sacrifice more than our lives to do good. When we must sacrifice our honor itself."

"Now you truly speak as a druid," Guttuatr said. "You speak as my equal."

"A sacrifice I forced *you* to make by descending into the world of strife to become my instrument, did I not?" Vercingetorix said softly. "And it weighs heavily upon my spirit."

Vercingetorix had never seen such a tender look in the Arch Druid's eyes. "Now," said Guttuatr, "you speak as my friend."

He had done what he could to restore the Great Hall of Gergovia, but still it seemed to Vercingetorix a sad specter of a past that could never return. The white-paint wattle had been scraped from the outside walls, but most of the ancient carvings of vines and flowers had gone with it. The colonnaded entrance portico had been torn down, but the scars still remained. The tinted glass had been removed from the window slits, the oil lamps had been replaced with torches, and the old banquet table had been brought back in, but there was nothing that could be done for the interior-wall paintings, which had been half destroyed by Gobanit's "repairs" in Roman style with paints whose hues had never been used in the originals.

The shields and swords and skulls of dead enemies had never been removed, but this boast of bygone glories now mocked the present circumstances. The chests of jewels and gold had been drained of most of their treasure to pay the people of the countryside for the loss of their crops and property, so Vercingetorix had had the empty ones removed to avoid being reminded of the extent to which the war had depleted the wealth of what had once been one of the richest tribes in Gaul.

Gathered at the old wooden table were Critognat, Cottos of the Carnutes, Comm of the Atrebates, Epirod of the Santons, Velaun of the

Parisii, Kassiv of the Turons, and Netod of the Belovaques—the leaders of what remained of the army of Gaul.

"According to the scouts, if the Romans continue at their present pace, they will arrive before the sun goes down tomorrow," Vercingetorix was forced to tell them.

"We are ready for them!" declared Critognat.

"As ready as we will ever be," Vercingetorix said, and immediately chastised himself for it. Keltill would not have spoken thusly in a council of war.

"The fortifications are completed," said Critognat. "Every sword has been sharpened, every helmet has been polished till it gleams. We are ready to destroy them!"

"No," blurted Vercingetorix, regretting his words even as he uttered them, "we are ready to *fight* them."

"What, then, do we lack?" Netod demanded.

"A path to victory," said Vercingetorix, and again was dismayed by his own words.

"What kind of talk is that?" said Critognat.

"You are saying I should flee with my warriors?" Comm said sarcastically.

"Perhaps we should," said Velaun, "rather than fight at the side of a general who sees no path to victory."

"Why *should* we allow ourselves to be trapped inside this Arverne city by the legions of Caesar?" demanded Cottos.

"He is right!"

"Indeed he is!" exclaimed Vercingetorix. "We should not!"

It was as if he had stood upon a mist-shrouded crag and the fog had suddenly lifted to reveal the valley below with perfect clarity.

A logical clarity. This must be how Caesar thinks, Vercingetorix surmised. And now I am beginning to understand it.

"You look as if the gods have granted you a vision," said Rhia.

"Not the gods," Vercingetorix said. *"Cottos."*

Cottos gave him a perplexed look.

"You asked why we should allow ourselves to be trapped in Gergovia by Caesar. The answer is we should not!"

"What?" roared Critognat. "You would abandon *our own city* to Caesar's butchery without a fight?"

"No," said Vercingetorix. "You will stay here with enough warriors to put up some kind of defense. I will leave with the greater part of our forces, and most of the cavalry."

At this, Critognat's face purpled.

Vercingetorix laughed. "What did Caesar hope to achieve at Bourges?" he asked.

No one said anything for a long moment.

"What he *did* achieve?" Epirod finally ventured.

"No," said Vercingetorix. "Resupplying his army was what he was able to achieve. What he *hoped* to achieve was to trap us inside the city."

"And now he seeks to do the same thing again . . ." said Velaun.

"*That* is why he destroyed Bourges and massacred its people, to force us to defend Gergovia against his siege."

"But, by the gods, we already knew that!" exclaimed Comm.

"We must not do what Caesar *expects* us to do," Vercingetorix said. "We cannot prevail defending a city against a Roman siege. He would either confine us until we starved to death or crush us like an egg inside a fist of iron. We must fight attacking, not defending! Not like rats in Caesar's trap, but in the open, like *Gauls*!"

"Well spoken!" said Critognat. "For the first time in too long a while!"

At least we can fight with *some* hope in our hearts, Vercingetorix thought grimly. But a commander of Gauls should speak like Keltill. And so, affixing a mask of fierce determination upon his visage, he leapt to his feet, drawing his sword.

"And even if we are defeated," he declared, "when the bards tell the tale, they will be proud to say that as Gauls did we die!"

"Given what resources he commands and the time he had to do it, even Gallius could not have done a better job of fortifying the city," Caesar told Brutus as he gazed admiringly at a fellow general's well-crafted piece of work.

From the forefront of his army's position on the plain below the unforested hill upon which Gergovia was built, Caesar could make out warriors on the walls and formations of men on horseback coming and going through the open gates and riding around the city like cavalry on parade.

He could not see the entrenchments dug around the city, but he had the reports of the men he had sent to reconnoiter. The first ditch they had encountered was too wide for them to cross and filled with the sharpened stakes generally employed to impale cavalry, so they were unable to determine how many more such ditches there were, but they had seen at least three more. And the outermost ditch put the walls beyond catapult range.

"See how he has neutralized our catapults, our siege towers, and even our battering ram, Brutus? With nothing more than shovels! We'd have to build heavy mobile bridges and throw them across at least four ditches to bring them into play, so it's not going to be worth the effort to try. Gallius will be furious."

"You almost sound *proud* of Vercingetorix," said Brutus, abashed at the petulance he heard in his own voice.

"I suppose I am, Brutus. I've been in this country too long. There are times when I find myself thinking like a Gaul. Mars help me, I'm beginning to weigh *glory*. And there is more of it to be had in defeating a worthy enemy than in overcoming a fool."

Decimus Junius Brutus had come to Gaul with buoyant high hopes of grand adventure and rapid advance in serving under the wing of a great man.

Caesar—the greatest man he had met and probably the greatest living Roman—was possessed of a pedagogical passion to explain, to instruct, to speak his mind to someone he might consider worthy of hearing it all, a function normally fulfilled by a son. And so, having no son, Caesar adopted substitutes.

Brutus had not understood this until Vercingetorix had for his time replaced him as the object of such attentions. But the jealousy this had called up within him—so like that between brothers for paternal favor—had made it plain. Thus his shameful secret satisfaction when Vercingetorix became the enemy.

If Brutus did not truly love Caesar, he had admired him as would the son of a great and brilliant father, who sought to earn his approval in turn. But the war against this barbarian chieftain, who burned men alive to seal pacts with blood-rite magic and thought nothing of destroying the countryside of his own people to starve his enemies, had changed the man Brutus had so admired.

Perhaps Caesar had been in Gaul too long, for, if he had not truly come to think like a Gallic barbarian, he had come to act like one. Vercingetorix seemed to have drawn him into a duel of ruthless atrocities, culminating in the butchery of Bourges, where Caesar had not only proved himself the harder man but entrapped the hapless Litivak with his display of utter ruthlessness, and apparently sealed Vercingetorix's doom.

Brutus understood the brilliance of this as strategy and by now had seen enough of war to understand the truth of what Caesar had told him long ago in Rome, that war was but a huge number of individual murders. He had no love for the Gauls, but now, though he still admired the great Caesar's brilliance of mind and godlike energy, he had seen in him something that made him shudder, that he had no desire to emulate at all.

Caesar often enough had instructed him to shed his innocence. And now he had succeeded. But not in the manner he had intended. Perhaps not even in a manner that Brutus' great mentor could even comprehend.

"He seems to have left us only two choices," said Caesar. "Lay siege, or storm the city with our infantry alone, using simple planks to get across the ditches and ladders to scale the walls. Which would *you* choose to do, Brutus?"

"A massive infantry assault would cost us many casualties and might even fail, but a siege would bring sure victory eventually, so I suppose . . ." Brutus shrugged like a diffident student.

A dim answer, Caesar thought irritably. Something seems to have gone out of Brutus of late.

"Think, Brutus, think!" he said. "The winter could be upon us before a siege succeeded. Our supplies would become exhausted again and we might be forced to break it off. And Vercingetorix *knows* this. And knows that I know it. So . . . ?"

The glassy-eyed stare that was Brutus' only response was dimmer still.

"He only *seems* invite a siege because he wants us to attack!" Caesar told him. "He means for me to see through it."

"He does?"

"Neither of us can afford a long siege. I because I am operating on hostile soil with a time limit, and Vercingetorix because the one military virtue an army of Gauls has the least of is—"

"—patience!"

Brutus seemed at last to have been shaken out of his trance.

"Very good, my young friend!" Caesar was finally able to tell him.

"The virtue most needed to withstand a siege. And therefore a leader of Gauls will avoid a siege at almost any cost. Vercingetorix let us have Bourges without a fight to avoid one."

"But . . . we . . . committed that . . . massacre at Bourges to *force* him to defend his own city."

"Oh, he must *defend* Gergovia all right. But not necessarily from inside."

"But his army *is* up in there! We've seen—"

"Warriors on the walls and cavalry on parade. We have no way of knowing how many men are actually inside. Or whether Vercingetorix is in there with them."

"You think he's not?"

"*I* would not sit inside the walls if I were him. I would leave enough forces inside to make it appear I was there, and hide somewhere with the one element in which I was superior to the Romans, my cavalry, and wait for Caesar to storm the city, and then, when his infantry is enmeshed in fighting its way across those defensive ditches to the walls—"

"—attack from the rear!"

Caesar nodded. "About the only chance he really has. And it might even work. The only logical battle plan under the circumstances."

"But he doesn't really know the true circumstances. . . ."

"No, he does not, the poor bastard," Caesar said almost wistfully. "And when he finds out, the knowledge itself will be the cruelest blow of all."

An owl hooted; sparks from a campfire drifted up like fireflies toward a starry night above the overhanging tree boughs. Rhia lay tantalizingly close with her back turned to him, and were it not for the whinnies and nickers of the horses and the snores and sleepy mutters of thousands of men, Vercingetorix could have imagined that he was back in the time when his entire army consisted of himself and his sister of the sword camped out like this in the forest.

But that time seemed like the long ago. Since then, he had killed more men than he could count, laid waste to more countryside than had Brenn or Caesar, commanded the army of Gaul, become a druid, and seen his life entire.

"Rhia . . ." he muttered softly. And then, when there was no answer, in a more normal voice, "Rhia? Are you asleep?"

"No longer," came her voice, but with a little laugh that softened the reproach.

"Perhaps the battle will come tomorrow, or if not, certainly soon, and so we cannot know whether this will be our last night together. . . ."

"And so . . . ?"

"And so . . ." crooned Vercingetorix, laying a hand on her shoulder.

Rhia pulled away. "This from the man who cannot die on the soil of Gaul?"

"But what if visions are but snares sent by the gods to perplex us?"

"You may have reason to *want* to believe that at this moment, and perhaps so do I, but neither of us really does—now, do we, silver-tongued Vercingetorix?" Rhia said banteringly.

And of course this was so. Nevertheless, Vercingetorix found himself rolling closer to her, so that he could hear her breathing, smell her musky odor mingled with the nighttime forest perfumes.

"Right now, I find it impossible to believe that I will ever be king of Gaul," he said. "And if *that* vision is false, of what value is—"

"—our vow as brother and sister of the sword?" said Rhia, and she laughed. And Vercingetorix was forced to laugh with her.

"You see through my strategy better than Caesar ever has," he said. Nevertheless, he inched closer, until their bodies were almost touching.

"It is less than subtle."

"Well, why not?" said Vercingetorix, laying a hand on the small of her back. She did not roll over to face him, but this time she did not pull away.

"Because our destinies would not have it such," Rhia told him, her voice now gone somber.

"But if our destiny is to die tomorrow, what matters what we do tonight?"

Rhia did not answer. The silence was long. Vercingetorix feared to move his hand farther, nor would he take it away. At length, Rhia sighed deeply—mournfully, or so to him it seemed.

"What is it, Rhia?"

"I would not speak of this," Rhia whispered.

"Of what?"

"Of . . . of love and death and destiny . . . yours and mine. Of why we cannot, of why we must not—"

Vercingetorix reached out his other hand to her shoulder and rolled her over to face him. She did not resist. "This may be my last night on earth, and I may die a virgin, and you will not even tell me why?"

"Some things are better left unsaid."

"But this is not one of them!" Vercingetorix declared vexatiously. Then, pleadingly, "Please, Rhia, at least this much . . ."

"It will not please you," she said sadly, but now, even in the darkness, Vercingetorix could read in her eyes the softening of her heart. And so he waited patiently, listening to her breathing, listening to the distant song of a night bird.

"I too have seen my death in a vision," she finally said. "And . . . and . . ."

"And?" Vercingetorix asked with as much gentleness as his vexation would let him muster.

"And I die a warrior's death," said Rhia.

"Is that not what you would have wished?"

Vercingetorix could see Rhia's head nod, but she looked away and would not meet his gaze.

"My death is everything I would wish for," she said in a strange, tender tone Vercingetorix had never heard her use before. "I die fighting at your side. And you . . . you . . ."

Vercingetorix touched her cheek. "And I?" he whispered.

"And you go on. . . ."

Vercingetorix did not know what to say, or what to feel, and so he put his other hand on her other cheek, and pulled her to him, and kissed her, however inexpertly, long and deep, as a man should kiss a woman.

Rhia returned the kiss in like manner, and took him into her arms, and held him close, gently at first, then fiercely. Her breasts pressed against his chest, her hips against his, which began to move against hers with a will of their own, and he felt hers respond, joining in the dance, and all thought was gone, and—

—she suddenly pulled away, rolled from his embrace, and turned her back to him. And then this warrior woman began to sob.

"What is it?" Vercingetorix asked tenderly, afraid now even to reach out a comforting hand.

"I should not tell you this. . . ."

"But now you surely must. . . ."

Rhia gave a great sigh. "Must I . . . ?" And she sighed again. And Vercingetorix could sense the vibration of a shudder go through her.

"Like all such visions, mine did not speak plain," said Rhia. "I saw . . . I saw . . . a night of love with you . . . and on its morrow, my death at your side in battle. A *lost* battle, Vercingetorix."

And she turned back to him, her eyes shiny with tears, her lower lip trembling. "*Now* do you understand why we *must* not break our vow . . . ?"

Vercingetorix could only nod, and touch a finger to her lips, for, however chastely, he dared not kiss her.

"I would not be the death of you . . ." he whispered.

"Still you do not understand," said Rhia. "I would gladly die for you. I would almost die for that one night of love with you."

And this he knew was the woman speaking.

"But the battle for Gergovia *must not be lost!*" she said fiercely. "For if it is Gaul is lost with it!"

And that was the warrior.

In that moment Vercingetorix did not know which he loved more.

Caesar sat on horseback in the midst of a score of signalmen, studying the sky and wishing for a bit more cloud. But the *perfect* night might never come, and the very starlight that would make the maneuver more visible from Gergovia would allow his men to see what they were doing without lighting torches.

Besides, the whole thing—the cover of darkness, no torches, orders given by messengers rather than trumpets—was a charade to match the charade of the Gauls in the city, who Caesar firmly believed would not emerge now if he were marching on the fortifications at high noon with banners flying and trumpets blasting out fanfares.

Still, he thought wryly, they *would* be disappointed if I didn't play along—now, wouldn't they?

"Tell them to begin," he ordered, and three of the signalmen departed to relay the orders.

Trebonius, Tulius, and Galba would now send three narrow spearheads of legionnaires to bridge the first ditch with planking. Then a single cohort of infantry would cross each bridgehead to guard the bridging squads. The second ditch would then be bridged in like manner, and the cohorts would advance, but no more troops would advance until the third ditch was bridged and crossed and the planking across all three ditches widened to accommodate any need for a rapid retreat. Only then would a larger force be sent across the first three ditches, with scaling ladders, axes, light battering rams, and archers. But this would not be the bulk of the army either.

Beginning an assault involving bridging entrenchments two hours before dawn was not something Caesar would ordinarily have done.

But the Gauls had never descended to challenge any of his probes, so it did not seem imprudent to proceed on the assumption that they were *inviting* him to advance beyond at least the first of the ditches without hindrance, and would do nothing until as much of his army as he was foolish enough to deploy was spread out crossing the rings of entrenchments.

Caesar was not quite sure what the Gauls in Gergovia would do then, save attack his front somehow, but he was almost certain that Vercingetorix's main force would emerge from wherever it was hiding, no doubt hoping to find the Roman army vulnerable to the surprise attack on its rear.

A wan sun rose through a grayish-white cloud layer over Gergovia, revealing eight cohorts of Roman infantry standing in tight formation inside the third ring of ditches and facing the city gates across the fourth. On the other side of the fourth ditch, some hundred Gallic archers lay prone. A plank bridge crossed the innermost defensive ditch behind them. On the other side were twice as many archers.

A thousand or so Gallic warriors rode back and forth before the city, shouting, cursing, banging swords and lances on their shields, raising a thunderous din; atop the ramparts, more warriors did the same.

With them were women, some of them young and fair, but most of them older and a good deal less so, wriggling their bare breasts as they shouted, turning and lifting their skirts to expose their buttocks. Trumpeters blew on Gallic carnaxes, tall brass horns curved like the necks of swans, accompanying this dance with mournful and flat blattings, creating the illusion that enormous farts were emerging therefrom.

The Romans did not break good order or military discipline to reply to this taunting, but contented themselves with shouting and cursing without moving while their own outnumbered trumpeters vainly attempted to match the volume of the Gauls.

Vercingetorix nodded to the nearest signalman, who blew a long, low warbling note on his carnax, which was picked up by another and another and another, until the woods resounded with what seemed like the honking of a great flock of brazen geese.

When the warriors were mounted, Rhia raised his standard high and Vercingetorix nodded again. The signalman blew three shorter and higher notes, and then he began to lead his army out of the forest. The dispersed force rode at a walk through the trees, then at a trot as the forest thinned out, and then a mighty horde rode at a full gallop across open grassland toward Gergovia.

Oranix's scouts had reported that, though the Romans had crossed the first three ditches during the night, they had proceeded no farther, nor had Caesar brought up his main force as yet.

This was disquieting, for the whole desperate strategy counted on Critognat to lure the Roman army into crossing all the ditches to attack his heavily outnumbered forces, so that Vercingetorix's own outnumbered forces could surprise them with an attack on their unprepared rear. And even if Critognat had thus far followed orders not to attack until the main Roman force attempted to cross the first fire ditch, how long he would hold his patience Vercingetorix could not know until he rode into the battle.

But the time for thought was over and the time for action had begun. Now that the final battle was beginning, it would be sword against sword, man against man. At last Vercingetorix could fight as the name his father had given him bade—as a Leader of Great Warriors. Great warriors fighting, not as an army of ants like Romans, but as a horde of heroes riding into battle with war cries in their throats, and the tales the bards would tell of this day already singing in their hearts.

Thousands of hooves thundered a stirring drumbeat and sent up a cloud of dust, thousands of voices roared out battle cries, and the rhythm of his horse galloping beneath him, and the rhythm of his heart beating in his chest, and the hot blood pounding through him stopped all thought, and Vercingetorix let out a mighty, wordless battle cry from the pit of his stomach that sent his spirit soaring.

Caesar had moved as much of his forces across the first three ditches as he was going to, and even though it might be risky, when a real battle started he could never resist leading from the front—else why wear a brilliant crimson cloak that made him the most conspicuous figure on any battlefield? So he rode through cheering legionnaires to the outermost ditch, handed his horse over to a centurion, and scrambled across the succession of plank bridges with his sword drawn like the youngest and spriest soldier in the ranks. And then there he was—standing sword in hand, crimson cloak blowing in the breeze—at the very forefront, glaring up at the city on the hill, while legionnaires cheered, grinned, and shouted excitedly to each other, "Caesar himself fights among us!"

Then a half-dozen of his men put their shields together to form a stage and helped him to mount it, and he stood there, sword raised high above his head to challenge the enemy, as thousands of voices chanted *"Hail, Caesar!"*

I may be getting a little long in the tooth for this sort of thing, Caesar reluctantly admitted to himself, but, gods help me, the older I get, the more I love it.

The shouting and cursing and shield-banging of the warriors atop the walls of Gergovia increased in volume and intensity as the crimson-cloaked figure was raised up like a tribal standard. The carnaxes blew out a furious cacophony. The women presented a solid wall of insulting buttocks. The cavalry in front of the walls descended toward the rear of the innermost defensive ditch in raging disorder.

Caesar raised his sword high above his head with his straightened right arm. Then he crossed the pit of his elbow with his left forearm, bending it into a right angle, a gesture anyone familiar with the Romans could recognize was the very opposite of their salute of honor.

And for anyone who was not, the thousands of jeering Romans emulating it made it all too clear.

Critognat, at the forefront of the Gallic cavalry crowding up to the archers behind the innermost ditch, shouted out something. With a quick series of puffs and whooshes and sudden gouts of black smoke, the pitch-soaked hay in the inner two ditches burst into flame and became walls of fire.

Moments later, a flock of arrows flew in a high arc toward the Romans.

The sudden ignition of a wall of flame before him staggered Caesar, sent him tumbling to his knees atop the shaky stage of shields, which suddenly collapsed, dumping him rudely on the ground amidst a forest of limbs. That probably saved his life, for arrows hummed through the space where he had stood the moment before.

He scrambled to his feet, while being shoved under a roof of shields already erected against the next fusillade of arrows, which clattered off them like a summer hailstorm on a tile roof. He felt heat far stronger

than even the Spanish summer sun, and then was caught up in the
backward rush of his men away from the fiery ditch.

Bravery might be a personal virtue, but it was a vice for a commander in a situation like this. He was operating blind in this front-line
melee. He had to get back to his horse to see some overall picture of the
battlefield.

So Caesar called half a dozen men to him and had them form a
small turtle with their shields around him, so they could escort him
through the crush and confusion, the curses and shouts, the cries of
pain, all the way back across the planking over the first of the stake-
filled pits.

Seeing that orders had been followed and the other side was clear of
his troops, he dismissed his escort, rejoined the main body of his forces,
mounted his horse, galloped back to where he had left his signalmen,
and only then turned to study the battlefield. There wasn't much of a
battle going on, since the armies were separated by two ditches of fire.
Arrows were ineffective at this range.

"Tell Gallius to bring up some catapults and bombard their archers
and that cavalry milling around behind them," he ordered a signalman.
"Rocks and stones for now, but have him ready that Greek fire of his."

The catapults might not be able to reach the city itself, but the Gallic
archers would be forced back or destroyed, and the cavalry behind
them would have to retreat.

Or, being Gauls, might begin whatever attack they had planned. The
concept of strategic retreat was entirely foreign to their nature. Only
Vercingetorix understood its uses. And Caesar was more certain than
ever that he was not among them.

A cloud of jagged rocks arced high over the main body of Roman
troops, over three ditches filled with stakes and two with fire, and fell on
the Gallic archers and the front ranks of their cavalry like the wrath of
the gods. Fist-sized, head-sized, barrel-sized, a thunderstorm of stones
began, then became a continuous torrent, smashing skulls, cracking
limbs, knocking men from horses, and sending horses writhing and
whinnying in agony to the ground.

In short minutes, all was a confusion of wounded men and horses.
Some of the archers bravely sought to return fire; others panicked into
retreat but were blocked by the cavalry behind them, some of whom
were themselves trying to retreat while struggling to control rearing

horses—some of whom even seemed determined to charge forward into the flaming pits.

From within the chaotic ranks of the Gauls, a trumpet sounded. Then it was answered by the deeper voice of a carnax up on the city walls, and Caesar beheld the sight he had been hoping for.

The gates of Gergovia opened, and a mob of Gauls emerged, hundreds of them, many of them women, hauling ungainly constructions of logs and planking—crude mobile bridges heavy enough to bear horses at least briefly, by the look of them. There were about a dozen of the things, lugged by scores of townspeople running, staggering, tumbling down the hill, a sight that Caesar found both comical and heartwarming.

What followed was even better. As the first of the mobile bridges neared the innermost fire ditch, horsemen began to gallop out of the city, hundreds, perhaps thousands—surely all the cavalry left in Gergovia.

What a glorious sight! Shouting, screaming, a mighty barbarian horde in full battle frenzy riding straight for their own fire ditch!

Perhaps they were even drunk, Caesar surmised. If not on beer, certainly drunk enough on their own battle ecstasy to find it quite credible that a mere Roman army would flee from them in terror.

"Catapults to cease fire!" he ordered. "Sound the retreat!"

As the front line of Romans began visibly to retreat and the rain of stones suddenly ceased, a great cheer went up from all the Gauls: the archers, the cavalry behind the guttering fire ditches, the people of Gergovia running down the hill with the portable bridges, and loudest of all from the horsemen charging triumphantly into the fray behind them.

By the time the first of the mobile bridges reached the inner fire ditch, the Romans beyond the outer one were in full, rapid retreat. Heedless of the flames still burning in the ditch below, the Gauls threw their mobile bridges across it, and the Gallic cavalry began galloping over them. The bridges creaked and groaned under the weight and impact, planks cracked and splintered, horses tripped in the holes and went crashing down with their screaming riders into the flames. Some of the bridges began to burn; three collapsed entirely.

But the majority of the Gallic cavalry got across, followed by towns-people on foot, who had an easier time of it, and who then began dragging smoldering, cracked, splintering mobile bridges toward the outermost fire ditch. By the time the process was repeated, the mobile bridges were wreckage, and hundreds of warriors had fallen to fiery deaths.

But the Roman army was in full retreat and seemingly in disarray now. They had abandoned their forward positions across the innermost stake-filled ditch, and had retreated back across the outer two ditches and half a league back across the plain in such a terrorized panic that they had neglected to withdraw or destroy their own bridges behind them.

Rearing his horse, waving his sword, Critognat led his triumphant forces in pursuit across the bridges the Romans had left behind.

Caesar hadn't expected the Gauls to make such a mess of crossing the bridges he had so thoughtfully left behind. Gallius had constructed them to pass infantry, but they were probably sturdy enough to allow horses to be walked across one at a time. Instead, the Gauls had tried to gallop across in a great howling horde, and several of the bridges had immediately collapsed, filling the ditches with screaming men and piteously neighing horses impaled on stakes.

This seemed to be enough to instill a modicum of prudence even in Gauls, and the succeeding waves had made more gingerly and successful crossings, unmolested by Roman archers or catapults.

Caesar had used the time it took them to do it to make some final redeployments. The force confronting the Gauls now consisted of infantry only five lines deep, the front line armed with spears, the rest with swords. Behind them were five lines of infantry furnished with plenty of javelins. There was cavalry behind that, but Caesar planned to hold it in reserve. And behind the cavalry, amidst more infantry, were the catapults.

The rest of his army, fully half of it, had been turned around to face the plain across which Caesar expected Vercingetorix's cavalry to charge at any time now. Judging from how few Gauls had actually emerged from the city and were now working themselves up for a cavalry charge against his own much larger force, the "surprise attack on his rear" was surely going to be the main attack, and they were only the diversion.

Still, it would be nice to dispose of the diversion before the main attack came.

"Order the Greek fire," Caesar told a signalman. "But tell Gallius to make sure to drop it well behind them, the second ditch or so," he added, remembering it had taken the catapults a bit of time to get the range at Bourges. It wouldn't do to have errant amphorae fall among his own troops when they closed with the Gauls.

Critognat raised his sword high above his head and brought it down. With a great collective shout, thousands of Gauls charged toward the line of Roman infantry at a full gallop—

—eight large clay amphorae whistled high over their heads, and impacted amidst the ditches behind them. Some burst into flame, some released spreading puddles of fire that set grass burning and flowed down into the ditches, setting stakes aflame and roasting the horses and men impaled on them, burning alive those who had not yet mercifully died.

Caesar had ridden in among the cavalry just behind his javelin men. He couldn't really see much, but he was close enough to the front to smell the horses of the onrushing Gauls, to hear their ferocious battle cries, and then the screams of horses gutted by spears, the clang and shatter of swords on shields, the howls of the dead and dying.

Javelin after javelin was thrown from just forward of where he sat, amphora after amphora passed overhead, and now so much Greek fire had been dropped behind the Gauls that he could smell its sharp reek as it mingled with the odor of blood, horseshit, and sour, fearful sweat that formed the perfume of the battlefield.

The fighting was intense, as he had known it would be, but a line of horsemen thrusting down at a wall of shields was far less effective than legionnaires thrusting upward from behind it and his infantry held the line against the Gallic cavalry charge, while the javelins took their toll on the Gallic rear.

Caesar waited until he was sure his front line had broken the charge, then rode back among his signalmen and ordered a trumpeter to sound the advance.

· · ·

Behind a solid wall of shields and spears, the front line of Roman infantry, slowly but implacably, step by orderly marching step, began to advance against the disorganized chaos of Critognat's cavalry.

Rather than retreat, the Gauls fought back. Some few tried to leap their horses over the palisade of spears, felling some Romans, but impaling their own mounts in the process. Most reared their horses, smashing hooves on shields and helmets, leaning low in their saddles to slash at necks and faces, but as soon as a legionnaire in the front rank fell, one from the rank behind replaced him, and should he fall, one from the third rank replaced *him*.

Inexorably, like a millstone grinding hard grain to powdery flour, the legions of Caesar pushed the stubbornly defiant Gauls backward toward the ditches, back toward the flames fed by the ceaseless bombardment of Greek fire.

As he led his cavalry out onto the plain in a broad ragged front, Vercingetorix was dismayed to behold a heavy pall of black smoke hanging over the hilltop on which Gergovia was built, and the huge Roman army before it. But his hopes rose as, galloping farther, he saw that, no, the city was not burning; rather, the smoke was rising from a wall of flame on the plain below it.

He raised his sword high above his head and gave a mighty, wordless war cry. Beside him, Rhia did likewise, waving his bear standard higher than any sword. The shouting was joined by the front line of the charging Gauls and spread backward through the ranks; then it was no longer an army, but thousands of howling warriors avid for the blood of the enemy, fearless of death in their lust for glory.

The time of true battle had come.

From the Roman army came a tremendous brassy blare of massed trumpets: four high, piercing notes, repeated four times. From the ramparts of Gergovia, in mocking reply, carnaxes blew deeper notes, a short tune of musical laughter, a fanfare of triumph.

The Gauls fighting the Romans suddenly wheeled their horses, broke away, galloped back toward the outermost ditch and the flames beyond.

· · ·

Titus Labienus had not been pleased when Caesar had withdrawn his command of the Gallic auxiliaries invading Britain in favor of Tulius, then handed it back to him when it was clear that it would turn into a travesty. He knew that Caesar trusted him as a general, but he also knew that there were matters on which Caesar did not trust him—political matters and, worse, matters on which his closest confidant had been that odious reptile Gisstus, dirty and dishonorable tasks he handed off to Tulius.

But Labienus had viewed this as mercy and wisdom. Mercy because he was a man of honor and a soldier with no desire to be anything more, and certainly no desire to be anything less. Wisdom because Caesar seemed to understand this and employ him accordingly.

Until now.

Now, however, Labienus found himself in the middle of one of Caesar's slimiest machinations. Here he was, with a squad of only forty of his own cavalrymen and that only a bodyguard, perched on a ridgeline to the northwest of the battle with the glowering Litivak, whose Eduen cavalry covered the slope behind them, muttering and cursing.

As a general, Labienus had just barely been able to swallow the butchery at Bourges as a necessary and clever stratagem. That was war. But this was forcing an honorable enemy into committing despicable treason. Most distasteful of all was that Labienus knew that Caesar had burdened him with this foul "command" precisely because the Gauls respected *him* as an honorable enemy, Roman or not.

Labienus sighed deeply.

Litivak, perhaps hearing his sigh and understanding its import, looked his way. It was a baleful glance, and Labienus returned it with a wan, regretful shrug, hoping for some sign of forgiveness but not receiving it. It was hardly a proper manner in which to deliver a decisive command. Nevertheless . . .

"Now," said Titus Labienus.

His blood afire, his body aglow with glorious strength, whirling his sword above his head as though it were a willow wand, and all but laughing with the wild joy of it, Vercingetorix led his warriors toward the rear of Caesar's army.

Closer, and closer, and closer. Now he could make out the catapults slinging something in the direction of the city, and the sunlight glinting off the shields of the infantry—

A moan so great and terrible that it could be heard above the din of the hoofbeats of thousands of horses arose from his own men, a sound so mournful and outraged that it sapped Vercingetorix's spirit as a sudden unexpected blow to the stomach might knock the air from his lungs.

He looked to the northwest and saw an army of horsemen almost as large as his own cresting the ridgeline and galloping down the slope toward his right flank, wearing the blue cloaks of Eduen warriors, waving swords and spears and axes and shouting battle cries.

The features of the figure leading the charge were not yet visible. But Vercingetorix did not need to see the traitor's face to know who it was, for it surely could be no other.

"Litivak!" he screamed in soul-deep agony.

This was just too good!

Vercingetorix was turning his army to meet the charge of Litivak's force on his right flank, or perhaps, like the schooling of fish or the flocking of birds, this was no more than the spontaneous reaction of a chaotic horde, but either way it exposed his *left* flank to Caesar as invitingly as a coquettish whore presents her succulent rump.

"Advance!" Caesar cried.

And without waiting for his word to be turned into a trumpet call, he raised his sword and rode through the ranks of his infantry to the front and beyond. Crimson cloak waving in the breeze of his passage as the ensign of his long-sought triumph, he led his legions as this fateful and glorious moment would have him do, from the front.

Vercingetorix found himself galloping ahead of his warriors, one horse length, two, five, eight, oblivious to all that was behind him, for now he had eyes only for what lay ahead—a rider wearing the blue cape of the treacherous Edui galloping ahead of his army too, sword held high in challenge.

And now he could see his face.

It was indeed Litivak.

Worse still, the swine was *smiling*.

And then Litivak reached across his body with his left hand and flipped his cloak over to turn its underside upward.

Vercingetorix gasped. Tears came to his eyes.

It was orange.

"The *Arverne* who would have burned Bourges was my enemy!" Litivak shouted. "But the *Gaul* who paid the price to spare it is forever my brother!"

As Caesar gaped in dismay, there in the distance before him, Litivak and Vercingetorix locked arms in a comradely embrace. And to a man, the Eduen warriors descending upon the right flank of Vercingetorix's army flipped their blue cloaks over to display Arverne orange. And wheeled around, as did Vercingetorix's cavalry.

And the trap he had set suddenly became the trap in which he was caught, as the two armies combined forces, and Vercingetorix and Litivak, side by side, led the whole horde straight toward him.

A huge cheer went up from the women and old men and children on the ramparts of Gergovia. In lieu of shields and swords or spears, they began a rhythmic beating of knives and tradesman's tools on pots and rocks and the walls of the city itself, accompanied by carnaxes.

Critognat's cavalry, outnumbered though it still was, charged what a moment before had been the orderly advancing Roman army, suddenly transformed into a melee of confusion as it found itself caught now between the hammer and the anvil.

There was no time to rage at Litivak's treachery; though Caesar's army might still outnumber the Gauls, that very treachery had turned what had been a winning deployment into an impending fiasco. Caesar wheeled his horse around and dashed five ranks back into his infantry from his totally exposed position before the charging Gauls.

After which it was a pandemonium such as he had never before experienced in battle.

The Gallic cavalry charge hit the front rank of Roman infantry along a fairly broad front, but not nearly as broad as the line of legionnaires. They at once broke through by the sheer shock of their concentrated numbers.

Hacking and slashing, they quickly penetrated a dozen ranks deep before encountering the heavily outnumbered Roman cavalry, who were able only to slow their advance briefly.

It was long enough, however, for Roman infantry on either flank of the Gallic spearhead to wheel around, come together in a pincer movement, cut it off, and then form a new line behind it. But this new Roman line was immediately broken by more charging Gallic cavalry and the rear of the Roman army began to fragment into isolated fighting units under assault of the unexpectedly massive cavalry charge.

Meanwhile, Critognat's cavalry was held back by the Roman line facing the city, taking and giving heavy casualties. But not for very long: elements of the combined forces of Vercingetorix and Litivak, fighting their way through the shattered Roman army, attacked them from the rear, and broke through to Critognat's warriors in several places.

It was no longer an organized combat between two armies on a coherent battlefield. It was now warriors fighting each other in small groups on a vast plain of chaotic slaughter.

With a sweep of his sword, Vercingetorix slashed across the throat of a Roman cavalryman, and blood fountained as the Roman fell from his horse to be trampled by scores of hooves. Rhia, regaining his side and hugging her horse with her thighs, sent a head flying into the air to bounce off the shield of a laughing Arverne.

Half a dozen Roman infantrymen charged at them from the left with swords; from somewhere a spear pierced one of them through the eye; as Rhia thrust her sword through a neck, Vercingetorix hacked an arm, reared his horse, smashing a skull with the full weight of its front hooves. A terrified horse galloped by with a headless Gaul tumbling from its saddle; Rhia leaned far down and struck upward at a Roman crotch; Vercingetorix slashed a centurion across the face, slitting it from cheek to eyeball.

Caesar had never experienced such combat, and found that everything was happening too fast, too furiously, too disconnectedly, for there to be space for thought or time for terror or even anger. Slash, duck, wheel, turn, thrust—he was no longer a general, hardly even a man, but fighting as an animal would for its life and the blood of its enemies, his sword his tooth and claw.

Out of the corner of his eye, he saw a catapult tumble over in a crash of wood and iron, even as he struck at one attacking Gaul's throat while another slashed his right arm. But the pain was far away, the line of blood strangely beautiful. So did the combat come to seem, a graceful dance of steel and flesh, of blood and guts oozing from wounds to the music of clanging swords and ululating screams, the rhythmic clatter of metal on metal, the drumming of stomping hooves. . . .

Thrust, parry, slice a neck; Vercingetorix seems to see everything the moment before it happens. Just as he wields his sword, so does destiny wield him.

A pair of Romans attack from the right and another three at the left, but they are moving so slowly, slower than the passage of time. He brings his shield down on a head, kicks a chin, turns to slash a throat.

It is as his vision beneath the Tree of Knowledge, as if there is a Tree of Action too, and he dreams this battle beneath it, for just as he stood outside of time and saw his life entire, so now does he see this battle entire, even while immersed in the blood and death and screams of it.

He sees dying Gauls and dying Romans, he sees catapults tumble and fall. He sees fire and blood and steel. He sees this battlefield strewn with the corpses of horses and men, littered with limbs and heads and guts. He sees dogs and wolves gnawing meat from the bones as clouds of carrion birds descend to join the feast.

He sees himself upon his horse, cutting, kicking, maiming, killing, bathed in the commingled blood of himself and his enemies. Beside him is Rhia, likewise incarnadine, eyes burning like those of the feral wolf-child she once was, and never more beautiful.

He sees the Roman army slowly retreating afoot across the plain, harried by Gallic horsemen, enclosed by its shields, slinking away in defeat like an enormous vanquished but impenetrable tortoise yapped at by frustrated foxes.

He sees himself holding a bloody sword high above his head in triumph.

Caesar brought up his shield as a huge Arverne warrior, eyes wild, blond hair and beard streaked with blood, came at him with an ax. The ax hit the shield with tremendous force, embedding itself in it, then the shield was ripped from his hands, his horse reared in panic, and Caesar was dumped on the ground, still clutching his sword.

Even as he scrambled to his feet, a dozen or more legionnaires, seeing him fall, dashed to protect him.

The rearing horses and the writhing men, the clash of sword upon sword, the shouts and cries and screams of the battlefield seem to Vercingetorix to dissolve into mist. Not the white mist out of which emerged his vision at Bourges, but a blood-red mist out of which emerges—

—a bright crimson banner snapping and whipping about in a storm of slashing metal.

A bright crimson cloak.

The standard of Gaius Julius Caesar.

Draped across the shoulders of Caesar as he rises from the blood-soaked ground, sword in hand, as legionnaires gather to him, like some demonic serpent who may be defeated, who may be brought down, but who will not die.

Vercingetorix urges his horse toward that undying monster, toward this moment of shared destiny, and, as if the gods would have it so, he glides forward, untouched and untouchable, as if all is unreal here save himself and Caesar.

Through the red fog of battle, a figure on horseback rides toward Caesar; young, blond, blood-spattered, Great Alexander as savage nemesis. But it is Vercingetorix, not Alexander, and as he draws closer, Caesar sees that his eyes gaze out from elsewhere, and he rides forward as he might in a dream.

Caesar cannot look away from those eyes as Vercingetorix approaches. They trap him in the nightmare of defeat which this day has become, as if he himself has become but a figment in the dream of glory of its victor. Yet Vercingetorix seems unable to look away from his eyes too. As if this is a dream they both share, a dance of death or of destiny, an eternal moment outside of time.

Caesar hardly notices when a mighty blow from somewhere strikes his sword from his hand and sends it tumbling through the air.

As a boy once caught the Crown of Brenn falling from the brow of his father before it could touch the floor, so now, without thought, does Vercingetorix pluck from the air the sword of Gaius Julius Caesar.

. . .

Time stops for Caesar as he stands swordless and defenseless before Vercingetorix, staring transfixed into the eyes of his conqueror, into the eyes of the man who will now slay him with his own sword.

And yet in those eyes he sees . . .

How can this be?

Before Vercingetorix stands his defeated and defenseless enemy, gazing unwaveringly into his eyes as if accepting his fate.

Yet what Vercingetorix sees in his vision of the next moment, in a moment outside of time, is not himself plunging the captured sword into the heart of Caesar, but himself holding a sword in both hands before him as an offering.

A token of surrender.

Caesar wonders if Vercingetorix sees what he sees.

But how can he?

For what Caesar sees is not his own impending death, but Vercingetorix, today's victor, meekly handing him back his sword as if *he* were the vanquished.

Caesar nods, as if to acknowledge the vision of unknown destiny which in this moment they share.

Without knowing why, but without being able to do otherwise, Vercingetorix nods back.

And raises the hilt of Caesar's sword before his lips in salute.

And then, holding it aloft, he gives a wordless cry of triumph that sounds hollow in his own ears, turns, and rides away.

XVII

RHIA RODE on Vercingetorix's right hand, holding high the Arverne bear. Litivak rode on his left with a standard-bearer displaying the Eduen boar. Behind them paraded a wonder unknown since the days of Brenn—a united and triumphant army of Gaul.

The gates of Bibracte were open wide, the ramparts were crowded with shield-banging warriors and cheering citizens, garlands were tossed, and carnaxes blew welcoming salutes. Vercingetorix entered the Eduen capital to the acclaim of its inhabitants, basking in the greatest glory known to a Gaul since Brenn had held Rome itself to ransom.

Yet his enjoyment of the greatest moment of his life was shadowed. He had spared the life of Caesar. He knew not why, save that he had followed a vision which had commanded him far more surely than he had ever commanded this army. And so Caesar had lived to rally his battered and bloodied army, to withdraw it from the battlefield of its defeat and shame in an orderly manner, a feat that Vercingetorix could not imagine himself performing had Caesar been the victor.

Now Caesar was probably marching the remains of his army back across the Alps and already planning to raise an even greater force with which to return. For Vercingetorix knew that to accept his failure to conquer Gaul would doom Caesar's ambition to rule Rome itself. And Caesar would die before he would accept that.

The Gauls believed that they had won the war. In truth, all that had been won was a battle. But Vercingetorix could hardly voice such misgivings, least of all to Litivak.

Litivak had risked all—not just his ambition to succeed Liscos as

Eduen vergobret, but the turning of Caesar's wrath against his own people, and hence his honor—to unite the Edui and the Arverni in the blood rite of victorious battle, creating thereby the beginning of a nation proud to call itself Gaul.

Vercingetorix knew he must now repay that debt of honor. He must hold this army together and use this victory to enlarge it, to draw in those who had defected, and those who had held back. He must play the man of destiny who knew no doubt.

Bibracte was somewhat larger than Gergovia and enriched far beyond the wealth of the Arverne capital by the commerce with Rome that Diviacx had brought the Edui before the war began. Now no one dared wear Roman garb, but the marketplace of the main plaza still abounded in Roman goods.

Some of the original Gallic buildings that had been given Roman facings and decorations had been cleansed thereof, save for the ghosts of men and women and strange gods still showing through where they had been painted over too lightly. But there were large new buildings—temples, markets, a mint, a treasury—built in the Roman style with marble and stone, which stood unchanged, save for the empty niches where Roman gods had been removed. And there were many elaborate dwellings in a new style too—square buildings with smooth tan walls, some with the crowns of trees visible above flat roofs of reddish tile, as if growing within.

The aqueduct on its narrow bridge of stone arches that the Romans had built had been preserved, and so too the system of piping that distributed the water to clean wells and pleasant fountains, nor had the new sewage drains been abandoned in favor of the old open ditches. The baths that the Romans had built across the plaza from the Assembly Hall likewise remained.

The Assembly Hall of Bibracte itself retained its entrance portico and the broad stairs leading up to it, apparently added in an attempt at Roman grandeur, but they had been stripped to plain oak.

The plaza was thronged with Edui when Vercingetorix, Litivak, and Rhia arrived, and Vercingetorix was pleased to see among the crowd quite a few nobles in the colors of other tribes. For, although he had brought his army here to repay Litivak by assuring that Bibracte would not be left defenseless against Caesar's promised vengeance, this had been done with a leisurely parade through the countryside, and he had dispatched invitations far and wide, hoping to make it a victory celebration not of Arverni and Edui but of *Gauls*.

The plaza was far too small for the army to enter it even had it been empty, so Vercingetorix dismissed his men for some well-deserved revelry, and he, Litivak, and Rhia dismounted and began to make their way to the gathering in the Assembly Hall afoot. But they had hardly begun to cross the plaza when Vercingetorix and Litivak were recognized, and hoisted up on shoulders, and then on shields, and then deposited on the portico atop the stairs leading into the Assembly Hall like the main dishes on a banquet table.

As, in a way, we are, Vercingetorix thought as the crowd banged swords and daggers on shields, feet upon stone, hands upon each other, shouting *"Vercingetorix! Vercingetorix!"* And he knew that he could not escape inside the building without speaking. So he held up both arms high above his head, and the din swiftly became an expectant hush.

"We have defeated the legions of Rome!" Vercingetorix shouted. "Julius Caesar himself has fled before us! We—"

"Vercingetorix! Vercingetorix! Vercingetorix!"

On and on and on it went, those who had been calling for him to speak now making it impossible for anything but their own voices to be heard.

"Vercingetorix! Vercingetorix! Vercingetorix!"

They were drunk on it, and Vercingetorix would have had to be a man of stone not to feel the seduction himself. At length he raised his hand to quiet both the crowd and the tumultuous clamor of his own heart.

"Cheer if you would for Vercingetorix of the Arverni!" he cried out, placing his right hand on the shoulder of Litivak. "Cheer if you would for Litivak of the Edui!"

They did, and Litivak grinned at him as the crowd shouted both their names, drowning out the syllables in a wordless confusion. At last the shouting gave way to another silence, and Vercingetorix decided to fill it with words that came as close as he might dare to what was in his heart.

"Cheer for the victory of the warriors of Gaul, but cheer not for tribes whose names will soon be forgotten," he said, perhaps more somberly than he had intended, and certainly more somberly than the crowd wished to hear, for these words were greeted with nothing better than guttural muttering. And so Vercingetorix finished by combining what he knew they wanted to hear with what *he* wanted them to acclaim:

"Cheer for what, with this victory, has now been born, and whose spirit shall never die! Cheer for *Gaul*!"

And they did.

"Vercingetorix! King of Gaul!" someone shouted out.

And the rhythmic banging resumed. But the song the multitude now sang was different:

"Vercingetorix! King of Gaul! Vercingetorix! King of Gaul!"

The words that the silver-tongued Vercingetorix had extracted from them. The words from the vision that had brought him to its fulfillment in the here and now. All he had to do was accept them and they would come true.

And yet, when at length the chanting had died away, he found that he could not.

"I shall not wear the Crown of Brenn," he found himself saying, "while there is a victory yet to be won! We have won a great battle, but not the war!"

No great cheer greeted this. Litivak gave him a lidded sidelong glance and the subtlest shaking of his head. Vercingetorix knew that he could not end it with those words. Yet he could not take them back. And so he must find a way to make them sing.

He drew his sword and held it high above his head.

"No king shall rule Gaul while Roman troops remain on our soil!"

The light drizzle falling on the encampment seemed appropriate to Caesar's mood as he stood in the entrance to his tent, observing his army. Legionnaires huddled just inside their own tents before fires rendered smoky by the rain, tending to wounded survivors, hammering dents out of armor, resharpening swords, cooking field porridge in blackened pots, tossing dice, arguing, grumbling, drinking.

There was no joy in this bitter aftermath, but Caesar took a grim satisfaction in commanding such an army, rendered dour by ignominious defeat, but licking its wounded pride and gathering its remaining strength to fight and win another day.

And win we will, for have I not seen Vercingetorix hand over his sword in a battlefield vision? Caesar told himself sardonically.

The disaster at Gergovia had taught him three very expensive but useful lessons that he would not forget:

Never, ever, not even in the most tempting circumstances, trust a force of Gallic auxiliaries or mercenaries.

Never, ever, allow a Gallic army to attack your rear with cavalry.

And, finally, do whatever it takes to trap Vercingetorix's main force in a siege. For Gergovia, even more than Bourges, has proved that this is what he fears the most.

Caesar turned and strode back into the warmth and comfort of his tent—large enough so a fire could burn within, and cleverly vented to release most of the smoke; equipped with oil lamps, a decent bed, and camp stools. Within, Tulius, Labienus, Gallius, Galba, and Glavius, his new so-called spymaster, sat over hot porridge salted with bits of meat and goblets of rough Gallic beer in lieu of wine, glumly waiting to report.

Quartermasters had piled up a dozen swords for his selection as replacement for the one he had lost, and Caesar sat down before them, hefting each in turn as they spoke.

"Well, how bad is it?" he demanded, lifting a sword speculatively.

"Our cavalry took the worst of it," said Galba. "Now, if it came to our cavalry against theirs in the open, we wouldn't have a chance."

Caesar merely nodded, trying another sword for weight and balance, having already assumed this and taken it into account.

"Our infantry was decimated," said Tulius. "Somewhat worse. The tenth part or so killed, another tenth part rendered useless for combat."

Caesar tried out yet another sword.

"Food could be a problem," said Galba. "We lost a lot when we retreated. We can probably last *until* winter with what we have if we are careful, but not *through* it."

"Butcher the dead or useless horses and smoke the meat," said Caesar.

The Gauls would never think of doing such a thing. They might have carnal intercourse with their mounts if they were drunk enough, but they'd sooner eat their own feces. They believed their horses had souls like their own.

"Equipment?" said Caesar, lifting a fourth sword.

"We lost all the siege towers and catapults, but not what we need to make more," said Gallius.

Caesar picked up a fifth sword, shrugged, and slipped it into his empty scabbard. These swords were all similarly crafted; one was as good as another, more or less. Including the one Vercingetorix had captured, though he probably thought its loss was some sort of blow to its former master's manhood.

"What do you think the Gauls will do now, Caesar?" asked Labienus.

"Were I Vercingetorix, I would avoid another battle at all costs. I would declare victory, crown myself king, continue to burn everything before our path and harry our rear and flanks until we finally ran out of food and fodder again and were forced to slink back over the Alps. Where Caesar would spend the winter trying to keep the Senate from recalling him to Rome and probably failing."

"A clever strategy," muttered Tulius. "If they pursue it, we are probably lost."

"Indeed," said Caesar. "But that's what *I* would do. What I believe *they* will do is try to finish us off."

"Wishful thinking, I'm afraid," said Galba.

"Finish us off?" scoffed Tulius. "They win one battle thanks to treachery, and they suppose they have defeated Rome?"

"Vercingetorix is clever," Caesar told him, "but patience is no Gallic virtue, and he doesn't command a true army but a horde of warriors, few of whom are likely to obey orders they do not want to hear."

"The question is, what do we do now?" said Labienus.

"Not quite," said Caesar. "The question is, what do the Gauls *expect* us to do now?" He cocked an inquisitive eyebrow at Glavius. The spymaster shrugged. Caesar scowled. What a lame replacement for Gisstus this man was!

"Where is Vercingetorix's army now?" Caesar asked, sighing, in the tone of a Socratic teacher addressing a dim student.

"At Bibracte."

"Doing what?"

Glavius, looking disquieted, shrugged once more. "Celebrating their victory?" he ventured.

"And what else?"

"What else?"

"By the buttocks of the gods, man, *why Bibracte?*" Caesar shouted in no little exasperation. "Why does Vercingetorix not celebrate the great victory of Gergovia in the place where it happened—which just happens to be the capital of his own tribe?"

The blank stare that greeted this made Caesar pine for the counsel of Gisstus.

"Because Litivak betrayed you?" Labienus suggested. "You forced him to fight with us at Gergovia only by vowing to destroy Bibracte if he did not, so when he betrayed *you* instead of his own people—"

"You're right!" cried Caesar. "Vercingetorix brought his army to Bibracte to protect it from my expected wrath!"

He sprang to his feet and began pacing in small circles. "Well done, Labienus!" he exclaimed. "*That's* thinking like a Gaul!"

"But if we do march on Bibracte in our current state, he'll bring his cavalry out of the city and slaughter us," said Tulius. "We wouldn't have a chance."

"Vercingetorix takes me for a fool," said Caesar. He laughed. "Or at least for a Gaul."

The quizzical looks they all gave him were choice, and he found himself wishing once more for the company of Gisstus: his sardonic friend would surely have enjoyed this.

"Were I a Gaul, I would be honor-bound to seek vengeance on Litivak to fulfill my vow, no matter that it would be an act of military idiocy," Caesar said. "And therefore a Gaul will be taken in when I pretend to do it."

"You have quite lost me, Caesar," Tulius said.

"Get me a map of eastern Gaul that goes as far as the Rhine, Glavius," Caesar ordered, and then, when Glavius brought it, he dropped to his knees and spread it excitedly on the bare earth.

"Look!" he cried, planting his right forefinger on Bibracte. "Here is Bibracte!" He moved it to the southwest. "And here *we* are, more or less."

He began moving his finger northeast, along a line that would take it somewhat east of Bibracte. "We march north, making it appear that the plan is to pass northeast of the city, and circle round to attack from the northwest—"

"But Vercingetorix will surely ride out and—"

"—and chase us down!"

"Do you really think so?" Caesar purred. "Chase us *eastward*?"

"East, west, north, south, it doesn't matter, he's got five times the cavalry we have left now, he'll chase us down wherever we go and slaughter us!"

"Not if we hire enough mercenary reinforcements to give him a very unpleasant surprise when we allow him to catch us," said Caesar.

"*Mercenaries!*" exclaimed Tulius. "Look what happened with Litivak! Nowhere in this cursed land are there mercenaries we can trust!"

"But there are, Tulius, there are!"

The din of talk and laughter in the Assembly Hall redoubled when Vercingetorix and Litivak entered, then guttered away to an expectant moment of silence as Vercingetorix stood there frozen by a bittersweet memory.

For the scene reminded him of Keltill's last feast in the Great Hall of Gergovia, when he was but his father's proud son in the long ago. This place might be larger and it might be lit by brazen oil lamps rather than torchlight, but the walls were also hung with the arms and skulls of defeated enemies, and a boar spitted in a fireplace at one end and an ox in one at the other filled the air with the same savory tang of roasting meat and burning wood. Here too the vergobrets and tribal leaders sat at a big table in the center of the room, and though this feasting table was covered with a cloth of blue, the fare laid out upon it was much the same: boar and mutton, bread and poultry, kegs and tankards of good yeasty beer. Vercingetorix could almost see Keltill seated in the central place of honor with a horn of beer in his hand, and a welcoming smile on his lips.

But here the seat of honor was to be his, on its right hand an empty place for Litivak, and on its left—

The center table was surrounded by smaller tables crammed into the hall to accommodate as great a crowd as the place would hold—craftsmen, warriors, traders—and now they were on their feet, banging tankards on the table, chanting his name, and expecting some words as he made his way to his seat of honor. But the sight of who it was who already sat at the left hand thereof rendered Vercingetorix indifferent to all else.

For it was Marah.

She wore a plain white linen Gallic shift trimmed with the red and black of the Carnutes, though her long blond hair was elaborately coiffed and held high off her neck by a golden tiara in the Roman style, and her cheeks rendered rosier than natural by artifice, and her eyes dramatically framed by black kohl.

Once more, the Great Leader of Warriors was transported back to the long ago, when a young boy's manhood had risen to salute his first sight of a budding beauty.

"Vercingetorix! Vercingetorix! Vercingetorix!"

But since then, Marah had lain with Caesar, become half a Roman, and scorned him as a barbarian. The "barbarian" who was now the hero of Gergovia and could have himself acclaimed king with a word. And to Marah's left sat her mother, Epona, who he doubted had brought her here for entirely sentimental purposes.

No, he was no longer that beardless boy, and she was no longer that young virgin. It was the eyes of a woman into which he gazed now, and behind them he saw neither innocence nor simplicity.

Nor were they alone.

Other eyes were watching this tender reunion. The eyes of the Carnutes, via the mother who had arranged it. The eyes of the Edui, who had hosted it. The smiling eyes of Litivak, who would seem to have had his friendly hand in it too. The eyes of Rhia, across the table a few places down, looking upon him with a face of stone.

And ears were listening. The ears of those at the table, the ears of those in the Assembly Hall, to whom what was said would be swiftly relayed, and unseen ears far beyond who would hear later, through the distorting ripples of word-of-mouth. No, thought Vercingetorix, we are not alone. We can never be that boy and girl again. We have become a tale the bards will tell.

"You have come to bask in the glory of the hero of Gergovia?" were the first words he spoke.

"To salute the man who spared Bourges," said Marah. "For *that* man would be a worthy king."

Well spoken! thought Vercingetorix. From the heart? Or carefully crafted to seem so?

"And you would be his queen?" he said.

"I laughed when I was asked by the boy, but I would be honored to be asked by the man."

The words seemed to hang in the air. Vercingetorix became even more acutely aware that the words they spoke were being spoken for thousands of ears not present, perhaps for ears yet unborn.

"I have vowed that there shall be no king in Gaul while a single Roman soldier stands upon our soil," he said.

"I can wait," said Marah, and kissed him lightly on the lips.

Which brought a cheer of acclaim from those at the table.

All save Rhia.

And Vercingetorix himself.

With all the guests at the table straining their ears to overhear whatever he might say to Marah, Vercingetorix pretended to give his full attention to food and drink, forcing himself to gobble down great chunks of meat for which he felt no real appetite, and appearing to quaff more beer than he was really drinking, observing with sidelong glances that she seemed to be doing the same.

Only when he saw that their tablemates had consumed enough beer so that even Litivak and Epona allowed their attention to drift elsewhere did Vercingetorix seek to converse with Marah, and then softly and without meeting her eyes, still pretending to be concentrating on his meat and beer.

"Why did you really come here?"

"I spoke the truth."

"Did you?"

"Sparing the granaries of Bourges was a noble act. The man who risked all to do it proved he had a noble heart."

"But the consequences for the city were disastrous."

"But not for Gaul. Had you destroyed Bourges, Litivak would not have returned to your side, the battle of Gergovia would have been lost, and—"

"And you would now be sidling up to Caesar?" Vercingetorix blurted, and immediately wished he had bitten his treacherous tongue off instead.

But Marah took no umbrage. "I deserved to hear that," she said in a gentle voice, "and it is only just that I hear it from you." And Vercingetorix felt his heart soften toward her at that forthright admission. But was it crafted to achieve such an effect?

"Then you no longer deem me a petulant barbarian?" he said, and softened his own words by adding jestingly: "Or at least I have become one with a silver tongue?"

"The man who burned people alive *was* a barbarian who made me ashamed to be born a Gaul. But the man who spared Bourges and accepted the consequences made me ashamed to have been seduced by the allure of Rome."

"And by Caesar?"

"I would be lying if I told you I regretted . . . knowing such a great man," said Marah.

"You can call the man who butchered Bourges 'great'?"

"Great as Rome is great, Vercingetorix. A great man determined to rule the greatest civilization the world has known."

"The greatest civilization the world has known!" Vercingetorix hissed, so that his anger would be heard by Marah alone. "Which seeks to conquer and despoil and enslave every people it encounters! Including your own!"

"To conquer, yes, but not to despoil. You have seen this city and you have seen Bourges. Can you truly say that either was left poorer by its commerce with Rome? Less rich in worldly goods or learning or the arts? Provided with a less abundant supply of water? Less . . . civilized?"

"But at what cost?" demanded Vercingetorix. "And if you find the *civilization* of Rome so admirable, why are you here among such rough Gallic barbarians?"

"Because," said Marah, "though Rome, like Caesar, is great in all the things of the world and therefore to be emulated and admired, it is not great at heart, and therefore, like Caesar, not to be loved. But Gaul *is* great at heart. As is the man who taught me this lesson, not with silver-tongued words or a mighty victory, but with a foul deed nobly left undone."

Vercingetorix's heart begged him to trust these honeyed words, but he could not be sure they weren't just silver-tongued words of a woman who would be queen.

"Vercingetorix! Vercingetorix! Vercingetorix!"

Bellies had been filled to the point of torpor, beer had been drunk to the point of red-eyed intoxication, and there was nothing left but to hear the words of the victor of Gergovia and the conqueror of Caesar, the silver-tongued Vercingetorix.

"Vercingetorix! Vercingetorix! Vercingetorix!"

Tankards slammed on tables, spilling beer. Feet stomped on the floor, scattering the dogs who were gorging on scraps. Dagger and sword pommels banged on shields as if they were Roman heads.

"Vercingetorix! Vercingetorix! Vercingetorix!"

"Listen to that!" exulted Litivak, his bloodshot eyes shining with battle lust. "Speak to them of glory and they'll be ready to follow you off the edge of the world!"

"That's what I'm afraid of," muttered Vercingetorix, having dreaded the coming of this moment all through the feasting. For he knew what he *should* say, and glory had no part in it.

He was rescued from having to answer Litivak's befuddlement by Liscos. His blond hair half gray, his heavy face weighed down by more than fatigue, the Eduen vergobret had tried to play the overjoyed host of the feast, to pretend that he had commanded Litivak and his warriors to the rescue of Gergovia. No one really believed it, but no one had yet found it useful to deny this unifying falsehood. Now Liscos leapt up onto the big table unsteadily, knocking several platters of meaty remains onto the floor. No one seemed to notice save the dogs that commenced squabbling for them under the table as he began to speak.

"Are you enjoying our feast?" he shouted in a voice a good deal less than sober. "Are you enjoying the magnificent hospitality of Liscos, vergobret of the Edui?"

The chanting and rhythmic pounding only became more insistent.

"Vercingetorix! Vercingetorix! Vercingetorix!"

Liscos made a rather vain attempt to mask his envious scowl. "Are you enjoying the greatest victory since the time of Brenn?" he bellowed at the top of his voice.

At this, Critognat leapt to his feet down at the end of the table and roared even louder: "The greatest victory in the history of the world! We have done what no one has ever done before! We have defeated the greatest army of the greatest general of the greatest army of the greatest—"

At this, the hall burst into good-natured laughter, rescuing Critognat from his drunken befuddlement.

"Six legions of them!" someone shouted.

"Ten!"

"A hundred!"

This was a boast ridiculous enough to draw laughter even from well-beered Gauls. But also enough to allow Liscos a graceful exit.

"A thousand legions and we would still have sent them fleeing before us!" Liscos declaimed grandly. "Our women could slaughter a hundred legions, our children a hundred, and our dogs could take care of the rest!"

At this there was more raucous laughter.

"We have defeated the despoiler of our land and the scourge of our people—Julius Caesar himself!"

Jeers, hissings, feigned fartings.

"Defeated by a greater general still—"

"Vercingetorix! Vercingetorix! Vercingetorix!"

The chanting began again, and Liscos, frowning, surrendered at last to the inevitable and shouted: "Vercingetorix! Who has brought us this greatest of victories! Vercingetorix! In whose honor I, Liscos, vergobret of the Edui, will now treat you all to three full days of the greatest *feast* in the history of Gaul!"

This was enough to earn him such a loud cheer that he could return to his seat with his hostly dignity more or less intact. But it was not quite enough to bring order.

"After which we'll ride out of here and smash the Romans once and for all!" Critognat shouted.

"Death to Caesar!"

"Why wait? Let's do it now!"

Many men were rising woozily from their seats, drawing swords, waving them wildly, drunk enough on beer and glory to ride out right now and try.

"*Vercingetorix! King of Gaul!*" some shouted.

"*Vercingetorix! King of Gaul!*"

"*No!*" shouted Vercingetorix as loudly as he was able, leaping up onto the table. The tumult died down into confused mutterings, and he decided to at least try to say what he must.

"I have sworn not to wear the Crown of Brenn while Roman legions still shame the soil of Gaul, and though we have won a great victory, we have not yet won the war."

"Well spoken!" shouted Critognat. "Let's ride after them and finish them off!"

"Well spoken yourself, Critognat!" said Vercingetorix, seeking to bend Critognat's words back to his own purpose. "Critognat is right— we must finish what we have begun. But our victory at Gergovia must be the last battle of the war."

"You speak in riddles!" shouted Critognat. "The war is not won, but there must be no more battles? How can this be?"

"We cannot win this war in Gaul," said Vercingetorix. "We must win it in Rome."

Once more, Critognat deflected his words from their intended purpose. "Now you're speaking like a *real* Gaul! Let's march on Rome! Burn it to the ground!"

Vercingetorix saw nothing for it but to press on as if these words had not been spoken.

"Caesar is desperate for a victory that he can take triumphantly back to Rome. We would be fools to give him such a second chance. All we need do to win the war is deny him both battle and supplies until winter approaches once more. Then will he be forced to retreat over the mountains with a starving army as the humiliated victim of a famous defeat. After which it will be a long time if ever before any Roman general thinks to make his reputation as conqueror of Gaul!"

"Now you're speaking like a cowardly Roman!" Critognat bellowed.

"When you've speared a wild boar through the lungs, do you give it a chance to charge at you with its tusks, or do you stand back and watch it die?"

"Stand back and watch your enemy die? Where is the glory in that?" said Critognat. "I would give any enemy the chance to die fighting! Even Caesar! The same chance I would want him to give me!"

This was met with a roar of approval, such as no words of Vercingetorix had drawn forth, for he had tried to speak to their minds the worldly wisdom they *needed* to hear, but Critognat had spoken what they *wanted* to hear to their spirits and so touched their warriors' hearts.

"*You* must choose," said Vercingetorix, making one last foredoomed try, but treading carefully this time. "Do we fight the Romans for victory or for glory?"

When the people will not follow where you would lead, you must go with them or walk alone.

It was Litivak who answered. "They are one and the same! We fight for the glorious victory of Gaul!"

The cheering that went up fairly shook the walls.

"So be it," Vercingetorix whispered softly to himself.

"So be it!" he cried aloud when the clamor finally subsided. "You have chosen to fight not for victory without glory, but for the glory of Gaul, and so I will lead you into the jaws of death with a battle song in my heart!"

He drew his sword, and sliced his left forearm lightly. "I pledge my life to the last drop of blood to lead Gaul and its cause no matter what sacrifice destiny may call upon me to make!"

Swords were drawn, arms were blooded and held aloft, and the chanting of his name rang out yet again.

But when Vercingetorix stole a sidelong glance at Marah and saw what was written in her eyes, he knew that she alone understood the hollowness of his words. She alone knew that there was no joyous battle song singing in his heart.

The silver-tongued Vercingetorix had only given them what he knew they wanted to hear.

XVIII

Ι T WAS AN OVERCAST NIGHT, and the only light from the sky was
the wan, pearly smear of the moon, but the streets below glittered
with bonfires, with cookfires, with torches dancing in the dark.
From the walkway atop Bibracte's wall, Vercingetorix could hear the
distant strains of music, talk, and laughter, merging into a song of revelry. But he was in no mood for celebration.

"You spoke well today."

Rhia had come up beside him.

"I lied," he said. "I have become practiced at it. I will lead them into
the jaws of death because I must, but there is no battle song in my heart.
I fear that the winning of one battle will bring the losing of the war."

Rhia shook her head in chastisement. "Now, *there* is a thought that
should be stopped before it slows your mind."

"Tell me how!" Vercingetorix demanded. "I gave them the choice of
fighting for victory or fighting for glory, and you saw what they chose."

"But Litivak declared that we fight for the glorious victory of Gaul,"
Rhia protested, though Vercingetorix detected no conviction in it.

"Beer talking, and, worse, the stronger drink of glory," he said. "I
can but love Litivak for what he did, but were I Caesar, I would be calling it treachery. Our victory was won not by superior force of arms but
by an act of betrayal."

Rhia regarded him as if he were some strange beast. "You fault your
friend for a courageous act of loyalty to you because it betrayed your
enemy?"

If there were any humor in him this night, Vercingetorix might have
laughed at that. "Of course not," he said instead. "But had Litivak

played his part as Caesar expected, you and I would probably be dead, and Gaul would now be a province of Rome."

"Is that not a clear sign that destiny smiles on our cause? And Caesar's losses were heavy. Perhaps we *can* defeat what he has left in open battle."

"Nothing is impossible," Vercingetorix admitted, "nor do I fear heavy odds against me—"

"Then what weighs so heavily upon you that you cannot bear a feast?"

Vercingetorix nodded back toward the lights and sound of the celebration below.

"The knowledge that, because of those greathearted fools down there, I must throw away a sure victory so that we can chase after honor and glory!" Vercingetorix said, giving vent to the anger he had not dared to display in the Assembly Hall.

"Am I interrupting something?"

Marah had come up onto the walkway, wrapped in a woolen cloak of Carnute red and black, but somehow contriving to drape it around herself like a silken Roman toga.

"Nothing not *better* interrupted," said Rhia.

"You were subtle as any Roman today, Vercingetorix," said Marah. "Caesar could not have spoken better."

"Am I supposed to take that as praise?" Vercingetorix asked petulantly.

"Caesar studied rhetoric under a master," Marah told him. "And logic as well."

"But they were swayed by neither my subtle rhetoric nor . . . Roman logic."

"Perhaps because you were wrong," said Marah.

"Oh, was I?" Vercingetorix snapped testily.

"Even if you *did* harry Caesar out of Gaul in disgrace, even if you killed him, *Rome* would never accept unavenged defeat. When the Carthaginian Hannibal defeated them, it took them a hundred years, but they destroyed even the memory of Carthage and plowed salt into the soil so nothing would grow there again. And this I was told by Caesar himself. He was very proud of it."

"You have learned much from Caesar," said Vercingetorix.

"And so have you," said Marah. "Enough to battle him as an equal. Enough to have the people you lead proclaim you king if you let them. More than Caesar has ever done."

And then, in a strange wistful tone: "Or sought to."

This sent a pang of jealousy through Vercingetorix's heart, and when he looked into Marah's eyes there was no denial to be seen there of the esteem in which she still held the great Caesar. Did she *seek* to arouse his jealousy? Or did she wish to see in *his* eyes acknowledgment that he too harbored admiration for his mortal enemy?

Vercingetorix found that this he could not quite deny. But he was determined not to let it show, and it was Marah who turned away, and spoke to Rhia in a bantering tone:

"Once, he promised to make me his queen, you know," she said. "Has he promised the same to you?"

"I will not live to see a king in Gaul," Rhia said somberly.

"And I fear I will never rule as one," muttered Vercingetorix.

Marah looked at him, back at Rhia, shook her head.

"What a sorry pair of lovers!"

Vercingetorix felt heat at the back of his neck and below his cheekbones, a blush of emotions—longing, embarrassment, somehow even shame.

"We are not lovers!" he blurted.

Marah eyed him narrowly. "She bears your standard, she rides by your side into every battle, I have heard it told that she has been seen sleeping by your side in the forest, and you expect me to believe—"

"Brother and sister of the sword," Rhia told her with a passion that belied her truthful words, "that is what we are, and all we will ever be."

And Marah laughed.

"Oh, come now, you have no need to hide it from me," she said good-naturedly. "I saw no reason to hide my dalliance with Caesar from *him*, so I cannot fault him for his dalliance with you, for the truth of it is that we have never yet been lovers, and I could hardly expect him to—"

"Nor have we!" Rhia insisted.

"You think what you feel for him doesn't show?"

This was becoming more than Vercingetorix could bear.

"I think I will return to the feast after all," he said. "Perhaps some beer will cheer my mood."

Marah laughed. "If it does, I should have no trouble finding you, O Great Leader of Warriors."

It was late morning after the second night of feasting, and the bright sunlight cut through the shadows like knives, cruelly revealing the remains of human revelry on the tables, and the gnawed bones left by the dogs on the floor.

Litivak, Liscos, Cottos, Kassiv, Epirod, Netod, Comm, and Velaun were already slumped around the central table when Vercingetorix brought Oranix into the Assembly Hall. The air was stale with the smell of old beer and roasting grease, and they were red-eyed, puffy-faced, and in an ill temper at being summoned before noon.

But Oranix had awakened Vercingetorix even earlier with news they must all hear. Caesar's army was not retreating south, toward the Alps. It was apparently marching north, toward Bibracte. But in a strange manner.

"Where is Critognat?" demanded Vercingetorix.

"Still sleeping it off, no doubt," grumbled Comm. "And why aren't we?"

"Caesar is moving north," Vercingetorix told the bleary assembly.

"North?"

That was enough to rouse their attention.

"Marching on Bibracte as he vowed to do?" Litivak said nervously, glancing furtively at Liscos.

The scowl that the current Eduen vergobret gave his suddenly not-so-certain successor seemed more one of vindication than of terror. "As you have *caused* Caesar to do, Litivak."

"Couldn't he have had the decency to wait until our feast was over?" groaned a hoarse voice at the entrance. Critognat, looking very much the worse for wear, staggered into the Assembly Hall to half-ironic laughter.

"We'd better gather our forces and march south to meet him," said Comm.

"Oh no," said Liscos. "It's the army of Gaul that is bringing Caesar's wrath down on this city, and honor demands that the army of Gaul stay here to defend it."

"The last thing we want is to be trapped in a siege!" said Cottos.

"He's right! Look what happened to Bourges!"

"Look what happened to *Caesar* when he tried to besiege Gergovia!"

"What is happening here?" Luctor had arrived at last and was making his way through the detritus.

"Caesar is marching on Bibracte—"

"I didn't say that," said Vercingetorix.

"Then he isn't?"

"I didn't say that either—"

"What, then—"

Vercingetorix picked up an overturned tankard and slammed it down loudly on the tabletop.

"We don't *know* what Caesar's doing!" he shouted. "So, before we start arguing about what to do about it, let Oranix tell you what our scouts have actually seen!"

"Caesar has split his forces," Oranix told them. "Labienus, with two legions and what seems to be all of their remaining cavalry, is moving northwest toward Bibracte. They have wagons that appear to be carrying the parts of siege engines."

Hearing this befuddled his lieutenants no less than it had Vercingetorix.

"Where, then, is Caesar?" asked Litivak.

"Caesar appears to be in command of the rest of his army, almost all afoot, moving more slowly to the north, on a line that will approach Bibracte from the east."

"Why would he do such a thing?" said Comm. "Without cavalry, we'll cut him to pieces!"

"But before you can reach him, Labienus will reach Bibracte," said Liscos. "You can't leave the city defenseless."

"What can even Labienus do with only two legions?" scoffed Cottos.

"Besiege the city!" said Liscos.

"We could break through easily—"

"You're forgetting he has all that cavalry—"

"—useless in a siege—"

"It's a ploy to get us to divide our forces," said Litivak.

"So we crush Labienus on the march and then turn east to finish off Caesar," said Critognat.

"That would make sense," said Vercingetorix. "But it makes Caesar seem far too stupid. . . ."

"It *is* stupid!" exclaimed Luctor.

"Too stupid to be credited," said Vercingetorix. "Caesar is *inviting* us to destroy Labienus' weak force and then turn on him. The question is, what does Caesar *not* want us to do?"

"This is getting to be too subtle for me," said Netod.

"You sound as if you're thinking like a Roman again, Vercingetorix," said Litivak.

"Perhaps *Caesar* has started thinking like *Vercingetorix*," muttered Critognat.

"What?"

"I'm just a simple old warrior whose brain may be dimmed by last night's beer, but it seems to me that Caesar might have learned a trick or two from you, Vercingetorix. Labienus' force is mostly cavalry, and as you say, he really can't besiege Bibracte with what he has, so—"

"Of course!" said Litivak. "As soon as we come after Labienus, he retreats—"

"—as you had us do for so long," said Critognat.

"Long enough to lead us far enough away from Bibracte so that Caesar's main force can destroy the city before we can return to defend it," said Litivak.

"Or take Bibracte and hold it *hostage* instead of destroying it," said Liscos.

Now Vercingetorix saw Caesar's plan. If he could capture the Eduen capital, he could threaten to destroy it and massacre its inhabitants unless his demands were met. At the very least, he could force the Edui to turn Litivak over to him and withdraw their warriors from the army of Gaul. And after what he did to Bourges, Liscos would have no other alternative.

"It is as I said, we must keep the whole army here to defend the city," said the Eduen vergobret, and Vercingetorix was inclined to agree with him now. But . . .

"But then won't we be trapped in a siege when both Labienus and Caesar arrive?" said Cottos. "Perhaps all this is designed to trick us into doing just that."

"One thing is certain at least," said Litivak, "we must not go chasing after Labienus."

"On that much we are in agreement, Litivak," Liscos told him sourly.

"If we attack *Caesar's infantry* with our full force and destroy him on the march, Labienus will be easy enough to deal with afterward," said Netod.

"Let's do it, then, and stop talking about it!" said Critognat.

"All we have to do is destroy Caesar's depleted forces and final victory is ours!"

"So it would seem," said Vercingetorix, feeling that he was missing something vital, but unable to see what.

"You intend to leave Bibracte defenseless against Labienus while you chase after Caesar?" asked Liscos.

"So stay behind to defend it," Critognat told him contemptuously. "*I* held Gergovia against a full army with a few thousand men. Of course, they *were* Arverni. But double the number of Edui should be enough to defend Bibracte against two little legions."

"You say Edui are lesser men than Arverni?" snarled Liscos.

Vercingetorix knew he had better end this before they were at each other's throats instead of the Romans'. "Enough!" he cried. "You shall have the great battle you've been waiting for! But against the Romans, not each other. Liscos, keep behind as many men as you deem necessary to defend Bibracte. The rest of us will go east to confront—"

And then it came to him.

"No," he said, "first we go *south* so as to pass *west* of Caesar and then attack his western flank, driving him *east*—"

"Toward the Rhine!" exclaimed Kassiv.

"Toward the lands of the Teutons!"

Vercingetorix nodded. "Who, if destiny smiles upon us, will believe he's invading and attack him from the other side."

"And become our unwitting allies!"

Vercingetorix knew that if he joined the revelry Marah need only follow the crowd that would accumulate around him as surely as torches attracted their admiring night moths. Perhaps that was why he had avoided the festivities of the first two nights, for the hero of Gergovia could hardly walk the streets of Bibracte with a tankard of beer in one hand and Marah's hand in the other like an ordinary man. Any words they spoke to each other among the revelers would enter the Land of Legend through every passing ear. Should they steal off together, that too would be noted and be sung by the bards.

Why should this so trouble him? Because she had arrived back in his life at such an opportune moment? Because he distrusted her as much as he desired her? Or could it be that he did not trust *himself* with a woman of such amatory experience, that he feared to either admit that he had none when the time came, or to reveal the embarrassing truth by ineptitude?

But this was the last night of the feast, the last night before they rode out to battle, and it could be the last time they would ever meet. So Vercingetorix went out into the streets, allowed a tankard to be pressed into his hand, allowed men to hail him and women to flirt, and both to follow in his aimless wake as he wandered from bonfire to bonfire, ate proffered boar and venison, listened to bards and musicians, even joined for brief moments in dance.

But he moved through the celebration without feeling part of it, and when Marah did find him, she seemed the only one in the whole fête to be entirely a creature of flesh and blood.

The street was smoky with the cookfires of stalls offering slices of spitted boar, whole roast pigeons, and brochettes of tiny ortolans. On one side of the street, a bard recited odes to a small crowd; on the other, a piper played for a group of wildly drunk dancers.

Marah approached through the cookfire smoke clothed in a plain white shift, reminding Vercingetorix of the nameless woman who had appeared to him out of the luminous mist in Bourges. And bent the path of his destiny.

"I see that tonight you descended to the feast," Marah said dryly.

"And I see that you have had little trouble finding me."

"All eyes and ears lead to the hero of Gergovia. You would be hard not to find tonight, Vercingetorix."

Then she sighed, and a wistful look replaced her air of mildly mocking banter.

"But it has certainly been a long journey from a boy and a girl kissing beside a stream to where we find ourselves now, has it not?" she said, moving closer, so that he could smell the floral sweetness of the perfume she wore, mingled with the tangier musk of her body.

"And where do that boy and girl find themselves now?"

Marah sighed once more, close enough for Vercingetorix to feel the breeze of her breath, taste its warmth.

"Why ask me?" she said softly. "I have lost myself often enough along the way. I lost that girl who kissed you when I became the sophisticated student in a Roman grammaticus. I lost that woman when Caesar became a worse barbarian than any Teuton."

"And now?" Vercingetorix asked testily. "*Now* who are you?"

"Who do you wish me to be?" said Marah.

No answer could have been worse. This woman whom his body longed to embrace had embraced Caesar when it seemed expedient, had embraced Rome as the future of Gaul when it had seemed inevitable, would embrace him now as its future king if destiny gave him the victory that made it so.

"Someone I can trust!" said Vercingetorix, speaking the angry truth.

"You do not trust me?" Marah asked in a voice so even and with eyes so devoid of any hint of emotion that Vercingetorix could not begin to guess what feelings were behind them.

"How can I?" he said. "Are you the girl I longed for as a boy? Are you the bait Caesar dangled before me? Are you the woman who arrived here two days ago to publicly accept an offer I made to you as a boy? Who are you, Marah?"

"She who has been all those things, one after another. Who else could I be?"

"And *this* you ask me to trust?"

"Remember, Vercingetorix?" Marah said softly. "We were walking on the beach, and you asked me if I trusted Caesar. And I said, yes, I trusted him to be Gaius Julius Caesar. To be what he was. As I trusted you to be the Great Leader of Warriors. To be what you are."

She shrugged, and Vercingetorix could see her nipples caress the fabric of her dress with the motion. "Can you not trust me in like manner?"

And he wanted to.

"Between a boy and a girl there should be something more than that," he found himself saying instead.

"Long live Vercingetorix, king of Gaul!" gabbled a glazed-eyed woman in middle years, one of a group of dancers whirling up the street, as she grabbed Vercingetorix by the hand, whipped him around once, twice, thrice, and threw him off balance into the arms of Marah.

"The hand of destiny!" Marah exclaimed with a laugh, and kissed him deeply, and Vercingetorix found himself returning the kiss. He felt her breasts, and then her thighs, pressing against him.

But then there was raucous and lubricious laughter.

Vercingetorix pulled away, his ears burning, as he discovered to his mortification that a circle of warriors and townspeople, good-naturedly drunk, had surrounded them and were cheering them on.

The black look with which Vercingetorix regarded the onlookers cleared them away as surely as the threatening sweep of a sword.

"If you cannot trust me, let me prove myself," Marah said in a voice loud enough for the closest of the crowd to overhear. "Give me a horse, and a weapon, and a shield, and let me ride to battle beside you as your warrior woman does."

To his chagrin, Vercingetorix heard a few mutters of encouragement and approval. Was she doing this for the benefit of their ears and the tales to be told by generations of bards? Or was this truly the offer of a brave and loving heart?

And why not both?

"You cannot be serious!" Vercingetorix whispered.

"But I am!" Marah declared, and this time for his ears alone, and when Vercingetorix saw the ferocity in her eyes, it sent his spirit soaring.

But what he saw also was a soft woman in a clean white dress without a battle scar on her body, who had probably never even lifted a weapon, let alone wielded one.

"It cannot be," he said.

"Why not?" Marah demanded.

"Because you are a woman, and you would not last five minutes on a field of battle."

"Then so be it. Let me die at your side."

"No!"

"And what is your warrior lover, Rhia?"

"She is not my lover!" Vercingetorix fairly shouted, then was mortified to realize that they were being overheard once more.

"And *I* am supposed to trust *you*? What would you have me believe next, that Rhia is really a man?"

"We swore a blood oath—"

"Yet another blood oath!" Marah shouted for all to hear. "Very well, then, why should I not swear my own?"

The music had stopped. The dancing had ceased. At once they were surrounded by a crowd that openly pressed in upon them, and it was to them that she spoke, and through them to Bibracte, and to Gaul beyond, and to the bards who would bear her words into the Land of Legend.

And Vercingetorix could do nothing to stop her. And when he heard them, he did not know if he would if he could.

"I do love you, Vercingetorix, future king of Gaul, and if you would not have me as your queen, I would be your whore. Like it or not, where you go, so go I, and no one shall prevent me, not Gaius Julius Caesar, not the gods themselves, not even *you*!"

And to a roar of approval, with a swirl of her robe, and her head held high, and with Vercingetorix's ears burning and his heart aflame with both love and fury, she turned on her heel and marched off into the night.

As might a queen.

Marah had gone to her bedchamber and doffed her robe, and was sitting on the chamberpot when there was an insistent knocking on the heavy oaken door.

"A moment, please, Vercingetorix," she said in a voice crafted not to sound flustered but failing to succeed.

She finished pissing as quickly as she could, slid the chamberpot into a far corner well away from the bed, put on her robe, did the best she was able to rearrange her hair with her fingers, then went to the door and opened it.

Rhia stood in the doorway.

"What do *you* want?" Marah demanded.

"To help you keep the oath you have made," said Rhia. "May I enter?"

She was dressed as a warrior and wearing a sword, though not a helmet. In her arms she carried a shirt of mail armor, a pair of orange-and-gray-striped pantaloons, a horned helmet, a heavy cloak of Arverne orange, and a scabbarded sword with its buckler.

With a bemused expression, Marah nodded. Rhia entered, and laid out what she had been carrying on the bed as Marah closed the door behind them.

"Take off your robe," Rhia said.

"What!"

"Come, now, we are both women, are we not?"

"Why should I do such a thing?"

Rhia picked up the pantaloons in one hand and hefted the heavy mail shirt in the other. "So that we may dress you as a man."

"As a man. . . ?" Marah said slowly.

"As one of thousands of warriors following the man you too have vowed to follow tomorrow," said Rhia.

"Why . . . why are you doing this? Why would *you* help *me*?"

"Did you not say there is no reason why we cannot be friends?"

Marah regarded Rhia suspiciously.

"You have nothing to fear by standing naked before me," said Rhia. "I am not a man, nor am I your rival."

"The former I can believe," said Marah, "the latter . . . ?" She shrugged, but she took off her robe and stood there naked, looking questioningly into Rhia's eyes.

Rhia stared back, gazed slowly down the contours of Marah's soft-muscled but well-formed body, then smiled, if only wanly, for the first time. "And even if I *could* be your rival . . ."

She handed Marah the mail shirt. Marah put it on. Then the pantaloons. Rhia picked up the sword and its belt, put her arms around Marah, and buckled the weapon around her waist. She took the helmet in one hand, balled the train of Marah's long hair into an untidy fistful with the other, and held it atop her head while she jammed the helmet down over it.

Rhia stepped back and studied her appraisingly.

"Now put on the cloak," she said.

Marah draped the orange cloak around her shoulders. Rhia shook her head. "Close it across your body to hide the bulges of your breasts, and keep it that way," she said.

Marah did as she was told.

Rhia cocked her head, left, right, left.

"Pick up some dirt and rub it on your cheeks tomorrow," she said, "and keep your head down when you ride, as if fatigued. It's the best we can do to hide your lack of beard."

"I ask you again, why would you help me?" said Marah. "I tell you truly, in your place I would not help my rival."

"And *I* tell *you* truly, Marah, I am not your rival," said Rhia.

"And will you tell me that you do not love him?"

Rhia sighed. "I am his sister of the sword. Is that love? Who am I to say? Who am I to know? I am but the flower."

"I do not understand what that means," said Marah.

"Then understand and believe this," Rhia told her. "I have an oath to keep and so do you. And by aiding you in keeping yours, I aid myself in keeping mine. So we are not rivals, Marah, we are oath-sisters."

And the warrior woman kissed Marah on the cheek and was gone.

Once more Vercingetorix found himself taking refuge from the fête high up on the ramparts. For those seeking them, the sky held a surfeit of portents, for it was as clear as the waters of a still lake and full of stars. One might read anything in the pictures they made, victory, defeat, love accepted or love spurned, destiny for good or ill.

But Vercingetorix had had his fill of omens and messages scrawled across the heavens. He had followed them since he was a boy, and where had they led him? To a fate that on the morrow, or on some day soon after that, would depend not on his ability to read the heavens like a druid but to read the mind of Caesar like a general. A man he feared was a greater general than himself, and certainly one who wielded an army that even in defeat was a keener-honed weapon than his own.

If he won, he would be king. And if he did not . . .

Enough of signs emblazoned across the heavens!

But at that very moment, the pale white trail of a falling star slipped across the sky toward the earth, and Vercingetorix's eyes, following it, were drawn to a figure standing outside the city gates.

It was the Arch Druid Guttuatr.

And in his right hand he held aloft the staff of his office, as if he had used the fallen star that crowned it to draw down another star from the heavens, and Vercingetorix to him thereby.

When Vercingetorix emerges from the city gates, he sees that Guttuatr seems to have aged decades, his visage thin, not in the manner of emaciation, but like that of a ghost on the verge of fading away. Only his eyes, sparkling starlight, seem to remain in the land of the living.

"Why did you summon me?" Vercingetorix asks.

"The time has come for me to say farewell," the Arch Druid tells him.

"You're leaving?" says Vercingetorix. "On the eve of battle?"

"My story is over; the victory is yours to win, not mine," Guttuatr tells him. "But walk my path with me one last time." He turns, and he walks down the slope of the hill toward the edge of the forest below— slowly, not like a frail old man, but deliberately, with a kind of majesty, using his staff as both a cane and a scepter.

"*Victory!*" says Vercingetorix as he walks a half-step behind. "The sure and easy victory I must throw away for the sake of what our people believe is honor and glory?"

"Did *I* not throw away the world of the spirit and come down into the world of strife when the voice of the people bade me?" says the Arch Druid. Vercingetorix hears no bitterness in his voice, only a questioning regret.

"As I now must do as the people demand and lead them into a battle in which even victory will be defeat," he replies in kind.

They have neared the margin of the forest, and the Arch Druid pauses, turns, regards Vercingetorix with eyes that seem pathetically imploring.

"If the man of action sees that victory will be defeat, then the man of knowledge—"

"—must find a way to turn defeat into victory," says Vercingetorix, completing his words. And Guttuatr seems pleased that he has.

"Fitting words of farewell," he says. He turns again, and continues walking toward the forest. "The time has come for me to go."

"To go where?"

"To where all men go," says Guttuatr.

They are at the margin of the forest now, and though the darkness is deep within, in the silvery starlight Vercingetorix sees, or imagines that he sees, shadows or shapes, moving among the trees—whether approaching or receding, he cannot tell.

"You would have been a worthy successor were it not my destiny to be the last Arch Druid," Guttuatr tells him.

"The last Arch Druid?"

"I too have stood at the Tree of Knowledge and seen the story of my life from beginning to end. If not with perfect clarity. Until now."

"And what have you seen?"

"Myself in this Arch Druid's robe," says Guttuatr. "And then just the robe marching on into the Land of Legend. With no one inside it."

The moving shapes in the forest have come forward so that Vercingetorix can see that they are druids, past and present, as numerous as the trees.

"The Great Wheel turns," says Guttuatr, and the druids of the forest begin to fade, their myriad faces becoming smoke, becoming fog that blows away with the passing breeze, until nothing remains but their robes. "And so the druids that were must depart to make way for the druid that must be."

And then Guttuatr too begins to dissolve within his robe, into the night, into the air, becoming one with the mists of time.

"The druid that must be?" whispers Vercingetorix.

"You, upon whose brow I will place the Crown of Brenn when we meet again in the Land of Legend," says Guttuatr.

He takes a step into the forest; he turns and looks back one last time. "The first and the last. The one and the only." And he hands to Vercingetorix the staff of his office.

And then nothing remains but his final words and Vercingetorix holding a scepter crowned with a fallen star.

"The Druid King."

XIX

A FOREST CLIMBS the gentle southern slope of a high ridge, fringing the crestline like the beard stubble of a giant. Below the crestline, the northern slope is a steep and rocky cliff tumbling to a broad grassy valley far below.

The Arch Druid Guttuatr stands just within the cover of the trees edging the forest, invisible from the valley floor, viewing the world of strife from just beyond it. To either side of him are Nividio, Salgax, Gwyndo, and Polgar, and behind them, a multitude of druids stretching back into the shadowy groves of the forest, into the mists of the Land of Legend.

Across the valley is another ridge. This one, adorned with scattered copses of trees, rises much more gently. To the north beyond it, a series of hills and valleys roll like the waves of a wind-whipped sea toward a horizon where black thunderheads are beginning to build.

A huge Roman army advances through the valley from the east, filling it with armored and helmeted men marching in square formations. The shadows of fast-moving clouds and the sunny gaps between them alternately deepen the hue of their helmets and armor and flash brilliant highlights from them, a disorderly natural pattern moving from north to south across the unnaturally perfect pattern of marching infantry squares. The only horsemen to be seen are a few officers accompanied by standard-bearers and small personal-guard units and trumpeters.

Most conspicuous among them and riding just behind the first rank of squares is the only man in the entire army wearing a bright crimson cloak.

"And so it begins," says Guttuatr.

"And so it ends," says the druid Nividio.

Vercingetorix had led his army out of Bibracte with Rhia bearing his bear standard at his right hand as always. But this was only the standard of the Arverni, not of Gaul. The only standard that Gaul entire might have was the scepter of the Arch Druid, which Guttuatr had passed into his hands. So this standard he had held aloft himself before the army of Gaul as it rode forth under its plethora of tribal emblems.

But now he lashed the staff crowned with the fallen star to his saddle and drew his sword, for, seeing the distant glints of sunlight off the shields and armor of the Romans marching toward him, he knew that the battle was about to begin.

And while the black clouds building toward the north seemed like an ill omen in the mind of the man of knowledge, the man of action found himself welcoming the impending decisive clash of arms.

Whether Caesar was offering this open battle and he was accepting, or the reverse, mattered not, for at long last the feints and strategies had finally come down to two great armies settling matters by simple force of arms.

His glad Gallic heart told Vercingetorix that this was as it should be. Here he was, riding in the front and center of a great wave of happy warriors, with Rhia at his right hand and Litivak at his left.

And now, amidst the metallic glimmerings of the front ranks of the Roman infantry, he could make out a bright crimson patch that must be the cloak of Caesar, and he felt a certain kinship with his enemy. Were they not brothers of the sword in this moment? Two opposing generals acknowledging the brotherhood that only they could share, by offering and accepting honorable and open battle.

As if Caesar were hearing his thoughts, a passing sunbeam at the other end of the valley flashed off a sword upraised as if in salute, a trumpet sounded, and as one man, the entire Roman army changed gait and broke into a trot toward him, a daunting yet also thrilling spectacle.

Vercingetorix raised his own sword, as much in salute as in signal, and brought his horse up into a full gallop. The carnaxes sounded, and, shouting battle cries, waving swords, lances, axes, laughing, screaming, grinning, the army of Gaul rode joyfully forward to meet its destiny.

Though he believed he had lied when he had promised to lead them into the jaws of death with a battle song in his heart, now that the time had come he found, to his own joy, that it had become true. There that song was, in the pounding of thousands of hooves, the pounding of his blood, in the cries and screams and yells of his comrades, even in the tramping of Roman feet now close enough to hear.

"For Gaul!" he screamed, waving his sword in celebration of the pure, simple pleasure of it.

"Gaul! Gaul! Gaul!" he cried in blissful abandon.

From the vantage of Guttuatr and the druids, all that can be seen is the distant and motionless rear of the Roman army and a cloud of dust arising in the west.

But the far-off ringing of metal on metal, the screams of horses and men in pain, the thumping of feet and hooves, the battle cries and grunts of anguish, the grim chorus of the world of strife, comes echoing back toward them like the surging of a distant sea.

Javelins slip past shields. Swords gash necks, slice arms from shoulders, rip out guts, open spurting arteries, reveal glistening bone. Axes cleave through helmets to crack open skulls. Horses rear and throw their riders, trample legionnaires, trample fallen Gauls, trample fallen horses. There is a grace to it that stills the thought that slows the mind, setting Vercingetorix beyond fear or remorse, making everything he does— slash a face, ward away a javelin with his shield, rear his horse to bring a Roman down—seem as if it is happening so slowly that he stands aside watching it flow through him.

At last Vercingetorix hears a shout over the battle din: *"They're retreating!"* As he presses his horse forward, he sees that, yes, the line of Roman shields and spears is marching backward, slowly, grudgingly, behind a rain of javelins, fighting doggedly for every bit of ground, but being forced back eastward by his army's assault.

Now the druids can clearly see the Roman army, and it is moving east, back down the valley toward them, the rear echelons marching away from the fray at a measured pace, their backs to the battle.

"Look, Guttuatr, our warriors are pushing them back!" exclaims Salgax.

"We're breaking the army of Rome!" Gwyndo cries with undruidly relish.

"So it would seem," the Arch Druid says dispassionately. And that does more to quell the martial enthusiasm than any word of reproach might.

From within the body of the retreating Roman army, Vercingetorix hears the mournful blare of a horn like the lowing of a mortally wounded ox. It is answered by more of the same, as if an entire herd of oxen has come to understand that it is being driven to slaughter.

It is a terrible sound, and it seems to strike terror into the hearts of the Romans, as a wave of motion spreads from the unseen rear of their army to the front. The Gauls greet it with an enormous cheer that reverberates through the valley, and together they become the purest note of the sweetest music he has ever heard—the sound of victory.

The line of Romans before him is staggering back as fast as it can, burdened by shields, armor, and spears—trotting, almost running, backward like a panicked porcupine attempting to cover its retreat behind a palisade of steel quills.

"Gaul! Gaul! Gaul!" Vercingetorix screams in ecstasy, and, heedless of all else—the flying javelins, the bristling swords, the cries of pain—he raises his sword high above his head, rears his horse, and plunges deeper into the maelstrom, into the midst of the crumbling Roman army, with no need to look back to know that his victorious warriors in their tens of thousands ride triumphantly into the Land of Legend behind him.

"Gaul is free!" exclaims Salgax.

"Rome is defeated!" cries Gwyndo.

"So it would seem," says the Arch Druid Guttuatr, and there is hope in his voice as he utters those four words.

In the valley below, the Roman army is streaming past them in full retreat, rank after rank, square after square of Roman infantry with their backs to their enemies, with their backs to the warriors of Gaul.

Running away.

Now the former front line of the Roman army, become a desperate rearguard, is coming into view as it battles the onrushing Gauls while trying to retreat backward. Between the backward-marching rearguard and the routed main body of the Roman forces there rides a single man, following his retreating men at an eerily serene canter, a bright crimson cloak trailing like a jauntily inappropriate banner behind him.

"Caesar," says Gwyndo, as if that were necessary.

As he passes directly beneath the druids, he pauses and seems to gaze right up at them.

"Does he see us?"

"How can he?"

But it seems that he does, for, far below, Caesar raises his sword aloft as if in salute.

"He's saluting us!"

"Why would Caesar ever do that?"

"He would not," answers the Arch Druid.

The distant figure in the crimson cloak brings down his sword. Five high-pitched trumpet notes sound as he rides past them, and then five more as the Roman rearguard passes.

And then there is a rumble of thunder, though the black clouds that have been approaching are still not overhead and there has been no lightning.

The thunder does not ebb, but becomes a continuous rolling, pounding rumble, growing louder and louder.

An enormous wave of horsemen breaks over the opposite ridge at a thunderous gallop, a front at least half as wide as the army of Gauls, and pours down the descending slope into the valley.

The Teutons are a fearsome sight.

Most wear helmets adorned with the horns of cattle or the antlers of deer, some with brass eagle-wings, a few with human ribs or femurs. Many of their leather shields are embellished with human skulls, whole or in pieces. They wield spears, swords, axes, lances, javelins. Most have long, unkempt hair, though some have greased it into extravagant crests with fat. Some wear earrings, some are crudely tattooed, some both. Perhaps the fourth part of the Teuton horses bear two riders, the one behind armed with a long spear or an equally long trident.

They scream as they reach the Gauls on the valley floor and tear into their flank, bowling over horses, smashing skulls, piercing bellies, slicing throats. They scream and howl, and many of them have achieved such a perfect battle rage that their mouths slobber as they howl, much of the foaming drool pinkened with the blood of their unheedingly bitten tongues and lips.

Vercingetorix fought now for simple survival. This was no graceful dance. There were only Teutons, and the world was full of them.

The shock of their sudden charge had immediately shattered his army into hundreds of small groups. There were no lines, and this was no true battle but thousands upon thousands of individual combats, each of which could last only seconds in such a melee of horsemen packed so closely together.

A blood-spewing Teuton stinking of rancid fat came at him with a spear whose point grazed his arm. Vercingetorix leaned over in his saddle to duck beneath it, and brought up the point of his sword into the Teuton's throat as something heavy thumped hard up against his back. As he righted himself, he saw three Teutons surrounding Rhia and struck one across the back of the neck with the edge of his sword as Rhia slipped the point of hers through a leather jerkin and into the belly of another.

What happened to the third, he didn't see, for there was a howl and a stench behind him, and he turned just in time to block an ax blow with his shield, sending a wave of pain down his left arm, as he reared his horse high enough to be able to kick its wielder, then stab him in his exposed throat as he screamed in agony.

It was impossible for Caesar to see what was happening from his limited vantage point east of the battle, but he could well imagine the bloody carnage as he gave the order for his army to halt, turn, hold position, and prepare to advance west.

The Teutons had always been a fractious lot, and even more so since he had driven them out of Gaul. The best he had been able to do was hire about fifteen thousand of them by agreeing to pay an uncouth mercenary chieftain named Ragar half of far too much on delivery and let him do the hiring. This had meant that the Gauls had outnumbered his Teuton "cavalry," and in a straightforward battle probably would have held the advantage. But the sudden and unexpected mass attack on their flank would have taken care of that, and now the Teutons were probably slaughtering them.

Of course, the Gauls were no doubt slaughtering their fair share of

Teutons too, and in the best outcome, they would all do a decent job of slaughtering each other, leaving his legions to mop up the surviving Gauls easily and persuade the surviving Teutons that the other side of the Rhine would be an ever so much more congenial place to count their money and lick their wounds.

High above the battle, the druids observe in still silence, only their ashen faces within the cowls of their robes betraying their dismay. Below, in the world of strife, the distant figures of Gauls and Teutons suffer, kill, die, but from here they are like two armies of ants, intermingled and indistinguishable from each other, the thousands of individual struggles lost in the seething maelstrom.

"Who is winning?" says Salgax, breaking the silence.

"Winning?" says Nividio. "Down there? The usual victors, of course—the crows and the buzzards, the rats and the worms."

"Were we wrong to have meddled in the world of strife?" mutters Salgax.

"So it would seem," says Guttuatr, and he sighs. "We raised up a boy to be a druid, but destiny called him to be a king."

"A druid king . . ."

Blood ran down his arm as he smashed his shield into the face of a Teuton, breaking his nose with a sickening crunch. Vercingetorix reared his horse to escape the thrust of a spear, wheeled around as a Teuton with a lance in his back charged clumsily by, looked up to swat away a javelin with his sword, and by chance saw—

By chance?

Saw?

Did he really see the white robe of a druid at the margin of the forest atop the far ridgeline?

A robe that might even be empty.

Waiting to be filled.

And if this is a sign, it is meant for him. And if it is not, he will make it so. Vercingetorix sheathes his sword and unties the Arch Druid's staff, entrusted to him, from his saddle.

He takes it by the tip and holds it at arm's length aloft as high as he can reach, so that the fallen star may be seen above the field of battle.

And as if that fallen piece of the heavens is possessed of the power to call upon them, a bolt of lightning lances across the cloud-blackened sky, there is a mighty clap of thunder, and a hard rain begins to fall.

Guttuatr stands back beneath the trees at the margin of the forest as the rain pours down, lightning bolts continue to flash across the roiling black sky, and thunderclaps drown out the noise of the battle below.

But the battle below is no longer quite a battle.

Vercingetorix holds his staff aloft, wheeling and rearing his horse in tight circles and shouting something. The Teutons immediately surrounding him, those who have seen him raise the fallen star and beheld the heavens answering, are shying away.

And the Gauls who have seen are rallying to him: four, eight, a dozen, a score ride and slash their way through the discombobulated Teutons to cluster around him, forming a circle of swords and lances.

Vercingetorix pumps his staff in the air—once, twice, thrice—and lightning illumines him as he rears his horse once more and points the fallen star westward.

With the swiftly following thunderclap, he rides where he has pointed, as oblivious to the Teutons around him as if they were ghosts, and the Gauls encircling him ride with him, slashing a way with their swords.

And as a comet or a falling star draws a train of light as it moves across the heavens, so do they begin to draw a widening train of men and horses, riding and fighting their way westward out of the valley, and onto the broad plain beyond.

"Behold the man of action defeated," says Guttuatr. "Behold the man of knowledge turning defeat into victory."

Then, sardonically: "Or at least into survival."

His staff once more lashed to his saddle and his sword sheathed, Vercingetorix galloped across the plain through the heavy downpour, leaning low onto his horse's neck, kicking its foam-flecked flanks to urge the all-but-spent animal onward. As if the heavens had withdrawn the favor of their magic, the lightning no longer flashed and the only thunder was that of the hooves of exhausted horses.

Behind him, the escaping remnant of the army of Gaul rode across the sodden and muddy plain, thousands of grim and soaked horsemen flaying their foamed and panting mounts into exhaustion and beyond.

A league or so behind *them,* and not losing ground, were the Teutons, and those whose horses could still gallop could see the gory fate of the many whose horses had given out.

A few leagues before them, they could see refuge, the vague silhouette of the city walls of Alesia atop its hill, tantalizingly close through the gauzy curtains of rain.

Before Caesar, the leading ranks of his legions marched stoically through the mud, cursing and muttering but in good order. Several leagues ahead of them, the Teuton horde chased the escaping Gauls, no doubt muttering entreaties to whatever dim and bloody gods they worshipped to protect them from the magic of the man whose army they had routed.

And from the look on Brutus' face, his eyes and expression glazed over with more than the miserable rain, Caesar had the feeling that, left alone, his young friend might be likewise entreating Mars. From Teutons one might expect such superstition, but for a Roman to credit it went beyond the irksome and into the realm of farce.

"Surely *you* do not believe such nonsense, Brutus," he said.

"Surely not . . ." said Brutus unconvincingly.

"But . . . ?" he said for him, in a good humor despite the foul weather, and the temporary escape of the better part of Vercingetorix's army. If things had not gone according to his fondest hope, they were certainly proceeding according to plan. A man of reason could hardly demand more of the gods, let alone count on their fickle favor.

"But many Teutons saw it happen. . . ."

"Saw exactly what happen, Brutus?"

"The, uh, druid weather magic," said Brutus, so embarrassed by his words that he was constrained to avert his gaze as he uttered them.

"No, that is *not* what anyone saw," Caesar told him. "They saw a man hold up a stick with a rock on top of it under a sky full of thunderheads. They saw thunder and lightning, and then it began to rain. What an enormous surprise! I too could make such magic if I chose. I need only hold up my arm as the first ray peers over the morning's horizon and command the sun to rise, and, behold, it shall obey, to the stupefaction of savages and barbarians!"

Brutus laughed wanly. Caesar laughed heartily.

"Be of good cheer, Brutus," he said.

"*You* certainly seem to be of good cheer, considering the circumstances, Caesar."

"And why should I not be?"

"Call it chance, call it magic—Vercingetorix and the greater part of his army are escaping—"

"No, Brutus, no more than a herd of cattle running before drovers is escaping. They are being driven into the slaughterhouse corral."

XX

VERCINGETORIX STOOD STILL and silent on the ramparts of Alesia under a dirty gray sky from which sheets of rain had not yet ceased to fall. No one would speak to him—not Critognat, not Rhia, not Litivak, not any of the thousands of inhabitants of the Carnute capital who gathered on the walls to gaze down in terror.

Below the ramparts, thousands of sodden Teutons huddled sullenly around damply smoldering fires, some under crude makeshift tents of horse or cowhide. Throughout this vast and unruly encampment they had planted lances as standard poles so that the emblems atop them would be plainly visible from the city walls. But these were not animals carved of wood or cast in metal.

They were the severed heads of thousands of Gauls.

Hundreds more Teutons, angrily drunk, rode back and forth, waving swords, axes, spears, fists, cursing and shouting like a pack of hunting dogs, which, having treed its bear, can only circle, yipping and baying in frustration at being deprived of its kill.

And at the limit of his vision, Vercingetorix could just make out the thin gray line of Caesar's army approaching at a measured and leisurely pace across a once-verdant plain whose grass had been soaked by the rain and trodden into a muck of mud and blood by the hooves of thousands of horses and the deaths of thousands of men.

The Teuton hunting pack had treed its bear. Their Roman masters could take their time arriving to finish it off.

Indeed, the Teutons might very well have done it for them had it not been for Baravax.

Not even their own vergobret Cottos had been able to persuade the Carnutes within Alesia to open the city gates to admit the shattered army of Gaul. The warriors on the wall above had pointed in terror at the onrushing Teutons and refused to obey Cottos' order.

It had been the plainspoken Baravax, not the silver-tongued Vercingetorix, who had ordered two of his guards to hold up a shield, leapt upon it, and made the noble speech that shamed the Alesians into opening their gates.

"I am Baravax, no mighty warrior, no brave hero, only the longtime captain of the guards of Gergovia, a man, like yourselves, whose job it is to protect the lives of those I am commissioned to guard," he declared to the warriors above the gates. "And I know how to do my job. Do you know how to do *yours*?"

He turned to address his own men, fewer than a hundred of them, drew his sword, and pointed it at the Teutons, now less than a league away, close enough for the hoofbeats of their galloping horses to be heard as a low, grumbling rumble.

"Our task, as always, is to guard those under our protection from miscreants who would harm them. Sometimes it is easy, sometimes it is not. Now our task is to delay those bastards long enough for the *heroes* inside this city to summon up the courage to open their gates, for Vercingetorix to get our army inside, and for the Carnutes to get them closed again. It's a simple job, so now let's get it done."

With that, he leapt down from the shield, mounted his horse, and galloped off toward the Teutons, toward certain death, without even looking back to assure himself that his men were following.

Seeing this, thousands of Gauls, men of all tribes, singly and in small groups, spontaneously rode off to join them before Vercingetorix could even think of an order to give.

And, seeing *that,* the Alesians could only open the gates, and Vercingetorix led his army, riding only six or seven abreast and crowded together like peas in a pod, to safety inside.

But not all of it. Baravax's rearguard had been overcome before all the army could make it into Alesia, and the tail end had been attacked by the Teuton vanguard while the gates were still open. Hundreds of warriors had then turned their backs to safety to stand off the Teutons long enough for Cottos to give the order that Vercingetorix could not bear to give.

The order to close the gates behind them.

Vercingetorix had watched from the cowardly safety of this wall while they were cut down, disemboweled, beheaded, torn to pieces by the Teutons right beneath his eyes. So close that each dying scream was a personal reproach. He had held aloft a fallen star and by chance or destiny had thereby brought his army out of Caesar's deathtrap valley, but *those* men had been the true heroes.

And now here he stood, alive and beholding what his pursuit of destiny had wrought, while Baravax's head was out there somewhere impaled on a Teuton lance.

It was Cottos who finally screwed up the courage, or the ire, to speak to him, for it was *his* people who found themselves playing hosts to an army that brought with it their doom.

"Well, what do we do now, Vercingetorix?" he demanded in a grim voice that seemed emptied of rancor only by act of will.

"I would not blame you if you surrendered the city," Vercingetorix told him.

"To the *Teutons*? That would do about as much good as a lamb offering its surrender to a pack of ravenous wolves!"

Vercingetorix nodded toward the horizon, where the Romans were an orderly advancing forest of metal and men.

"To Caesar," he said, hoping this offer would be spurned, and ashamed of his guile in making it. "He might show mercy to Alesia if we left the city—"

"Your army would surely be slaughtered!"

"We'll all be slaughtered like rats caught in the grain barrel if we stay here anyway!" Critognat declared. "Better to ride out and die with honor!"

"And where would the honor of the Carnutes be if I allowed you to do such a thing in the hope of extracting mercy for us from Caesar?" said Cottos. "Which would not be forthcoming anyway. No, we're all in this together."

"As the cockroaches said to each other in the dung pit," Critognat muttered, at which enough spirit was summoned up to produce general wan laughter.

"As Gauls," said Cottos.

Gallius had already sent logging crews into the surrounding forests, and Labienus had turned away from Bibracte as planned and would arrive shortly, so Caesar had been quite content until Ragar arrived outside his tent, announcing that his men were going to leave and demanding the rest of their pay right now.

The Teuton warlord was a huge man a decade younger than Caesar, with enormous muscles on the battle-scarred arms emerging from his ill-tanned leather tunic. His helmet was adorned with a yellowed human skull, his long blond hair was worn uncombed and filthy, and if he wasn't belligerently drunk he was doing a fair imitation. The iresome bloodshot eyes were not those of a dimwitted lout, however, but of a reasonably clever warlord.

"The task for which you were hired is not completed," Caesar told him evenly.

"We routed the Gauls for you, Caesar!"

"True," said Caesar, nodding toward the city walls looming beyond the disorderly and odoriferous Teuton encampment, "but there's still an army of Gauls in there."

"*Your* problem, Caesar!"

"True too, my friend, and I promise you it will be taken care of," Caesar told him, "but before it is, a final service is required of you."

"The gold, Caesar! Now!"

Caesar held his temper and favored Ragar with a smarmy grin. "All that is required of you is that you camp here for a few weeks or so, enjoying our wine and terrifying the Gauls. Surely your men will not find that an excessively onerous task."

"This is not what you promised, Caesar!"

Caesar hadn't really expected to destroy Vercingetorix's whole army with the Teuton flank attack, but the chance confluence of Vercingetorix's pass at so-called "druid weather magic" with the breaking of the storm and the Teutons' superstitious dread had allowed a larger force than expected to fort itself up inside Alesia. Too large to be easily contained by his legions alone while Gallius did his work. He needed the Teutons to remain. He didn't need them to fight, but he *did* need them outside the walls of Alesia looking ferocious and numerous.

"Surely the greatest warriors on earth cannot be afraid of a rock on a stick?" he ventured.

"We are afraid of nothing on earth!" roared Ragar. Then, in a much smaller voice: "But . . ."

"*But?*"

The Teuton's eyes became furtive, and his voice betrayed an undertone of fear. "But even the greatest warriors on earth would be fools not to fear a magician who can call down the powers of the heavens."

"*I* do not fear such nonsense," Caesar snapped at him. "You are telling me that you are a lesser man than I? You disappoint me, Ragar. I thought you my equal."

The Teuton warlord frowned, unable, no doubt, to decide whether he was being insulted or flattered. Caesar magnanimously rescued him from this arduous mental task.

"Of course, it may be that you speak thusly for your men and not yourself."

Ragar nodded in relief. "*My men* want their pay and they want to be far from this place."

Caesar nodded back in comradely commiseration. "Not all generals are as fortunate as I."

With a broad gesture of his arms, he invited Ragar to contemplate the Roman encampment: the thousands of tents, the catapults being constructed, the armories full of arrows and javelins and lances and Gallius' noxious incendiary brews, and the tens of thousands of well-armed, well-armored, well-disciplined troops now forming a ring around his own Teutons.

"What do you see, my friend?" he asked silkily.

"I'll tell you what you see," Caesar told him when the only reply was a dim look of befuddlement. "You see fifty thousand Roman legionnaires, all of whom will follow my every order as faithfully as the fingers of my own hand, none of whom fears anything on earth or in the heavens as long as they know they are commanded by Gaius Julius Caesar. You may tell your warriors that, Ragar, you may tell them that there are two reasons for such obedience. First, of course, because my men love me with open hearts as I love them."

He displayed a vulpine grimace that could be taken as threatening. "Second, because they know that *my* displeasure is much more to be feared than the wrath of any other power on earth *or* in the heavens."

He smiled and clapped Ragar on the shoulder. "I'm sure a great leader such as yourself will be able to make your warriors understand."

Alesia was a city hosting an unwelcome army that had put it under perilous siege, and so Cottos had summoned up a guard of some score warriors as well as a bearer displaying the horse standard of the Carnutes before escorting Vercingetorix, Litivak, Rhia, and Critognat through the streets to their quarters in his own "villa."

At Gergovia, Vercingetorix's main force had been out in the forest, and at Bibracte, those troops who could not be accommodated within the walls had found hospitality in the countryside. Here, however, the gates were closed, and stones, wood, rubble, and earth were being heaped up behind them against a Roman battering-ram assault, and the countryside was in the hands of the Romans and Teutons. So warriors were bivouacking everywhere. In the market. In the plaza. In people's houses when they were given leave, sometimes when they were not. Some were constrained to camp in the streets, clogging them with cookfires. Mobs of idle armed men wandered the streets, and the only women to be seen abroad were crones too aged to be endangered.

Alesia, a city that had not expected a siege and therefore had laid up no extra supplies, had suddenly had its population doubled.

Tens of thousands of horses had also been trapped inside the city, and Vercingetorix saw them everywhere, gobbling what little grass there was, rapidly devouring stored-up fodder, and converting it all to abundant quantities of flyspecked dung liberally distributed wherever one sought to set foot. The wells too were being drained. The reek of horse piss was everywhere.

And most of the warriors packing the city were from foreign tribes, bringing not victory, or even hope, but noise, stench, chaos, and impending disaster.

And the siege had only just begun.

Cottos' villa, though constructed of wood and wattle, was built around an interior court in the Roman style, to judge by the crown of a great old oak peering up from behind its walls.

Vercingetorix scarcely considered the grim mockery of this, concerned as he was with matters of siegecraft. Did the city's water come from wells, or springs inside the wall? How much food was stored up? How much fodder? How long could they last?

But when Cottos led them through heavy wooden gates and into the central courtyard, all else was forgotten as Vercingetorix beheld who awaited him there:

Marah, bareheaded, but otherwise bizarrely garbed as an Arverne warrior.

"What are you doing here?" Vercingetorix demanded. "And dressed like *that*?"

"Did I not promise that I would go where you go? And that not even you could prevent me?"

Indeed she had. And now here she was, to the grinning pleasure of Cottos, who had arranged this surprise. Litivak was obviously pleased too, and Critognat regarded the couple with avuncular approval. The smile on Rhia's lips was less than genuine, but was that not a fleeting look of complicity passing between her and Marah?

"Who better to welcome you to the city of the Carnutes than your future queen?" said Cottos, breaking the awkward silence in a manner that amazed Vercingetorix but pleased him not at all. "Surely you are pleased to see her here?"

Even in the midst of a siege likely to end in disaster, the Carnutes still thought to use her to seal their primacy with the man who might emerge as king of Gaul!

"Surely I am not," Vercingetorix found himself blurting boorishly. "For I would not have wished to see her put in such mortal danger."

"Where you go, so go I," said Marah gazing at him with a daunting intensity. "And if it is into the jaws of death, so be it."

"This is certainly no moment to dwell on danger and death, Vercingetorix," Litivak said with forced gaiety. He nodded at Cottos. "Surely even the Great Leader of Warriors deserves a few moments of happiness alone with his betrothed."

"Surely," said Cottos. "Let me show the rest of you your quarters." He escorted Litivak, Critognat, and Rhia to a series of doors opening onto the courtyard. One by one, they disappeared inside, leaving Vercingetorix and Marah alone.

Awkwardly alone.

"When were we betrothed?" Vercingetorix finally said.

"You asked me to be your queen. And I accepted."

"I was a boy then. And you did not accept until years later, and then before the world."

"And that is what troubles you? That I proclaimed my love for you before the world?"

What *is* it about her that troubles me? Vercingetorix asked himself. That her tongue is as silver as mine? That she presumes to use it in public? That she loves the king I am supposedly destined to become rather than the boy that I was or the man that I am? But these explanations rang hollow, excuses for something that felt uncomfortably like fear. But that was ridiculous.

"Between a man and a woman there should be something more than that," he said.

Marah took both of his hands in hers. "Let me share your chamber, and I can promise you the something more."

Before he could speak, she drew him to her and kissed him, prizing open his lips with her own, gliding her tongue into his mouth, first gently and gracefully, then deeply, and commandingly, as a man might enter a woman.

Vercingetorix found his body responding as might a woman to a man, opening to her, pressing against her, trembling at the knees. He *was*, after all, a virgin, and she was the experienced one.

It inflamed him, and yet he found himself weakened, as if some magic were being drained from him. He now began to understand what Rhia had never been quite able to make clear. Virgins both, their unslaked lust was somehow a source of power.

"What's wrong?" said Marah, pulling away.

What could he say? That her amorous sophistication unmanned the virgin boy hidden within the Great Leader of Warriors? That he feared the loss of magic whose price destiny demanded that he must still continue to pay?

No man could say such things to a woman.

Where is your silver tongue now, Vercingetorix?

"I . . . I do not have the heart for such pleasures the day so many of my men have been slain," he said.

He expected anger, scorn, reproach, but Marah instead favored him with a soft, tender smile, and Vercingetorix came to feel what love between a man and a woman might truly be.

"I understand," she told him. "Though it pleases me not, I can only love you for it."

"How long until the city is completely enclosed, Gallius?" Caesar asked peevishly as he and the chief engineer rode along a section of the fortifications under construction by grunting legionnaires pressed into service more suitable for slaves.

Gallius shrugged. "A week or two. Possibly three."

"Too long."

"The logs have to be dragged long distances, Caesar, and these cavalry mounts are far from ideal dray horses. Nor do we have slaves to dig the ditches and pits, and—"

"It's not *you*, Gallius," Caesar said, cutting him off before he could launch into an engineering discourse that could go on for hours. "It's the Teutons. I don't know if I can keep them here that long."

Dressed tree trunks were planted in deep postholes to form a stout palisade, cross-braced with long split logs. Immediately in front of the palisade was a deep and wide ditch, which Gallius planned to fill with water from the River Ose once the work was completed. Before this trench, the plain had been sown with pits bristling with sharpened stakes, and before *that*, yet another ditch, this one to be filled with larger stakes to impale horses. Gallius' plan called for a second wall to be erected outside the first and a walkway between them to connect towers. And, if time permitted, for the space between them to be filled with packed earth. And between Alesia and the construction, protecting it from attack, at least for now, were the Teutons.

As far as Caesar knew, no one had ever before besieged a fortified city by surrounding it with his own fortification. It was a task that might have daunted Hercules. But Gallius displayed as much enthusiasm for the project as a man commissioned to slake the lust of a bordello-full of courtesans.

His architectural ambitions knew no bounds. A wall. A double wall. A double wall filled with rammed earth. Small catapults or ballistae atop its towers. Given time and left to his own devices, he no doubt would clad the whole thing in armor and surround it with a moat full of crocodiles brought up from Egypt.

But time *was* a factor. The Teutons were getting more restless, bored, drunk, quarrelsome, and obstreperous day by day.

The Teuton encampment was a hideous and ominous vista whose stench was nearly overpowering even from here. Twelve thousand or so barbarians and an equal number of their horses. No proper latrines. Hundreds of rotting heads impaled on spears. Back and forth they rode when they were sober enough to mount, sometimes staging mock battles, which often got out of hand.

Caesar had already been constrained to pay Ragar half of what he still owed to keep them from fleeing "druid magic" and the reeking midden they had made of their own camp, and he had no doubt they would depart the moment he let go of the rest.

Even with the arrival of Labienus and the Roman cavalry, he needed the Teutons, for the Gallic cavalry inside Alesia greatly outnumbered his own. If the Gauls sought to escape now, a significant number of them would almost certainly elude death or destruction to fight another day, and all too probably with Vercingetorix among them.

"How much is completed now?" Caesar asked nervously.

"You mean *fully* completed, double walls, watchtowers—"

"I mean how many gaps remain open?"

"Oh, a dozen or so . . ."

"A *dozen!*"

"But none more than half a league wide."

"Concentrate all your efforts on closing them," Caesar ordered. "Doubling the walls and the rest of it can wait."

Gallius frowned, his artistic sensibilities injured, but the sooner the Teutons were rendered superfluous, the sooner Caesar could breathe easy, and then Gallius could indulge whatever fancies he liked.

Caesar worried that future military historians might criticize this strategy for lack of elegance, but certainty was what he now required. Though there might be no drama or glory in it, once the fortifications were completed Roman military engineering would ensure victory. Vercingetorix and his army could starve to death in there or squash themselves like bugs against impregnable fortifications if they liked, but the military conquest of Gaul *would* be completed.

Vercingetorix, Litivak, and Critognat, wrapped in heavy cloaks, paced the ramparts of Alesia, watching the Teutons and Romans. It was raining again, a cold, steady downpour that dampened the enthusiasm of the Teutons for riding around and cursing in favor of huddling under their cloaks or hide tents, and, of course, drinking. But the Romans seemed indifferent to the rain, working busily on their fortifications like a enormous tribe of beavers building an immense dam. Thousands of warriors doing the work of peasants or slaves without complaint, enlarging the ditches encircling the city, and beginning to build a second wall of logs only two man-lengths behind the first.

What were they doing? Vercingetorix had been asking himself this since the Roman construction began, and it had been the subject of endless discussion, but no one had come up with a convincing answer.

Vercingetorix had expected Caesar either to storm Alesia as he had Bourges or to lay siege. When the attack didn't come, he had assumed that Caesar had chosen the surer strategy. But then the Romans had started building these fortifications, a mighty yet seemingly pointless undertaking.

"Could it be that Caesar seeks to force us to attack him?" suggested Litivak, hardly the first time Vercingetorix had heard this explanation.

Perhaps Caesar supposed that, once the nature of what he had started to build became clear, impatient Gauls would rush from the city to be slaughtered by the Teutons and finished off by the Roman infantry behind them.

"Well, why don't we give him what he wants and break out of here now!" declared Critognat.

"If we try to fight our way out, we'll be destroyed," Vercingetorix told him, "and Caesar will do to Alesia what he did to Bourges."

"But if we don't, we'll die of hunger or thirst," said Litivak. "The water from the Ose won't be enough when the wells run dry, the horses are already running out of fodder, and Alesia hadn't laid up enough food to feed even its own people for very long."

"So let's die like men with our swords in our hands, not starving to death like cowards!" said Critognat.

"And be remembered as the heroes who abandoned the city they were defending to slaughter to purchase their own glorious deaths in battle?" Vercingetorix said. "No, Critognat, I don't think the bards would find much honor in that."

"Well, then, what *do* we do?"

"Whatever it is," said Litivak, "we had better do it soon, before they finish their wall and—"

"Why?" blurted Vercingetorix.

"Why what?"

Vercingetorix nodded toward the Roman wall, where thousands of warriors were swarming busily over the fortifications under construction. Day and night. In the mud. In the rain.

"Why are they in such a hurry to finish it?" he muttered. "It cannot be because of anything Caesar fears *we* might do first, so it must be . . ."

"*The Teutons. . . ?*" said Litivak. "Caesar fears they might turn on him?"

Vercingetorix speculatively studied the Teuton encampment sprawling below the walls of Alesia. Thousands of them with nothing to do but ride around threateningly or hunker miserably in the mud. He imagined an army of Gauls constrained to endure such sodden boredom. An army of Critognats. Add an ocean of drink and subtract all sense of a cause, and you had the Teutons surrounding Alesia and keeping his army inside its walls.

"Or just leave!" Vercingetorix exclaimed, groaning with the mortifyingly belated realization of the obvious. "The Teutons are there to defend the construction! And the fortifications are being built to replace them!"

"A wall replaces the Teutons?" said Critognat. "Have you gone mad?"

"Without Caesar's Teuton mercenaries, we could fight our way out with enough of our army to continue the war. But now it's too late. The wall is nearly complete. And the Teutons are still there."

"So there's no way out?" said Critognat.

"Not for us," said Vercingetorix. And hearing his own words, it came to him. No, not for *us* . . . "But perhaps for the horses . . ."

"The horses?"

"Horses are useless and worse in surviving a siege. They soon starve to death, draining supplies before they do. We should really kill them now and smoke the meat to eat later."

"Eat our horses!" Critognat cried in utter horror. "I'd sooner eat . . . I'd sooner eat . . ." He threw up his hands in outraged frustration.

"Shit?" suggested Litivak.

"It's that or give them their freedom," said Vercingetorix.

"What's all this sudden concern about the fate of our horses?" asked Litivak, eyeing him suspiciously.

"I have heard a story about a siege and a horse," said Vercingetorix. "Some Greeks built a great horse of wood and hid men within to get them *inside* a city they were besieging. Why can we not hide men within a herd of our horses to get them *out*?"

The light of the nearly full moon sharpened shadows and silvered the backs of the great herd of horses assembled before the gates of Alesia. Behind the horses were dozens of warriors with carnaxes, and behind the warriors, a dense crowd of townspeople had gathered. The rubble reinforcing the gates had been temporarily cleared by townspeople eager to be quit of the useless horses draining the water supply and fouling the city with their dung.

All of the horses had been stripped of saddles, bridles, blankets, and all other human accouterments, save some three dozen fitted with simple reins of rope, and more ropes tied under their bellies to be gripped by their riders.

Most of these were the vergobrets and war leaders of all the tribes trapped in the city—Litivak, Netod, Epirod, Comm, Luctor, and the

rest. Only the Arverni and Alesia's own Carnutes were not so repre-
sented. Among them were also Oranix and a dozen of his scouts, who
had begged to leave a walled city where their huntsman's skills were
useless, in favor of escaping to the countryside, where at least they
might track the movements of the enemy. Vercingetorix could not imagine how they could possibly report back, but he had not had the heart to
point this out.

Vercingetorix stood high on the stairs leading up to the parapet, his
sword sheathed, the staff of the Arch Druid lying on the step beneath
him.

"Stay as low on your horses as you can, make for the gaps in the
wall, and, once beyond, take care to split up," Vercingetorix said. "Ride
to the four winds! Let all Gaul know that here we stand!"

"Why not escape with us?" cried Litivak, as they had planned.

"I will not leave another city defenseless for Caesar to butcher as he
did Bourges; come what may, my destiny is here."

"Without your voice to unite us, who is to say whether *ours* will be
heeded? And if not, you will die here and our cause will be lost."

This he and Litivak had *not* arranged beforehand, and Vercingetorix
found it vexatious: there might be all too much truth in it.

"I have seen in a vision that I cannot die on the soil of Gaul. And
even if that vision should prove false, if one man's death can defeat our
cause, does it not *deserve* to be lost?"

He drew his sword and held it high.

"Go, and bring me back an army of Gauls! When you return, you
will be the hammer and we the anvil, and we will crush the Romans
between us!"

Even so, Litivak persisted. "You know what we are like, Vercingetorix," he said pleadingly. "Who is to say how many will answer the call?"

And Vercingetorix finally perceived what Litivak was pleading for. If
he and the others were to risk their lives to bear a message that would
bring an army of Gauls to the rescue, that message must possess a
magic sufficient to call such an army into being.

And so . . .

"I swore a blood oath to lead Gaul and its cause no matter the sacrifice!" Vercingetorix shouted. "Tell them of *this* oath that I now swear in
blood!"

He sliced his forearm lightly, waited for the red blood to anoint his
sword clearly, then held it aloft.

"Tell them that Vercingetorix, whom they would acclaim their king, swears not to leave Alesia alive before an army of true Gauls arrives! Death before dishonor! If they fail to arrive, the dishonor will be *theirs*, not mine!"

He sheathed his sword, picked up the staff of the Arch Druid, turned, and ascended the parapet.

A warrior appears atop the wall of Alesia, the bright moonlight burnishing his armor a lucent silver. He bears not a sword but a staff of wood crowned with a fallen star of black and pocked iron, the dark sister of the queen of this brilliant starry night.

Vercingetorix turns to face the Teuton encampment. He takes the Arch Druid's staff by the tip, raises it high above his head with a bloody arm, and stands there immobile as a statue.

And then a sound begins to stir the sleeping Teutons. A multitudinous chorus of the same low and ominous carnax note, like the angry, wakening buzz of a hive of unthinkably enormous bees.

Louder and louder. Coming from within the walls of Alesia.

Louder and louder still, rousing Teuton after Teuton from drink-befuddled sleep. Until at length thousands of Teuton warriors stand uneasily enthralled by the monotonous music, muttering to each other as they stare up at the apparition atop the wall, its arm dripping blood as it holds up a fallen star to reflect the light of the heavens.

Or to call something down?

And then the music suddenly stops.

In its abrupt absence, the silence is total.

Vercingetorix does not move.

The Teutons dare not.

Somewhere an owl hoots.

Vercingetorix sweeps his staff down and across his body and points its fallen star threateningly at the Teutons like the point of a lance.

A tremendous blaring—far louder than what has been heard before—issues forth from Alesia. And a cacophony of whinnying, neighing, and nickering as the gates suddenly fly open.

And out pours a stream of horses. A surging river of horses. Black ones, brown ones, white ones, piebald, dappled, roan. Stallions and mares and geldings. Eyes rolling, hooves pounding, nipping, kicking, and bucking in their shoulder-to-shoulder panic, a mighty fountain of horses spouting from the gates of Alesia, spreading out to inundate the Teuton camp in a rushing tide.

Vercingetorix stood atop the wall, his staff lowered now, watching the horses galloping through the Teuton camp as the gates were slammed shut. They smashed down tents, kicked over fires, trampled men, panicked the Teutons' own horses.

The Teutons themselves seemed to be in several different kinds of panic. Some fled the flying hooves. Some scrambled to seize equine booty for themselves. Some lashed out in a fury at horses with swords and axes. Some tried to retrieve their own mounts.

Few of them seemed to notice that groups of horses were galloping through gaps in the Roman wall, and none sought to stop them. Now, for the first time since the gates of Alesia had been closed behind his army, there was hope.

"You do realize that you've trapped us all in here?"

Vercingetorix had not noticed Marah coming out on the parapet beside him; he turned at the sound of her voice.

"Hope rides with them to the four winds," Vercingetorix told her, but even he could hear the lack of conviction in his voice.

"You know what the chances really are," Marah said scornfully. "You know what the Gauls are like. They'll argue, they'll bicker, they'll fight over who is to lead. . . ."

"I stay here to challenge them to become something more than that," Vercingetorix told her, and in these words was the clear ring of truth.

"And if they do not?"

"Then perhaps I may achieve in legend what I failed to do in life."

Rhia, who had also come up onto the wall, held her distance as she saw Vercingetorix and Marah kiss briefly. She did not approach until he had descended, leaving Marah standing alone looking pensively up into the heavens.

"What did he say to you?" Rhia ventured.

"What you would expect a man of destiny to say under these circumstances," Marah said sardonically. "Something about becoming in death a legend that might achieve what he failed to do in life."

"You must be good to him in the time he has left," Rhia said imploringly.

"I would if he would let me . . . but I think he would rather . . . have you."

"You understand nothing, Marah."

"You can't tell me you don't want him!"

Rhia seemed to hesitate, seemed about to say something, then choked it back, and replaced it with something else.

"I will be his till my death and beyond," she said with a sad wistfulness. "But whenever his story is told, he will belong to you."

XXI

C AESAR HAD BEEN JOLTED AWAKE by a hideous reveille of Gallic carnaxes, had found himself dodging maddened horses, and finally had watched half a dozen of them trample down his tent.

Then the Teutons had decamped like the feckless barbarians they were. Those who had captured horses had no further thought of fighting Gauls for Roman gold, since horses counted as a far more manly form of wealth among them. Those who had not caught horses had left to chase after their fair share. And none of them wanted anything more to do with Vercingetorix and his "druid magic."

But once it was all over and calm descended, Caesar realized that the loss of the Teutons was after all no more than a minor annoyance: the fortifications were all but completed, and his own legions could easily enough hold what gaps remained against any attempt by the Gauls to break through. And the sacrifice of his cavalry surely meant that Vercingetorix had given up all hope of doing so.

In a better mood, Caesar curled up on the ground in his cloak, resolving to sleep the rest of the night in the open, which, after all, he had done more times in his life than he could count. He had dozed off when Tulius awoke him with a prisoner.

"Now what?" he grunted, rubbing sleep from his eyes and rising irritably to his feet. "This had better be important, Tulius!"

"I'm afraid it is, Caesar. We spotted men lashed to some of the horses. Most of them escaped, but we slew three of them: a Santon, an Atrebate, and a Cadurque by their garb. This is the only one we captured alive."

The prisoner wore roughly tanned leather pantaloons and jerkin, ripped here and there, and bloodied. His hands were tied in front of him. The scratches, blackened eyes, and facial bruises might have been the result of the stampede, but it was difficult to imagine how his left thumb had become a bloody stump before capture.

"This man has been tortured?" asked Caesar.

Tulius nodded.

"What did you get out of him?"

"Not much more than his name and his tribe. Not *yet*. This is Oranix of the Arverni."

So this was the great and terrible Caesar, the prey he had pursued in the longest hunt of his life, the prey that now would turn on him and make it his last. Oranix was not impressed. Indeed, he was disappointed.

Having lived his life as a hunter, Oranix had always hoped he would die a good hunter's death, felled by a noble beast, as an old man by a great bear if the gods favored him, or even a lion if he was truly fortunate.

But this was no lion. This was a balding man in middle years, the top of whose head rose no farther than Oranix's chin.

"Why were you and those men tied to horses?" Caesar demanded.

Oranix knew he was going to die. Any hunter must accept such a possibility in every hunt. It was a pact of honor between hunter and prey. Hunting a stag, you could always find yourself hunted by a bear.

"To keep from falling off," Oranix told him. The knowledge that he would be denied a proper hunter's death hurt more than the beatings or the throbbing stump of his left thumb.

"Who were the those men?"

"Gauls," said Oranix.

"Speak plainly if you want to keep the right thumb," said the torturer, whom Caesar had called Tulius.

"Why should I?" Oranix said defiantly. "I won't have the use of it for very long—now, will I?"

"Don't be a fool," Caesar told him. "We could always start in on your testicles. . . ."

Oranix felt his scrotum contract.

To be denied a hunter's death was to be denied a hunter's honor. But there was no honor in betraying your fellows out of fear. If he was to die in fear like a cornered doe, perhaps in so doing he could at least inflict some fear on Caesar.

"I am Oranix the hunter," he said. "You were my prey, and now I am yours. But soon enough you will be hunted down to your death by others. You will kill me now, we will kill you later, and there is nothing either of us can do about it."

"We?" said Caesar. "A handful of men tied to—"

Caesar suddenly silenced himself, and what Oranix saw in his eyes told him that this man had a cunning that made a fox seem like the dimmest of cows.

"Emissaries!" Caesar cried.

A fox who pounced on Oranix's vainglorious words as if he were a foolish chicken.

"I must have still been half asleep not to realize it immediately. He didn't release his horses just to relieve himself of their useless and hungry mouths. There was no need to torture this man. Vercingetorix used his stampede as cover! The men tied to the horses were emissaries! He's trying to raise a relief army."

Caesar turned to Oranix and favored him with the smile of a lynx toying with its prey.

"Thank you, Oranix the hunter, you've been most helpful," he purred, to Oranix's utter mortification.

"Shall I have him executed now?"

"Oh no, Tulius, this fellow has earned Roman gratitude. He has earned himself a choice."

"A choice?" Oranix said miserably.

"A glorious but possibly short career as a gladiator in the arena, or a much longer but surely less rewarding one in the lead mines."

Caesar's face showed no pity as he said this, and Oranix froze his own into a mask of dismay, for he would not show this man gratitude. But he had heard what went on in Roman arenas.

Caesar had not offered him this boon sincerely.

But boon it was.

Oranix the hunter might yet meet his lion.

Caesar slept little the rest of the night, and what sleep he managed to steal was haunted by the same dream repeated over and over again in different guises. His army was besieging a city. Bombarding it with catapults from behind a wall. Or storming it with siege towers, scaling ladders, and battering rams. Or just waiting. Sometimes the city seemed to be Bourges, sometimes Gergovia, sometimes Alesia. Each time, victory was within his grasp. Each time, his buttocks were one way or another suddenly exposed to the open air, and his army was attacked from the rear: by Eduen cavalry led by Litivak, by Arverni led by Vercingetorix, by bare-breasted women led by Vercingetorix's amazon.

Finally, it was Rome itself he found himself besieging, and the army cravenly attacking from behind was one of senators armed with knives, and that was enough to have him bolting awake and upright at dawn. He needed no soothsayer to scry out the meaning, for the visions of sleep only told him what in the waking world he already knew:

Cover your rear!

If the Gauls succeeded in raising their relieving army, he would surely be attacked from the rear by a vastly superior cavalry force. He would be trapped between them and his own fortifications. And so he called a meeting of his chief lieutenants outside the wreckage of his tent in the bleak early-morning light to consider how to compensate for the defection of the Teutons.

Labienus was there, and Tulius. Trebonius, and Antony, and half a dozen others. Glavius and young Brutus as well. But among them all, only Gallius had come up with any idea at all, and his notion was ridiculous.

"Build another wall."

"A *wall* to replace the Teutons?" said Labienus. "Why not dig a canal to the Mediterranean and bring up a fleet of galleys?"

Everyone laughed but Gallius and Caesar.

"Kindly confine yourself to engineering, Gallius, of which you are a master," Caesar said irritably, "and leave strategy, of which you are ignorant, to the field officers!"

"We should storm the city now," insisted Labienus. "We can capture it long before the Gauls can assemble another army."

"And then what?" said Galba. "Then we trap ourselves inside."

"*If* this second army ever materializes."

"Why not sack Alesia and burn it to the ground like Bourges?"

On and on it went, and Junius Gallius could see that Caesar liked none of it, as well he should not. These *generals* believed that war was a con- test of physical or tactical prowess like the Greek Olympics, or what went on in the Senate. Throw men at the enemy and overwhelm them, outwit the opposing general with your brilliance. To them, the power of Rome lay in their strategy and the numbers and discipline of their legions.

Gallius knew better.

The Persians and their barbarous ilk had larger armies, and no doubt their generals were no dimmer than this collection of bravos. But Rome had defeated them. Because Roman military engineering was so superior. And getting better year by year, war by war. Catapults. Ballistae. Mobile siege towers. Greek fire, which he was well on the way to perfecting. Even on the march, Roman battlefield engineers threw up palisades and enclosed them in entrenchments. These Gallic barbarians had no military engineers at all.

War was a *craft,* and superior military engineering would win out every time. *This* was the future of war, *this* was why Rome was destined to rule those who did not even comprehend the concept. It was mostly a pleasure working for Caesar because Caesar understood this, as his lieutenants did not.

Right now, though, he was letting these generals babble on uselessly, and by his deepening frown, by the impatient tapping of his right foot on the ground, Gallius could tell that Caesar's frustration was ripening. Best to try again now.

"A second wall!" he shouted.

"I told you to keep out of it, Gallius!" Caesar shouted back.

Gallius steeled himself and presumed to shout down the great man himself.

"An impregnable fortress!"

"What?" grunted Caesar, and Gallius sighed in relief.

"What I have been trying to tell you all along, Caesar," he said peevishly. "A fortress impregnable to attack from both the Gauls inside Alesia and any army outside."

He picked up a twig and began scrawling with it in the dirt.

"Look!"

He drew a rough circle.

"Alesia . . ."

He drew another circle around it.

"Our present fortifications . . ."

He poked repeatedly at the ground behind the wall, stippling the ground with dots.

"The present position of our forces . . ."

He drew a third ring, a wider one, so that the pocked earth was now contained within it.

"A double palisade with our entire army inside!" exclaimed Caesar. "And Alesia a prisoner within it!"

Gallius nodded.

Caesar had come to his senses.

"But *we'd* be trapped inside!" said Labienus.

"No," said Caesar. Now that he understood what Gallius had been trying to tell him, he saw at once that this was the surest solution. "Not unless and until this relief army appears, and then inside an impregnable fortress will be exactly where we want to be."

"Besieged within our own siege," said Labienus. "I like it not."

"I have not heard a better idea from you, Labienus," said Caesar.

"You'd render our cavalry useless by penning it up within walls? Look what happened to Vercingetorix!"

"What would you do with our cavalry, Labienus?"

"Ride after the Teutons. Bring them back to fight at our side."

"And how do you propose to accomplish that feat?"

Labienus' mien displayed a certain lack of certitude.

"I'd . . . well, shame them into it."

"You'd do what?" said Galba.

"They count themselves fearless. So I'd . . . I'd challenge their courage . . . by . . . by riding off to attack this relieving army myself—"

"Into certain death!" said Trebonius.

"Exactly!" declared Labienus, and now Caesar could see his fervor arise. "They must either follow, or count themselves cowards and lesser men than Romans!"

Caesar considered it. If anyone could pull off such a thing, it would be Labienus. And even if he didn't, he was certainly right about one thing—the cavalry would be worse than useless within the walls of a siege.

"Try it if you like, Labienus, and promise them as much gold as you like," he said, and turned his attention back to Gallius, whose design seemed more elegant, more infallible, more *Roman* the more he pondered it.

"How long would it take you to build this thing, Gallius?"

"The basic structure? A lot less time than it would take Gauls to put together another army and get it here," Gallius said. "Of course, the refinements . . ."

"Refinements?"

Gallius nodded happily and began sketching in the dirt again. "We'll want towers with light catapults and ballistae atop them, of course. We'll need to put the heavy ones on platforms inside the fortress, so they can fire over the walls with usable trajectories—the calculations will not be so easy—and we'll have to forge enough proper kettles for the boiling pitch, and build an underground aqueduct from the Ose at some distance in case they try blocking the river, perhaps dig wells inside too, and I'd like to construct as many wheeled barricades as possible to seal the river entrance and any breaches. . . ."

"What about baths and a theater for dramatic performances?" Caesar suggested dryly.

Gallius regarded him humorlessly.

"Do you really think that's necessary, Caesar?" he said. "It would make more sense to build a proper sewer system first."

A thin, misty rain hung in the air as Vercingetorix stood with Cottos atop the highest tower on the ramparts of Alesia, watching the Roman army, rank after orderly rank, moving into its enormous and strange fortress.

"What is it?" Cottos demanded of him, not for the first time. "What are they *doing*?"

And, not for the first time, Vercingetorix refused to utter aloud the words in his mind. What the Romans had now completed was a structure that no Gaul could have even imagined, and it filled him with a grudging admiration for the power of Rome.

What Caesar had built was more than a fortress. It was more than what Gauls deemed a city, for it enclosed a city entire. No matter how hard he tried to put the thought from his mind, Vercingetorix could not keep from thinking that the Romans had built a Great Wheel.

The Great Roman Wheel's rim contained a circular Roman city imperiously implanted in the soil of Gaul. A city of tents and sheds and smithies, of catapults and ballistae and armories, and its population was a Roman army, and at its hub and dwarfed by it was Alesia.

As Vercingetorix beholds it, the Great Wheel seems to turn, and a pitiless sun arises over a wasteland where nothing moves but skeletal figures crawling their last across a charnel plain of corpses so emaciated that they dry to leather before they can rot.

The Great Wheel turns, but Alesia does not turn with it, and its walls creak and crumble. Fire falls upon the city of the Gauls, upon the lands of the Gauls, searing them brown, burning them black, replacing them with streets of stone and buildings of marble, with arenas and fountains and colonnaded avenues, with gladiators and legionnaires and slaves.

With that which is Rome.

"What are *we* to do, Vercingetorix?" said Cottos. "The food is running out. Perhaps we *should* surrender."

Vercingetorix came mercifully blinking out of that cruel vision.

"Surrender?" Vercingetorix said. "Surrender to *that?*"

"You do not think Caesar might show mercy?"

"Perhaps *Caesar* might," said Vercingetorix. If given his victory to ride in triumph back to Rome, he might let the people of Alesia live, because he would have no reason not to. But not as Gauls.

"But *Rome* will not let Gaul live," he told Cottos. "For Rome is like a millstone crushing and grinding all beneath it, rock into mortar like grain into flour, to turn it into more of itself."

"This you have seen in a vision?"

"Yes," said Vercingetorix, "but did I have to?"

Day and night, rocks fell from the sky—here a fusillade of fist-sized ones scattering the fortunate and wounding the less lucky, there a great boulder crushing a man, a woman, a child, a house, whatever it chanced to fall upon. They were as impossible to evade as sudden hailstorms or the capricious will of the gods.

The Roman catapults rained down fire too, though less generously, the amphorae bursting in the plazas or the centers of the wider streets doing relatively little damage, those hitting houses or marketplaces or nearly empty granaries setting whole quarters ablaze, for the Romans had blocked the waters of the Ose, and the wells were running too dry to allow water to be spent on fire fighting.

Of late the Romans had taken to flinging dead animals over the walls of Alesia as well—horses, pigs, dogs, whole or crudely butchered. But those of the famished Carnutes who fell upon Caesar's largesse found that the carcasses had been left to rot for days beforehand, perhaps in water, so that the guts were a mass of gelatinous putridity and the flesh crawled with maggots. Those sufficiently maddened by hunger to attempt to eat them sickened and died, and even many who did not fell ill with unknown and terrible diseases.

Vercingetorix had taken to roaming the smoldering streets, the staff of the Arch Druid in his hand, to show the Alesians that he shared their danger as his army shared their meager rations, perhaps in the hope of rallying their spirits by reminding them of the druid magic that had scattered the Teutons.

But that hope had become more and more forlorn as the siege ground on and the rations dwindled away and the wells began to run dry, and the people of Alesia eyed the warriors of foreign tribes with sullen and desperate anger.

As the sun set on the nightmarish streets this evening, Vercingetorix sensed that the staff with the fallen star atop it had become more of a protective talisman than a scepter the starving Carnutes respected. Wherever he went, eyes looked away, or down, or to the side, and whenever he chanced upon a gaze not averted in time to conceal what was written within it, he saw not awe, or comradeship, or hope, but dread and hatred.

And could he justly blame them?

This eve he had seen children no older than nine come to blows over a moldy crust of bread, the victor gulping it down while holding off the others with a knife. And now he saw a wild-eyed man holding a squirming rat by the throat spear it up the anus with his knife and thrust the still-squirming and squealing creature directly into the flames of an empty market stall while a woman, perhaps his wife, knelt beside him, all but drooling.

"Where is this famous rescuing army of yours, *King Vercingetorix*?" the man snarled. "I'm a loyal Gaul, after all, and as proof, I'll save the tail for those cowardly bastards!"

"Oh no, you won't!" the woman cried. "Even a rat's *balls* are too much meat to waste on them! We'll cut off *theirs* and eat them if they ever get here!"

"Not much danger of that—now, is there?"

Vercingetorix found that his silver tongue had deserted him, and all he could do was slink off disconsolately like one more cur dog haunting the ruins. And it came to him that perhaps he walked these streets to dare the gods or destiny or the Romans to slay him with a rock or fire from the sky.

He who—

A whooshing roar above and behind him interrupted his thoughts.

Whirling around, he saw a hail of jagged rocks, dozens of them the size of a man's head and more, fall from the sky upon the man, the burning rat, and the woman, smashing them all to abrupt and bloody silence, and half burying them in the ground where he himself had stood a moment before.

He who destiny had decreed could not be slain on the soil of Gaul.

A trestle table had been set out in the courtyard of Cottos' house, shaded from the afternoon sun by the boughs of the great oak, and around it sat Vercingetorix, Marah, Rhia, Critognat, and Cottos, sharing the day's singular meal. Vercingetorix's heart left him no appetite for the meager handful of boiled millet on the plate before him, though his growling stomach commanded him to choke it down. It was not the paucity and tastelessness of the fare that so offended his palate, but the grim variance between the blue sky, the gay sunlight, the overarching oak, and the acrid odor of fire and the stench of rot and death that choked the air even here.

"This is all for today?" said Marah.

Cottos nodded disconsolately. "Tomorrow there will be less, and less the day after that, until . . ." He shrugged, unwilling to complete the thought.

But Vercingetorix had to know. "How long before there is nothing?" he demanded.

"Days, not weeks."

"We should have slaughtered and smoked the horses," said Critognat.

"You were the one who said he would sooner eat shit, as I remember," Vercingetorix reminded him.

Critognat picked the millet off his plate with his hand, squeezed it, held up an object roughly the size and color of a pallid turd. "This is any better?" he said. "Perhaps we should . . ."

He hesitated, seemingly horrified at the thought that had invaded his mind.

"Should *what?*" said Rhia.

"Slaughter everyone who cannot fight and eat *their* flesh!" Critognat blurted.

"You cannot be serious!" exclaimed Cottos.

"He has a point," said Vercingetorix. "We cannot *feed* them any longer—"

"Surely you don't mean—"

"Of course not!" Vercingetorix said quickly, to quell the unanimous looks of outrage. "We cannot *eat* the women and the children and the less-than-able-bodied men, and so we have no choice but to trust them to the mercies of Caesar."

"Caesar!" exclaimed Marah.

"If we keep them here, they will all starve to death within a week for certain, and so will we," Vercingetorix said coldly. "We send them out, and at least they have *some* chance."

"And we can hold out twice as long," said Rhia.

"Do you really believe Caesar will feed them?" said Marah.

"Why not?" Vercingetorix told her bitterly. "After all, we may be barbarians, but Rome is an enlightened civilization, is it not? And Caesar is a great man. . . ."

"Better to attack now, while we still have the strength, and die like heroes!" declared Critognat.

"No, Critognat, we would not die as heroes if an army coming to our rescue found itself fighting the Romans alone over our corpses."

"You really still believe they will come?" Cottos said dubiously.

Vercingetorix weighed both his thoughts and his words carefully, searching for a truth that would not dishearten them, for surely he owed them better than a silver-tongued lie.

"It matters not what *I* believe," he finally told them, "for surely *Caesar* fears that they will, else why would he have built his mighty fortifications? Sometimes it takes more courage to endure suffering for a cause than to die for it."

"What a horror!" groaned Tulius.

"But what does it mean?" asked Brutus.

"It means they're running out of food and water," Caesar told him. "The question is, what do we do about it?"

From this vantage atop a tower facing the gates of the city, Caesar could see the whole ghastly spectacle. Thousands of Gauls wandered disconsolately about the plain between the walls of Alesia and his own inner fortifications, the more enterprising among them, or the more desperately famished, crawling around the grass searching for worms or bugs or edible roots. Still more of them were emerging through the open gates, though the exodus seemed to be reaching its conclusion.

Women, children, old men, the sick, the lame, the blind—it was obvious what Vercingetorix was doing and why, for there was not a warrior among them, or a man able-bodied enough to be pressed into service even in desperation.

"Why must we do *anything*?" said Tulius.

"Because," said Caesar, "doing nothing would still be doing something. All these people would starve to death in plain sight of the army left in the city."

"Excellent for that army's morale," Tulius said sarcastically.

"And if we try to feed them all?" said Brutus.

"Entirely out of the question," said Caesar. "We must husband our supplies against the possibility that another army of Gauls might arrive in time to besiege *us*. The question is, how much mercy can we afford to show?"

"That wasn't a question at Bourges," Brutus blurted.

"Bourges was an atrocity committed for a strategic purpose," Caesar told him coolly. "Ruthless, perhaps, but rational. But to commit an atrocity for no rational purpose is simply the act of a madman or a monster."

Something of which I do well to remind myself of in this barbarous country, Caesar told himself. In a war against barbarians, the commission of barbarous acts may be inevitable, but now that the war is about to be won, a display of mercy would prove more useful than another atrocity. Of course, I had better not go too far, lest mercy be interpreted as weakness. And better that mercy turn a reasonable profit.

"Send out squads to make a selection, Tulius," he ordered. "The women young and comely enough to be salable as slaves and please the troops in the meantime, we feed and keep. Also craftsmen and the like, who will pay back their keep on the slave market."

"And the children?" Brutus asked, with more than a hint of pleading in his voice.

"Useless mouths to feed?" Caesar said teasingly. Poor Brutus looked aghast at what he believed he would hear next.

Caesar laughed. "Oh, all right, for your sake, I'll feed the able-bodied children too, Brutus," he said. "If we keep them healthy, we should be able to sell them to the slave merchants."

While training up the best and the brightest and most pliable of them as a corps of Romanized Gauls to administer the province and serve as teachers to turn the next generation into more of themselves.

"You are not as hard a man as you pretend, Caesar," Brutus told him.

"I am as hard or as soft as circumstances require, my young friend. Anyone who does otherwise is a beast or a fool or both."

"And the rest of them?" asked Brutus. "The old men, the sick, the cripples?"

Caesar pondered that one carefully. He would certainly not feed them. The question was where to let them starve. If he kept them trapped within full sight of those in the city, it would sap their morale, to be sure, and it might even sow discord between Vercingetorix and some faction wishing to readmit them. But it would probably also harden resistance. If he allowed them passage through into the open countryside to expire out of sight, *not* knowing their fate might be more disheartening to the Gauls. Worse than the horror you see onstage, as the Greek dramaturges well knew, is the offstage one your mind's eye is forced to imagine.

"We will let them choose their own fates," Caesar said. "We will give those who wish to try their luck in the countryside an hour to pass through our fortifications. After which those who remain can try begging scraps from Vercingetorix. Let the gods decide. Those who survive in the countryside may spread the tale of Caesar's relative mercy. Any of the others who might manage to survive on bugs and the corpses of their fellows will only tell the tale of Vercingetorix's cruelty."

"But the rest . . . ?" said Brutus, obviously appalled.

Caesar shrugged.

"The rest, of course," he said, "will not be around to say anything."

The only sounds in the night were the impacts of Roman stones and amphorae and the cracking collapse of burnt-out buildings, for dogs and cats and even the birds were gone. Marah sat alone by the table under the oak, gazing longingly across the courtyard at the closed door to Vercingetorix's chamber.

Then a door did open, but it was not his, it was Rhia's. She emerged,

wearing her armor and sword but not her helmet, crossed the courtyard, and sat down unbidden beside Marah.

"There is little time left," said Rhia. "Why do you sit here alone?
Why don't you go to him?"

"Because he won't have me!" Marah said angrily. "It's *you* he wants!
Why don't *you* go to him?"

"That is not why he won't have you."

"You deny that he wants you?"

"No."

"You deny that you want him?"

"No," said Rhia, averting her gaze. "The truth of it is, he wants both
of us. And we both want him. But I cannot have him, and he cannot
have me."

"Because of this stupid blood oath?"

Rhia looked down and nodded.

"Because you are sworn to virginity?"

Rhia nodded silently again.

"Well, I am certainly sworn to no such thing!" said Marah. "If it's
really true that he wants me, he can have me, so why—"

"Because *he* is," Rhia said in a whisper.

"What?"

Rhia hesitated, nibbled on her lower lip, slowly looked up to meet
Marah's disbelieving gaze.

"Vercingetorix is a virgin," she finally said.

"Vercingetorix is sworn to virginity?" exclaimed Marah. "I don't
believe it!"

"Vercingetorix swore no oath of virginity," Rhia told her, "but we
did swear a blood oath as brother and sister of the sword together, an
oath to honor *my* oath of virginity while fighting and even sleeping side
by side, and thus sharing its warrior's power. I think, without quite
knowing it, Vercingetorix swore a secret silent oath within his own heart
to retain the power of his own virginity as long as his destiny required."

Marah groaned, shook her head. "You don't know very much about
men, do you, Rhia?"

"I lay no claim to your . . . Roman sophistication."

"You don't have to have been educated in the amatory arts by a
master to know that, shorn of its blood oaths and magical powers, what
your little tale really tells is that Vercingetorix has so far remained a virgin because he is afraid."

"Afraid!" said Rhia. "Never have I known of a man more fearless in battle!"

Marah laughed. "Vercingetorix is afraid to make love to a woman, in large part *because* he is the Great Leader of Warriors. Fearless in battle! Commander of the army of Gaul! Chosen by destiny to be king! Perhaps even you, Rhia, have noticed that their pride is what men hold most dear?"

"It has from time to time come to my attention," Rhia admitted.

"Well, then, consider what such a man, with so much to be justly proud of, must feel at imagining himself exposed before a woman he would impress with his manly prowess as a virgin as innocent of skill in the necessary art as a fresh-faced girl handed a sword and told to do battle with Hercules."

"There are things about which *you* know nothing, Marah," Rhia told her coldly.

"No doubt," said Marah. "But one thing I *do* know now is that Vercingetorix has failed to make love to me not because he spurns me, but because he fears to face the moment when he must expose his virginity."

Shaking her head, Rhia stood up, took Marah by both hands, and drew her to her feet. "I do not understand a woman like you, Marah, and I do not think I want to," she told her. "And perhaps I do not truly understand Vercingetorix either. But I do know that the end approaches, and you must go to him now, while there is yet time."

And Rhia began tugging the not reluctant Marah across the courtyard toward the door to Vercingetorix's chamber.

"Knowing what I now know, so I shall," said Marah. "But I don't understand you any more than you understand me. You love him, do you not?"

"With all my heart."

"Then why—"

They had reached the closed door. Rhia took her hands from Marah's and poised them to push it open.

"I am his flower destined to die. But you are destined to bear his fruit," she said. "I ask only one thing. . . ."

She paused, hesitated.

"Give this to him from me," she said, and then kissed Marah tenderly but squarely on the lips.

Marah stared at her in shock for a short moment, then regarded

Rhia silently for a much longer one, long enough for tears to come to her eyes. Then she took Rhia's hands.

"No," she said. "For one single night, can we not be the two women who love him, nothing less and nothing more?"

And she pulled Rhia to her and kissed her back. "Come with me," she said, "and give it to him yourself."

Together they pushed open the door.

And entered, hand in hand.

When the door to his chamber opened, startling him out of his uneasy reveries in the borderland between wakefulness and sleep, Vercingetorix at first thought he had been awakened, but when he saw the silhouettes of two women standing hand in hand in the moonlight, he believed he must be in the realm of dreams.

When they approached his bed and stood over him and he saw that they were Marah and Rhia, he knew not where he was; and when they sat down on either side of him, and Marah kissed him tenderly on the lips while opening the fastenings of his tunic, he found that he didn't care.

"What is this?" he said softly as she drew it off, if only out of the need to say something.

"This is the most natural thing in the world," Marah told him.

And after all, in the waking world, this was of course true, else there would be no men or women to inhabit it. It was his denial of this simplest of truths, known to the lowest beasts in the fields, that was unnatural.

"Two . . . two women and the man we both love," said Rhia, in a voice that seemed constricted by reluctance, or even the *fear* that he had never seen this warrior woman show.

And if it was fear, the courage it must have taken to lie down beside him and kiss him too, hesitantly at first, then roughly, uncertain perhaps how to do it properly, but still as a woman should kiss a man, must be greater than any she had shown in battle.

The greater the magic, the greater the price that must be paid. Now he began to understand the terrible price he had paid for the magic, such as it was, to become the Druid King of Gaul. Nor had he paid it alone. These two women, each of whom loved him after her different fashion, had paid it with him.

The magic might have failed, the war might be lost, death might be near, and the Gaul they had known might soon perish, but on this night, which might be their last in the world of strife, he at least *did* have the power to break the spell.

By doing the most natural thing in the world.

Vercingetorix arises, and he draws Marah to her feet and undresses her tenderly with a grace he has never imagined, though he has imagined doing this many times. But never, in the perfection of his dreams or reveries, was she as lovely as now, in the fleshly truth of her little imperfections. Nor had he ever envisioned her standing so tall and proud and unashamed before him.

Nor had he ever imagined that there would be an onlooker.

Rhia sits on the bed in her warrior's garb, regarding them with a face of stone. In the world of flesh, Vercingetorix finds that her presence redoubles the arousal of his manhood, but in the world of the spirit, he is unmanned, for the three of them are frozen there like a tableau carved in marble, and neither the man of action straining at his pantaloons, nor the man of knowledge with his divided heart, has any idea of what to do.

But Marah does. With one hand, she leads Vercingetorix back to the bed, and draws Rhia to her feet with the other. Then she kneels before this woman dressed as a man, and unbuckles her sword. She nods at Vercingetorix, who now understands, and who begins to remove Rhia's armor.

And then, at last, the two women he has wanted since he began his life's journey into manhood stand fully revealed. Marah, with the softly perfect body and smooth, clear skin of the goddess Venus as rendered by a Roman sculptor. Rhia, with the battle-hardened and scarred body of a mighty woman warrior. Both, in their utterly different ways, equally beautiful.

Gently Marah pushes him back onto the bed, gently she guides Rhia as the two of them, Rhia on the left leg, Marah on the right, peel off his pantaloons. And now Vercingetorix's manhood is fully revealed, to Marah, to Rhia, and indeed to himself in a way it has never been before. As the most natural thing in the world.

Nor does it seem anything but natural when Rhia and Marah lie down beside him, wrap their arms around him, and press their breasts against him, covering his face, the nape of his neck, his chest, his nipples, with caresses. And though their kisses dance over him in ever-moving profusion, he can easily tell one from the other: Rhia artless and bold like a warrior entering an unknown country, Marah cunning and knowing, each kiss artfully placed to elicit his pleasure, to inflame his arousal.

But then there comes a moment that is not natural at all, the inevitable moment of choice between them, a choice he finds he cannot make, for it seems to Vercingetorix that to choose the one would be to spurn the other, and in this moment he loves them both, differently but equally.

It is Marah who lovingly makes the choice for him.

She reaches down and takes the burning quick of him firmly in hand, kisses him deeply with her lips and tongue, then rolls him over.

"First you must give her this from me," she says, and guides him into Rhia.

As soon as Vercingetorix enters his sister of the sword, he transforms her into something less and something more, a natural woman of Gaul knowing her first lover. And, transformed himself, he knows that this is right, for the spell that has bound the three of them has been broken by this gift of love from Marah.

Marah embraces the two of them as Vercingetorix finds his rhythm, as he rides Rhia, as she rides him, side by side, strongly, plainly, insistently, neither and both horse and rider.

Lovers now yet still brother and sister of the sword, they make love like comrades, and as Vercingetorix's thoughts dissolve, the smell of Rhia is of warm grass and the sweat of battle, and his vision is of deep, shadowy forests and the starry heavens, and he soars across them borne on Rhia's hearty cry of ecstasy and joins it with his own.

But as he glides back down into the world of flesh, into her arms, he senses that something is departing; the bright glow of the greatest pleasure he has ever known gutters down into the smoldering embers of a sad longing for a world entire which is passing, never to return.

The greater the price that is paid, the greater the magic.

But what is bought when the price is the magic itself?

"Now you must give her what is hers, Vercingetorix," says Rhia. "For mine is to be but the flower. Hers is to be the fruit."

Vercingetorix does not understand these words, but Marah does. "No, Rhia," she says, "if there is to be fruit, the love that quickens the seed is yours as well."

And she kisses Rhia tenderly on the lips.

And Rhia kisses her back.

And it seems to Vercingetorix that a new magic is made.

Women's magic, never to be understood by men.

Marah then kisses him, her tongue tasting the depths of him, lapping at his soul as the tongue of a bee drinks nectar from a flower, so deeply that she reaches beyond to his sated manhood, magically filling it with herself, commanding it to arise again.

Unseen hands urge it upward and onward, the smooth soft knowing hands of Marah's gentle and subtle caresses, the strong rough hands of Rhia gripping it like the pommel of a sword, and together they temper its metal once more.

Then Marah rolls over onto him, and those hands wield his manhood together as Marah mounts and rides.

With Rhia it had been the rough-hewn consummation of all those nights lying together on the fragrant forest floor and a magic that was passing. With Marah it is a reluctant yet exquisite surrender to a mistress of a magic he has never known, a passage into a world being born.

Yet, as Rhia kisses him roughly once more, but with some of the knowing and artful tenderness of Marah, it seems to Vercingetorix that some magic is passing between them, from the world that will be to the world that was, from a world being lost to a world to come, and in that moment, the three of them become one, a circle completing itself.

And as Vercingetorix's seed surges through him and beyond him, he knows that *this* is somehow the moment of the Wheel's Great Turning, as all thought that fills the mind stops, and there is only a great white light.

XXII

WHEN THE SUN ROSE above the distant silhouette of Alesia, it looked down upon a mighty army of Gauls moving across the plain in a broad front, like an ocean of men flowing inexorably toward the city. Nearly forty thousand mounted warriors rode at a frustratingly slow walk, so as not to outdistance an almost equal number of men afoot—a ragtag collection of farmers, townsmen, artisans, smiths, even beggars. The fortunate were armed with swords, pikes, lances, axes, and equipped with shields, helmets, bits and pieces of Roman and Gallic armor; the rest made do with scythes, hoes, hayforks, whatever came to hand.

Gaul itself had risen up as one to come to the rescue.

But, riding in the center and front of this second "army of Gaul," Litivak knew all too well that this was a unity so fragile as to be close to an illusion. He rode in the center only because the Edui were the largest contingent. Each tribal army rode and marched behind its own standard, and the leaders of *all* the tribal contingents rode in the front line to either side of him, casting measuring glances from time to time to assure themselves that none of the others had presumed to move to the forefront.

Litivak had only obtained the leadership of the Eduen forces by renouncing all ambition to election as vergobret. That had been the price he had to pay to still the opposition of Liscos to what he had privately called "the whole doomed enterprise."

As for Vercingetorix's druid magic, Litivak knew only what he had seen, and what he had professed to believe, and must continue to profess.

He had seen what every man who had escaped from Alesia with the horses had seen—Vercingetorix holding high the Arch Druid's staff and calling down the lightning and thunder, Vercingetorix pointing the staff at the Teutons surrounding Alesia and scattering them in terror.

After escaping from Alesia, some eighteen men had reached the sanctuary of the forest within sight or earshot of each other. Not daring to light a fire, they had huddled close to find the words to rally the forces of their peoples. But none of them knew what words might accomplish such a feat until at length Litivak spoke up.

"Tell them of the blood oath that Vercingetorix made. Tell them that he himself could have escaped, but swore that he would not leave Alesia alive until an army of Gauls arrived to relieve the siege. Say that he proclaimed that if no such army came the dishonor would not be *his* but Gaul's."

"True enough, perhaps," said Comm, "but—"

"Remind those fortunate enough *not* to be trapped in Alesia that *all of our tribes* have thousands of men in there who are!" Litivak had said peevishly. "And if they all die or are dragged off to Rome as slaves because of the cowardice of their brothers, what Gaul of *any* tribe will ever be able to look another in the eye and see a man of honor?"

No one had had anything to say to that except a few grunts and mutters of disconsolate agreement. Litivak had sensed that something more was required.

Magic.

"Tell them that Vercingetorix drew down the wrath of the gods on the Teutons. Tell them he so terrified the Teutons with druid magic that they fled in terror without so much as a single blow being struck against them. We were all there. We saw it. Tell the people of Gaul that destiny is with us because our cause is just. Tell them that not even Caesar and all the legions of Rome can stand against druid magic!"

Magic? Who was to say what was magic and what was fortune, save a druid? Certainly this great army of Gauls could only have been conjured up by, if not magic itself, then the tales thereof. Magic? Perhaps magic could only be made by those who believed in it. As these Gauls, his brothers, in their thousands upon thousands, surely did, or it would not have brought them here to win the war and their freedom.

Carnaxes blared.

Fists pounded on a wooden door.

"They're here!" a voice shouted.

Cottos' voice.

"They've come at last!"

Vercingetorix awoke bolt upright as Cottos burst in the room, and such was the Carnute vergobret's exhilarated excitement that he barely blinked at the sight of the two women rubbing sleep from their eyes.

"There's an army of Gauls arriving! We're saved!"

Such was Vercingetorix's own excitement that he threw off the bed-clothes and leapt out of bed, forgetting his nakedness, and forgetting too the nakedness of Marah and Rhia.

Marah pulled the bedclothes up over her breasts, but Rhia was so indifferent to her nudity, except when it came to regaining her sword and armor, that she almost put them on before she had clothed herself.

"So many!" groaned Brutus.

Caesar, Tulius, and Brutus had mounted the most convenient tower on the outer wall to observe the arrival of this new "army of Gaul," and Caesar had to admit that it was an impressive spectacle. The sheer number would have been daunting, had the outer fortifications not been completed.

But since they had been, it was the Gauls who were clearly daunted. They had arrived as a massive and vengeful charge in full battle frenzy, expecting to overwhelm the exposed rear of a besieging Roman army. Instead, they found themselves confronting a mighty fortress, their enemy snug inside it, and not a man outside to be intimidated by any amount of screaming and shield-beating and horn-blowing.

Now the battle cries and carnax blares guttered away to a discombob-ulated silence, and the Gauls, infantry and cavalry alike, milled around half a league or so beyond the outer defensive ditch, visibly at a loss.

"What would you do if you were their commander, Brutus?" Caesar asked in a playful pedagogical mood.

Brutus shrugged eloquently.

"Exactly," said Caesar. "Their only rational strategy is to sit there, do nothing, and hope that they can starve *us* out before *Alesia* starves."

"I can't imagine them doing that," said Tulius.

"Neither can I," said Caesar. "But just in case they are smitten by an uncharacteristic attack of rationality . . ."

· · ·

Vercingetorix stood on the ramparts of Alesia watching helplessly, as did Critognat, Rhia, Marah, Cottos, and as many warriors and townspeople as had been able to crowd atop the wall to greet the arrival of their rescuers. Who, in their scores of thousands, massed along a wide front, well beyond the Romans' outer defensive ditch, doing nothing.

Until—

A gate in the outer Roman wall opened, and square after square of Roman legionnaires emerged, at least two full legions, bridging and crossing their narrow inner entrenchment, then spreading out to form a skirmish line three ranks deep. Behind the first rank were javelin-throwers. Behind the second rank were archers. Behind the third were five small wheeled catapults, light enough to be maneuvered by men.

The Roman infantry marched slowly and carefully across the pit-strewn field toward the outer defensive ditch and the Gauls beyond it, the catapults being drawn up behind them more gingerly still.

When they were barely in range, the Roman archers fired a volley of arrows on a high arc that just reached the front ranks of the Gauls, doing little damage. Some archers within the body of Gallic foot soldiers answered to even less effect, their arrows clattering weakly off the Roman shields.

The Roman archers continued to fire, moving behind the Roman infantry marching to the edge of their own defensive ditch. At this range, their arrows had more deadly effect, piercing scores of Gallic horsemen with each volley—deadlier still because the front line of the Gauls was prevented from retreating out of range by the great mass of men behind them. The result was milling, rearing confusion.

When the Romans reached the ditch, they began throwing javelins as well, and what order there had been in the Gallic front line disintegrated as hundreds of men were struck from their horses, as horses went down, as warriors rode this way and that in futile attempts to avoid the rain of arrows and javelins.

"Retreat! Retreat!" Vercingetorix shouted from the ramparts, but he was far too distant to be heard. The Great Leader of Warriors was reduced to groaning in dismay like everyone else.

On the left flank, a hundred or so Gauls, Santons by their green cloaks, galloped senselessly across the plain toward the Romans. Not to be outdone in suicidal bravery, a contingent of Atrebates on the right flank did likewise. And then Turons, Cadurques, Parisii, hundreds of each tribal army, some led by their vergobrets, some with their vergobrets remaining behind desperately trying to maintain their armies' cohesion.

In the center, where the Edui were grouped, Litivak reared around to face his troops, shouted something Vercingetorix could not hear, then rode with his standard-bearer into the gap on their left flank opened by the charge of some Turons; and the Edui retreated behind him in more or less good order.

Meanwhile, perhaps two thousand galloping Gauls reached the outer ditch, many of the front rank realizing too late their mad folly and falling into it in a melee of whinnying horses and screaming men. Some of those behind managed to pull up short. Others did not and tumbled into the ditch atop the mass of broken men and horses already there. A hundred or so, farther back, tried to charge across this bridge of writhing flesh, and a few even succeeded.

The Roman infantry inexplicably retreated backward before the scattered horsemen who had successfully crossed, inflaming them into a screaming suicidal charge into the field of pits. The horses tripped, splintered their legs, and fell, dumping their riders to the ground.

Then the Roman catapults began lobbing amphorae into the main mass of the Gauls on the other side of the ditch. They burst into flame, scattering burning globs that fired everything they touched and stuck like mud. Volley after volley of the fiery death.

This was enough to send the makeshift infantry fleeing back across the plain after Litivak's Edui—hundreds of them aflame and screaming—followed by the tribal cavalry, many horsemen likewise turned into torches spreading fiery death.

Behind the ghastly rout, a steaming pall of grayish smoke mercifully obscured the field of blackening corpses. But there was no escape from the stench of it.

So eager was Caesar to see what dawn would reveal of the deployment of the Gauls that he was up on the battlements while it was still dark and no one else was abroad but the guards. The first rays of the sun revealed a plain seared to ash in many patches, strewn with the corpses of men and horses so thoroughly crisped that it was difficult to tell the one from the other. Across the plain, the army of Gauls was encamped atop a hill about two leagues from his outer fortifications, still a force larger than his own.

What would I do now, were I their commander? Caesar asked himself.

I would keep my army up there except for foragers to keep it supplied and wait for starvation to finally force the outnumbered Romans to emerge from their fortress. Would whoever commanded the Gauls up there have the sense to do that? Would he be able to convince his fractious forces to follow such a sure but plodding strategy if he did?

The former could be expected of any commander who was less than a fool. The latter, though, might only be achieved by the "druid magic" of Vercingetorix.

Caesar turned to regard the walls of Alesia and smiled in satisfaction. For in his mind's eye he saw his only worthy adversary among the Gauls looking back at him in frustration, removed from all communication with the larger part of his forces up on the hilltop, and therefore removed from command.

"What will Litivak do now?" said Cottos.

"Assuming he's in command . . ." muttered Critognat.

"He's in command up there if anyone is," said Vercingetorix. "He was leading the Edui, and the Edui led the retreat. If they hadn't, there'd be little left out there to command at all."

"Who's in command up there is not the question," said Critognat. "The question is, what will *we* do?"

"What would you have us do, Critognat?" asked Vercingetorix, knowing what the futile answer would be.

"What we all want to do!" declared Critognat, opening his arms to embrace the demands of the warriors who had been gathering atop the ramparts since dawn. "Attack!"

"Attack *where*? Attack *how*?"

At this, Critognat fell silent.

"All we can do now is prepare ourselves to attack the inner Roman wall if and when Litivak's army attacks the outer one," Vercingetorix told them. "Like . . ."

"A hammer and an anvil," muttered Cottos.

"If and when!" said Critognat. "What if there *is* no if and when?"

At this, it was Vercingetorix who was forced into silence, and he doubted that the frustration of his two chief lieutenants could match his own. He was powerless to order such a coordinated attack, and if he emerged from the city with his weaker force to attack the inner Roman fortifications alone, they would surely be met by the same Roman tactics and thrown back reeling.

Worse, Vercingetorix knew full well that his smaller and half-starved force would not retain the strength and numbers to attack again effectively in coordination with Litivak.

Worse still, he knew that there was one strategy that Litivak could pursue on his own that *would* bring victory, but it was so dire that he could scarcely bring himself to think it. Litivak *could* besiege Caesar as Caesar besieged Alesia: starve him out into open battle against superior forces. But the food supplies and the water inside Alesia would expire long before what the Romans had stored up was gone.

Everyone inside the city would die.

That would be the price of certain victory.

Vercingetorix was sure Litivak would never pay it.

Would he himself?

The sun had slid far past its zenith when the army of Gaul descended from its hilltop, and this time it appeared to Caesar to be more of a real army and less of a barbarian horde. It moved along a comparatively narrow front, with cavalry leading at a measured pace, so that what passed for infantry could keep up.

Two men in cloaks of Eduen blue rode at the point, a horse-length or two in advance—one a standard-bearer, and the other therefore the commander, that treacherous bastard Litivak, in command of the whole army now, by the look of this formation. And they were moving purposefully. They had a plan. What could it be?

From his observation tower, Caesar could see that Gallic infantrymen were bearing long wooden objects—poles, or logs, or planks—perhaps scaling ladders or something of the like, which might be able to get a useful portion of the infantry across the ditch. But not all that cavalry. Surely the fools had learned that horses could not leap the ditches that entirely surrounded the fortification—

Oh no, they didn't! Caesar suddenly remembered, and he ran to the ladder. When he reached the ground, he began shouting for signalmen, even as he ran for the nearest of the few horses left inside the fortress. "Another legion to the Ose! Bring up the barricades! Follow me!"

Gallius had left two gaps in the outer ditches and wall to allow the River Ose to flow through the encampment, to provide an inexhaustible supply of water. From the hilltop where the Gauls had been camped all day, those gaps had been clearly visible.

That's where they're going to attack! And if they get inside, they'll turn these impregnable fortifications into a slaughterhouse!

The Ose was not a broad river, and the gaps left in the Roman wall were only large enough to allow it to flow through them with banks no more than a half-dozen horsemen wide. The gaps in the two ditches beyond the wall were unguarded, but the gaps in the wall itself were flanked by low towers.

Litivak broke his cavalry into two wings to pass through the gaps in the ditches, leading the right wing himself. Roman archers on the wall took a heavy toll as they did, for only a score or so horsemen could advance at any one time.

When half the Gallic cavalry had passed the outer ditch, the two wings converged to form a battle line between the two gaps in the wall and began slowly threading their way through the field of pits, as the Gallic infantry poured through the gaps in the outer ditch behind them as fast as they could, bearing planks, poles, and hastily constructed scaling ladders, their archers firing wildly up at the wall.

Caesar leapt off his horse and ran to the nearest ladder, for there was nothing to be seen down here but well-organized frenzy: men forming bucket brigades, boiling pitch in great iron cauldrons, and, in the distance behind him, cohorts of legionnaires arriving at the dead run, and behind *them,* more men desperately wheeling up the heavy mobile barricades.

He scrambled up the ladder to the walkway, where even his crimson cloak failed to gain him immediate attention, for it was crammed with archers crouched down behind the protective parapet, firing as rapidly as the men behind could feed them arrows; legionnaires forming up the lethal end of the bucket brigades; javelin-throwers rushing to take their positions; and swordsmen crowding into place.

Fusillades of the Gauls' arrows clattered against the top of the wall, more flew on harmless high arcs over it, some reached their apogees and came tumbling down; none seemed to be doing more than forcing his own archers to keep their heads down and fire without taking meaningful aim.

Caesar elbowed and kneed his way through the crush to the first centurion he could find, who goggled at his sudden appearance and began to salute.

"Hail—"

"Never mind all that!" Caesar shouted. "What's happening down there?"

"They're trying to scale the wall and break through the gaps at the same time, Caesar."

"This I have to see for myself!"

"Keep your head down, and your cloak hidden. They can't hit very much from the angle they've got down there, but if they see it's you, every archer among them will be trying for a lucky shot."

Caesar nodded, swept his cloak well behind him, crept forward in a crouch, and peered carefully over the parapet.

A great mob of Gallic infantry—or, rather, armed peasants—crowded beyond the inner ditch immediately below the wall and as far along it to the left as Caesar's eye could see. This ditch was comparatively narrow, and Gauls were crawling across it on poles, planks, and scaling ladders. Many had already crossed, but the ditch was almost up against the foot of the wall, leaving only a very narrow strip of ground, where perhaps two or three men might stand, pressed front to back to wall. This strip was crowded with men trying to scale the wall with crude ladders set perforce at steep angles, and his own archers weren't doing much to thin them out, protected as the Gauls were from fire from the parapet by the very angle that made it all but impossible for them to reach it.

To Caesar's right, close by the right-hand gap in the wall, cavalry was massing to do something he could not quite fathom, a suicidal attempt to ride through on the embankments, perhaps. . . .

"Move aside! Coming through!"

A legionnaire carrying a steaming bucket barked orders at Caesar.

Caesar good-naturedly obeyed.

The poor fellow did not even see whom he was ordering around until he had poured his bucket of hot pitch down on the Gauls. Even then, he did not have time to stammer an apology before he was handed another bucket.

Litivak's cavalry contingent was now massed on both banks of the river where it flowed through the right-hand gap in the wall, and another such formation was poised by the left-hand gap. He looked around, raised his sword high; a carnax blew, then another, and another—

And Gallic cavalry, half a dozen horsemen wide and thousands deep on each embankment, broke into a gallop toward the gaps, waving swords and lances, shouting battle cries.

As the front ranks neared the walls, the ranks behind the first score suddenly wheeled and rode into the river, which in moments became filled with swimming horses reaching far back beyond the outer Roman ditch—an attempt to breach the fortifications in force via the river flowing through them.

The spearheads of the cavalry formations on the embankments reached the towers guarding the gaps in the wall, surged beneath them, and—

Palisades of stout wooden logs suddenly wheeled into place, entirely blocking their way. And from the towers flanking the gaps, torrents of steaming black pitch came pouring down.

Litivak, near the river's edge, escaped by diving his horse into the Ose. More than half of the others in the leading ranks were not so fortunate. Covered with the sticky boiling stuff, horses and men crashed into each other half blinded, spattered by flesh-searing gouts, raising a horrid clamor of screams and neighs of agony. The horsemen behind them either wheeled around to flee, or rode their horses into the river, many of them knocked off their mounts in the panic and confusion. Litivak, as it turned out, was twice fortunate, for he was knocked off his horse, had to swim frantically to catch another mount, and thus was spared the further disaster that followed.

The now leaderless cavalry already in the river heroically kept their mounts swimming toward the open gaps. As the front ranks passed the guard towers, more pitch was poured, to roll down the banks and into the river, setting it steaming; arrows and javelins rained down at close range and favorable angle.

Still the swimming cavalry pressed desperately forward, those behind eagerly replacing those who had fallen, even those aflame urging their mounts on with their dying breaths, and a spearhead of some hundred made it through the wall—

—where the embankments were lined with Roman legionnaires afoot, who caught them in a deadly crossfire of javelins.

Some of them bravely kept their horses swimming forward through the crossfire to make room for more Gallic cavalry swimming in behind them. But the farther the Gauls advanced up the river, the more of them were slain by the Romans on the embankments.

Some tried to climb up the embankments to push back the Romans and hold the river breach open, but the embankments were too steep for their horses, and the Romans easily slaughtered them.

The Romans then wheeled up more mobile barricades, these to the riverbanks *behind* the Gauls who had penetrated their fortifications. They tumbled them into the Ose, where they splintered and cracked but blocked the river like beaver dams, cutting off the Gallic spearhead and trapping them within the fortress. Legionnaires dashed up with buckets of some greasy liquid, threw it on the barrages, and set them ablaze.

More of the stuff was poured on the river behind the burning dams, where it floated on the surface until it touched the flames. Then it ignited, sending walls of fire floating toward the cavalry still outside the fortifications, who now found themselves swimming right toward the flames.

From the walls of Alesia, Vercingetorix had seen the Gauls moving toward the outer Roman wall where the Ose flowed through, had seen them pause, had seen them mass before the defensive ditches, had seen the cavalry then advance toward the fortifications with infantry behind them.

But from this angle, there was a blind area reaching from the outer Roman wall halfway to the gaps in the outer ditch, so all he had been able to see of what was obviously a battle was a rising pall of oily black smoke, cavalry in the river swimming toward the fortifications, a sudden eruption of distant orange flame, yet more smoke, and then horsemen in the river turning to flee in unruly confusion, followed by thousands of running men.

Vercingetorix might not have seen what had happened, but he and everyone else on the city walls had certainly seen enough to know that the attack had somehow ended in a catastrophe, sending Litivak's army of Gauls reeling back toward their hilltop sanctuary in desperate disarray.

There was not even a dirgelike banging of swords on shields. No shouts or cries of anger or grief. Only hundreds of accusatory eyes and grim faces turned toward Vercingetorix, and the terrible chastisement of utter silence.

It was Critognat who finally broke it, but in words meant for the ears of Vercingetorix alone.

"No more if and when," he said. "No more hammers and anvils. No more clever strategy. The next time our brothers out there attack, you lead us out of here or I will do it myself."

Caesar had been awakened at the first glimmerings of dawn by a breathless Brutus, who had informed him that the entire army of Gaul had magically crossed the outer defensive ditch.

Caesar had ascended to the walkway atop his outer wall and walked a quarter of the way around, surveying what the Gauls had done. Spread out before him, just inside the outer ditch and around its curve to either side as far as his eye could see, were the Gauls in their tens of thousands, both cavalry and infantry, apparently waiting for enough light to traverse the field of pits, and apparently transported there by druid magic.

But now, as the sun rose halfway above the horizon line, Caesar saw, hardly to his surprise, that the only magic that had been involved was of the usual sort—well-directed muscle and sweat—though he had to admit that it was rather amazing what thousands of men without any better equipment than battle-axes, swords, shields, tree limbs, and bare hands had been able to do between sunset and dawn.

The whole sector of the outer ditch behind the Gauls had been filled in with earth, branches, and brush, compacted into a mass sufficiently strong for horses as well as men to cross.

As if spotting his presence on the wall, the Gallic cavalrymen began banging their swords on their shields, the foot soldiers doing likewise if they had them, or thumping lances, scaling ladders, logs, and feet on the ground if they didn't. The tens of thousands of them yelled ferociously, and those flat, ominous carnaxes blared, a hideous din certain to awaken every Roman still sleeping.

"What're they *doing*, Caesar?"

"No doubt working up their courage to cross the field of pits and storm the wall."

"I mean, why would they bring up all that useless cavalry?"

Caesar shrugged. "Because they're *Gauls*. The nobles and warriors believe it beneath their dignity to fight afoot."

Tulius clucked his tongue against the roof of his mouth and shook his head.

Caesar glanced at the nearest tower, atop which was a small catapult with its piles of stones and amphorae, its crew rubbing the sleep from their eyes and making it ready. All along the walkway, bleary archers and javelin-throwers were ascending to their positions.

"Look on the bright side, Tulius," he said. "They *do* make excellent targets."

A volley of arrows flew from the top of the Roman wall, then another, and another, a ceaseless barrage that at this range mostly clattered off the shields of the cavalry and those of the infantry who had them, but skewered scores of those who did not, and discouraged all from advancing any closer.

Then heavy ballistae and catapults inside the Roman camp, and lighter ones on the wall, began to hurl long spearlike bolts, showers of rocks, large stones, clay amphorae. Their effects were far more terrible.

Ballista bolts went through men's breastplates and bodies to emerge from the other side with enough force to kill another man or even a horse. The clouds of light rock took out eyes, cracked noses. The heavy rocks crushed all whom they fell upon. And the amphorae burst on impact, releasing a gush of sticky burning stuff that could not be brushed off and could not be extinguished.

Litivak waved his sword above his head and shouted something to his standard-bearer, who raised the boar high; the two of them retreated through the field of pits and began riding at a trot around the inner edge of the outer Roman entrenchment. Eduen cavalrymen began to follow, then more cavalry, then infantry, and finally the whole army, horsemen circling just slowly enough for running men more or less to keep up.

This did not put them out of range of the catapults and ballistae, but, as a flock of birds wheeling in unison might present less of a collective target than the same birds sitting in a tree, in motion each individual was less vulnerable, or at least seemed to be so.

Instead of disintegrating under the fearsome bombardment, the army of Gaul held together.

"What are they doing *now*?"

Caesar laughed. "It would appear that they're running around in circles," he said.

"Seriously . . ."

"Seriously, they're keeping in motion to present less easy targets, and circling our fortifications searching for a weak point that they are not going to find."

"What do you think they'll do then?" asked Tulius.

"They can charge our fortifications and be annihilated," said Caesar. "Or they could besiege us, in which case we would be in dire trouble unless Labienus succeeds in rounding up enough Teuton cavalry to break through. But I doubt they'd have the discipline to do that, since it would mean that Vercingetorix's army in the city would die of starvation long before we feel the pain. Or they could give up and go home."

"You are saying that the war is won?"

"Yes, Tulius, I do believe I am."

"Well?" demanded Critognat.

As much of Vercingetorix's army as could had crowded up onto the ramparts, watching Litivak's force turning round and round the Great Wheel of fortifications.

Rhia stood beside him silently, holding up his standard, which now, rather than being a rallying point, was the focus of grumbling impatience.

"They're waiting for you to give the order," said Cottos.

"And I am waiting for Litivak to realize that he must pick a spot, mass his force, and attack the outer Roman wall."

"And if he does not?"

From somewhere around the curve of the ramparts, where Vercingetorix could not see, someone began banging his sword on his shield, and then someone else, and then another, and another, and another, and then it seemed that the whole army was beating out a rhythm. It was neither a triumphant cadence nor a threatening one, nor one to raise a battle spirit, but a slow, heavy, somber beat, almost what one would hear around a funeral pyre.

"You must order the attack now, or they'll just run out there on their own to be slaughtered," Rhia whispered in his ear.

When the people will not follow where you would lead, you must go with them or walk alone.

"So be it," said Vercingetorix. "Perhaps Litivak is waiting for a sign—"

"A sign!" groaned Critognat. "Have we not had enough of signs and omens?"

"A sign from *us*," said Vercingetorix. "It would appear we must attack first, and hope that he will understand what we are doing, and thus what *he* must then do."

Vercingetorix made his way to the nearest watchtower and mounted it, so that as many of his troops as possible could see him and directly hear his words.

He drew his sword, held it high above his head, and stood there silently until the beating of shields had ceased, and the silence had spread all around the wall, as the words he was to speak would spread from mouth to ear to mouth.

Words that he had spoken before. Words that he could not find silver enough in his tongue to better now.

"So be it! I will lead you into the jaws of death with a battle song in my heart!"

And they cheered. And the cheering spread. And swords on shields began to pound out a mighty rhythm.

The barricading rubble had been cleared from the gates of Alesia, and Vercingetorix's army was assembled before them, a long column no more than a dozen men across at its widest, stretching far back out of sight into the smoldering ruins of the city.

Vercingetorix stood at the head of the column, flanked by Critognat and Rhia, and directly behind him a score of warriors carried a battering ram crafted from the trunk of the great oak that had stood in Cottos' courtyard. They had tipped it with an iron cauldron reinforced by lead.

Behind the ram, twoscore warriors carried logs, bales of straw, pots of pitch, and burning torches. Learning from the Romans, Vercingetorix had positioned around this spearhead force fifty warriors with the largest shields to be found.

Everything was in readiness. Or as ready as it could be.

There was nothing left to say, save perhaps the words that might still the dark thoughts that slowed his mind.

And so he drew his sword and declaimed them:

"Open the gates! Do we want to live forever? Or would we rather become immortal?"

. . .

Vercingetorix, Rhia, and Critognat, bunched tightly together with their shields forming a roof above them, ran down the slope toward the inner Roman wall. Behind them came the warriors carrying the battering ram, and then those with the logs and straw bales and torches and pitch pots, surrounded by more warriors, who likewise roofed them over with shields, a larger, Gallic version of a Roman turtle.

Pouring out of the city after them, fanning out from the open gates into a human avalanche, came the rest of the Gauls.

Caesar left Tulius in command of the outer fortifications and rushed to the top of the inner ones, where Galba was in charge. When he had clambered up the ladder to the top of the command tower, he saw that Brutus was there with Galba and the signalmen. He also saw that the front line of the Gauls from Alesia charging the wall was already within arrow range, but moving too fast for catapults or ballistae to adjust their ranges rapidly enough to be effective. Soon enough, the Gauls would be so close to the wall that the angle would render these weapons useless.

"Brilliant!" he exclaimed when he saw how the advance spearhead with the battering ram was being protected from the archery barrage by auxiliaries with shields. Nor did he have to bother to look to know that Vercingetorix himself would be leading it.

"Brilliant?" said Brutus.

"See how he has adapted our infantry's turtle formation to a specialized unit! Remember this, Brutus! What a pleasure it is to learn a new tactic from an enemy!"

"Pleasure?" grunted Brutus with a look of befuddlement that Caesar found almost as choice.

"Oh yes," he said, "and unfortunately a rare one. And one, of course, that you can only enjoy when you know you will defeat him anyway."

Under a brutal fusillade of arrows and javelins clattering off their shields, Vercingetorix, Rhia, and Critognat reached the ditch at the foot of the Roman wall, halted until men protected by the shields of others brought up logs to bridge it, then crossed.

Here the angle was difficult for the archers and javelin-throwers atop the wall, and the rain of arrows and javelins off his shield became a mere patter. But when Vercingetorix looked behind, he saw that the wave of warriors dashing toward the wall were using their shields in a much less organized manner and taking disheartening casualties.

"Straw! Logs!" Vercingetorix commanded, and the men bearing them piled up an untidy pyre.

"Pitch!"

Pots of sticky black pitch were poured and tossed upon it.

"Hand me a torch!"

A torch was passed to Vercingetorix. He stepped back to what he deemed a prudent distance and tossed it onto the pyre, which exploded into bright-orange flame, sending billowing black smoke aloft, and a mighty cheer from the Gauls who saw it.

"The ram!"

A pillar of black smoke boiled skyward from the inner wall, not far from the tower where Caesar stood.

"The wall's on fire!" cried Brutus.

Caesar leaned over the edge to get a better angle, and saw that the Gauls had built a roaring bonfire beside the wall.

"No, Brutus," he called out, "the wall's not on fire. But it soon will be."

And indeed the wall by the bonfire was beginning to smolder as Caesar righted himself and returned to Brutus and the signalmen.

"They're trying to *burn* through the wall?" asked Galba.

"Yes, they're—"

He was interrupted by a great thump that shook the tower and became the first blow of a continuous rhythmic pounding.

Litivak, riding around the curve of the ditch, raised his hand into the air to signal a halt to the circling as the pillar of boiling black smoke came into view, slowed his horse to a walk, waited for the army behind him to do likewise, and then stopped entirely as the tips of tongues of flame licked teasingly at the top of the inner fortifications.

Vercingetorix slung his shield and, trusting in the wall of shields above him, joined the crew at the ram battering the now burning section of the wall steadily and relentlessly through the roaring flames of the bonfire.

"I've got to get to a closer tower," said Caesar, scrambling down the ladder.

"Caesar, don't—"

"You're in command here, Galba! I'm going where I belong! Commanding from the front!"

The scene within his fortifications was an admirably orderly contrast to the chaos outside.

The infantry was lined up in neat cohorts positioned at regular intervals all around the circumference of the circular fortress, ready to reinforce any section of either wall at short notice in the event of a scaling or breakthrough. Cauldrons of pitch and some stinking sulfurous stuff that he could not identify were boiling merrily away, surrounded by soldiers ready to relay their contents to the parapets. Chains of legionnaires extended from the armories, up ladders, to the tops of the walls, constantly resupplying the archers, javelin-throwers, and catapults. Gallius' mobile barricades, a score of them, were waiting along both walls to be wheeled into position to block any breach if needed.

A complex and smoothly functioning war machine hidden from sight of the Gauls, Caesar thought in no little satisfaction. I myself have said I do not like what I do not understand. And I doubt that any Gaul, even Vercingetorix, could truly understand *this*, even if he *could* see it.

Litivak's army stood motionless, watching black smoke piling up like a small thunderhead into the clear blue sky. A distant tide of Gauls poured down from the city toward the inner wall, antlike at this distance, their deaths barely visible as they fell by the hundreds under fusillade after fusillade of Roman arrows and javelins, which were so numerous, and so grayed by the distance, that they appeared as a storm of driving rain.

No one moved for a long moment. Then Litivak trotted his horse a few lengths to the fore and turned to them.

"Are we lesser men than our brothers?" he screamed. "Do we fear death more than dishonor?"

Few were close enough to hear his words. But none were so distant that they could not discern his meaning as Litivak wheeled his horse around and galloped toward the battle without looking back.

Had he done so, he would have seen an army of Gauls charging into the jaws of death behind him.

Caesar felt the pounding of Vercingetorix's battering ram through the soles of his feet as he ascended the tower nearest to it. The whole structure shook with each blow, and when he reached the top, the acrid smell of burning pitch and wood seared the back of his throat, and the thick black smoke obscured what was happening below.

But the eyes of the catapult crew and the signalmen were fixed on what lay beyond the outer wall, and when Caesar followed their gaze, he saw Litivak's entire force, cavalry and infantry alike, charging the fortification. Horses by the hundreds stumbled into pits and fell, and still they came. Men by the hundreds were pierced by arrows, and still they came. Amphorae of Greek fire burst in their midst, and even burning men pressed on.

Here, he thought, comes Gaul itself. A vast pride of lionhearted warriors dashing gloriously into certain destruction. Fearless as a lion and just as simple. But beautiful as a lion is beautiful.

Titus Labienus' spirits soared as soon as he was close enough to confirm that the smoke he had seen before Alesia became visible was indeed a sign of battle. And a great one, by the looks of it from here! And it was not too late to join in and assure final victory.

Labienus rode beside his general's standard in the center of an orderly formation of Roman cavalry, some five thousand in identical crested helmets, reddish-brown cloaks, well-tended armor.

Up there, Caesar had ten times as many men, but, to judge from the smoke, and the fires, and the extent of the human anthills boiling and roiling around the bottom of the hill on both sides of Junius Gallius' precious fortifications, Labienus was sure that a second army of Gauls had indeed arrived.

He knew that his five thousand cavalrymen would make little difference. But half a league behind rode something like twenty thousand Teutons.

Caesar could never have done what was needed to bring Ragar and his mercenaries this far. For, famed as an orator as Caesar was, Labienus knew that Caesar would never have found the simple words and simple deed necessary to win the Teutons over.

Gaius Julius Caesar was a complex man—warrior, yes, but also general, statesman, cunning politician. The Teutons were simple warriors. And so was Titus Labienus. And proud of it.

Labienus had finally offered Ragar a chest of gold denarii, all he had with him, just to gather at least ten thousand Teutons to hear him speak. He assembled his cavalry on horseback in a tight, orderly formation—a mere five thousand facing a good deal more than ten thousand well-armed Teutons.

"On this chariot, you see a chest of gold you could easily seize, and you wonder how I could be so stupid as to believe I could prevent you from just taking it," Labienus told them. "The answer is simple."

He nodded to the charioteer and standard-bearer, who, groaning with the weight of it, hefted the chest and laid it on the ground before the Teutons.

"I prevent you from seizing it by *giving it to you*. My men and I will now ride off to fight in the great and glorious battle I tried to pay you to join. My mistake. I insulted your pride. True warriors do not fight for money. True warriors fight for pride and glory and the pleasure of it. So I *give* you the money. Ride after us, and if the battle is to your liking, join us. If you see no pleasure or glory in it, you now have plenty of gold with which to gamble on the outcome as you stand aside like old men and watch."

And without another word, Titus Labienus wheeled his horse, turned his back on the dumbfounded Teutons, and rode off at the head of his men, not deigning to look back to see if they were following.

Nor did Labienus deign to look back now as he ordered his trumpeter to sound the charge, and one trumpet blared, and then many, and five thousand Roman cavalrymen galloped across the plain toward death or glory.

After a few minutes, the drumming rumble of their hooves was drowned out by a far greater thunder.

Thousands of men and horses fell to arrows and then javelins before the sea of Gauls could reach the defensive ditch at the foot of the outer Roman wall, and then it seemed to pause, to pile up, to crest into a foaming breaker like a rolling wave against a rocky coast.

Horses, unable to check their momentum, stumbled into the ditch, their riders thrown; more horses piled up behind them, fell atop them;

and in moments the ditch was filled with the dead and the dying, with screams and whinnies and cries, with the mingled blood of horses and men.

But more horses and men crossed over this bridge of flesh and gore, and reached the wall. Scaling ladders were thrown against it, and men fought with each other to climb them, but the angles were too steep for the weight by the time anyone reached the top, and they mostly fell down. Foot soldiers battered madly at the logs of the wall with swords, spears, and battle-axes. Cavalrymen tried to stand up on their saddles. Gauls tried to form human pyramids.

Had any of those battling at the Roman fortifications thought to glance to the northwest, they would have seen a gleaming line of armor moving toward Alesia.

And then, behind it and flanking it on either side, and wider still, darker and more indistinct, something like billowing clouds of dust, or a storm front moving in.

Caesar was torn between two equally grotesque spectacles, for atop this tower he was high enough to see over both walls of his fortress.

On the far side, a vast pile of corpses was already heaped up, and had many of them not been steeped in burning pitch and Greek fire or whatever other noxious stuff Gallius had cooked up, the Gauls probably would have tried to use this pile as a human scaling ladder, yet they kept coming and coming, even as more death poured down, even as catapults and ballistae devastated their rear.

When would the poor fools break or run? Or was their idea of honorable glory to be slaughtered to the last man?

"Look! Look!" cried a signalman, presuming to grab Caesar by the arm with one hand, and direct his attention westward by pointing with the other.

"By the balls of Mars, he did it!" exclaimed Caesar.

There, descending on the rear of an army of Gauls too valorous to admit that it was already defeated, was a formation of Roman cavalry led by the standard of Titus Labienus and followed by a vast horde of Teutons.

In a way, it was a double mercy. Even though the battle was already won, Mars had granted Labienus his moment of glory. And perhaps what was about to happen would finally convince those poor brave bastards that Gaul was conquered.

Caesar crossed the platform and turned his attention to the state of things on the Alesian side. It was much the same, except for the lack of an onrushing Teuton horde. The Gauls crowded as close as they could behind Vercingetorix and his battering ram, where the wall was on fire, virtually right below Caesar's own position.

Somewhat concerned at this, Caesar surveyed the situation between the walls of his fortress. It was quite reassuring. He saw the backstage machineries of his army grinding smoothly and purposefully on, boiling more pitch and water, relaying ammunition to the walls, and bringing up two cohorts of infantry to face the section of the inner wall beneath him.

Which had blackened and begun to smolder clear through and was now beginning to splinter under the blows of the battering ram.

The earth rumbled with the thunder of onrushing hooves, and finally eyes at the back of the crumbling army of Gauls turned to behold a small formation of Roman cavalry leading a mighty wave of Teuton horsemen descending on their rear.

So great was the collective cry of despair that it could be heard above the din of the battle.

The rear ranks of Gauls—those who saw what was coming—turned to flee, cavalry and infantry alike scrambling back across the filled-in section of the outer ditch, then scattering in all directions.

The army of Gauls disintegrated from the rear, each rank turning in confusion as the rank behind disappeared, then fleeing in terror. It did not take long for the process to reach the carnage beneath the wall, for all to realize that they were about to be caught between the merciless Roman war machine and the onrushing Teutons, whose massed hoof-beats could now be heard above the din of the lost battle.

Courage abandoned those vergobrets still living, those standard-bearers still holding their tribal ensigns aloft. One by one, the Santon hawk, the Parisii wolf, the Cadurque stag, the Atrebate eagle, and the rest turned to flee, dispersing as widely as they could, their tribesmen running, riding, smashing into each other, in their desperation to follow the standard of their own people.

Seeing this, Litivak could only wave his sword in a rage, screaming and cursing in a futile attempt to rally the Gauls to continue their suicidal attack on the Romans—

He reared his horse, wheeling it and—

A ballista bolt struck him in the throat and passed clear through, ripping his head almost free from his neck in a fountain of bright, spurting blood, and struck his standard-bearer in the navel, knocking him off his horse, and the standard of the Edui to the blood-soaked ground.

"Now I have finally conquered them," Caesar muttered to himself, as he saw Litivak fall and the Eduen standard fall with him.

If this ghastly rout could be dignified by such a military term. The battle was won, the war was over, and he should have felt triumphant elation.

There was that, but there was also something akin to what those who suffered from it described as postcoital sadness. In which state Caesar realized that the poor Gauls were still being bombarded to no useful purpose by ballistae and catapults.

"Tell them to cease firing and let the poor bastards go," he ordered a signalman.

Am I becoming soft in my maturity? he wondered. But no; for while mercilessness might be a virtue while there was a war to be fought, it was unseemly once it was won.

Turning his attention to the other front in this war that was already won, Caesar saw that Vercingetorix and his army didn't yet know it.

They were still there being slaughtered, and Vercingetorix was still humping away with his battering ram like a dutiful but insensitive lover.

Then, with a final shattering crack, the ram *did* breach the fire-weakened wall, and to the cheers of all the Gauls who saw it, a whole blackened section fell away in shards to reveal—

A solid wall of Roman shields blocking the breach and bristling with the swords of the legionnaires behind them.

For a moment, Vercingetorix froze.

And then he glanced upward.

And his eyes chanced to meet Caesar's atop the tower.

Gazing into the eyes of Vercingetorix, Caesar sees a little smile of grim acknowledgment.

He knows.

Vercingetorix raises his sword in mocking salute.

"We who are about to die salute you, Caesar!" he shouts.

Mockingly?

Perhaps not, thinks Caesar, as he finds himself raising his own sword and saluting his worthy vanquished foe with total sincerity.

Vercingetorix lowers his sword, and with his amazon at his side, and his defeated Gauls rallying to him, lunges at the cohort of legionnaires blocking the breach in the fortress of Rome. And so the final battle of the conquest of Gaul begins after the war is already won, a meaningless combat of man against man and sword against sword.

Meaningless, or as it is meant to be? Caesar asks himself. Shall history say that Gaius Julius Caesar was a lesser man than the king of the Gauls?

As, with no further thought, he descends from on high to join it.

Action mercifully stops the thought that blackens his mind as Vercingetorix slashes away at Roman shields, a mindless clatter and clash of metal against metal, of muscle against muscle, of the sheer weight of bodies, of the mass of his warriors expending their strength and their lives against the armored mass of Roman legionnaires. Of all that was once Gaul against all that is Rome.

With Rhia, his sister of the sword, fighting beside him to the very end.

Caesar reaches the rear of the fray and sees a squad of his men wheeling a mobile barricade toward the breach, but sees too that the Gauls have pushed his legionnaires back, and a line of them stands just inside the blackened and jagged hole, defending and blocking it with their bodies.

"Take heart, legionnaires!" he shouts as he presses forward, sword held high, the ensign of his crimson cloak streaming behind him. "Caesar himself fights at your side!"

And they do. They cheer. They attack with renewed vigor. Four javelin men from a reinforcing cohort rushing up behind him break ranks to escort him through the crush to the front.

"The battle is won!" Caesar shouts triumphantly as he breaks through the ranks of his own men to face the Gauls.

To face Vercingetorix.

"The Gauls flee to the four winds!" he shouts. "The war is over! Gaul is conquered."

Vercingetorix looks right at him. His sword hangs limp.

The Gauls surrounding him seem to cringe backward in dismay. Caesar's legionnaires stand motionless for an instant, so that it seems that he and Vercingetorix stand alone facing each other on their own private battlefield.

As it was meant to be.

Dreamily, Caesar finds himself moving forward. To accept the unspoken challenge.

As was destined—

From behind him, a javelin whistles toward Vercingetorix—

His amazon leaps in front of him—

And the javelin pierces her breast straight through to the heart.

She falls backward into the arms of Vercingetorix.

Who holds her tenderly as he gazes at Caesar. Who cannot look away from those eyes until—

He senses the wind of a motion behind him.

And sees a legionnaire in the act of throwing his javelin.

"No!" he shouts angrily as he smashes it from the man's hand with the flat of his sword. "He has lost everything but his life and his honor."

And he looks back at Vercingetorix with the tenderness of the father he has never been for the son he has never had.

"Those he may keep. The triumphant conqueror of Gaul owes that much to . . . its king."

And the mobile barricade slides shut across the breach between them.

XXIII

VERCINGETORIX CARRIES the lifeless body of Rhia across a plain piled with corpses and drenched with blood, toward a burning city, through its shattered gates, and into a plaza thronged with warriors beating a dirge on their shields with their swords.

The faces of the warriors are bone-white skulls, a funeral pyre is already burning, somehow Rhia already lies upon it, and within the fire Vercingetorix sees the eyes of Keltill, brighter than the flames, as his father's voice speaks to him from the place beyond them.

"In fire do you become the tale the bards will sing.
In fire shall you enter the Land of Legend as a king."

Vercingetorix walks into the flames, burning but unconsumed.

He knows that this is a dream, that he has passed through the flames into the Land of Legend, where the Great Wheel turns and a new Great Age is born. And he can see now what will be.

He sees himself catching the falling body of Rhia, and Caesar staying the hand that would slay him, and he hears the words that Caesar spoke, which never reached his ear in the timebound world of strife.

"You have lost everything but your life and your honor."

Now the corpse that he holds is his own. And Caesar stands before him in a stone prison cell, a sword in one hand, and the Crown of Brenn in the other.

"One or the other," says Caesar. "Which shall it be?"

The voices of a multitude chant: *"Vercingetorix! King of Gaul! Vercingetorix! King of Gaul!"*

Vercingetorix reaches for the Crown of Brenn.

"Hail, Vercingetorix, king of Gaul," Caesar says sardonically, and places it upon his brow.

"Vercingetorix! King of Gaul! Vercingetorix! King of Gaul!"

The chanting is mocking now, larded with laughter. Vercingetorix wears only a filthy loincloth and the Crown of Brenn. His hands are chained before him, and the chain is fastened to a gilded chariot, and he is afoot. The chariot is dragging him down a wide avenue in Rome, and Caesar rides in the chariot, a wreath of laurel on his brow, waving triumphantly to the crowds lining the way.

"Vercingetorix!" they cheer sardonically. *"Vercingetorix! King of Gaul!"*

Vercingetorix stands once more in the dank stone cell, the Crown of Brenn heavy on his head, as Caesar kneels and now offers him the sword.

"I owe this much to the king of Gaul," he says tenderly.

Vercingetorix accepts the sword, and he turns it inward, and plunges it into his own heart.

As he does, he becomes an eagle soaring once more above the magic city of his vision beneath the Tree of Knowledge.

But now it is night. A magical night in the Land of Legend such as has never been known in the world of strife. The city is alive with light, as if the gods have sprinkled it with jewels of every color, as numerous as a winter snowfall. Lights soar across the heavens. Lights move along the avenues like falling stars which will never touch ground. The tower of metal wickerwork glows with lights like the Tree of Knowledge set ablaze, so bright that it outshines the stars, burning yet unconsumed.

"Vercingetorix! King of Gaul!"

The eagle he has become swoops down to alight on the pedestal of the statue of the warrior on horseback he has seen before, but now, in this magical night, it is illumined a brilliant greenish white, like old copper shining under a full moon. There is writing engraved on the pedestal in the lettering of the Romans, yet in a language he somehow knows that neither he nor Caesar could ever read.

But he can read clearly enough what is written on the face of the statue, his own face ennobled in stone. It is a face that has seen far too much for its years. It is not the face of a victor, and yet its grim smile is triumphant.

"Vercingetorix! King of Gaul!"

Somehow he knows that this City of Light is in a land that will one day be called Gaul. This is a city built by *Gauls,* built by a people far greater than the Arverni, Edui, Carnutes, Santons, Atrebates, tribes whose names they have forgotten, a city whose glory outshines even that which once was Rome.

"*Vercingetorix! King of Gaul!*"

This is what the magic of his death has made. Will make. Must make.

"*Vercingetorix! King of Gaul!*"

The king who must die that his people might live.

"*Vercingetorix! King of Gaul!*"

He who must die that his people might truly be born.

Caesar has had visions before, in the burning white light of the falling sickness, in the blood-throbbing heat of battle, in the moment of orgasmic completion, in the depths of fatigue. This is like all of those, and yet it is not, for he awakens out of the bright white light onto a battlefield of dreams.

This *must* be a dream, else how could Great Alexander, blond and radiantly glowing, be riding toward him through the battle of Gergovia upon a horse as white as that light?

Through the red fog of battle he rides, godlike, untouchable, immortal, and Caesar strides forth to meet him, as is his destiny. They come together, their eyes meet, and Caesar looks into those fierce blue depths and is filled with envy, with awe, with pity, and, yes, with love, for he knows that somehow each of them, one to the other, is both father and son.

"When I was your age," says Alexander the Great, "I had conquered the world."

"When you are my age," Caesar tells him, "you will be long since dead."

For those are the eyes of Vercingetorix in the face of Alexander. He dismounts, and holds out a sword, one hand on the hilt, the other on the blade. Caesar's own sword.

Vercingetorix kneels before him and holds it up as an offering. "In the name of my people, I surrender my life and my sword."

"In the name of the Senate and people of Rome, I accept your surrender," says Caesar, as he takes the sword and places the Crown of Brenn upon the brow of the defeated. "*Vercingetorix, King of Gaul.*"

· · ·

Vercingetorix stands in a clearing in the great forest beneath the Tree of Knowledge. He wears the robe of an Arch Druid over the armor of a warrior. In his right hand is a sword, in his left the scepter of the fallen star. Within the forest stand the shapes of druids; faceless, numberless, hidden in plain sight.

Vercingetorix raises the sword, and an empty white robe comes forth. He raises the Arch Druid's staff and the face of Guttuatr appears within its cowl.

"And have you seen the story of your life entire now, Vercingetorix, man of action?" he says.

Vercingetorix holds up his sword. "I have seen my death and the triumph its magic will make."

"The triumph, man of knowledge?"

Vercingetorix holds up his Arch Druid's staff. "The age of the tribes of Gaul is over, the age of druids has passed, and the age of Rome has begun," he says. "And when that age passes, there will come another, far greater than any man of knowledge born in this age can hope to understand."

Vercingetorix raises his sword and crosses it with the Arch Druid's staff. "I was never destined to do more than carry the spirit of that which is passing from this Great Age into the next."

From the ethereal folds of his robe, Guttuatr withdraws the Crown of Brenn. Vercingetorix kneels and allows him to place it upon his head.

Vercingetorix rises. "All kings must die," he says, "but a *druid* king, having encompassed the moment of his death while he yet lives, may wield it as a mighty sword."

He holds the Arch Druid's staff aloft by the tip. And the fallen star thereon rises on a tail of fire back into the heavens from whence it came. To become a bright new star as the Wheel turns from one Great Age into the next.

Caesar approaches a circular clearing. In the center of the clearing is a great oak. Beneath the oak is a man. He wears the armor of a warrior beneath the cloak of a druid. Upon his head is the Crown of Brenn. In his left hand is a wooden staff. In his right is a sword.

The sword is Caesar's own.

"Hail, Caesar, Conqueror of Gaul," says Vercingetorix.

"Hail, Vercingetorix . . . my young friend," Caesar finds himself saying. "Do I wake or do I dream?"

"This is the Land of Legend, Caesar. And we are both in it."

"But why are we here?" Caesar finds himself saying, as if he is an actor playing the part of himself in a drama that has played out many times before.

"To give you what you need," says Vercingetorix.

"You would surrender Alesia and save the city from further carnage?" says Caesar.

"Is that what you need, Caesar?" says Vercingetorix. "Do you need to pass the rest of your life as an object of ridicule chasing barbarian tribes through the forest?"

"No," says Caesar. "What *do* I need?" he asks Vercingetorix.

"You must have a *King* to surrender *Gaul*," says Vercingetorix. "Thereby creating a Gaul for you to conquer."

And Caesar understands. After all, this is the man he sought to make that king before this war began.

"So be it, my young friend," he says. "You may rule Gaul as Roman proconsul subject to no man but Caesar. And you may keep the crown you wear if it pleases you to also be called a king."

"This cannot be," Vercingetorix tells him. "I have sworn a blood oath never to rule as king while a single Roman soldier remains on the soil of Gaul. No Gaul would obey a traitor who broke such an oath."

"But then what *do* you offer me?"

"The surrender of a king to take back to Rome in chains as proof that Gaius Julius Caesar can at last be hailed as conqueror of Gaul. That is the part I play in the legend of Caesar."

"And what part do I play in the legend of Vercingetorix?"

"They are one and the same," Vercingetorix tells him. "We open the door to the Land of Legend, each for the other, and each of us walks through it."

And Caesar knows that this is true. Will be true. Is destined to be true.

"The king who must die salutes you," says Vercingetorix, and hands Caesar back his own sword.

Vercingetorix awoke with the warmth of Marah's body close beside him and a weighty burden upon his brow.

He did not need to reach up and touch it to know that it was the Crown of Brenn.

XXIV

MUST YOU?" Marah asked Vercingetorix after they had made love, but he heard no true questioning in her voice.

This second and last time had been far different from the first. That had been the opening of a door, a magic of a kind, and while it had lasted, he could believe that it was a beginning.

This had been a simple, natural act of love between a man and a woman, as he supposed it was meant to be, as it would have been a thousand times and more down through their years together, had destiny not robbed them of those years. Had he been favored by the gods with another life, the life of Keltill perhaps, a noble of the Arverni on his homestead with his wife by his side and a son to love him.

But that way of life was passing, and that simple happiness would never be his. The final act of love that they had shared had been a farewell, and both of them had known it. And if this had tinged it with a hint of the bitter, it had sweetened it with poignancy as well.

"You above all others know that I must," he told her as he rose from the bed to dress himself.

Marah could only sigh, and nod, and somehow that little nod of brave acceptance touched his heart more deeply than she ever had before, making what he must do both easier and more arduous.

"Rome is the future," she said. "And Gaul is the past."

"No," Vercingetorix told her as he donned his pantaloons and tunic and armor. "The Age of Rome has come, but when the Wheel makes its next Great Turning, Rome too shall pass. The Gaul that was a forest of tribes, which the druids would have preserved forever like a fly in amber, is gone, but the Gaul that will be is a great oak with many branches that will bear seeds that will flower when the names of those branches have been forgotten and Rome has become a fading memory."

"You have seen this in a vision?" asked Marah.

"I have seen another time and place, where the very tongues of Gaul and Rome are no longer spoken. In the end, Rome and Gaul will make this Great Age as . . . as . . ."

Vercingetorix paused, unable to say the words, and his eyes burned with tears when Marah said them for him.

"As a father and mother make the child that is neither of them and the heir of both."

Vercingetorix could only nod. "That is the future I must do this thing to make," he said in a whisper. "If I must be its father, you will always be its mother."

He picked up the Crown of Brenn. He paused.

"I swore an oath not to don the Crown of Brenn while a single Roman soldier remained on the soil of Gaul, and yet now I must break that vow, that Gaul might be born. . . ."

"Then let its mother, who loves not honor more than the boy who first kissed her by a stream, break it for you and leave your honor unblemished," said Marah.

She rose from the bed, and as Vercingetorix gazed upon her naked loveliness for the last time, she took the crown from his hands, and he beheld all that he would lose, all the joys of the long life together that he must now throw away.

The greater the magic, the greater the price that must be paid.

Marah kissed him for the last time.

"Take that with you into the Land of Legend . . ." she said, and placed the Crown of Brenn upon on his head.

". . . Vercingetorix, king of Gaul."

Carnaxes blow a solemn note as the gates of Alesia open and Vercingetorix rides through them alone, mounted on a white horse and wearing the Crown of Brenn. From within the city comes the slow, steady beating of unseen swords on shields as he rides across the corpse-strewn battlefield to the inner wall of the Roman fortification, where a portal has been opened to grant him passage.

Roman trumpets answer as he rides through it, parading down an aisle formed by two lines of centurions—their armor polished to a spot-less gleam, their swords raised in salute—across the Roman encamp-ment, and through the outer wall.

Beyond is a much greater battlefield, stretching to the outer defen-sive ditches and far beyond, heaped with twice as many corpses, the green grass soaked with still-congealing brown-red blood.

In the midst of this vast field of unburied dead, picked at by tri-umphantly cawing crows and silent and unseen but victorious worms and insects, have been planted the tribal standards of the Arverni, and the Edui, of the Atrebates, and the Santons, of the Turons and the Parisii, of all the many tribes of Gaul.

Under truce, sullenly and forlornly standing behind them, and guarded by legionnaires are surviving vergobrets and nobles of the scattered tribal forces of what was once the army of Gaul. Behind their leaders are hundreds of ordinary warriors and peasants, each contin-gent cleaving to the standard of its own tribe, gathered by the Romans to bear witness and the word of that witness throughout the lands of the Gauls.

Before these witnesses the Romans have laid out a path of crimson carpeting through another aisle of centurions, and at the end of it sits Caesar, beneath a crimson awning upon a chair gilded like a throne.

Vercingetorix slowly rides through the battlefield to the lip of this carpeted passage, then stops. He looks out at the Gauls standing in iso-lated groups under the standards of tribes whose names will soon be forgotten. And the silver-tongued Vercingetorix speaks to them one last time.

"All of you know that I have sworn a blood oath never to rule as king in Gaul while one Roman soldier remains on our soil. But here they stand in their scores of thousands. And here I stand before you wearing the Crown of Brenn. Yet I will keep the oath I swore in my own blood. I will not rule as your king in Gaul. I will die as your king in Rome."

He gestures down at the midden of corpses and severed body parts and drying blood, all mingled and mangled together, among which the men of every tribe stand.

"Behold, here are Gauls of every tribe, whole and in parts, united at last as brothers. As I keep the oath I have sworn in my blood, I call upon you to keep the oath they have sworn with theirs, for they have entered the Land of Legend as *Gauls,* and so as Gauls must you remember them. Surely here is enough spilled blood to seal that oath till the end of time."

Before him, the tribesmen squirm and mutter uncertainly.

"As they lie here together as Gauls in the brotherhood of death, so must the living now come together, that by their blood and mine the Gaul they died for might be born. Gaul is defeated! Long live Gaul!"

Vercingetorix speaks no more. No one speaks. He glares at the tribesmen for a long moment that begins to seem eternal. No one moves.

Then the vergobret of the Parisii silently strides to the standard of the Santons. And the vergobret of the Atrebates takes a place behind the standard of the Turons. And a noble of the Turons moves to the standard of the Cadurques. And then more tribal leaders change places. And behind them, warriors and peasants mix together.

There is no cheering. There is no chanting. There is nothing to be heard but the slow, steady stamping of feet upon the ground.

And there is nothing to be seen but Gauls.

Vercingetorix rides slowly down the Roman carpet toward the conqueror of Gaul. Three times do Roman trumpets blow fanfares as three times does Vercingetorix ride around the throne of Gaius Julius Caesar.

The Roman trumpets sound one more time as he halts before Caesar and dismounts, and now they are joined by a bass harmonic of carnaxes from the distant ramparts of Alesia.

Vercingetorix draws his sword and holds it before him in both hands as an offering as he approaches Caesar.

"In the name of the Kingdom of Gaul, I offer the surrender of my life and my sword," Vercingetorix declaims.

He does not kneel.

"But not your honor, my young friend," Caesar whispers in a voice that only the two of them can hear.

Then he reaches out to take the sword.

He hesitates.

And then he rises to accept it.

And proclaims in the stentorian voice of a well-schooled Roman orator for all the world to hear:

"In the name of the Senate and people of Rome, I accept your surrender . . . Vercingetorix, King of Gaul."

EPILOGUE

BENEATH THE SHADE of a copse of trees overhanging the stream below the hill upon which stands the city of Gergovia, a small boy plays with a staff of wood taller than a man, unsure whether to pretend it is a scepter or a sword, while his mother watches with a wistful smile.

"Tell me the story of my father again, Momma," he asks.

Marah sighs, as if she has told it too many times, but then, as she speaks, her eyes soften with tears, even as they seem to be gazing elsewhere in pride, as if she never truly tires of telling it nevertheless.

"Your father was a great king," she says. "Out of tribes whose names will soon be forgotten, he made a nation whose spirit will live forever. Your father was a druid—"

"—he made magic!"

"He made magic. He conjured victory out of defeat. And there is no greater magic than that."

Acknowledgments

I would like to thank the following people who were instrumental, one way or another, in inspiring the creation of *The Druid King* or making this novel what it has become.

Jacques Dorfmann, without whom I would never have begun this journey, nor, in the end, been compelled to continue.

My literary agent, Russell Galen, and my foreign rights agent, Danny Baror, whose belief in *The Druid King* was initially even stronger than my own.

Martin Asher at Vintage Books and Sonny Mehta at Alfred A. Knopf, who took a chance on a most unusual project by a writer who had never written such a novel before.

Edward Kastenmeier, my editor, who persisted so diligently and in such a detailed manner during the long and arduous process of putting the novel into its final form.

Most of all, I would like to thank my late great friend Richard Shorr, who brought me to this story at the outset, and who argued so passionately and so forcefully, as only Richie could, that what I had done in an early version of a screenplay should not be lost in what a film had become, that not only could I write this novel, but I *must*.

Once again, you were right, Richie. I only wish you were around to read the result and tell me "I *told* you so!" one last time.

A NOTE ABOUT THE AUTHOR

Norman Spinrad is the author of *Bug Jack Barron, The Iron Dream, Child of Fortune, The Void Captain's Tale,* and numerous other novels. He has also written literary criticism, political commentary, and the screenplays for two feature films. He lives in Paris.

NOTE ON THE TYPE

The text of this book was set in Plantin, a typeface first cut in 1913 by the Monotype Corporation of London. Though the face bears the name of the great Christopher Plantin (ca. 1520–1589), who in the latter part of the sixteenth century owned, in Antwerp, the largest printing and publishing firm in Europe, it is a rather free adaptation of designs by Claude Garamond made for that firm. With its strong, simple lines, Plantin is a no-nonsense face of exceptional legibility.

Composed by Stratford Publishing Services, Brattleboro, Vermont
Printed and bound by Berryville Graphics, Berryville, Virginia
Designed by Robert C. Olsson

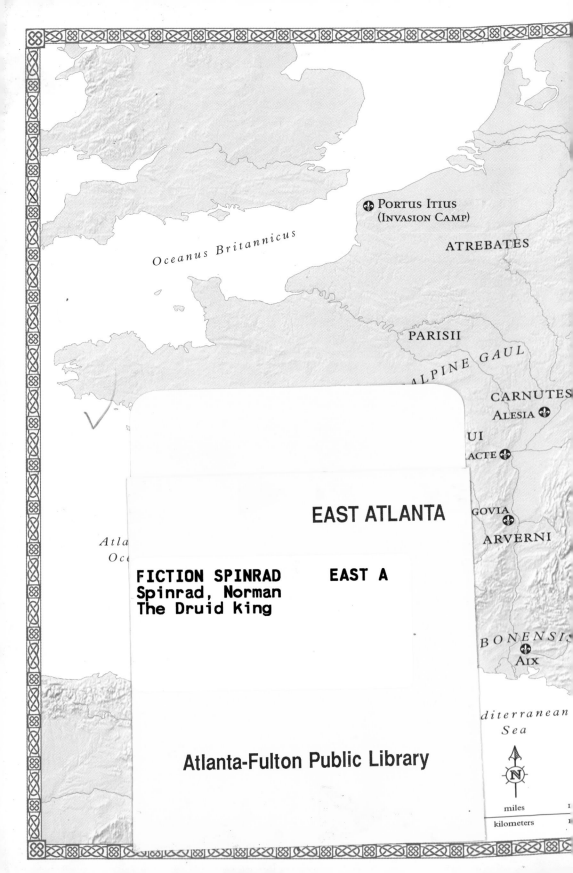

Portus Itius
(Invasion Camp)

ATREBATES

Oceanus Britannicus

PARISII

ALPINE GAUL

CARNUTES

ALESIA

UI

ACTE

GOVIA

ARVERNI

Atla
Oce

EAST ATLANTA

BONENSIS

AIX

diterranean
Sea

N

miles

kilometers